PRAISE FOR

Paul Kearney

"Fantastic . . . a wonderful blend of *Treasure Island* and classic fantasy. It is the beginning of what looks to be an incredible voyage and presents a refreshing twist on the classic fantasy story. . . . So splice those mainsails, feel the wind in your hair, let the salt-sea fill your nostrils and set a course for The Sea Beggars."

—*Outland* (UK) on *The Mark of Ran*

"Kearney's new novel marks a triumphant return for one of the very best British writers of hard-edged, visceral, gritty fantasy fiction. . . . Kearney has never been one to bow to the conventions and stereotypical tropes of fantasy fiction; he's always left the bog-standard kiddie-quest lying trampled in the dirt where it belongs and struck out in a new direction [with] a focus on high-quality world-building and great strength of characterization. . . . He was writing [like this] even before Martin began his Song of Ice and Fire or Erikson embarked on his Malazan Books of the Fallen, and *The Mark of Ran* will certainly appeal to fans of both these series, as well as readers who enjoy the likes of David Gemmell or Glen Cook as well."

—The Alien Online

"If there is a sub-genre of naval fantasy, Paul Kearney is its master and commander. With provocative, complex characters and written in a language evoking the sea's own rhythm—a language that is, quite simply, beautiful. Kearney is to my mind one of the very best writers of fantasy around. And recognition of that is long overdue. His previous series, Monarchies of God, delivered a raw, uncompromising world and some of the most memorable characters in fantasy—memorable for their imperfections as much as their deeds, courageous and otherwise. As with Glen Cook's Black Company series, there's no romantic gloss to Kearney's fantasy worlds. He delivers a much-needed dose of reality to fantasy, and I eagerly await the next installment."

—Steven Erikson

"Kearney injects an enthusiasm into his tale that makes it new and exciting. There are echoes of the best in other fantasists . . . and yet it's all Kearney's own delicious style. . . . I can hardly wait for the next volume."
—*SF Site*

"Think *Master and Commander* with added magic . . . Kearney writes well, his prose roars along like a riptide and he delivers plot broadsides with panache." —Jon Courtenay Grimwood, *Guardian*

"A triumphant return for one of the very best British writers of hard-edged, visceral, gritty, fantasy fiction . . . Kearney's prose is consistently and typically excellent . . . you are in for a treat."
—The Alien Online

"Gorgeous . . . about as three dimensional as a fantasy world can be. You can taste the salt in the air of this barbaric, corrupt expanse, smell the blood . . . an immersive joy in which you must bathe. Full gudgeons ahead!"
—*SFX*

"Everything a fantasy reader could possibly want . . . Kearney's handling of this page-turning, atmospheric tale is never less than expert."
—*Starburst*

"Finally, a fantasy novel that lives up to the billing . . . Kearney's novel is every bit as good as it promises to be . . . a cracking story."
—*Birmingham Post*

"Dark, compelling . . . bodes well for the next book." —*Interzone*

"One of the most exciting of fantasy storytellers returns with a suspenseful and well-crafted tale in a sub-genre that could well be called nautical fantasy—if so, he is the admiral of the fleet. . . . There is a brilliant twist at the end . . . and you're left eagerly awaiting the next installment."
—*Western Daily Press*

ALSO BY PAUL KEARNEY

The Way to Babylon

A Different Kingdom

Riding the Unicorn

Hawkwood's Voyage

The Heretic Kings

The Iron Wars

The Second Empire

Ships from the West

THE MARK *of* RAN

BOOK ONE *of* THE SEA BEGGARS

Paul Kearney

BANTAM BOOKS

THE MARK OF RAN
A Bantam Spectra Book / December 2005
Originally published 2004 by Bantam Press,
a division of Transworld Publishers (UK)

Published by Bantam Dell
A Division of Random House, Inc.
New York, New York

Cover illustration by Steve Stone
Cover design by Jamie S. Warren Youll
Decorative map © Neil Gower

Book design by Sarah Smith

Library of Congress Cataloging-in-Publication Data
Kearney, Paul.
The Mark of Ran / Paul Kearney.
p. cm.—(The sea beggars ; bk. 1)
ISBN-10: 0-553-38361-2
ISBN-13: 978-0-553-38361-4
I. Title. II. Fantasy fiction.

PR6061.E2156 M37 2005
823′.914—dc22
2005047238

Printed in the United States of America
Published simultaneously in Canada

www.bantamdell.com

BVG 10 9 8 7 6 5 4 3 2 1

For my mother,
Mary Teresa Kearney

ACKNOWLEDGMENTS

I would like to acknowledge the encouragement, the patience, and the sheer forbearance of several people without whom this book could not have been written. Firstly, Steve Erikson, who helped put me on the right track writing-wise again. Secondly, Simon Taylor, who is a pearl amongst editors and all-round nice guy. Thirdly, my agent, John McLaughlin, without whose help and advice I would be lost.

And finally my wife, Marie, the best thing in my life.

0 100 200 300
Leagues
Limit of Winter Pack
WINTERPACK SEA
STAFFIN
GIDIOR
Cadmus
GALT
MAPRIAN
Achoris
OSCA
BIONESE SEA
BIONAR STRAITS
ANDELYS
GASCAR
Ascari
The SEVEN ISLES
ALDIBOR
ARBIONAR
CORSO
Phidon
MYCONAN
WESTEREASE SEA
Arbion
Urbonetto
BIONAR
MTNS.
PERILAR
Perdios
Mycon
GANESH
Omer
The GOLIAD
Ganesh Ka
GOLORON MTNS.
Golgos
Athir
Ordos
ORONTHIR
INNER REACH
THE GUT
OUTER REACH
Cavarr
THE ISTHIS
UNCHARTED
AVOSK
Uruban
Vosk Delta
Vosk River
ORR
Jungles of the Vosk
GONDAR SEA
Sonen Ka
Pharos
GONDOPHAR
Gondopharian Jungles
Mysol
Tukos
TUKELAR
UNKNOWN
UMER (WEST)

UMER (EAST)

Gower '04
Limit of Winter Pack
KRESCIR
HELDRIAN SEA
HELDRICS
VRYHEYD
Vrydiol
Nast
Graillor
WRYWIND SEA
GASCAR
Ascari
DENNIFREY
BORHOL
TETHIS
UNCHARTED
ABOR
OSMER
Aornos
KULL
MAMERTINE
Omer
ARMIDON BANKS
ARMIDON
Perigord
AUGSMARK
Augshar
Armidia
Mamertos
AUXIERRE
Fengos
ARINGIA
LEAGUE
CAVERRIC STRAITS
CAVERRIC SEA
Lodorin
CAVAILLON
Kentta
LAUGRO
KASSIC SEA
WESTERN CAVERRIC SEA
KASSA
TUKELAR
Khasos
Tukos
Gokran Desert
UNKNOWN

THE MARK *of* RAN

PART ONE

THE TOWER

One

SALT-BLOODED

"THERE WAS A GOD ONCE, OF COURSE THERE WAS. AN ALL-Father who created everything and each race to inhabit the earth. But He left us long ago, disgusted by the way-wardness of His creation, and the wanton appetites of the creatures He had populated His world with. We are forsaken now, children abandoned by their father. And when God withdrew from the world, to punish us He took with Him all hope of life after death. So nothing but the worm awaits us all. No justice for the persecuted, no punishment for the wicked. And thus our world turns, spun on its axis by the greedy dreams of men."

"But there are other gods, surely," Rol said. "There is Ussa, and Ran her spouse. And Gibniu of the Anvil—"

"Lesser deities, bound to the earth even as we are, my boy. They are powerful, yes, and immortal, but they cannot create. They can only destroy, or warp what has already been made by the One God who abandoned us."

"And the Weren, what of them?"

Rol's grandfather paused, frowned. It was a long moment before he answered.

"Some say that the Weren are fallen angels, exiled here on earth in punishment for an ancient sin, others that they are Man before his Fall, Man as he should have been. But the Lesser Gods, in jealousy, broke them down and enfeebled them and produced the mankind we know now. In either case the peoples of the world are but shadows of angels, just as the Ur-men, the Unfinished Ones, are shattered travesties of humanity. For this much is true about Umer, the wheeling earth we inhabit: all things are in decay now that God has left us. The world spins ever more slowly on its axis and the sun cools year by year, century upon century. One day Umer will be a frozen ball of mud, its turning stilled at last, and it shall drift about an ashen sun in which all light has died."

The boy named Rol considered this. The evening light off the Wrywind Sea set his red-gold hair alight in a momentary kinship of color. His eyes were green as amethyst, pale as the shallows of a tropical lagoon. He was nine years old, and his arms were wrapped around his filthy, scabbed knees. An urchin with the face of an archangel.

"When did God leave the world?" he asked the old man.

"Eons ago. Before even the first of the Lesser Men opened his eyes, in the time of the Old World, before the New was born."

"How do you know all this, Grandfather?"

The old man indulged in another one of his silences. He thumbed down the glowing whitherb in his black pipe with one horny thumb, long burnt past sensibility. Behind him, in the west, the dying sun ignited a gaudy cauldron of fire on the brim of the horizon. In the shadow of the headland the waves reached languidly for the black rocks below, caressing the same stone that in winter they would pound with white fury.

"Our people have always known these things," the old man said at last, reluctantly. He turned rheumy eyes upon the bright young face beside him, and smiled. In that instant it was possible to see that in his youth he, too, had been beautiful.

"The Dennifreians? Why do farmers and fishermen keep all this lore to themselves? Why—"

"For the last time, Rol, you and I, and Morin and Ayd who watch over you, we are not from Dennifrey. We come from—elsewhere."

"So you say. But where, Grandfather?" The boy's face had hardened into stubbornness as all children's will at the wheedling of some secret knowledge.

His grandfather puffed thoughtfully on his pipe, and stared up at the first stars that had come chasing the sunset. He seemed to be looking for something in the empurpling sky, and when he found it he pointed with one brown, corded arm. "See that star there?"

"The one that flashes blue? That's Quintillian. *Bíonar's Guard* they call him too. Set your course by him and you'll come in the end to Urbonetto of the Wharves, the Free City."

Grandfather smiled. "Well done. But he was once called something else. Or-Desyr he was to me, when I was as young as you are now. Don't you be telling that to no one now. That's a secret, the name of our star, for us alone to know."

The boy nodded solemnly, deflated because the secret had been so small a thing as a name that meant nothing to him. And whom could he tell?

"You said we were not from Dennifrey," he pointed out sulkily. "What's a star got to do with that?"

"The star points home," his grandfather said patiently.

"We're from Urbonetto, then?"

"No! We're far beyond that, beyond mighty Bionar and Perilar and even fabled Uruban of the Silk. Remember this: Or-Desyr, or the Guard as they call him, he points over the Oronthic

Sea, at the edge of Tethis herself. In those great waters it is said he can be followed to a place where ones such as us may be safe, for a little while at least. But never mind that. It's a matter for another day. Look, the night has come upon us unawares."

It was indeed dark now, and behind them Morin and Ayd had lit the lamps so that kindly yellow light flickered out of the doorway of the cottage they all shared. They heard the click of wooden plates, Ayd's sharp voice berating Morin for some domestic infraction. A yellow rectangle of firelight flooded out of the doorway, waxing steadily as the darkness deepened around them and the coastal kirwits began to rasp their nightsong.

"Tethis sleeps," the old man said, staring out at the quiet sea. "See the swell? Ussa is combing her hair."

They watched the starlight as it glittered on the successive small waves lapping the rocks.

"I will sail the sea one day," Rol whispered fiercely. "I will visit every country and kingdom in the world. I will captain the finest ship ever built."

"Perhaps you will," said Rol's grandfather softly. "It is in your blood, after all. And all things came out of the sea in the Beginning. Even the mountains once were mud in the dark of Ussa's Womb. To the sea shall it all return before the end of days. Only when the sun grows cold will Ussa herself die, and the surface of the earth know stillness at last."

He stood up, gripping the shoulder of the boy beside him and groaning. The bowl of his pipe glowed red and he spat fragrant smoke into the night air.

"Come, Rol. Ussa will wait for you and that ship of yours, but it's time for supper and Ayd is not so patient. The pigs have seen too many of my meals lately."

Dennifrey of the Nets, easternmost of the Seven Isles, and most insular of the seven. The shallow water of the Wrywind

Sea lapped its dour shores, famed for fogs and the treacherous Severed Banks that never twice appeared on the same longitude. The Dennifreians were wedded in a bitch-marriage to the sea, a nation canny with small boats, near with their welcome to strangers, giving grudging obeisance to Ussa of the Swells, sometimes slaughtering a kid to her consort, vicious Ran, to placate his winter storms. It was as though they hated the element upon which their craft floated. They rode it as warily as a man might a skittish horse. But their fishing grounds were the richest in the northern world, and the Dennifreians had done well out of their hag-ridden union. They had become prosperous, and yet their wealth had not rendered them any more receptive to the matters of the world beyond their shores. Almost they gloried in their ignorance, and viewed the Fisher-Merchants who took the salted choice of their catch abroad with disdain.

A small payment for this fish-fueled prosperity of theirs—a steady trickle of lives every year lost to Ran's Nets, the blood-price for their tenure of the sea's riches. Perhaps it was that which made them dour, for they were a folk apt to strike hard bargains, and to resent it when in their turn they had one forced upon themselves. But one does not argue with the gods. So they cursed the sea when they were not out upon her breast, and their offerings were made with ill grace.

Rol's family—for so he thought of them though Morin and Ayd were no kin to him—had lived on Dennifrey for many years. And yet still they were outsiders, and Grandfather could bring stillness to a packed tavern in Driol merely by peering across the threshold.

"We are the flotsam of an old hatred," he had told Rol, "set adrift by the fear and ignorance of men." He said many things of that sort, so many that even Rol now barely heard them. Grandfather had a rolling, lilted voice as deep as a barrel, musical as a lark, but he did so love to listen to it, and to make sonorous pronouncements about things Rol had no hope of ever understanding. So he and Morin would sit by the cottage wall mending the nets, nodding without knowing, for they loved the old man.

They lived separate and apart, the odd quartet, their cottage built by Morin out of wherzstone blocks, and set on a jutting promontory from which the shipping of the Twelve Seas could be seen in skeins of sails on the turquoise horizon. *Eyrie,* Grandfather had long before named their little dwelling, insisting that a house needed a name much as did a ship. And the house was good to them, as if appreciative of the thought. Roofed with turves and constructed as squarely as a redoubt, Eyrie shrugged off winter gales and crackling summer heat alike. It was the only home Rol had ever known, or would ever really know, a solid permanence at the center of his young life.

Below the cottage was a tiny crescent-shaped cove where they beached the wherry in winter, and behind it Ayd had crafted a rood of good soil with infinite labor and tons of seaweed, so they had fresh vegetables without haggling over them in town. Beyond it, in a small plashed wood, two pigs rooted in genial ignorance of their approaching fate, their black-striped offspring squealing for their teats.

On the very crumbling tip of the promontory loomed a hagrolith, cold even on the hottest Midsummer Day, and casting no shadow at sunset. The local folk refused to go near it, and yet Rol's family had made their home within sight of its mossy flanks, and Rol thought of the stone as one might of a distant and seldom-seen relative, neither good nor ill, but part of the mental landscape. Grandfather often sat with his back to the stone, even in winter, and watched the endless progression of the sea-swells as they came traveling across the Wrywind.

The familiar landscape was circumscribed by the emptiness of the high moorland about the promontory. This was a wide waste of heather and scrub and bracken, soft going underfoot, and in wet seasons treacherous to those who did not know about the bogs and quagmires it spawned. No one lived there; it was left to the deer and the rabbits and the buzzards.

There were only intermittent contacts with the local people. Serioc the Headman of Driol would drop by once a year for the Tollcount, and though he would not enter the house, he would share a flagon of barley beer with Grandfather in something of an annual ritual, and would ask the same polite questions, then leave with the sweat cold upon his brow and the relief staring out of his eyes. But it would raise his standing in town for him to say he had dared to sup with the folk on the headland, and his re-election as Headman would be assured.

And Ayd would tramp the muddy miles into Driol once every few months to barter for those necessities that they could not make or grow or catch for themselves. Yarn for net-making, whitherb for Grandfather's pipe, a new axe blade or kitchen knife to replace one worn to the quick, and always a great sack of yellow flour for their twice-weekly loaves. On her return the strap of her back-basket would leave a red bar across her forehead for days to mark the trip, and she would be slightly less cross-grained and irritable than usual, either because she liked going into town, or because she was glad to have it over with. After each trip she would always spend the following night out on the moors—to clear her head, she said—and would invariably return in the morning muddy and scratched, but with a brace of conies dangling from one fist, or more rarely a young deer, its neck broken and dangling.

One clear autumn afternoon Rol had fared farther afield than usual, blackberrying on the western slopes of the headland, when he had come across a knot of the local boys engaged in the same quest. He was large, and broad-shouldered for his age, but even he could do little when they pounced on him en masse and commenced pummeling his head into the springy short-grassed turf. His baffled astonishment gave way to fury, and he managed to plant his fist between the eyes of their sandy-haired ringleader. This merely fed their viciousness, however, and they were casting about for a suitable stone with which to crush his skull when out of nowhere Morin appeared. Rol lifted his bloodied head from the grass to see their faces go gray with terror, and abandoning their berry baskets, they fled, pelting back toward the town with a collective wail and nary a backward glance. But when Rol had looked at his rescuer, Morin was merely smiling his vacant-minded smile, like an amiable bear. Only for a second did he think he saw something else in the big man's face, an emerald gleam in the eye, a strange blurred definition to his countenance. He put it down to the ringing in his head, and forgot it in the wealth of blackberry jam that ensued.

They avoided him after that, the village boys, and often as he tramped about the sere upland moors above the headland with his birding bow and game bag, he would see them at their play, and feel an odd pang as they took to their heels when they sighted him. He was not solitary by nature, and as he grew older he wearied of Ayd's carping, Morin's simpleminded placidity, his grandfather's absurd tales and dark mutterings. It was a great joy to him when he was pronounced old enough to go out in the wherry with Morin, and take his chances with the whims of Ran and Ussa on the Wrywind.

The *Gannet* was a decked, shallow-draft inshore boat with a single mast that carried a loose-footed gaff mainsail. Broad-beamed as an old whore's hips (so Grandfather said), she made a great deal of leeway, but made up for it with a ducklike stability. There was no style about her, but she had a fine, simple heart, and Grandfather repainted the sea-eyes on her bow every spring with great care, murmuring incomprehensibly as he did so. At the beginning, Rol could not raise her mainsail without Morin's help, strain though he might at the halliards, but he had (so Morin said) a nose for the wind, and he was quick and deft with the tiller. In the autumn the southeasterlies came barreling up from Abor one after another, making the outward trip to the fishing grounds a swift pleasure, but beating back in their teeth was hard, intense work, and it called for fine judgment on the helm to keep the wind on the port bow.

The work on the boat, the hauling in of the nets, broadened the boy's shoulders and toughened his muscles, so that within a year Rol was capable of handling *Gannet* alone, though this was not yet permitted. Most of their catch was ablaroni, the long, silver-flanked fish that was the staple of the Seven Isles. But they would also haul in squid, herrin, and Bank's Monk, the fearsome-looking delicacy that in Bionar, Grandfather said, sold for its weight in silver minims.

Some fish they ate as part of their everyday diet. More went to feed the pigs, and a large proportion was dried or salted or smoked or pickled against the darkness of winter, when few fishermen would put out to chance Ran's Rages. There was an earth cellar below the boards of the cottage, and by the solstice its shelves were a gleaming parade of jars and pots, and racks of ablaroni fillet salted to the consistency of wood. Soon the two pigs made their contribution, and there was blood pudding in the evenings after the slaughter—Grandfather's favorite—as well as sausages and cured hams and jellied trotters and great sides of bacon smoked in the outhouse. There was dried seaweed to chew when the whitherb ran low, and wicker panniers of turnip and carrots and beet, harvested by the tireless Ayd before the first frosts cracked open the ground. There were pots of nuts, beaten off the limbs of the hazels in the pigs' copse, and—a rare windfall—combs of honey raided by Morin from the trunk of a hollow oak farther down the headland, sealed with their own wax in an earthen pot and guarded by Ayd as though it were a worm's hoard.

So with autumn late upon the world the foursome would sit about the driftwood fire as it spat and sparked blue in the hearth, and beyond the stout walls of Eyrie, Ran in his tantrums began to batter the stony coast in his annual dance.

It was more burdensome to Rol than past years, this autumn, and the long northern winter to follow. After they had hauled the wherry up on the beach and made her fast, and Grandfather had blessed her labors with a libation of barley ale, the whole other world of the sea was closed until the turning of the year, and for Rol it was like a small bereavement. There were only the well-worn features of the headland and the bleak moors about it, and beyond it, lights twinkling in the early dark of the evenings, the lamplit windows of Driol where he had never been and was not allowed to go. Not yet. So he tramped the moors with his birding bow like the exile his grandfather insisted he was, hunting what game had not gone to earth. Or he and Morin sat mending nets in the house when the weather was too grim for wildfowling, and spliced rope endlessly, and when the winds abated for a while they would scale the surrounding cliffs and bring back baskets of late seabird eggs to brighten Ayd's day and make Grandfather rub his bony hands together. Over gull-egg omelette they would sit about the table listening to Grandfather's tales of the wider world.

He spoke of the rise of Bionar, greatest nation of the earth, but one that had been cursed by the endless wars over the fate of the barren Goliad, wherein legend had it mankind had woken and taken its first steps under the watchful eyes of the last angels. He recalled with narrowed stare the white wastes of the Winterpack Sea, the pancake ice crackling past his bows and on the horizon the blinding peaks of the Krescir, which no man had ever climbed. And then, puffing smoke, he would switch tack, and wax lyrical about the souks of Kassa, the spice-tang heavy in the hot air about the stalls, the silk-clad *jeremdhar* of the Khalif striding by with golden apples on the butts of their spears, and beyond the ochre walls of ancient Khasos the shimmering expanse of the Gokran, birthplace of scorpions.

He would speak freely about any country, kingdom, or sea lane in the world, but when Rol asked the questions he most wanted answering, Grandfather's seamed face would shut. Of his own origins, Rol knew only that his parents were dead, and that he had been born at sea, and was thus a citizen of no land in the world. The rest was hints and riddles, and not even overindulgence in barley beer could pry more out of the old man.

So the first dark half of the winter passed, the fifteenth of Rol's life.

Two

RAN'S HUMOR

THE STORMS WERE BAD THAT YEAR, RUNNING IN FRENZIED abandon across the face of the sea and battening onto the ragged coast as though determined to drag it down into the deeps. All across the Seven Isles, men made sacrifice to Ussa, imploring her to restrain her wild husband, and even Grandfather slit a runt piglet's throat in deference to the Storm-Lord, though he did so as grudgingly as a Dennifreian, and tossed its little carcass over the sea cliffs with surly reluctance.

So high were the waves that Rol and Morin had to haul *Gannet* farther up the beach and make for her a new berth well above the high watermark. There she lay moored fore and aft to great boulders while the sea foamed four fathoms astern in impotent rage and a northwesterly gale shrieked about the sea cliffs. The *Gannet* was no light craft, and for perhaps the first time Rol realized just how strong Morin was. The big man grasped her bowline and hauled her up the shingle by main force. Rol had to shout at him to slow down, as the stones had begun to rasp splinters off her keel and bottom timbers to expose the white wood.

He examined the damage while Morin stood by rubbing his palms together in contrition. "I hurt *Gannet*?"

"No great problem, I think. A spot of pitch here and there will cover it. You go on home. It's getting dark anyway. The pitch pot is down in the hold. I'll root it out and bring it back with me. We'll never get a fire started here."

Morin nodded obediently. He ran one huge hand over *Gannet*'s gunwale apologetically, and then turned to put the screaming wind at his back and begin the climb back up out of the cove to Eyrie.

The hold was dark and evil-smelling and Rol located the sticky pitch pot by touch alone. A crab scuttled out from under his questing fingers and the accumulated miasma of a million netted fish tempted his gorge to rise. He clambered out into the storm-tossed air with relief, glad of the clean howl of the wind.

And stopped as he caught sight of the figure leaning casually against *Gannet*'s sternpost.

A small man dressed in odd, shimmering gray garments the like of which Rol had never seen before. Grandfather had described such material, though, or something like it. Fishpelt, the skin of a semilegendary deep-sea creature. The man was dark and bearded, and he stared out to sea as though this were his own boat he was leaning against and he was contemplating her proper element. Rol froze, the pitch pot swinging heavy in his hand.

"There will be a good haul of drift in the morning," the man said. His voice was light, yet it carried over the wind effortlessly, as though made way for. "The Banks are on the move; there will be men drowned by sunrise." He turned and smiled, and Rol saw that his eyes were the color of the wind-sped waves he had been watching, cold as a night on the Winterpack.

"You have hauled up your craft in good time. I congratulate you."

Rol found his voice, and straightened so that he was looking down on the stranger from the height of *Gannet*'s tilting deck. "Ran is greedy for ships. They are his playthings. You have to keep them out of his reach."

One black brow rose, amused. "And who told you that, I wonder?"

"My grandfather. He was at sea all his life."

"Hard-won wisdom. He is right, your grandfather. But Ran is not an evil god. Merely capricious."

Rol dropped from the boat down onto the wet shingle. He was taller than the stranger, and a good deal broader, but there was something intimidating about the man.

"You are from Driol, along the coast?" he asked politely.

"No." The stranger did not elaborate, but studied Rol with an appraising air. "You are a long way from home, young Ordiseyn, and I see ten million waves yet to roll under your keel. Many is the green sea that you will go over, and in the end many a green sea will go over you; but not yet."

"My name is Cortishane," Rol said, somewhat alarmed to find that he was talking to a babbling lunatic. He backed away, weighing the pitch pot in his fist and calculating the distance to the man's head. The dirk in his bootleg seemed suddenly too far from his fingers.

The stranger grinned, a gesture that transformed his countenance into something bright and feral.

"Old Ardisan has been discreet," he said in a low voice that the storm should have rendered inaudible. "Perhaps too much so. Listen here. There is a dead city in the delta of the Vosk. It was named after you, and you will go there one day. When you do, I shall be waiting." He raised his head to stare at the black cloud that towered over the headland. "There is a storm coming by land as well as sea, and you will be in the eye of it. This cockleshell of yours had best be a weatherly craft."

"I have to go now," Rol said uneasily. "They'll be missing me up at the house."

The stranger nodded, and his manner brightened, became mocking. "One thing more, my lad. This idyll of Ardisan's is at an end. Fate has come knocking at the door. I have a gift for you now that may ease your passage in the world. Hold out your hand."

Rol immediately closed his free fingers into a fist and backed away. "Stay back, or you'll have a face full of pitch."

"I doubt it. The stuff in that pot is cold as a witch's cunny."

And somehow the man had darted forward, quick as a heron's lunge, and had grasped Rol's free hand in his own. His fingers were like cold iron, and they burned. Rol cried out and fell to his knees in the shingle. The stranger bent over him and forced open the fist, matched palm for palm. It felt as though the flesh of Rol's hand were being seared through the very bone to the marrow. He screamed, but the sound was lost in the omnivorous roar of the wind. When he was released he fell backwards and a foaming wave crashed over him, the salt water pouring into his eyes, his ears and mouth. He rolled onto his side, staggered to his feet, and the next wave smashed into the backs of his thighs, toppling him once more. The man was gone, but Rol was sure he saw something sleek and black and shining leap into the rabid waves and disappear, before the salt spray blinded him once more.

He was floundering in waist-deep water—somehow he had rolled down the beach into the riotous breakers. He fought himself upright, his whole world a black and white storm of fuming water. The waves seemed to be trying to drag him out to sea, and there was cold laughter in their thunder. Finally he found himself by *Gannet* again, and he wrapped an arm about the wood of her sternpost. Staring at his pain-racked hand he thought he could make out a shape, a scallop of scar on the palm, but the light was going fast and his eyes were stinging with salt. He stumbled inland, up the face of the little cove, and did not stop until he had grass under his feet again and the bellow of the sea was muffled by the frowning cliffs below.

Lightning played about the headland, and there was a bright red glow that perplexed Rol. Then he heard shouting over the wind and the pelting rain, and broke into a run toward Eyrie.

A mob of men with torches were milling there, perhaps a hundred on foot and another score on horseback, their cuirasses shining in the stormlit rain. They had surrounded the shuttered house and various of them were hammering at the closed door. Rol saw Serioc the Headman of Driol there, carrying a half pike and hitching at the weight of an ancient mail shirt on his back. He looked both self-important and embarrassed, like a man caught out giving charity. But the obvious leader of the crowd was a fully armored figure on a black destrier, his face almost invisible beneath the bedraggled plumes of his helm, which he kept twitching aside in irritation. Now and again he would lean in the saddle and speak to one of the other horsemen who clustered deferentially about him, and they would nod solemnly.

Rol wondered if he had slipped into some fevered, dream-lit madness. Clutching his injured hand to his breast, he dropped into the sodden heather a cable from the house, and watched as the pigs were run off squealing, Ayd's vegetable garden was trampled, and Eyrie's stout shutters were dunted and thumped by the butts of pikes and halberds. The more enterprising of the mob scrambled up onto the roof of the cottage and began thrusting pike-points down through the turves of the roof. However, they all scrambled hastily to the ground again when one of the penetrating pike-shafts was whipped out of its owner's grasp and disappeared, only to re-emerge point first and with startling rapidity close to his backside.

"Come out now and we will be lenient, Cortishane," the plumed horseman shouted, and the ill-tempered growl of the crowd went quiet. "It is the law. You are suspected of brewing witchery and must answer for it before the Marschal. By resisting arrest you will only make it worse."

A silence, except for the billowing whine of the wind and the rattle of rain off armor. Out to sea thunder rumbled, like the bad-tempered muttering of some subterranean god. Then the entire throng of men jumped as the bars of Eyrie's only door were drawn back within, and Rol's grandfather stepped out into the rain. At once a score of crossbowmen put their foot in the stirrups of their weapons and pulled back the bow-cords to set their quarrels.

"Lord Vasst. To think you should be out on such a night over such a trifling misunderstanding." Rol's grandfather smiled reasonably. Behind him, lamp- and firelight streamed out, to make of his bent frame a wizened silhouette. He leaned heavily on a blackthorn stick and in his free hand was nothing more threatening than an unlit pipe.

Nonetheless, the mass of men backed away from him, murmuring.

"Gossip and rumor make a fool's justice, my lord. I have been here twenty years, and never yet harmed a soul, nor will I, if left in peace."

"That ape-armed giant of yours scared my boy half to death," a voice shouted fiercely from back in the crowd. "And do you think we don't see the woman prowling the moors at night with those eyes of hers?"

An angry snarl of agreement eddied through the ranks of armed men. Lord Vasst held up a gauntleted hand.

"If you are innocent, Cortishane, then you and your family

have nothing to fear from Dennifreian justice. But we are here to take you by force, if need be. Do not compel us to shed blood."

The mob made way for a file of the liveried crossbowmen, their weapons now cocked and ready. Lying where he was, Rol could no longer make out the expression on his grandfather's face, but he was sure beyond all doubt that for a moment the old man looked straight at him as he lay shivering in the heather, the lines about his eyes tightening.

Then Grandfather straightened, and leaned on his stick no more. When he spoke again, it was with a strong, carrying voice that seemed that of a much younger man.

"You are a gaggle of ignorant barbarians. I have encountered what you term *justice* on half the continents of the world; always it ends with a rope or a pitch-soaked stake. Leave this place now, or by Ran's blood, I shall lay you dead."

With that, he raised his arms skyward as if to try and grasp the lightning. Behind him, the gleam from within the cottage was blotted out by the huge bulk of Morin, and in Morin's head two hungry green lights burned that had nothing human about them.

"Shoot him!" Lord Vasst screamed, his horse bucking under him. "He'll spell us all!"

Rol found it hard to follow what happened next. There was a flash of emerald light, so brief it might have been tinted lightning. He distinctly heard the *thock* of the crossbows releasing. Men screamed and shouted and streamed away from Eyrie, knocking one another down. The horses shrieked and reared. Above them all, Morin reared up tall as a tree, his face transformed into the mask of a ravening beast—and behind him another, smaller shape sped out of the cottage with the same inhuman light in its eyes. It was prick-eared and feline with a twitching tail, but ran on two legs and yowled insanely before launching itself on Lord Vasst's men.

The horsemen mastered their mounts and charged the two figures, swords swinging. The crossbowmen paused fifty yards from Rol's hiding place and began to reload their weapons. Serioc was shouting at his fellow villagers to stand fast. A loose phalanx of the more resolute among them leveled their pikes and advanced back the way they had run, fear white in their faces under the branched flare of the lightning.

It could not be real. These things were impossible.

Rol started to his feet, but a strong hand grasped the back of his neck and forced his face down into the scratch and drip of the heather, and his grandfather's voice said hoarsely, "Be still."

They both watched as the villagers and horsemen closed in on whatever it was Morin and Ayd had become. Bodies and parts of bodies went flying through the air. Crossbow bolts rained down on a choked, writhing, screaming mass of boiling humanity and horseflesh, and the lightning played garishly overhead. The crossbowmen reloaded time after time, and edged closer to the cottage, the better to aim into the melee. Grandfather seized Rol's hand. "Come with me."

He ran like a young man, trailing Rol after him. The pair went unnoticed in the glare and the murk and the shining curtain of the rain. They did not stop until they were at the foot of the hagrolith that watched over the headland, some quarter mile from the house. Eyrie was burning from within by then, flames licking brightly out of the front door and curling up into the turf of the roof. Up on the roof the cat-thing that might have been Ayd snapped and snarled as the crossbow bolts rained down on her. Morin was a great broken carcass lying before the house, a beached whale that men flensed to pieces with sword and pike and halberd, the dark blood splashing up past their knees.

Grandfather leaned with his back to the hagrolith, and there was pain in the rasp of his breath. He put a hand to his side and Rol saw a crossbow bolt protruding obscenely there, the white flights blackened with the old man's blood. Rol thought to take hold of it, but the old man slapped away his hands irritably. "No good. Leave it be."

They watched the bright flames roar up in the night as Eyrie's roof timbers gave with a groan, the house dying in agony whilst about it the surviving Dennifreians thrashed the heather with their weapons, and a knot set up two dark, dripping trophies upon stakes fashioned out of hewn saplings. Some men were still mounted, though most of the horses lay torn and lifeless about the house. One that was thrashing blindly in its own entrails was put out of its misery with a sword-thrust.

"They'll find us," Rol whispered. He was wet through and shivering. "We have to get away."

"No. She'll protect us. She'll hide us from them." And Grandfather looked up at the tip of the mossy stone above him and smiled through his pain. "Twenty years she has kept them from our door. But times change, it seems." He shut his eyes for a moment and some kind of febrile strength left him. He was an old, withered man shot through the guts and bleeding his life out in the rain.

"Take *Gannet,* Rol. Leave this place and never come back."

"Where shall we go?" Amazing that he could sit and talk calmly like this, when his whole life was burning down in front of his eyes, and all he knew lay dying or dead about him. But his mind seemed remarkably clear. The palm of his left hand had ceased its burning.

"I stay here. You must go alone"—a hand held up to silence Rol's protest—"and go now. You must go to Gascar. It's six days' sail with a fair wind, and this storm could not have been pointed better; you'll have it on the larboard quarter. Steer west-nor'west—" He coughed, and something black as crushed berries was spat into his beard. Rol wiped it away, dry-eyed and staring.

"In the capital, Ascari, you must ask about the wharves for a man named Michal Psellos. Tell him you are a Cortishane. He is—he is a friend."

"Why?" Rol asked. "Why did all this happen? Morin and Ayd—"

"You are not human," the old man said harshly. "Morin and Ayd were your guardians. I summoned them for that purpose."

"What am I?"

But the old man's eyes were glazing over. "The pain is going now," he whispered. "Never a good sign. Leave me, Rol." And he shoved the boy away with surprising strength. Rol knelt and watched him struggle to breathe through the blood that was flooding his lungs. Once he said clearly, *"Emilia,"* and smiled up at the lightning.

When God withdrew from the world, to punish us He took with Him all hope of life after death. So nothing but the worm awaits us all. No justice for the persecuted, no punishment for the wicked...

He died with his eyes open, and there was a distinct tremor in the ground about the hagrolith. Rol clenched his fists in his hair, and the rain beat the tears from his eyes. Behind him, he heard the shouts of the men who had destroyed his family carry over the burgeoning roar of the storm. He turned. With the death of the old man they had seen him at last, and at least two dozen were laboring through the knee-deep heather to the tip of the headland.

When Rol turned back to look at his grandfather, the old man's body was gone. In its place was a great leaning stone, a second hagrolith that had erupted out of the ground beside the first. Now the two leaned in against each other as if exchanging a kiss.

Rol got to his feet and began to run.

He could not take *Gannet*—she had been beached too high, and was too heavy for him alone to shift. He ran with no clear idea in his head except to get away from the men with bloody swords, to find some black corner wherein he could collect his thoughts.

But they had spread out like beaters flushing game onto the spears of the hunters, and behind them now half a dozen men on horseback came riding, their mounts stumbling and tripping on the heather roots but making a good pace all the same. Rol halted. There was nothing for it but the sea, then, nowhere else to go.

The wind was a heavier roar as he came over the lip of the higher ground, toward the cove where *Gannet* lay beached. It smote his face in spiteful glee, and drove rain into his eyes. The tide would be far in—there was only a black moon tonight, but it would still be high.

Lightning struck the turf ten yards ahead of him as though lighting his way, and with that he felt the wind backing and noted its changed direction with the automatic seagoing part of his mind. He scrambled down the steep clifflike bank where swifts nested in summer, and slid down the slick grass to the black rocks below.

The sea was before him, dancing to Ran's Music in the wind. It looked stark black and white, furious, explosive. Rol had never seen breakers so high. So far up the shingle had it come that *Gannet* was lurching and bobbing there, fighting her anchor rope. She was afloat, ungrounded—the storm had been good for that much at least.

He heard the shouts up the slope behind him, turned, and saw a man in armor standing outlined against the sky, pointing down. Rol waited no more. He waded into the sea, the white cold shock of it clearing his brain of all thought. The waves buffeted him, swung *Gannet* broadside on. He grabbed her side and pulled himself up over the rail. The wherry leaped and bucked under him like a wild, sentient thing. He crawled to the bow and began sawing at the wet anchor rope with his dirk. The rope was thick, wet, and stubborn; it came apart strand by strand.

A crowd of men at the edge of the breakers, the spray dancing and leaping about them. They hesitated, confronted by the sheer naked violence of the waves, but then one mustered his courage and began wading out, sword upraised.

The rope was only half cut through. Rol wiped seawater out of his eyes and glared at the approaching soldier with pure hatred. He abandoned the rope, and reached for the gaff instead, lifting it out of its slot in *Gannet*'s rail. As the man approached the wherry's pitching side, Rol judged the movement perfectly, and with the downroll he stabbed the hooked point of the gaff into the top of the man's head. It broke through his skull and stuck there. The man sank under the water without a sound, dragging the gaff with him.

No one else came out to try to stop him, though a pair of crossbowmen arrived and fired ineffectual bolts into the wind. Rol cut the anchor rope at last, unfrapped the mainsail, and hauled up first the throat and then the peak halliards. The mainsail broke open and *Gannet* began to cease her mindless wallowing and move with more purpose. The wind was a southerly, and the bulk of Dennifrey was mitigating its blast along this northern coast. Out at sea the swells would be unimaginable. Drenched, Rol sat by the tiller and brought the wherry's head round to larboard. West-nor'west perhaps, he was not sure. He only knew that the wind was now striking the boat from somewhere behind his left ear. The little vessel staggered as the mainsail filled out with a sharp crack, and the mast itself groaned. But the sickening roll had stopped, and *Gannet*'s stem was laboring up and down like a rational thing. She was moving out past the murderous foam-smashed rocks, toward the open ocean. Rol sat at her tiller like a thing made out of stone.

You are not human.

Three

THE STERN MAIDEN

BLACK WAVES, WHITE-TIPPED WITH FURY IN THE HOWLing night. Rol had outsailed the sheltering promontories of the deep-bitten north Dennifreian coast, and he was truly out in the open ocean now. The great swells that were looming astern had come all the length of the Wrywind and were monsters of their kind—or so it seemed to him with nothing but coastal squalls to compare them to. A numbness had set itself about Rol's mind, and he watched the pitching horizon with a kind of dulled stubbornness, the tiller clamped grimly in one armpit. He ought to shorten sail, but the numbness kept him sitting there at the steering bench, and below him *Gannet* was hurled forward recklessly. In the hollow of the great waves it grew almost calm, but as the wherry coursed manfully up the side of the next swell the wind would take hold again, and the boat would stagger, the stem digging deep in the flanks of the sea, water foaming aft and flooding down into the hold. Already, she was lower in the water than she had a right to be, and her painful dance was becoming jerky as that of a mishandled puppet.

There came a moment when Rol finally realized that he must see to his craft or perish there in the heaving night. Painfully, he rose and slipped the deadman's lines about the tiller to hold the course, and then methodically set about reducing sail. As he loosed the halliards the gaff struggled against him, beating about the mainmast, but finally he had it lowered on deck and began gathering in the loose bunt of the mainsail. The canvas thrashed him in the face as it flapped and fought his fists but he managed to secure it to the gaff and then square away the yard, *Gannet* pitching and rolling under him like a wild horse all the while. Finally he set up a little triangle of a storm-jib that they kept in the forward locker for emergencies, and that was just enough to keep the wherry's head to the wind and prevent her from broaching-to. The effort left him bleeding, bruised, and exhausted. He stumbled aft like a man who has been flogged, and then set about sealing the mainhatch with a swatch of tarred canvas. That done, he was able to collapse on the steering bench once more, securing himself there with a length of cordage.

West-nor'west, the wind on the larboard quarter. Rol had no idea what speed *Gannet* was making, but even with the mainsail taken in, it was greater than any he had ever seen her achieve before. The wherry, broad-beamed as a duck, seemed to skate across the great swells, moving now with a more rational purpose. Rol bent and kissed the smooth wood of the tiller, momentarily loving the sturdy little craft and her valiant heart. She had not been designed for deep water, but seemed to revel in the challenge all the same. Some of the numbness that had fogged his brain seemed to lift, and his mind began turning again. He looked up and saw the stars glittering cold and white above him, found the Mariner, and the five points of Gabriel's

Fist. Still on course, then. Some new life awaited him out there along the winking pathways of the nighttime sky, and he knew now that he was ready for it.

The storm blew itself out in the watch before the dawn, the sun rising over a succession of long, blue swells. Seen from land, even a stormy sea is flat, a featureless horizon. But to one at sea in a small boat, the ocean is a moving landscape of hills and valleys, mountains and canyons. When *Gannet* rode up the side of the tall waves Rol was able to look straight into the eyes of swimming fish, as though they lived in some great-walled tank of glass. Then the wherry would be over the crest, and he would be as it were sliding down a steep hill into the windless valley at the bottom.

A clay beaker of water and some sheaves of dried fish were kept always in the boat's stern locker. The water was weeks old, but it tasted sweet and cool to Rol as he sluiced the salt out of his mouth and nibbled on ablaroni fillet. It would last some days, with care. The welcome sunlight began to dry out his sodden frame, and a curious gull circled the wherry, perching for a while on the truck of the mainmast and preening itself unconcernedly. The sight was somehow reassuring—the wider world had not disappeared in the chaos of the night. Umer wheeled on as always amid the vast gulfs of the stars. Life continued on the other side of the storm.

Twice during the days that followed, Rol caught sight of other vessels abroad upon the Wrywind. They were high-seas ships, tall carracks flying pennants of silk. One sailed close enough to become hull-up on the horizon, and he could actually glimpse the tiny forms of mariners about her decks. He watched them with a strange mixture of fear and longing. He trusted no man now—whatever his heritage was, men obviously feared and hated it. Could they even sense it, like a horse smelling fire?

And yet he would have given much to be one of those mariners, no longer alone, but part of a ship's company abroad upon the open ocean. Belonging to something.

The carrack passed, until even her masts had disappeared beyond the curve of the earth. They could not have seen the tiny scrap of jib that was all the canvas on *Gannet*'s yards. Rol's horizon was empty again. These were well-traveled waters, full of the sea trade of the Seven Isles, policed by oceangoing enforcers in the pay of the Mercanters. He need not, at least, fear pirates here; they cruised in the warmer waters of the Westerease Sea, and down in the Inner Reach. So Grandfather had said, back in saner days.

Rol studied his left palm in the clear morning light. It was white, pale as the inside of a shell, and scalloped in ridges. A cluttered tangle of tiny lines, darker than the skin about them, wound about the scar like the blind trails of sea-worms. Almost he thought there was a pattern to them. The thing that had done this to him—it was no man, of that he was certain—had said things, called him by a name that he could not now remember, so much having happened after. So many things.

He thumped *Gannet*'s timbers in frustration, shouted at the empty sky, cursing his grandfather's riddles and mysteries; and finally bent his head and wept for the ending of the world he had known. Angry tears, full of salt.

Four days he sailed along, keeping rigidly to his course. He set the mainsail again as the wind fell and *Gannet* began to wallow, and dozed shivering on the hard steering bench by night, the deadman's lines securing the tiller. His clothes he took off and flew from the mast to try to dry them. On his naked skin the salt sat dusty and ash-gray, and his hair was harsh as a horse's mane with it, his eyes red-rimmed and smarting. He grew sick of the very sight of dried fish.

The skies remained clear, the wind backing a point now and again, but always veering round once more, as though under orders to remain constant. It was cold, but bright, as if spring had come early to the Wrywind. The swell never grew taller than half a fathom, and *Gannet* puddled along equably, as though she had been made for this crossing of the open sea.

On the fifth morning Rol sighted land fine on the larboard bow, a tall blue line of hills, and a white-tipped mountain in their midst. He was in the coastal waters of Gascar now, at the center of the Seven Isles. Some eighty leagues he had sailed, and a few more would see his landfall. He studied the sunlit hills as though he might decipher the answers to all his questions on their slopes.

The wind dropped to a moderate breeze, and as *Gannet* coasted with Gascar's hills to port, Rol passed a few late inshore fishermen taking advantage of the unseasonally clement weather. They stopped and stared at the strange sail before continuing to haul in their catch. There was little enough in the coastal grounds this late in the year, but a last netful might mean the difference between hunger and plenty at the tail end of winter.

Rol rounded a long promontory, wooded with tall green pine and fir and girded with gray rock. A square-rigged caravel went by, beating into the wind, her crew singing in the shrouds. Thanks to his grandfather's endless stories Rol knew that the gilded porpoise at her stem meant she was out of Corso, to the southwest. The Corsoans, short and dark as seals, were consummate deepwater sailors, and their pilots were in high demand over all the Twelve Seas. He felt a momentary thrill of excitement. All those tall tales, they had been an education, in a way. Perhaps Grandfather had been preparing him for a day such as this.

Ascari, capital of Gascar. It shone bright in the sunlight at the foot of its long bay. White houses with red clay roofs, a haze of smoke hanging over them, and in the harbor at the city's foot half a hundred vessels of all ports and builds, cradled by a white-washed mole of squared stone that arced protectively into the glittering waters of the bay. He had made very good time, and Grandfather's sailing directions, brief though they had been, were still accurate.

The hills surrounding the port killed the wind, and the water in the bay was calm as glass. Rol broke out *Gannet*'s heavy sweeps, and for a sweating couple of hours labored first at one and then the other, as if propelling an oversized rowing boat. A swift six-man cutter put out into the bay and hailed him as he worked. The helmsman was grinning through a salt-gray beard.

"Hot work, even on a cold day, young 'un! We'll tow you in, if you have a mind, take you right snug up to the wharves. What say you?"

Rol wiped his forehead, panting. "How much?"

The men in the cutter looked at one another. The helmsman's grin widened. "No more than you can afford, with a pretty face like that. Give me, Aradas, a roll in the hold and we'll scull you to port in style."

Rol bared his teeth, and spat over the side. "Too dear for my liking. I'd sooner sweat."

Aradas laughed. "Suit yourself, my proud one!" and the cutter was sculled rapidly away with its crew hooting and calling derisively.

It was late evening by the time Rol had finally made *Gannet* fast fore and aft to stone bollards set in the harbor mole. By that time he was spent, his back aching and his hands blistered—except where the strange scar had somehow protected one palm. The first stars were out, and his breath was a pale fog before his face. He sat on the mole by *Gannet* for a while, feeling the cold stiffen his sore muscles and start to work a chill within his sweat-soaked clothing. At the base of the mole Ascari was a maze of yellow lights, and he could hear raucous laughter, shouts, clattering cart-wheels. A burst of song from the open door of a tavern. At his feet the waters of the bay plopped and hissed and *Gannet* floated, creaking. It was the ebb of the tide.

Rol had never felt so alone.

A lantern-bearing shape loomed up out of the night, the fragrance of whitherb wound about it. A bearded man with a short pipe jutting from his mouth, and eyes black as bubbles of pitch in the lantern-light. He took his pipe out of his mouth and spat on the whitened stone of the mole. "When'd you get in, younker?"

"Just now. Just this moment."

"Berthing fee to be paid. Five minims a day, unless you're kin to one of the fisherfolk. What's the name?"

Rol rubbed his face. "I'm a friend of Michal Psellos. Would you know where to find him?"

The man's pipe paused on its way back to the reeking hole in his beard. He glared. "Ten minims a day for such as you, then, and make it quick or I'll have the Harbor Watch impound that cockleshell o' yourn."

Rol stared at him, smelling the dislike. A few short days ago he might have been cowed, but not now. He stood up, hand on the dirk in his belt. "You'll have your money and more if you tell me where Psellos is to be found."

He was eyed narrowly. "You're not of Gascar. There's a tang of Dennifrey in your accent, and something else maybe. What would you be wanting with a creature like that? Do you know Psellos at all?"

"I was to look him up here."

The man seemed to study him closely. "You didn't sail from Dennifrey in that thing, did you?"

Rol shrugged, too tired to elaborate.

"You want my advice, then set sail for home again. You don't want to go mixing with folk such as that. You're only a boy—I see now. Ascari's no place for a youngster alone."

"I've nowhere else to go."

The man hesitated, and then: "Go to the top of the town, up the hill. There's a gray tower there in the eaves of the wood. Psellos is there some of the time at least."

"What about the ten minims?"

"Pay me tomorrow, if you see tomorrow. If you don't, I'll take your boat."

Rol was too weary to argue further. He nodded wordlessly. The man gave him a last stare, spat over the side of the mole, and walked away shaking his head.

The life of Ascari, even in winter, seemed to take place on the streets. Everywhere along the narrow cobbled ways, braziers burned outside open shopfronts, and men sat drinking by them. Once a drunkard lunged for Rol, and he whipped out his dirk, eyes blazing. The man's companions reeled him back in, laughing and bowing mockingly. Women called to him from upper windows, blew him kisses, promised him all manner of carnal services. Urchins pawed at his waist, eyes bright in wasted faces. He thrust them aside, loathing and pitying them at the same time. He passed fevered knots of copulation in wet alleyways, and once a group of feather-capped men bending over a body sprawled on the cobbles. Music eddied out into the night, cooking smells brought the water into his salt-tainted mouth. He was famished and parched, but knew better than to enter any of the dank taverns he passed. He walked his slow, obstructed way up the hill upon which Ascari sprawled and felt that he was being assaulted by a whole new range of experience, a different world that his mind struggled to take in. This beetling hive of humanity was at once fascinating and repulsive. He wondered how men could live like this—piled atop one another—without going mad.

Farther up the hill the town became less congested, the houses larger and better made. Trees were planted in stately avenues and banners flapped atop the spires of tall towers. The streets became wider, and Rol began to breathe more easily, though with his travel-worn clothes he was more remarked by the better-dressed strollers who passed him by. When he paused and looked back he was able to see the lights of the port strung out down the hillside and along the shore to the northwest and southeast. He realized that the hill and harbor made up only a portion of the entire town; it extended in haphazard fashion for thousands of yards along the coast with no order or design to its layout.

Ascari was unwalled, as were all of the cities of the Seven Isles. They relied on their navies to keep out invaders. Grandfather had said that though the Isles might war amongst themselves from time to time, when an outsider threatened any of the seven he would find himself attacked by all. Not even Bionar had ever felt strong enough to assault the Isles by sea, though Arbionar had been a colony of hers once upon a time.

The last building before the wooded summits of the nearer hills was a stone tower, although the term did not do justice to its gaunt massiveness. Unlike the rest of the town, it was unpainted and unadorned, constructed of massive courses of dark masonry, and it seemed to be built into the hill itself, with low wings extending back from the cylindrical base of the main structure. Not so much a dwelling as a fortress. A light shone high up in a window, and near the conical roof Rol thought he could make out an open space, a balcony of some kind. There was a huge double door a fathom from its foot, reached by a steep wooden staircase. Set within it, a smaller postern was framed in iron. Clambering up, Rol hammered on the wood of the postern with his fist, not allowing himself time to think or hesitate.

He waited. Nothing. He stood unsure and afraid, hand on the hilt of his dirk. The tower seemed dead and empty despite the light he had glimpsed far up its flank.

All this way he had come for this, and if it turned out to be a barren errand, what then would he do? The night seemed vast and empty and alien to him. He knew of nowhere else in the world he might go.

The door scraped back on its jamb, startling him. A hooded figure stood holding a candle-lantern. He stepped back, and came close to falling off the stairway.

A woman—no, a girl. She was not hooded but had a heavy mane of black hair that fell down on either side of her white face. Her eyes were so pale as to be almost colorless, with no whit of warmth to soften their hue. She stood silent, as severely beautiful as a marble statue.

"I'm here to see Michal Psellos," Rol stammered.

The cold eyes looked him up and down, and then the door was slammed shut in his face.

He stood gaping for a moment, and then began hammering on the door with his fist. "Open up!" When that failed he drew his dirk and pounded on the stout timbers with the pommel, suddenly furious.

The door opened again. The hard white face was unchanged, but something glittered at the girl's waist. Before it could register, Rol felt a hard punch to his midriff, and his legs turned to water. He fell to his knees. There was no pain, simply a sense of utter weakness. He had no idea what could have happened, even when he bowed his head and saw the dark stain on his shirt.

He looked up again. The girl seemed to be studying him. Then her foot came up and kicked him in the chest. He toppled backwards, off the wooden stairway, and thumped to the earth six feet below. Lying on his back he looked up at the distant brilliance of the stars until, one by one, they went out.

Four

THE HOUSE OF MICHAL PSELLOS

"YOU ARE A RARITY, MY YOUNG FRIEND; A LIFE WHICH sidled past the edge of Rowen's blade. Perhaps she likes you." A laugh, unpleasant to hear.

Rol opened his eyes. His vision was filled by a face. A bearded man, hair dark and shiny as jet, the beard oiled and waxed into a curled point. His eyes were the color of a skua's breast, and they changed even as Rol watched. His eyeteeth were made of fang-sharp silver. He smelled of perfume.

The man withdrew. Rol tried to sit up and found that he was naked, bound hand and foot to the posts of a heavy iron bed. A dull pain burned relentlessly below his rib cage. It was stuffy, and the sweat trickling into his eyes blurred his vision. He was in a candlelit stone room, windowless, circular, the ceiling upheld by heavy beams. More, he could not lift his head to see, but he thought he glimpsed a dark shape sitting at the corner of his eye, close to the bed. The girl? As he tried to twist his neck to look, the pain turned his bowels to water and left his dry mouth in a hiss. He closed his eyes until it passed.

"I must go to work," a low voice said, a woman's.

"Very well." It was the bearded man. "But be back after the middle hour—this fellow will need someone to watch over him, and I have appointments to keep." No answer but the sound of a door closing softly.

"Look at me," the man's voice said sharply.

Rol obeyed him. The man filled his vision again. The colors swirled in his eyes, like oil on water.

"You are Ardisan's kin—I would know that countenance anywhere. Perhaps it made Rowen turn her blade aside. She senses these things too. Hold still."

Something hot and moist was pressed against his sternum. A tingling spread from it, a warmth that invaded Rol's head and made him dizzy as if he were inhaling smoke.

"Well, you'll live, which proves my point. The Blood runs in you—but how true, I wonder?" Here the man raised a vial of scarlet liquid in the candlelight and studied it intently. Seeing Rol's bleary puzzlement, he smiled, his silver fangs catching the light in turn. "Call it payment, if you will. If it's as pure as I think, it'll keep us in bread and oil for many a day."

"Psellos?" Rol croaked.

The man bowed. "Indeed. Ardisan is dead at last, I take it. Well, he was a worthy fellow in his time, but he was a fool to bury himself out in the middle of nowhere as he did. We conceal ourselves more easily the more cattle we have around us."

He leaned close over Rol as though recording his features. "Yes—I see your mother in you." He glanced back at the door. "She was a beauty too."

"You knew my mother!"

"In a manner of speaking."

"How? How could—" Rol tried to raise an arm but failed. "Why am I bound?" he demanded.

"One must be cautious. You could be anything—a doppelganger out of Kull knocking on my door." And he gestured with one long-fingered hand to a shelf near the ceiling. It was lined with jars, and in each floated a face, a severed head in which the eyes glared brightly. One blinked, and its mouth opened in a soundless snarl, making Rol flinch.

"But I can loose you now, I think. Don't try to sit up—you must allow the poultice to do its work." He began untying the knots that held Rol to the bed. "They came for him in the end, did they, the local cattle?"

"They burned our home. And Morin and Ayd they killed too."

Psellos looked up at that. "I would not worry overmuch about golems, useful though they are. Your grandfather had a way with them, it's true. My talents lie elsewhere."

The poultice felt as though it were sinking through Rol's chest, dragging his ribs down to meet his backbone. He grimaced. "Talents? I understand none of this. What did they kill him for—why did they hate us so? How are we different?"

Psellos's strange eyes went dark. "That's for another time, I think, when your guts have stopped leaking out of your belly. Rest for now—and do not try to rise or even raise your head. Do not touch the poultice."

"I'm thirsty."

"You cannot drink, not yet."

"Why did she attack me—that girl?"

Psellos threw back his head and laughed. As he did, Rol could have sworn that for a moment a sharp, finger-thin tongue whipped out from between his lips. It was black.

"Ask her, if you dare. But if she had meant you to be dead,

you can be sure you would be, blood of Orr or no. Sleep now, my bonny boy, and be thankful I came home when I did."

He snapped his fingers with a *crack,* and Rol slept.

Movement on his chest woke him, something warm and heavy slithering there. Frozen by fear, he felt the thing crawl off him, plump onto the bed, and then land with a slap on the floor. His shaking hand felt the place where the girl had stabbed him. It was covered in some manner of slime, and there was a ridged scar, but the wound had closed. He felt clear-headed, incredibly thirsty. The room was dark, save for the guttering stump of a single tallow candle by the bed.

Rol sat up, and immediately a shadow came out of the corner and a cool hand shoved hard against his breastbone, pushing him supine once more. It was the girl, Rowen. He felt his heart thudding under her palm as she held him down. Her hair was hanging dark as a raven's wing over one eye; the other seemed almost to take on the yellow hue of the candlelight. She was older than he had thought, not a girl but a full-grown woman, his senior by ten years at least. There were shadows under her eyes, fine lines running from the corners of her nose to her mouth. Her lips were dark as a bruise, and on the back of the hand that pinioned him, blue veins stood out stark against the pale skin. Rol was strong for his age, his muscles hardened by work at sea and on land, but he realized that the strength in her slim arm was greater than his own.

All the same, she seemed to him one of the most beautiful things he had ever seen.

She took her hand away slowly, as if expecting him to spring up again. Her eyes never left his face. She reached at the side of the bed without looking and took hold of a clay cup. This she put to his lips and tilted backwards. Rol drank cool water greedily, some of it trickling down his chin and neck.

"Thank you," he gasped.

The girl said nothing, but laying aside the cup, she bent over his chest and examined the place where she had wounded him. Her hair brushed Rol's ribs and stomach, glided across his navel. He felt the cool fingers on his belly for a moment, before she straightened again.

"Get up," she said, turning away. "Get dressed."

He had become erect while she had been examining him, but she had given no sign. He turned his back on her, cheeks burning, and pulled on his clothes. They lay over a stool by the bed, and had been washed and their rents mended. A needle and thread sat to one side. Rol wondered if the neat stitching was his companion's work, but thought it better not to ask.

Now that he could see the room upright, he saw that it was larger than he had supposed, with several doors and alcoves set about the walls. Many shelves and bookcases stood about, all heavy with manuscripts, jars, pots, and leather-bound grimoires as thick as a man's bicep. A few small round tables sat here and there, and a yard-high brazier red with burning charcoal heated the place well enough to bring the sweat popping out on Rol's forehead.

On one empty part of the wall, heavy iron rings had been set into the stone, and from these shackles hung.

The girl drew back a chair from one of the tables and gestured for him to sit. There was a full pitcher of water thereon, bread, apples, cold mutton, and pickles. Rol wolfed it down with a will. He could barely remember the last time he had eaten a decent meal. Ayd would have scolded him for his table manners, but Ayd was dead now—and what manner of thing had she been anyway?

He looked at the girl, Rowen, with a new resolve. If there were princesses and queens in the world, he thought, they must look like her. But he had not forgotten the cold violence he had suffered at her hands.

"Who are you?" he asked, emboldened by the good food in his stomach and the close intimacy of the chamber.

"Who are you?" she asked in her turn, raising an eyebrow.

"I . . ." He hesitated. "I suppose I don't know, not anymore."

She shrugged as though that were answer enough, and taking a poniard from the scabbard at her waist began sharpening it deliberately with a small whetstone.

"Why did you attack me?"

She pointed the blade at his face. "You had a knife in your hand and were hammering at Psellos's door. That is enough, usually. In Ascari the questions come afterward."

"Were you trying to kill me?"

She paused in her work. "Yes."

"Psellos doesn't think so."

"He may think what he likes."

"Are you his daughter, or his wife?"

The unsettling eyes stabbed out at him, as cold and hostile as those of a spitting cat.

"No wife. No kin. I work for him."

"What do you do?"

She actually smiled, but there was no humor in it, a bitterness rather. "Whatever I have to."

"Psellos, then." The exasperation was fraying Rol's voice. "What kind of man is he? A man down on the wharves warned me against him. How did he know my grandfather, my mother?" The last words were a sobbing croak.

Rowen regarded him with mild interest. "I dare say you'll find out, in time."

After that Rol gave up on her. He rose from the rags of his meal and set about exploring the chamber. He was not altogether surprised when he found that every door leading out of it was locked. His dirk was gone, and there was nothing he could see in the place that might serve as a weapon. He did not relish the thought of tackling the girl bare-handed. Rubbing his chest, he leafed through the tattered books on the shelves. He could read, after a fashion, but the words within them were in languages he did not know, illustrated with arcane engravings. There was an unclean feel to some of the tomes, which made him wipe his fingers on his breeches after he had laid them back down.

Hours passed. Rowen sat watching him, patient and untiring as a stone. Rol wondered what time it was—surely the winter dawn could not be far off? He was exhausted. Finally he gave his companion a last glare, and fell asleep leaning against the wall. He disliked the idea of the bed with its ropes.

He was on the bed when he awoke, nonetheless. Sunlight streamed into the room through windows that had been hidden behind drapes the night before. The charcoal in the brazier had sunk into ash. Psellos and Rowen were standing by it with their backs to him.

"He's full-blooded," Psellos was saying. "I don't know how it can be, but old Grayven is never wrong. I knew Amerie must have cuckolded the fool, for all her protestations of love."

"Who was the father, then?" Rowen asked.

"You have me there. But I mean to find out, one way or another. In the meantime, he'll stay."

"Another stray to bleed dry?"

"No—he's much more than that." Here Psellos ran a hand up into the black mane of Rowen's hair. Grasping a fistful, he drew her head back sharply and set his mouth on hers. When he released her, there were red teethmarks about her dark lips. He held out his other hand, and without a word she placed something in it. A clink of coin. Psellos smiled into her pale face, rattled the gift in his palm. "A good night. You got the book?"

"Yes. Now I must change. I stink."

"I like it when you stink," he said, grinning. She tugged free, leaving black hairs in his fingers. Psellos's face twisted with mock contrition. "Everything must have a price, Rowen. It is the way of the world."

"I know. You taught me well." She left the room without a backward glance.

Psellos stood shaking his head. Smiling still. Then he pocketed his coinage and, turning, kicked the bed. "Up."

Rol sat up in the bed.

"Come. If you are to stay here, then we must make you useful."

The Tower was even more spacious than it looked from without. Rol followed his host up a series of corkscrew stairs until they came out on a wide-open space, the balcony he had glimpsed the night before. Morning had come. They were several hundred feet above the level of the sea here, and in the bright winter sunlight all of Ascari could be seen spread below, and beyond it the blue vastness of the Wrywind extending to the horizon. They were looking east, toward Dennifrey, and a life that already seemed part of the vanished past.

"Rol, is it?" Psellos asked casually. "Well, that will do. I am your master now, Rol. You may stay here under my tutelage as Rowen has, but in return I expect perfect obedience."

"My boat—"

"Sold this morning. It will help to defray your expenses."

Outraged into silence, Rol took a moment to master his voice. "What if I do not wish to stay?"

"Then you will never have your questions answered."

He glared at the man. And Psellos laughed.

"You dislike me. Good. That's well enough for a beginning."

Thus the education began.

It was enough, for the moment, that he had stopped running.

His mind accepted Psellos's patronage the more easily because he had nothing of familiarity left in the world, not one face he knew. It was easier to convince himself that there was no alternative. And so he submitted.

But he was not admitted to any degree of intimacy. In fact, Rol was at first little better than a scullion, set to all the menial tasks within the Tower that Psellos's whim dictated. Perhaps this was meant to humble him, but he had been raised to accept hard work without a murmur. So he scrubbed floors and gutted fish and cleared hearths equably enough, and all the while he watched and listened and learned the running of the Tower household.

It was a large establishment, for all that the Tower itself presented an austere frontage to the world. Psellos, Rol quickly discovered, was a man of wealth and influence, and he kept a certain style. To do so, he must needs surround himself with a small army of attendants and underlings.

There was the cook, Gibble—a short, rotund fellow with a bald pate and ferocious eyebrows. He was absolute master in the subterranean chambers that constituted the kitchens, but lived in mortal fear of his employer. He commanded a platoon of spry street urchins who shopped or stole for him according to the dictates of the day's menu. When the last course of the night was taken up to the Master's chambers, Gibble would sink back into a wide-bottomed carver and apply himself to the bottle with a dedication that was awesome to behold, while his stunted underlings gorged themselves on the table's leftovers as recompense for their errand-running.

A manservant there was also, thin as a fish. His name was Quare and he had long white fingers that left moist tracks on everything they touched. His black hair was greased back from his brow. Clad in sable hose, he padded about the stairways of the Tower as noiselessly as a spider. Rol learned early on to avoid meeting him alone, after a groping encounter in the wine cellars. Quare held a privileged position in that he had access to the Master at all times of the day and night. He was Psellos's ears and eyes in the lower quarters and was cordially hated by everyone.

There were other servants in ever-changing numbers. Valets, grooms, seamstresses. Maids who would arrive winsome and merry, and over time would become haggard, with haunted eyes, before disappearing to be replaced by yet more. And every week *associates* of Psellos (their own word) would come and go, uniformly obsequious to him and contemptuous of everyone else. A rigid hierarchy existed in Psellos's Tower, and though to all intents Rol was at the bottom of it (he slept on a pile of rags on the hot flagstones of the scullery) he was nonetheless marked out as different. Quare's attentions abruptly ceased after the first few days, and he regarded Rol with a mixture of wariness and hatred thereafter.

How Rowen fitted into the household Rol could not quite make out. Everyone deferred to her—out of fear if nothing else—but at the same time gave the impression that they despised her. Only Gibble was different. He treated her almost as a daughter and was always awake, if not entirely sober, when she returned from her nocturnal assignations. He would have food and hot water waiting for her and would see that she wanted for nothing before tottering off to his own bed. As for Rowen, she had a suite of richly appointed rooms in the upper third of the Tower and was often called to join Psellos at table, especially when he was entertaining, but she ate in the kitchen whenever she could and would often take some mundane chore upon herself on a kind of dark whim, working at the long oak table while Gibble clattered pans and chattered to her from the blaring heat of the stoves. She seemed to find the hot semidark of the kitchens soothing, and would sometimes stay there until dawn, sharpening Gibble's knives and skewers, boning joints with the deftness of a surgeon, or simply staring into the fire. No one but Gibble ever dared to address her.

One night, though, when the entire household was abed, Rol watched her through the scullery door as she stood drinking wine at the kitchen fire. She had just returned from one of her usual forays and was dressed mannishly, in breeches, doublet, and short cloak. Her hair was bound up and she looked almost like some delicate-featured boy. But there was a stiffness about her that marred her usual grace, a care in movement which spoke of some concealed pain.

Rol's breath stopped in his throat as she began to undress there and then, unaware of his wide eyes watching her. The raven hair was pulled out of its tight coiffure first, falling down onto her shoulders, and then the clothes were discarded with something akin to distaste. Her white skin was washed scarlet by the light of the dying fire, and the taut muscles moved in her thighs and calves, and along the curve of her back, as she examined herself. There was a series of vivid welts and what looked uncannily like bite marks running down her side and flanks, and she bathed them in Gibble's steaming water, wincing, her face drawn. The vision haunted Rol's dreams for weeks.

The Tower extended underground for almost as far as it loomed skyward. Days would go by when Rol would not even glimpse sunlight, his work confining him to the kitchens and cellars, the innumerable storerooms and pantries and workshops which were tunneled deep into the hill. He helped unload tall-sided wagons, which came in regularly, loaded with all manner of fruit and vegetable and game and barrel upon barrel of wine, brandy, and beer. These, he learned, were the produce of Psellos's own estates, vast tracts of arable land and pasture and hunting preserve lying farther inland beyond the Ellidon Hills, farmed by tenants, culled by gamekeepers. A private kingdom over which Michal Psellos was absolute monarch.

In quiet moments Rol would question Gibble and the longer-serving maids about their master and the Tower, but they were not forthcoming. To a man and woman, they were terrified of him, and yet something held them in thrall there, bound them to his service. Rol did discover that Psellos was not of noble blood. And though he speculated in various commodities and had cargoes in many a tall ship up and down the Twelve Seas, he was not a Mercanter. Where then did his immense wealth come from?

Often Rol thought of simply walking away, strolling down to the busy wharves of Ascari and hiring out to some skipper who needed an extra hand. He had recovered some kind of equilibrium now, and he had learned something of the wider world—it would not be difficult. But two things held him back.

Psellos knew his family, the story behind Rol's own origins perhaps. If Rol left, he might never find that out by himself no matter how much of the world he wandered.

And Rowen. There was something about her that drew him—not just her beauty, but a sadness sensed beneath the chill exterior. If Rol needed to know his own story, he hungered to discover hers.

After the initial few days there was little contact with the Master. Rol saw him often but never spoke to him, nor was he ever addressed. Both Psellos and Rowen seemed to have utterly forgotten his existence, and for the first few months of his new life, Rol did not especially mind. There was much to learn and see, other people to get to know. A routine to master, petty domestic politics to tax the brain with their real and imagined slights, their guessings and whisperings and petty baffling rules.

A couple of brief skirmishes with the other kitchen scullions soon established his physical superiority. Though they were older than him, Rol topped most by half a head and could crack their skulls together even when they came for him three at a time. The smallest and grimiest of them, Ratzo, then offered him a truce.

"There's one boat here, and we're all in it," he said, the sibilants lisping over the gap where his front teeth should have been. "It may be we could carve your guts for you in your sleep, but rumor has it the Master has took a special interest in you, so we'll forbear. You're on probation, mind, Fisheye." They had spat on each other's palms and shaken hands, and after that Rol was more or less accepted as one of them. The nickname stuck, and much though he hated it, Rol finally accepted the label. He had that in common with Psellos and Rowen, he realized: something in his eyes that made other folk uneasy. A strangeness.

Like all the other scullions, Rol tried to befriend Gibble, but unlike them he had some success, both because he was genuinely uninterested in cadging more kitchen scraps (life in Eyrie had always been frugal), and because he was unfazed by hard work, did not complain, and carried out his chores promptly, taking a perverse pride in performing the meanest of them to perfection.

One night, some two and a half months after he had joined the household, he sat up with Gibble as the stout cook cracked open his nightly bottle of *aguarputa*—the cheap but potent spirit of Ascari's slums—and listened patiently to his well-worn and oft-heard complaints about the poor quality of his underlings, the rapacity of the merchants in the upper city, the declining quality of imported nutmeg. Rol was only half listening. It was a spring night outside, under the open sky. Even here in the dungeonlike confines of the kitchens it was possible to sense the turning of the year. Rol was thinking of *Gannet,* wondering if she floated yet, and if her new owner had repainted her sea-eyes and anointed her bows as Grandfather had once done every year with the first primroses. And he was absentmindedly poking at the red hell of the fire in the immense black iron range which extended clear across one wall of the kitchen, keeping the coals bright to heat Rowen's water. As the hours passed Gibble grew drunker, and his rambling talk turned to subjects other than the matters of the kitchen. He described with great relish just what he had been doing to Mina, the oldest of the serving-maids, the night before in return for the princely bribe of one roast game hen. Generally a good-natured man, Gibble nonetheless felt the need every now and again to fathom the limits of his authority. The reluctant (but hungry) girl had succumbed, and that was that—his faith in his own place in the world was vindicated, and he would molest nothing more animate than a bottle for weeks to come. In truth, the maids did not much mind Gibble's advances, at least compared to Quare's. The bodyservant's attentions would leave them bruised and weeping for days, unable to speak of what had been done to them, unable to forget it either. Gibble at least tried not to hurt them.

Rol they had all swooned over from the beginning, and he had had his pick of the litter. He had lost his virginity in the first week, pumping the insistent girl hard up against a dark wall in the cellars, surprised by how little it meant to him. From time to time he had been importuned again, and had obliged. But every time he thrust into some squealing girl he was seeing Rowen in the kitchen that night, before the fire, and was imagining her dark lips pressed hungrily against his own.

Gibble moved on from his lecherous reminiscing. As he became drunker he grew more morose. He checked the dripping water-clock and seemed troubled. Rol dozed for a while—it was several hours past the middle of the night and his day had started before dawn. When he nodded out of sleep he found Gibble still talking, half to himself.

"It's not right what he makes her do—it's not as if the Master needs the money. No, he does it to shame her, to keep her in her place. And those creatures he makes her—" He stopped, stared down at a yawning Rol. "And you too. It's plain as a pikestaff all over your face, but he thinks he's the only one who notices. He's getting careless, is what." Gibble swallowed hard from the neck of his denuded bottle and wiped his mouth with one meaty forearm.

"What's plain on my face?" Rol asked softly.

"I've been here longer than anyone—eighteen years. I've seen it all. Two more and my time is done—he told me so. Two more and I'm free again. Not that it wasn't worth it, to see those whoresons choke on their own offal." Here Gibble grew maudlin, and began to weep. "So beautiful, she was. That was why. It's said they can't suffer after death. Gods above us, I hope it's true. True for her. But the Master put it to rights. He always keeps his word. He promised they would die slow, and they did. Twenty years. Half a life. She was nineteen when she died." Gibble began to sob quietly.

The door to the kitchens slammed back against the wall. Gibble and Rol both jumped. The bottle slipped through the cook's thick fingers to smash on the slick flags of the floor.

It was the Master himself, with Quare at his side. Psellos looked about the room, his gaze lingering on Rol with a frown, as though the boy's presence reminded him of something he would have sooner forgotten.

"Where is Rowen?" Psellos demanded. "Not back yet?"

Gibble was trying to stand up and failing. Psellos never came down here. "No, my lord. No sign of her—and she's hours late. I have her water ready here. I sat up waiting—"

"I can see that. Quare, go fetch Skewer, and a lantern. Be quick."

The bodyservant took off in silent haste.

Psellos stood looking into the flame-light of the range's open door. Taking a pair of gloves from his belt he drew them on thoughtfully, tugging the calfskin snugly over each knuckle.

There was a dangerous light in his shifting eyes. Rol sat silent and still with the reek of spilled *aguarputa* all about him, watching.

"My beautiful young apprentice has grease in his hair. How does he find life in Psellos's Tower?" The Master did not look away from the fire as he spoke.

"No worse and no better than in other places," Rol said, and he received a thump on the shoulder from Gibble.

Psellos smiled, and turned to regard him. "I have had men flayed for turning the word on me, boy."

"Why ask a question if you do not want to hear an honest answer?"

"Men rarely ask questions out of genuine curiosity. They want what they already know to be confirmed. Or they want the answer to the question they have not asked. It is good that you have spirit, boy, but be careful to whom you reveal it. Not all men of my station are as indulgent with their inferiors."

Rol was about to retort, but Psellos's eyes stopped him. The dark man smiled again, silver glimmering in the corners of his mouth. "That's better."

Quare returned, high forehead shining. "My lord."

Psellos took from him a long, slim sword with a guarded hilt. The scabbard was worked with silver and obsidian. He buckled it to his belt unhurriedly.

"Come with me," he said to Rol.

Psellos, Quare, and Rol took to the winding stairs that led up to ground level. They came out in the wide circular atrium which took up almost an entire floor of the Tower. Here Quare lit the lantern from a candle-sconce in the wall. Psellos spoke to Rol. His voice was cold and grim.

"You will stay here by the door and watch for our return. If any others seek to enter you must bar the door in their faces. Open for no one except me—not even Quare here. Do you understand?" Rol nodded dumbly, wondering what had happened.

The Master and his bodyservant slipped out of the postern Rowen had once opened to Rol, and quickly made their way down the winding street toward the lower city, the lantern throwing bars and wands of light about their feet.

Just before they disappeared, Rol stepped out of the postern himself. Motivated by he knew not what, he pulled the door to behind him, but did not let the big latched lock snick shut. Then he set off at a run in the wake of Psellos and Quare.

Five

THE KING OF THIEVES

IT WAS EXHILARATING TO BE OUT OF THE TOWER, TO BE running under the bright stars on a warm spring night, and Rol's feet fairly sped over the cobbles. He followed the fitful flash that was Quare's lantern, dodging behind corners and rain barrels when he thought that they were looking back. As they traveled further down into the city, the streets began to fill up with people, and he had to draw closer to Psellos so as not to lose sight of him in the nighttime throng.

Ascari, with spring unfolding about it, was like some noisome and garish flower. Every house in the city, it seemed, had disgorged some capering form of sprightly life upon the streets. The night seemed like exercise hour in some gray prison, when the inmates grasped the free air and bit off chunks of it with laughing mouths. A milling chaos, good-humored and dangerous, fascinating and repulsive. But after a time Rol wearied of the stopping and starting, the breathless push through the milling streetwalkers and beggars and drunks and peddlers. The streets stank of spilled wine, of spiced cooking and ordure and pulsing, crowded humanity. He began to wonder what mad notion had brought him here. Psellos and Quare showed no signs of halting, until at last Rol could see ahead of him the masts and yards of ships tied up to the wharves. They had come clear down to the seafront, a good half league from the Tower as a bird would fly, though their feet had walked twice that.

Finally the Master and his companion halted before a series of tall warehouses right on the wharves. There were fewer people abroad here, some drunken longshoremen and forlorn whores. Psellos drew his sword, and kicked open the side door of one of the buildings. There was a dim light within. He and Quare entered, shutting the door behind them.

Rol's curiosity peaked again. He dared not try the same door, but went round the back of the warehouse and clambered up a mound of junk: discarded barrels and crates, rolls of sodden canvas, frayed ship's rigging rotting in mounds. He was able to haul himself upon a sill and peer in a grimy window. He had to spit on the glass and wipe the filth off it to see through it. But it was dark inside. He swore softly to himself, hesitating, and at last tried the window. After a couple of sharp thumps it opened inward in a spray of rotten splinters and insect husks. Gulping at the noise, Rol crawled through and let himself down inside.

He was afraid now, and yet there was a bloody-mindedness at work in him too. All this had something to do with Rowen's lateness, he was sure.

He had an impression of thick beams rising above him. Stone under his feet, and dust hanging in the air. He stifled a sneeze. The warehouse seemed disused, partly derelict—he could see the stars through chinks in the roof—and there was all manner of rubbish strewn about it and heaped against the walls. Rol fumbled through the debris, disturbing a nest of mice, exploding a tight knot of cockroaches, until finally his fingers fastened on a length of wood that seemed free of worm. A belaying pin. It had all the satisfying heft of a club, and he slapped it into one palm with a little more confidence.

He was sure he could hear raised voices now, and he picked his way to a brightness by one wall: a passageway that led to some light source, and the reek of smoke. He crept along it as silently as if he were hunting quail up on the headland on Dennifrey.

And stopped. Somehow his eyes had caught the steel glitter and his legs had halted of their own accord before the import even registered with his brain. Now he crouched and studied intently the second's glimpse that had brought him up short. Two wires strung across the passageway at shin and neck height. He followed them to the walls and found they were wound about iron hooks set into the crumbling masonry. Before they reached the hooks, their steely length was hung with a row of small silvery bells.

Rol breathed out slowly. After a moment he mustered up the courage to move between the wires, and continue on his way—more slowly now, his eyes scanning the very air in front of him.

The passageway opened out onto a gallery that ran all the way round the walls of a long chamber, some ten feet from the ground. The wood of the gallery was crooked and worm-eaten, and Rol dropped to his belly and crawled out upon it gingerly. Finally he was able to look down on the space below.

A fire burned there on the stone floor of the chamber, the only illumination in the room, and the smoke of it smarted Rol's eyes. About it a tatterdemalion band of strange figures were warming their hands and passing an earthenware jug between them. They were clad in rags and oddments of leather byrnies, oilskin cloaks, even the tattered remnants of women's skirts. Some wore caps, others had grubby scarves tied about their heads, but all had feathers jutting from their headgear.

Their faces were black with filth, eyes white in the midst of it, mouths like red laughing holes. They were jabbering to one another in a language Rol did not understand, but as he listened, he thought that now and again he caught a gist of the meaning behind it—as though it was not an entirely foreign language but a debasement or dialect of one he knew. Gascarese was the common tongue of the Seven Isles, and this was an offshoot, or a corruption of it.

The men's talk died away as Psellos and Quare entered the chamber by a ground-level door. Rol shrank back into the shadows, and the rotten wood of the gallery creaked under him.

Psellos held up one empty hand in greeting, though his rapier was naked in the other. The lantern was shaking in Quare's fist, and the bodyservant's face was white as old ivory, ashine with sweat. Psellos appeared wholly at ease, except for the concentrated glitter of his eyes.

The raggedly caparisoned figures about the fire spread out at once, and from hidden places in their clothing they drew out knives and hammers. Psellos grinned.

"Canker! Is this the way to greet an old friend?"

One of the ragged men stepped forward. He had a mouth full of yellow teeth and his feathered cap was set at a jaunty angle on the back of his head. He held a long, slim knife.

"Well, well," he said in accented Gascarese, "the lordship himself. To what do we owe this honor?"

"You have something of mine here, Canker. An entire night was not in the deal."

Canker smiled, and spread his hands in a gesture of helplessness. "What can I say, my lord? We are bewitched, enthralled. And not all of us have had a turn yet."

Psellos looked about the chamber, as if counting heads. A flicker of distaste passed his countenance and was gone. He sheathed his sword. "Tell me you have some decent drink in this louse-hole."

Canker laughed, and the men in the chamber seemed to relax, their weapons sinking by their sides.

"The King of Thieves may be many things, but he is no barbarian. There is Bionese here, for those of discernment. If one so grand will deign to drink with the dregs of this world."

"I've drunk with worse," Psellos said, and stepped forward.

From somewhere a silver goblet inlaid with gold and set with lapis lazuli was produced. Canker waved a filthy hand and one of his subordinates filled it from a bulging wineskin. Psellos studied the proffered goblet with a connoisseur's eye, and drank deeply.

"Exquisite," he said. "The vintage of the year before last, and the skin has treated it surprisingly well. I congratulate you, Canker. I had no idea your cellar was so good."

"Not my cellar, my lord Psellos, but that of Lord Perrivale. Congratulate him if you must."

Psellos raised an eyebrow. "Well, I am doubly impressed. Perrivale is not the easiest mark on the street. They say his manse is a veritable fortress."

"Even a fortress must have a door."

"Indeed. In the midst of stealing fine wines and heirlooms I trust you have found time to attend to my errand. I do not usually make down payments in advance."

Canker bowed. From the breast of his ragged apparel he produced a scroll wound about a wooden spindle and sealed with black wax. He handed it to Psellos with something of a flourish.

Psellos's face did not change, but something came into his eyes, a blaze of hungry triumph. He held the scroll as though it were made of thousand-year-old glass. "Ah, Canker," he murmured, "you are an artist."

"The down payment is being enjoyed as we speak," Canker said. "When will the balance of the fee be delivered?"

Psellos's eyes did not leave the scroll. "Quare," he snapped.

The manservant came forward, reaching into a belt-pouch.

He produced a slip of paper. "Remius and Midd, on Pandreddin Street. You may have it in credit or in gold. They are expecting you."

Canker did not deign to read the paper. He stuffed it negligently into his tattered robe. "As always, a pleasure to do business with a professional," he said.

Psellos was wrapping the scroll in a lace handkerchief. "When will the down payment be available for other work?"

Canker shrugged. "My subjects are hale and hearty men beneath their rags. You are satisfied with their work, why not let us have her for another day? Call it a bonus."

Psellos was clutching the scroll to his bosom as though it were the holiest of relics. "Why not? But do not break her, Canker. She has sweetened many a deal for me."

Canker grinned. "She is perhaps a little bent, but nowhere near broken yet, never fear. Have some more wine, my lord. Perhaps we can discuss a little business."

Rol eased himself backwards off the wooden gallery inch by agonizing inch. The creaks and groans of the rotten wood were masked by a raucous babble of talk and laughter from the gathered men below. At last he reached the passageway behind him and was able to rise to his feet. He heard Psellos laugh, and for some reason a hot blaze of hatred rose up in his heart. He dodged the strung wires with supple swiftness, and clutching his makeshift club, he padded back into the darkness of the abandoned warehouse, his mind full of what he had seen and heard. Not even in his own thoughts did he admit or analyze what he intended to do. His heart knew without being told.

He circled round the firelit chamber wherein the King of Thieves entertained Psellos. The warehouse had been subdivided by moldering timber partitions and piled mounds of rubbish. Here and there pallets of straw lay upon the stone, little heaps of belongings, a dying fire aglow in a crudely made rock hearth. But there was no movement save for the small scurrying life of half-glimpsed vermin. It would seem that all those who made this place their home were drinking with their *king* and his guest.

Almost all. In the quiet dark Rol could still hear the buzz of talk from the firelit chamber, but he had grown accustomed to that. Now there were noises nearer at hand. Men gabbling, a snorted laugh, a beastlike grunting.

It was pitch-black, but Rol had not thought to wonder why it was he could see quite clearly. He followed the noises down a series of passages, and the gleam of the wires brought him up short again. Three of them this time. He held his breath as he twisted through them, and then went on.

Candlelight flickering out of an opening to his left in the passageway ahead. An odd smell, like that of a moldy herb being burned. He glided forward, drew a deep breath, and then risked a split-second glance round the corner.

He leaned back against the rough wall again, exhaled. In his mind's eye the picture was bright and hard and clear. Once again, his body knew what it would do with no prompting from his will. He closed his eyes for a second, evened out his breathing, then nodded once, and turned the corner.

Three men, one on the bed, another at its foot, the third at its head. The belaying pin cracked off the skull of the nearest before he even turned round, the noise sharp and startling. Not all Rol's strength had gone into the strike; he remembered Grandfather teaching him how to kill a pig. The placing of the blow was more important than the force.

As his striking arm completed its arc, snicking off the broken bone of the man's head, so Rol stepped forward alongside the bed. The second man was naked from the waist down, his member jutting out from under his ragged shirt. Rol reached below it, found the testes in their soft bag of skin, and clenched his fingers about them, squeezing with all the strength in his fist. He felt them squish and pop. The man's mouth opened in an O of agonized astonishment, but before a noise could issue from his throat Rol had thrust the blunt end of the belaying pin in over his teeth, breaking them, hammering through to the back of his throat.

He turned then to the third man who was disentangling himself from his activities on the bed, a blade naked in his hand. This one had had a moment more to collect his wits. The knife stabbed out for Rol's side but Rol was already turning, and the blade buried itself in his forearm instead. The belaying pin swung round and took the fellow under his left ear. The blow staggered him long enough for Rol to bring a final swing down on the top of his forehead. This last was delivered with every ounce of strength he had left. The front of the man's face caved in, nose and eyes destroyed as the hard wood went through to the brain.

A gurgling squeal from the floor from the wretch who lay cupping his genitalia. Rol stamped a boot down on the side of his neck, breaking the vertebrae there with an audible snap, and he was still.

He stood breathing evenly, the pain in his forearm beginning to make itself felt. Perhaps eight seconds had gone by since he had entered the room, and the noise of the fight had been no louder than the groans and grunts that had preceded it. There was no sudden uproar. Rol stared down at the bed, at Rowen, and something went out of him, some calm exaltation. He bent over, gasping, and was sick in a corner of the filthy little room.

Her body was very white in the dim candlelit gloom, which meant that the bruises and welts stood out on her skin all the more starkly. She was watching him, but there was a dulled detachment in her gaze he had never seen before. He had dreamed of her nakedness for weeks, but seeing her like this roused only pity in him, and outrage. He untied her arms and closed her legs to hide the glistening darkness at their crux, wiped some of the filth off her skin with the corner of a less-filthy blanket. She lay unresisting and limp, and he wondered what they had done to her, besides the obvious.

That smell in the air. He traced it to a small brass dish by the side of the bed. Within it were a number of tiny black cubes. As he touched one, part of it crumbled into powder and he coughed at the fragrant little cloud it produced. His head swam momentarily, and he spat to get the taste out of his mouth.

He stepped over the bodies on the floor. His forearm was dripping and numb, his left hand close to useless. He tore strips off the coverlet and tied them tight about the wound. Rowen's eyes followed him but she made no sound. He found her clothes to the right of the bed and set them on her stomach. "Get dressed. We have to go." This last in a racked whisper. Fear was rising up in his throat, the thought of what he had just done, the sinking realization that there would be consequences.

Rowen's hands twitched. Her mouth opened but only an inarticulate groan came out. He bent over her face and took her restless fingers in his own.

"What? What is it? Tell me."

A tear fled from the outside corner of her eye and trickled down to her neck. Rol leaned farther, until they were sharing each other's breath and he could feel the butterfly-kiss of her eyelashes on his cheek.

"Fool," she said, and pushed him away.

He straightened, looking down on her in bewilderment. "Get dressed," he repeated mechanically.

"Go," she said, baring her teeth.

"I came here to—to help you," he whispered. "Look what they were doing to you. He was going to let them have you another whole *day.*"

That made her pause. They stared into one another's eyes, burnished steel meeting a sea-storm. At last her fingers fastened upon the garments he had set atop her abdomen.

"Help."

With one hand at the back of her fluted neck, he raised her up and began to dress her. As they wrestled with her shirt his wounded forearm bled down her stomach, the blood trickling into the matted hair between her legs. With the shirt on he set his arm behind her knees and swung her feet over the side of the bed. She could sit up by herself, though her head still lolled forward, the magnificent black mane of her hair falling down over her bruised breasts.

Rol stopped to listen. Still that murmur of talk and laughter from the main chamber. But it would not be long before others came down for their turn at the night's sport.

He bent and retrieved the knife that had scored his forearm. It was a thick-bladed, slightly curved weapon with an ivory grip, well made and wickedly sharp. Tucking it into his belt, he took Rowen's arm and hauled her to her feet. "Come. We must go now, right now."

She demurred, mumbling, but he dragged her out of the room as a man might support a drunken comrade. She was not heavy, and he swung her up into his arms, some part of him relishing even at that moment the taut feel of her flesh under his hands. She stank of the men who had been abusing her, and of the drug by the bedside. For a moment she struggled in his grasp, trying to make him set her down. Then she gave up, and put her white arms about his neck, hiding her face in the hollow of his shoulder like a child afraid of the night. With that, something of his earlier detachment and calm returned. His heart slowed, and he seemed to see more clearly in the guttering dark beyond the candlelight. He walked along the passageway as sure-footed as a prowling cat, bent under and stepped over the warning wires as though performing part of some slow-stepped dance, and then picked up speed.

The warehouse was tall, echoing, and it stank with the debris of decades. Rol picked his way like a dancer, some adrenaline still singing through his blood. But after a while the reaction began to set in. Away from the voices, in a corner of the evil-smelling blackness, he went to one knee and set Rowen's weight atop the other to rest his injured arm, his heartbeat a rushing susurration in his throat. She raised her head, her mouth tickling his ear.

"Put me down. I can walk."

He let her slip out of his arms with an odd reluctance.

"Do you know a way out?" Her eyes seemed to shine faintly in the dark as she regarded him. Her speech was slow but clear, as though it was an effort for her to make each word distinct.

"Yes. A window. Not far now."

Kneeling, she swayed and leaned against him. Then she turned and vomited. He felt warm liquid spatter his boots. She wiped her mouth on the shoulder of the short-sleeved shirt he had put on her. Only three or four buttons held it closed over her breasts—the rest had been ripped away. She spat, then straightened, and began tying her long hair back from her face.

"Let us go, then."

He rose to his feet. She climbed up him as though he were a ladder, still unsteady. He put an arm about her waist and drew her along, sometimes taking all her weight when her knees buckled. She said no word, but put her left arm about his shoulders and her right hand on his where it gripped her hip.

Somehow he remembered the way he had come, and they staggered back through the blank darkness, the rats scurrying out from under their feet. Finally he saw starlight through the windows near the eaves, and sensed the greater height over his head. They were back in the rubbish-mounded space where he had made his entry.

A clamor. Shouting in the night, echoing behind them. Rowen looked at him. They nodded to each other without a sound, and began scrabbling up toward the grimy windows, Rol thrusting her ahead of him with his good hand. In his growing panic he could not see or remember which one he had come through. Rowen pounded at the stiff frame of the nearest with the ball of her fist, and there was the bright smash of breaking glass. He heard her curse under her breath, and then he was staring at the pale length of her legs as she went through the broken window headfirst. He followed her, the teeth of the broken pane ripping the belly of his tunic, tearing at his breeches. Then he was through, and fell down several feet to land on his shoulder and side. He lay winded for a second, until she gripped his collar and pulled him to his feet. They half ran, half tumbled down the midden of junk that was piled up against the high wall of the warehouse, and at last Rowen's bare feet were slapping on cobbles. It was raining, and the night air seemed clean and sweet and cold in their lungs. Rol turned inland, to where Ascari rose out of the bay in lamplit disorder, but Rowen took his hand. "No, not that way. They'll go there first. Come."

She was bleeding from glass-cuts across her belly and thighs, but she pulled Rol after her with some of her old strength until they stood at the edge of the wharf and were looking down at the black water. Without hesitation Rowen jumped in. He saw the white flash of foam as she went under, and stared half in disbelief. It was a few seconds before he could bring himself to dive in his turn.

The water was bitter, icy, and foul, its swells awash with the detritus of the port. Rol broke the surface and looked around.

"In here."

She was under the wharf, in among the enormous supporting timber piles. He swam to her, teeth chattering, and scrabbled through the slime and barnacles until he had ahold of the wood beneath. Rowen's face was livid, her eyes black holes. He could feel her shuddering against him in the water but as he tried to speak she slapped a palm over his mouth.

They raised their heads as one. There were boots clumping on the wood of the wharf above them, terse voices. Then the boots broke into staccato thumping as their wearers took off at a run, scattering.

Rowen eased Rol's newly acquired knife out of his belt.

A silent shadow was climbing down among the pilings. It was noiseless, sure-footed as an ape. Rowen's fist cocked back with the knife blade between her fingers. Her shivers stilled. She braced one foot against the timber pile they floated alongside.

The shadow drew closer. Rowen's arm snapped forward in a white blur. There was a solid, meaty *chunk,* and without a sound the shadow tumbled into the water headfirst. The splash seemed very loud in the night, and Rol and Rowen tensed against each other, waiting for some cry of inquiry. But nothing came, no sound, no curious comrade-shadow. Rowen began shuddering again.

"Can you climb up?" Rol whispered.

She shook her head. "Must swim farther along. Too close here."

They struck out together. Rol kicked off his boots. He felt as though he were swimming through soup. His entire body was shaking with cold and delayed reaction to the violence of the night. His left arm was a throbbing, swollen lump of meat. Looking up, he saw that the sky was lightening out to sea. Dawn was approaching. He had no idea what the coming day held for him, but he more than half wished he had never followed Psellos and Quare out of the door, and had merely done as he was told. He was no longer possessed of the calm certainty that had enabled him to kill three men in cold blood. And Rowen seemed untroubled by gratitude for her rescue.

They came to the base of Ascari's mole. There were stone steps here, leading down into the sea, and all about them rows of fishing smacks were moored. The pair paddled exhaustedly to the base of the steps and hauled themselves onto the chill stone, where they lay gasping like landed fish. The light was growing moment by moment, and there were people abroad on the waterfront.

"Run along the wharves and find a horse-cab," Rowen said. "We must get back to the Tower."

Rol stared at her. "Why? Why go back to him?"

She shot him a glare of pure irritation. Then her eyes dropped to his bloody arm. A strange look flitted across her face—a kind of bafflement. "Where else is there to go?"

Six

WORTHY OF HIS HIRE

"UP, FISHEYE; THE MASTER WANTS TO SEE YOU, AND HE'S not a patient fellow."

Rol opened his eyes to see Ratzo leaning over him grinning hideously, but with an odd respect.

"The kitchen boys have a wager on you'll be carrion by nightfall. Care to enter the pool?"

He sat up on his mattress of rags with a groan. All yesterday he had been expecting this, and through the night he had stared blankly at the kitchen firelight awaiting the summons, cursing himself for not having the courage to walk away from Psellos, from Rowen, from whatever family history this place contained. On his return, a day and a night ago, Gibble had stitched up his forearm and given him fresh clothes, but aside from that had asked no questions. He had seemed a little in awe of Rol, if truth be told. It was all over the servants' quarters; the kitchen scullion had disobeyed the Master's explicit orders, and had somehow become involved with the mistress of the Tower.

As he left, the kitchen staff turned their eyes from Rol as though he were the bearer of a contagious disease. Only Gibble spoke.

"Don't provoke him. Be meek and mild, and hold your tongue, for pity's sake."

"Has Rowen—"

"No, lad. Not a word." The portly cook set a hand on Rol's shoulder. "It's not in her nature. You must look out for yourself alone."

Quare was waiting for him at the foot of the main stairwell. He was smiling. "My young beauty. The Master awaits you. I will take you up to him." But he made no move. Instead he leaned forward and said: "Rowen is to fulfill the remainder of her contract with the King of Thieves within the week. How do you think his minions will receive her? Are they the type to bear grudges?" And he vented a curiously girlish giggle. Rol said nothing. The manservant shrugged slightly and led the way up the austere circular staircase, which led to the upper levels.

"Leave us, Quare," Psellos said, and Rol heard the door easing shut behind him. He was in a chamber he had never seen before, though his errands routinely carried him through almost every cranny of Psellos's Tower. One straight wall, the other a vast semicircle which had set along it the grandest series of glass windows Rol had ever seen. They were big enough for a man to step through and faced not downhill, toward Ascari, but away from the sea, so that Rol's vision was filled by the sun-dappled bulk of the Ellidon Hills. A slim silhouette stood before them.

And other things. Set between each pair of windows was a

small table of disturbing workmanship. The legs of these seemed twisted as though by some wasting disease, and set atop them were glass demi-johns. In each a murky shape shimmered and floated.

"Rowen told me all," Psellos said. He strode over to yet another table and poured himself some wine from a crystal decanter whose neck had been chiseled into the mouth of a leering fox. "I am surprised at you, young Cortishane, surprised and I must admit somewhat impressed. I knew you had murder in you, else I would not have wasted my time—but three of the Thief-King's Feathermen in one fell swoop, as it were? Now, that speaks to me of a certain style."

Back at the semicircular wall of windows, he sipped wine with one hand and the other he set upon one of the mysterious glass jars. At once a greenish light began to glow within its depths, revealing the contents. The head of a bearded man. The eyes within the head blinked and the mouth moved.

"Freidius of Auxierre, my old friend, look upon my latest apprentice and tell me what you see."

The voice that issued from the jar set Rol's hair on end. It was a tortured gargle. "Psellos, set me free, end this monstrous half-life, I beg of you—"

"Now, now, do as I say or I shall bring back our friend the rat."

The disembodied face twisted. "He is a child of the Blood, I can see it in his eyes."

"So can every other fool on the street. Use that brain of yours or I shall bruise it some more. This was your field when you were a man."

The thing in the jar shut its glazed eyes, and all at once Rol felt a peculiar sensation in his head, as though a cockroach were crawling beneath his scalp. He backed a step, but at a glare from Psellos stood fast.

"He is—he is more pure-blooded than I thought. Where did

you get him, Psellos? What has Grayven said? Have you sent him a sample?"

"Yes. But I wanted a second opinion. His powders and tubes are not always as accurate as I would like."

"He is of Orr, no doubt about it, but if I did not know better I would say he has the makeup of an Ancient."

"Impossible."

"I know, but—is there any taint in him?"

"I examined him myself. There is none."

"To have so much of the Blood, and yet be perfect, whole. I have not felt his like before save once—and so young! Where on earth did you find him?"

"He found me," Psellos said, and he grinned, exposing the silver canines.

"If there is no flaw in him—I do not know how a bloodline could have stayed so pure—do you realize that—"

"Enough," Psellos said, and the green light in the jar went out. The face slumped into the immobility of dead flesh. There was a silence in the splendidly lit room.

"What manner of man are you?" Rol asked, staring in disgust at the thing in the jar.

"Eh? Oh, strictly speaking I am not much of a man at all—but I am more of a human than you, my impertinent young friend." Psellos's manner was jaunty, but his eyes were humorless as a hangman's.

"You are a sorcerer."

"No, I am much more than that." Psellos raised his glass again, and finding it empty he repaired to the decanter. The neck of the crystal clinked twice against his goblet, and with a shock Rol realized that the Master's hands were shaking.

"Take a seat, youngster. It is time we had a talk. Man to man, or as close as you and I can come to that."

They sat thirty feet apart, the bright mountain view behind Psellos rendering his face inscrutable with shadow.

"You are not human; I told you that once before. The blood that runs within your veins, that which your heart pumps about your carcass, belongs to a race older than humanity." Psellos steepled his fingers together, resting his elbows on the stuffed arms of his chair. "What do you know of the history of the world?" And before Rol could answer, he laughed. "Forgive me. I should perhaps be a little more specific. Did Ardisan ever speak to you of the Weren?"

"My grandfather told me of the Elder Race, which existed in the time of the Old World, before the New was made. He said they were Man before his Fall—some thought of them as angels."

"Your grandfather was repeating only the superstitions of ignorant men. I suppose he had his reasons. In any case, he misled you. The Old World and the New coexist. They occupy the same space upon this earth, the Umer that we know. But they belong to different eras, and they rarely touch upon each other."

"I don't understand."

"There is a world beyond that which we see and touch in everyday discourse. It is not given to every creature to access it, but some can exist in both at once. You, Rol, are a creature of the Older World, as am I—and Rowen." Psellos paused, and seemed about to elaborate, but then changed tack altogether. "How did you kill those three Feathermen?"

"I don't know—it was very fast. I had them before they could move."

"The minions of the King of Thieves are chosen for their swiftness, for their instincts, their reflexes. Admittedly, they were busy at the time, but you bested three of them in one single combat. If it were luck, then it was like none I have ever seen before. Tell me, can you see in the dark?"

Rol started. "Sometimes."

"Have you always been able to see in the dark?"

"No. Listen, why do you make Rowen do these things—why do you torture her?"

"She is making payment."

"For what?"

"Knowledge."

"Where did you get all this knowledge that you withhold? What gives you the right to withhold it?"

Psellos waved a hand. "A man goes out into the fields, he harvests his crops, he takes them to market. Would you have him give them away for nothing? The laborer, we are told, is worthy of his hire."

"Your prices destroy people's lives."

"I do not force people to bargain with me. I name a price. Either they pay it or they do not."

Rol pushed the palm of one hand into his eye. It was the scarred palm, and it seemed to cool the hot tumult of his brain. "What are we?" he whispered.

"Ah, the matter in hand again. I believe I told you."

"No. I am just a man, like you. I don't believe in—" Rol stopped, realizing that his words were absurd, after the things he had seen and done even in the short span of his life hitherto. He no longer felt sure even of the ground beneath his feet.

"The world is not what you think," Psellos said, and there might even have been an edge of sympathy in his voice. Had he, too, once been a bewildered boy confronted by the strangeness of his own nature?

"What do you want with me?" Rol asked wearily.

"That is difficult to say," Psellos said. "I tell you what, young Cortishane, as a gesture of goodwill, I will give you some of this precious knowledge of mine for free. It may help your aching head. Now, bear with me.

"Once, this world of ours was a different place. The gods walked openly upon it, and the Weren communed with them, learning from them wisdom that had been handed down by the Creator Himself. The Word of God, if you will. But it is in the nature of all sentient things that they must remain dissatisfied with their lot, and mighty and noble though the Elder Race might be, yet they hungered after more knowledge always, and felt constrained by the waking world that bound them. The gods withdrew their friendship, and thus the spinning of the world was hastened, and all things within it felt their mortality more keenly."

Psellos paused. "What that must have been like, that Elder Time, when the stones still remembered the footfalls of the gods. It was so long ago that the ages since can barely be quantified in years. What a world to have lived in!" He smiled, eyes staring out into empty air. "But of course, it passed, as all things must." His voice changed, grew harder.

"Man came upon the world in this waning era—the last gift of the Creator, some say. Others believe he is a curse, set here to complete the destruction of the Weren, and short-lived though he might be, he is fecund, and curious, and impatient. At first the Elder Race tutored the early men, but as time went on a rivalry grew between them. Man was envious of the Weren even as they envied the gods. That is the nature of things. But many of the Weren, as they declined, interbred with Man. The two races are very close, physically, save that the Weren are more robust, longer-lived of course, and not subject to disease. In every way superior to the lesser race that came after. In every way but one. They were few, and mankind had become a teeming multitude. So they thought that by merging the two races they might have the best of both. But there was a problem with this . . . interbreeding. While it boosted the dwindling numbers of the Elder Race, it had its dangers. Some of the first hybrids went awry. They issued from their mothers' wombs as twisted monsters, sound in mind but warped in body. These Fallen ones were meant to have been destroyed at birth, but a parent's love is a strange thing. Many of the Weren who had these maimed creatures as children fled the cities of their peers to keep the changelings from being killed. They took to the seas, to compassionate Ussa of the Swells, and she took pity on them, and brought them to a place far in the south of the world where they began life anew, where their poor offspring might be raised without prejudice or ridicule. These Weren had a leader, a gray sorcerer whose children were all of the Fallen kind, but who loved them nonetheless. His name was Cambrius Orr."

Something in Rol stirred at the name. He looked up, frowning. Psellos nodded. "Always that name conjures up a shadow in the memories of men, even if they do not know why. He is a myth, a dark children's tale. He is a story, nothing more. I have been seeking out references to him in half a hundred libraries and word-hoards up and down the known world for over forty years now, and I can tell you that he actually existed, as did the kingdom he founded, out there in the wastes of the limitless sea. The kingdom of Orr existed, and the gods know Cambrius's great palaces and observatories and ballrooms may molder yet, stone upon stone in some lost jungle untrodden by man."

Psellos poured himself more wine, and paced up and down before the windows without tasting it. There was a passion about him, an honest enthusiasm Rol had never seen before, like that of a man chancing across a stranger who shares the secret obsession of his life.

"The Orrians dropped out of recorded history over ten thousand years ago, and in the rest of Umer their kin the Weren dwindled further, and intermarried with the sons of men, and declined, and became not much more than legend themselves. One by one the great kingdoms of the Weren fell into obscurity, their lands ruled by princelings and chieftains of the race of men. New kingdoms arose, and the world we know now came slowly into being. We were left merely with the ruins of their great cities, now jumbled piles of marble and stone dismantled and quarried by those who came after. But that was not the end. The Mage-King arose, in the land of Kull, and around him the creatures men name Banemasters. Some say they are the last of the Weren, others that they are some awful Third Race visited upon the world of men by the jealousy of the gods." Psellos paused again.

"They struggle among themselves, the Lesser Gods, now that the Maker has left them. They have their feuds, their cabals, their underlings flitting about the world and doing their business. But the Mage-King is not one of these. No mortal man has ever set foot on Kull, and the Banemasters go about their master's business for the most part in anonymity. What are they? What hidden knowledge does the Mage-King hoard in his Halls of Bronze? I believe he is a Were, the last great scion of an ancient race whose blood flows in you and me. But he and his minions frown upon the use of sorcery by anyone or anything not of Kull. And they do not like those who ask questions, who seek out the truth behind the myths. Thus have I had to keep one step ahead of them all down these years. But my time is running short."

Here Psellos paused in mid-stride, fixing Rol with a piercing eye. "The blood of the Elder Race still flows in the veins of a few who walk about our waking world. Stronger in some than in others. Our eyes give us away, it is said." He smiled. "It was in the man who called himself your grandfather, in Emilia, his lovely wife. The Lesser Men will kill you for the ichor that beats within your heart, Rol."

"Why?"

"It extends life."

"Extends— How old are you?"

"I have seen out two centuries. I hope to see a third, if the gods are kind."

Rol was dumbfounded. "Where are you from?"

Psellos's face closed over. "No place of significance. I am not a prince in waiting or the heir to a lost throne. I am not of noble blood—not as it is deemed noble in this day and age. I began as you, a lost boy. I was lucky enough to find a pair of mentors who trained me as I will—as I am training you."

"My grandparents."

"Emilia and Ardisan. Yes. Emilia died at the hands of a mob in Perilar. They collected her blood in pots. Her body Ardisan recovered and buried on Dennifrey, where he made his last home. He was always something of a romantic. I mourn his passing, but I am not surprised by it.

"So you see, Rol, we are brothers beneath the skin, you and I."

Rol was repulsed by the very thought. "You have taken my blood these last weeks, but not for some experiment or treatment—it is sold to the highest bidder." He remembered the sight of Rowen tied to a bed down on the waterfront. "Do not try to tell me you took me in out of charity. You set a price upon everything—one I will no longer pay."

Psellos halted, and in a heartbeat he had crossed the ten yards separating them and was leaning in close to Rol's face. There was a feral sheen to his eyes, and his lips were drawn back from his teeth.

"You ungrateful little wretch. Who do you think you are? I make the rules here. Others abide by them. Including you. Especially you."

Rol was not cowed. "What if I say you and your knowledge and your *training* can go bury yourselves?"

"You would be lying. And you are getting too old for such empty bravado. I see now that your education must be moved forward."

Rol hesitated. "Don't send Rowen back to those animals."

"Why not? Are you smitten with her, Cortishane? Best stick to the serving-maids. She's not good for you."

"If you send her back, I'll leave this Tower."

Psellos snarled audibly. "You simpleminded—I see Ardisan's

absurd romanticism has rubbed off. Better for you to do as you're told." A black snake of a tongue snapped out from between his teeth and disappeared again. His eyes glowed.

"No. You want something more than my blood from me, else I would be dead already. Sticking my head in a jar will not get you it, I think. So that is *my* price. Leave her alone. Don't send her out again."

Psellos straightened. His face grew calm. "Very well—by all means. Have your absurd chivalry. A piece of advice, though. You cannot bargain effectively when you do not know the value of that which you are selling."

He retreated, becoming a shadow limned by the light from the windows once more.

"I have told you a little of your history—"

"Who were my parents?"

"All in good time. We must save something for later."

"Killing those men down at the waterfront—was I able to do that because of—of what I am?"

"Had you been any ordinary stripling they'd have had your throat out before you made one step toward them. But do not think yourself some kind of champion. There was luck involved also. You are fortunate to be alive. As it is, your debt to me is increased."

"Why?" Rol asked angrily.

"Because, you young fool, I must find some other means of payment now that our dear Rowen is off the menu. And should they suspect that I had a connection with the killings—which they will in time—I will have to stump up weregilds to avoid having the King of Thieves at my door."

"What did they have that was worth so much anyway?" Rol did not mention the scroll that had so delighted Psellos two nights before.

"That is not your business." Psellos stared at Rol thoughtfully, sipping his wine. Finally he sighed, and said: "Rowen."

She stepped noiselessly from a curtained alcove behind Rol. He twisted round to stare at her in astonishment and dismay. She was dressed in a close-fitting suit of sable leather, long knives strapped to her thighs, her hair tied up behind her head. Her face was still bruised, and there were smudges the color of plums under her eyes. She did not look at Rol.

"Your shining knight has seen fit to preserve the rags of your chastity from the minions of the Thief-King. He is your responsibility now. Teach him well."

"What shall I teach him?" Her voice was as low as the beat of a swan's wing in flight.

"Everything, Rowen. Teach him everything."

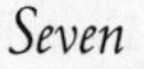

Seven

SCIMITARS AND SEAMSTRESSES

SWEATING, THEIR BODIES SLAPPED TOGETHER BRUISingly. His bare toes dug for purchase in the earth floor, gouging furrows. They strained breast to breast, each trying to overthrow the other by sheer force for half a second; realizing it would not work, they immediately began writhing for advantage, arms locked together, hot breath mingled, trying to hook their feet around the other's ankles.

She slipped fractionally, her grip slithering on his sweat-slick bicep. At once he shifted, committed his weight. She gave way smoothly, deliberately, and his balance tilted out of kilter. Somehow she spun in his grasp. Her thigh pushed between his legs, knocking one foot clear of the ground for a moment. Her tensed arm came round and the tricep impacted against the side of his neck. He went down face-first in the dirt and felt the weight of her foot set on his nape.

He slumped in defeat, and felt the pressure of her sole ease. As it did, he flipped onto his back, knocking her leg aside with his left elbow. His right fist came up in one smooth blur with all his remaining strength behind it. It connected with her abdomen in a sickening slap of meat, and the breath was concussed out of her lungs as her diaphragm buckled into her rib cage. She staggered backwards, and he rose unhurriedly. Her eyes remained fixed on his as she fought for breath, color rising red from her collarbones up. She fell to her knees, whooping, and he watched her dispassionately.

"Yield," he said.

She shook her head and began to rise to her feet, still struggling for air.

He hesitated only a second, and then the butt of his palm slammed into her forehead. She flipped over onto her back. Her body arced once, fists furrowing handfuls of earth. Then it flattened out, and she was still.

Rol stood breathing evenly. "Rowen?" And then more urgently: *"Rowen?"*

He darted forward, and her left heel snapped up with the speed of a hawk's strike with all his weight and all her force behind it, and smashed into his breastbone. He flailed backwards, red darkness pummeling his sight, lungs a sucking vacuum, and he never felt the kiss of the earth as he fell full-length upon it.

Air, life being blown brutally into his mouth, his chest rising as it filled. He felt the bite of her teeth on his lips, and opened his eyes, then turned on his side, coughing, heaving. Her hand passed through his hair, down his cheek, and then receded. When he had caught his breath—her breath in him—he looked up at her as she stood composed as a caryatid before him, white skin shining, naked save for the breechclout. A few damp tendrils of hair framed the triangular perfection of her face, and there was a rising lump on her forehead. She essayed a small smile, teeth white as a cat's. "Once again, eagerness is your downfall. Overconfidence will kill you yet, Fisheye."

He hated that name, and she knew it, which was why she never called him by anything else.

"I thought I'd damn well killed you for a second."

"I take a lot of killing." She offered him her hand and hauled him to his feet. Tall as she was, he towered over her now. Her small breasts, taut and glistening, brushed against him. They stood like that a moment, like two lovers sharing a whisper, and then she turned and left the earthen practice ring to fetch her towel.

They stood in the clammy dimness of the chamber in the bowels of Psellos's Tower, and stared silently at one another as they wiped the dirt from their bodies. Rol had a scratch above his left eye that oozed blood, and Rowen's forehead was bulging purple.

Fighting men, ordinary men, subjected to the force of the blows that had just been exchanged, would be dead by now, one with a broken skull, the other with a burst rib cage. For Rol and Rowen, however, there were only scratches and bruises. If anything had finally convinced Rol of his . . . inhumanity, it had been the last year in Psellos's house. He was not *cattle,* as Psellos jauntily referred to the mass of everyday humanity. He was something else. Part of him reveled in the sense of superiority—Psellos encouraged this—and part of him mourned the fact that he was set apart from the everyday concourse of life as surely as a freak in a traveling circus.

The main thing, though—he had finally accepted it.

This secret complex near the Tower's foundations was where the bulk of Rol's combat training took place. He and Rowen left the practice circle without exchanging another word, and limped down a candlelit corridor to the plunge-pool. Discarding their stinking breechclouts, they dived in within seconds of each other, as once they had leaped from the wharves of Ascari. The water was freezing cold, fed by some subterranean spring whose origins were in the roots of the mountains. The cold stole Rol's breath, but he was used to that now. It was good for his wrenched muscles and battered skull. He floated, staring up at the bare rock of the ceiling, and felt the kindly chill numb his aches and pains. He rubbed dirt from his limbs, emptying his mind as he had been taught, discarding whatever preoccupations floated there. Finally, at a nod from Rowen, he pulled himself heavily out of the water again. The pair padded naked across the bare stone toward the steam chamber. Within it, heated rocks had raised the temperature to the limits of endurance. They ladled water over the rocks and sat side by side in the scalding billow of steam that ensued. A single oil lamp guttered and fought for life, flashing out broiled shadows. The air was hot enough to sear the lungs, but Rol breathed in the steam deeply while fresh sweat popped out of every pore. Rowen scraped the running moisture from his body with a curved strigil, and her deft hands explored the places where she had hurt him, much as a farmer might feel over a horse he meant to buy at market. There was something soothing in the touch of her hands. Her business was killing, but her gift was in healing. She seemed to drain away the pain, leaving Rol limp and relaxed as seaweed abandoned by the ebbing tide.

"You fought well today," Rowen said quietly. "The impatience is that of youth, and will be remedied in time." Her strong fingers kneaded the flesh of his shoulders and he leaned into her, closing his eyes. For him, the pain of the practice bouts was worth this, the almost-dark of the steam chamber, the intimacy of their two bodies close in the stifling warmth. Perhaps Rowen felt the same way, for she was always a little less reticent after their contests. She would talk to him not quite as an equal, but as a favored subordinate. A fellow-traveler perhaps.

"I have broken more bones in the past year than I did in the fifteen that came before it," Rol said dryly. "If time does not remedy it, a broken neck will, one of these days." He twisted to meet her eye, and for a treasured instant she was smiling back at him. Then she eased his face away from her and began massaging the sore meat of his muscles again.

Psellos was not entertaining that evening, so they joined him for dinner on the balcony level of the Tower. Rol had counted eleven levels aboveground and seven below, but he knew there were yet more beneath those seven—seldom-visited caverns he would probably never see. Psellos had a laboratory somewhere below the training circles to which he would sometimes disappear for days at a time, and among the Tower servants there were rumors of secret strong-rooms stuffed with jewels, imprisoned demons festering in stone cells, forgotten prisoners eking out a starvation existence in the subterranean darkness. Sheer fancy, most of it, but if half the rumors and demi-legends could be proved true, Rol would not have been surprised. He had seen and done enough in his year within the Tower to know that anything was possible.

Psellos was in an expansive mood. He had bidden Rol and Rowen don their finest, and the long table was cluttered with crystal and silver, the centerpiece an exquisite rendition of a carrack in full sail crafted of thinnest gold plate. The model's main-hatch was full of salt, and silver barrels that lined the little deck were full of other condiments and sauces. It was a long way from dried fish and brackish water upon the *Gannet.*

Silent servants danced attendance on the trio, their comings and goings regulated by curt gestures, nods, and waves from Quare. They drank Armidian apple wine with fillets of Bank's Monk stuffed with anchovies and capers, hooked snail-shrimp from their long whorled shells with silver picks, and sliced into cutlets of lamb rare and bloody and mouth-melting with wild garlic and thyme. Finally they pushed back their chairs, dismissed the servants, and sat while Psellos broke open a bottle of Cavaillic brandy, the glass encrusted with age. Gibble had surpassed himself. It was a meal a king could not have found fault with. Psellos was austere in many ways, but not when it came to his belly.

"A year and a day you have been under my roof," Psellos said to Rol. "Doubtless, in your youth, it seems a long time. And yet your training has barely begun. Rol, your tutor tells me that you are close to besting her in combat, and you have no idea what praise that is." He paused awhile and looked both Rol and Rowen up and down. He seemed to be savoring some secret knowledge as a miser will gloat over his hoarded gold.

"But fighting is not everything. There are other disciplines which are not so easily mastered. I want you to learn them all. I want to see what you can do."

He was perhaps a little drunk, but not solely on wine. Psellos often slipped into moods like this. He would sit and plan their lives in vague terms which seemed nonetheless to please him inordinately, and sculpt visions of glorious futures. Sometimes Rol thought there were two natures warring within Psellos, one which was proud to teach, and another which was closed and ugly, hoarding its knowledge. One never knew which was strongest. Until one won out.

"My, what a handsome pair you are. What beauty sits at my table. Rol, you have the brow of a prince. Rowen, you are stainless, perfect. You shall remain with me. I wish to enjoy you tonight."

Rowen inclined her head, expressionless. Rol knew her well now, and he could see the tiny flicker in her eye. For a long time now, Psellos had not called her to his bed, or sent her out to lie in others'. It had been a tacit hope of Rol's that Psellos would hold to his word, and not do so again. He bowed his head. What was he to say, if Rowen said nothing?

Psellos had not missed the look in Rowen's eye either. It seemed to heighten his good humor.

"Rol, doubtless you have a comely kitchen maid awaiting you downstairs, but before you leave us, there is something I wish to present you with." Pushing back his chair, Psellos rose and from a nearby sideboard fetched a long, slim wooden case. He unlatched the lid and raised it. Whatever it contained flashed the reflected light of the candles across his face.

A sword. It came up in his hand like a sliver of blue water. With a twist of his wrist he sent it spinning end over end toward Rol's face. Rol twisted aside and plucked it out of the air as though he were catching a paper bird. Psellos laughed. "Good, good! Rowen's time has not been wasted, I see. Its name is—well, it does not matter what its name is. You must give it a new one now. It is yours to wield, for a while at least."

The surface of the blade was luminous as the shallows of a calm sea at evening. It was wickedly light, a snicker of cold laughter in Rol's fist. Almost he felt it had a voice, a whisper which crooned of carnage. The voice was avid as a famished rat—but there was a delight in the perfect balance of the steel. It seemed somehow to connect with the very sinews of his arm, its curved brightness an extension of his limb. A light scimitar, its trappings were unadorned and workmanlike, but the bright, marvelous blade was exquisite as a faceted jewel.

"You think he is ready for it?" Rowen asked the Master, and there was an odd, contained urgency in her voice.

"We will see. What think you of your gift, Rol?"

"I think I could fillet the north wind with it. Thank you, sir."

Rowen spoke. "It is an old blade, and it contains many memories. It will enhance your sword arm, but there is something—"

"Do not ruin the surprise, my dear," Psellos said with sharp levity. "Let the boy have his trinket." From the padded box he lifted a plain wood and leather scabbard chased with green bronze and tossed it to Rol. "You may go now." And as Rol rose and bowed, he added: "Keep it with you at all times, and do not unsheathe it again unless you intend to shed blood."

"But I will have to get to know it, to practice—"

"No. You will find that the blade adjusts to your style. There is no need to become accustomed to it. The sword will take care of that itself."

Rol felt a prickle of unease. "What kind of weapon is this?"

"An ancient and unique one, which should be treated with respect. Now leave us."

Rol did as he was told. He met Rowen's eyes for one flashing instant as he turned to go, and realized some light that had come into them of late had been quenched again. The realization darkened the simple, lustful joy of the scimitar's bright quiver in his hand, and he made his way down the Tower's endless stairs with heavy feet, some part of him still with her at Psellos's table.

He bedded Arexa that night, a tall, dark-haired girl from inland Gascar who worked in the middle regions of the Tower and had the neat hands of a seamstress. Her breath was quick and light under him as his pelvis slammed into her buttocks. He was staring at the sword as it hung on the wall before him, thinking of Rowen's steel-spring strength straining against him. Somehow the two were connected in his mind. Absurd and hopeless though it might be, he knew he loved Rowen. He loved her rare smiles, her silence, the sense of wholeness and quietude her presence gave him.

He spent himself viciously in the girl whose white back strained below him. Psellos had recently brought in a whole new crop of maidservants, and every one was tall and slim and dark.

The Master knew of Rol's infatuation, and it amused him.

Rol rolled the girl aside, wiping his forehead on the back of his arm. Arexa began dressing composedly. She was a placid girl, with a quick smile that lit up her face. How had she come to end up here? But Rol knew the answer to that question even as he asked it. Payment. Her father or her uncle or her brother would owe Psellos money, or a favor, or would want a certain deed done discreetly, and Arexa would go to the Tower to be subject to the whims therein. Rol felt suddenly ashamed, part of the machinery of Psellos's intrigues. He handed Arexa her skirt. It was plain and homespun, but she had embroidered interlocking leaves of ivy about the hem. Like her, it smelled of lavender.

He sat on the bed with her slickness still upon him, while she dressed and tied up her hair. When she had finished she ran nimble fingers down his cheek.

"Sad tonight. What goes on in that head of yours?"

He sprang up, swung her into his arms as though she were a feather pillow, and kissed her soundly. "Apple wine and lavender and pretty girl's thighs. Pay me no mind. And take something away with you so you may embroider more flowers about your ankles." He set her down and fished in his bedside chest, came up with a silver minim. A week's wages for a maid. Psellos tossed him a pouch of minims every month as a man will throw a bone to his dog, and he was told to spend it like a gentleman.

Rol dropped the coin between Arexa's creamy breasts where they rose in the V of her blouse. Then he slapped her taut rump and told her with a grin to be on her way.

The grin winked out like a snuffed candle-match as the door closed behind her. Rol's gaze was drawn inevitably to the sword on the wall. He crossed the small room in two strides and took it down. The curved blade was as long as his arm from fingertip to collarbone. He could not believe its lightness. It seemed to want to dance in his hand.

"What will I call you, then?" he asked it. How does one name a sword?

He thought of plunging the scimitar into Psellos's sneering

face, lopping off the aristocratic nose, putting out the eyes. The contemplation of killing dizzied him for a second. He tossed the sword onto the bed, frowning. And realizing that he was not going to make up a name for this sword, he was going to discover one.

He took to the streets in his journeyman attire. A shirt of unbleached wool, canvas breeches, high boots, and a comfortable sleeveless tunic of soft leather with large pockets. From his belt hung a stout hide purse, a double-edged dirk, and the scimitar in its ancient-looking scabbard. Over all he had thrown an oilskin cloak, black with age and long use. He would spend Psellos's minims like a gentleman. He would get drunk and pick a fight and make a whore moan. Or pay her to moan at least. He would . . .

He would do whatever it took to stop thinking of Psellos and Rowen making the two-backed beast. And he would give ear to the comforting whispers of his new sword.

No—was he drunk already? Or not drunk enough. "Iron does not speak," he said aloud, and for some reason the thought pleased him. He strode down the hilly streets of lamplit Ascari with the brisk pace of a man lucky in love.

Eight

NAMING A BLADE

HE HAD BEEN TAUGHT TO BE CAUTIOUS IN ASCARI, TO fade into the background. It had been part of his training. He and Rowen had slipped about a score of taverns and slop-houses up and down the city, their task to blend in, to remain so unnoticed that the other customers would not even spare them a comment on the weather. Rol had thought it an impossible feat, for Rowen was the most beautiful woman he had ever seen, and he himself was not so unremarkable.

"We use disguises, then," he had said to Rowen, "hooded cloaks and false beards and the like?"

"No. We go in as we are."

"Then it's impossible."

"Watch me first."

And she had glided into the Merry Leper, as quick and sure as an otter hunting eels. He had followed after, and the heads that had not turned at her passing now swiveled to regard him at once with a mixture of suspicion and hostility. No one drank in the Leper who was not a mariner or a longshoreman.

"How is it done?" he had asked her later, when she had extricated him from an ugly scene.

"It is in the mind, like a fence you put round yourself—or better yet, a veil of shadow. It blurs men's minds, turns them aside like a buckler turning the point of a sword."

"Yes, but *how is it done?*"

One of her priceless smiles. "That is something you will have to find out for yourself. It is enough to know that it can be done, that it is in you to do it."

Well, he had done it, on occasion, or thought he had. It was a case of visualizing that veil of shadow, and then seeing men's regard turn toward it like bright spears of interest. When that happened, the shadow hardened, and rebuffed them, and they slid away. Easier when the watchers were drunk, or when they came one and two at a time. What he had not yet mastered was the concentrated regard of an entire roomful of people turning to look at the latest incomer. All men did it; it was a habit of nature. The only way Rol could defend himself against that many eyes was to enter directly behind someone else, and let them take the brunt of the drinkers' curiosity.

But tonight he did not give a rat's behind how many men and women noted his coming and going. The sword was a comforting weight at his hip, and he could feel the eagerness in the blade, the hot desire to leave the scabbard. He laughed aloud for he knew not what, whilst the folk on the streets looked askance at the tall youth and his strange eyes, the black cloak rising in his wake.

A soft rain had come in off the sea so that the cobbles were shining at Rol's feet, but the street traders merely moved beneath their striped and checkered canvas awnings and the rest of the traffic ignored it. Cartsway, the main thoroughfare, wound through the hills like a silken sash abandoned on a rumpled bed. At the main crossroads iron braziers were flaming with charcoal, and the City Watch stood yawning and grumbling among themselves. The Watch had just changed, and these were the Nightmen. Higher paid than the Daywatch, they were also of more dubious character, and it was best to steer clear of them. Their captain was in Psellos's pay, but his hold over his subordinates was often tenuous.

They knew Rol, had been apprised of his identity by Psellos six months before. They watched him as he passed by, and Rol saw them spit, out of the corner of his eye. He smiled, the strange, fey mood still upon him.

He turned off Cartsway as the rain grew heavier. Crowds of cloaked, ill-smelling townsfolk jostled and cursed amid the narrower streets, all trying to steer clear of the open central drains which ran with ordure and were alive with rats. It was spring, and in the woods up in the foothills the primroses would be out, but here in the city the seasons counted for less. One could drink beer in the street in comfort if it was summer, and on the coldest winter nights many taverns charged an entrance fee for those desperate for warmth, but that was all.

A beggar, his eyes mere shriveled raisins in his head, held out a yellow-nailed hand in blind hope. Rol dropped a minim into it, and the beggar gaped, feeling the rare weight of silver. "Thanks to your honor! A blessing on your house!" He would be lucky not to be killed for it before the night was out.

Eastside, the lower quarter of the city that faced toward Dennifrey. Rowen had taken him here a few times, to let him grow accustomed to the brash streetlife, the insistent hawkers, the predatory gangs, the confidence tricksters. It seemed amazing sometimes that ordinary, honest traders and businessmen could operate in Ascari, but of course that was all down to the

King of Thieves, and the price of his protection. A feather pinned above the doorway of a shop meant that no footpad or urchin would trouble the place. If he did, he would be found with a slit throat in short order. Some of the older establishments, such as inns, had been under the Thief-King's protection so long that the feather had been carved in stone or wood, and was placed above the entrance as a badge of pride, a guarantee that no one within would be smothered in his bed. The Feathermen, as common folk often called those of the Guild of Thieves, could drink their way from hilltop to harbor (it was said) and never pay for a drop, such was the power of their patronage.

If Rol had known then what he did now, he would never have dared to follow Psellos and Quare out of the door that night. But then he might still be a scullion, kept only to be periodically milked of his blood.

He and Rowen both gave their blood to Psellos once a month. Their bed and board, the Master called it. He took it to the apothecary, Grayven, who had his shop here in Eastside, and it was auctioned off in secret. Thus the rich and noble of Ascari prolonged their lives, drinking the blood of those they secretly regarded as monsters. It was an odd world, odder than Rol would ever once have believed, for all his grandfather's tall tales.

He approached a fight in the street, and studied the combatants with some interest. Three footpads had set upon a scrawny man of middle years whose bald head was already speckled with his own worthless gore. The footpads wore blue rags about their necks which meant that they were licensed, and thus the Watch would leave them be—not that there were any of the Watch down here in Eastside after dark. The footpads were trying to be reasonable with their victim.

"Just give us the bloody purse, and you'll have nothing worse to show for it than a bump on the skull, mate."

"You're only making it worse for yourself," another said with an aggrieved air.

The little bald man was clutching his purse to his chest as though it were a child. His eyes were tight shut and his widely spaced teeth were clenched.

One of the footpads rose and produced a long knife. "Have it your way, then, you little bastard."

"Hold on there, lads," Rol said, prompted by he knew not what. The hilt of the scimitar was vibrating under his palm. He felt he must almost hold it down in the scabbard.

The quartet of struggling figures paused and looked at him. They saw a tall man—no, not much more than a boy, at second glance, but big for his age, and with oddly unsettling eyes. A worn cloak only partially concealed the fact that the rest of his clothes were of good quality. And a plump purse hung from his belt.

The three footpads released the little bald man and he slumped into the mud. A ribbon of blood coursed steadily from his crown, sealing one eye shut, dripping off his unshaven chin.

The one with the drawn knife grinned. "Slumming it tonight, are we, my young cock? Come to see how the lower half live? I'll wager it's silver that plumps out that purse of yours. No copper minims for the likes of you. Maybe even a gold ryal—ah, it's been a long time since Snick has seen the gleam of gold!"

The other two drew their knives also, though *knife* was an inoffensive term for a length of cruelly sharpened iron a foot long. Rol's heart began to throb in his throat. He was not afraid—there was a kind of gladness in him. He drew his sword, and it leaped up like a pinion of brightness in the street. The cloak he whipped round his left arm. He realized he had been looking for this, or something like it.

All about them the passersby were stopping to watch, and had begun to crowd against the walls of the nearby houses. It was an ancient form of entertainment, free to those who were not involved. Other folk were leaning out into the street from upstairs windows, crowing and clapping their hands and telling their children to come see.

Snick's eyes flicked to the blade of the scimitar. A moment of doubt, followed by a kind of lust. He and Rol smiled at each other in perfect understanding. Then the footpads moved.

Two to his front, one circling round to find his rear. Without conscious volition, Rol blocked two leaping thrusts of the knives, clashing them aside with little explosions of sparks. He moved in fast, following up. His left elbow caught the footpad leader below the nose, breaking teeth, snapping cartilage. The arm moved on, swooped over the thrusting blade of the second, caught the man's wrist. At the same time Rol was aware of the man behind him coming in for the kill, like a cloud sensed behind his shoulder. He spun the scimitar without looking back, felt it cut through something as yielding as clay. Attention back to the second man. He twisted the wrist, broke it with a loud snap, released it with the fellow yelling in his face, and sidestepped another stab from the third at his rear.

He was out of their circle. The leader was holding his face, blood pouring over his fingers. The second was retrieving his knife, one hand hanging useless and limp. The third was gasping, his hands pressed to the red rent where Rol had slashed open his bowels.

A smattering of derisive applause broke out around them. Someone threw half a cabbage head at the leader of the footpads, and there was hooted laughter. The two men who could stand helped each other away whilst the folk in the street bombarded them with catcalls and refuse. The third had collapsed, fists clenched in his lacerated intestines. He drew his legs up like a child going to sleep, and died there in the mud. Rol looked down at the blade of his sword. There was no blood thereon—it had cut too swiftly for that. He thought of the bright tool that Psellos used to draw blood every month.

"I shall call you *Fleam,*" he said, and the sword seemed to dip in his hand in answer. He sheathed it, unwrapped his cloak from his left arm—there was a rent in the oilskin—and looked about himself like a man waking from sleep.

The little knots of bystanders were unclotting already, going about their nightly business. Though the street was crowded, they made a space around Rol as though he had an unseen wall about him. He rubbed his hand over his face and bent over the little bald man who lay bloody-faced, still clutching his purse. He was grinning.

"That was as good as a play, my lad. Here, help me up." On his feet, he shook Rol's hand like a man pumping water. "Come with me and I'll buy you a drink—I can do that at least. I have never seen such swordplay. Come now—I have friends waiting for me."

Rol was about to refuse—the fey mood was gone now, and in its place was sinking the sick cold reaction. But then he thought of the Tower, and what was happening in there tonight, and he nodded. He was content to follow now, his passion spent.

The small man's name was Woodrin, and he was purser and part owner of an Andelysian brig which was bound for Osmer, far to the southwest of the world, beyond the Seven Isles. They had made landfall in Gascar to off-load half their cargo of walrus ivory and to let the ship's company cry a little havoc in the famed taverns of Ascari. The purse he had fought so recklessly to retain contained the proceeds of their cargo's auction, which in turn represented most of the sailors' pay for the outbound voyage.

"I am not the only one of the company who will be glad to

buy you a drink, I am sure." The little man laughed, wiping the blood out of his eye with a spotted bandanna.

The Merry Leper. Rol had to smile as Woodrin clapped him on the back and ushered him in.

The place was low-beamed, foggy with whitherb smoke, close and hot as a steam room, and fetid with the smell of spilled beer, ill-washed men, and stale food. The roar of noise from the motley throng within struck Rol like a wave as he entered, but it subsided somewhat as he was studied closely by those whose noses were not too deep in their tankards. No veil of shadow here. He stood an ordinary man amongst men, returning their stares warily.

A huge, startling shape rose from beside the fire, where it had been turning a spitted pig. "Woodrin—what's this with the blood and the shit and all? I told you I should have come with you."

The speaker was a thing the like of which Rol had never seen before. Some fathom and a half tall, it had to crouch under the beams of the Leper, its knotted knuckles resting on the flags of the floor. In its head burned two green lights which blinked under a frowning crag of bone, and blunt tusks arced out above the lower lip. Its flesh was a mottled olive, lighter on the chest, darker on the forearms and face. It wore loose cowhide breeches with the hair left on, and a hide waistcoat. The creature's great, splayed feet were bare, each toe as wide as Rol's wrist.

"Fear not, Gallico; I had an angel guarding me. This is—a man of the city—who saw fit to preserve me from some over-friendly footpads."

The thing called Gallico lumbered forward, rocking on its fists like a boat chopping through swell. Bent though it was, its eyes were on a level with Rol's. The light in them moderated somewhat, and Rol could see that there were golden flecks in the green, and black pupils which were not round, but lozenge-shaped. Surrounding the eyes was a massive frame of bone, the olive skin stretched tight across it, speckled with tiny golden hairs. The thing's scalp was entirely bald, but it had grown a sparse goatee on its chin, and there were gold rings in its earlobes, wide enough to settle comfortably about a man's thumb.

The creature raised its arm (thicker than Rol's thigh) and set a hand on his shoulder. "Well, now," it said, and its voice was low, like a bass lute. "What might this man of the city's name be?"

"My name is Rol, Rol Cortishane."

"Rol Cortishane, I am Peor Gallico." The thing grinned horribly. "I believe I shall buy you a beer."

The fight in the street was a story now, which found a worthy teller in Woodrin, once his comrades had stopped up his broken head and wiped the worst of the filth from his clothes. Rol drank the good beer that came foaming up from the cellar below in tall wooden pitchers. In Psellos's Tower the Master and Rol and Rowen drank wine, and beer, suitably watered, was the preserve of the lower orders. It tasted nothing like this.

Gallico was watching him, one paw turning the pig on the spit as easily as if it were a chicken.

"Why, Woodrin, he's naught but a boy. Are you sure it was three desperate thieves, not just some shirttailed urchin who caught you unawares?"

A gale of laughter met this sally. Woodrin was indignant. "I tell you it was three professionals, licensed and all. This boy took them on cool as you please, slew one and sent the others limping off with broken bones and busted noses."

"He's somewhat young to be a killer of men," Gallico said, but there was no humor in his voice now. The green glitter of his eyes had sharpened. "But, yes, I see it. I see—" He stopped, and supped mightily out of a wooden tankard which seemed small as a thimble in his fist. "I need some air, and to stretch the kinks out of my backbone. You there, our heroic rescuer, lend me a hand out of the door."

The talk and laughter fell, and Gallico looked round, smiled. "Why the long faces? I will not bite him. Come, Rol Cortishane. Bear with me."

For the first time in his life, Rol was reluctant to leave a tavern. It was something to be a hero, or at least it was something to be accepted, and brought into the edges of a brotherhood. It was new, and he liked it.

The streets were black and full of running water, but the rain had stopped, and in this lightless corner of the city it was possible to look up and see the stars. Gallico straightened to his full height upon leaving the tavern, and Rol stepped back a pace, shocked by the sheer bulk of the creature. His hand went to Fleam's hilt, naked training kicking in.

"Na, na," Gallico said equably, "you need not fear me. We are all in your debt, and mariners do not forget. Keep your sword blade hid." His nostrils widened as he sniffed the air. "A change is in the wind. It will have backed round to due east by morning. We will have it on the port beam."

"You sail tomorrow?"

"We sail today, youngster, at dawn."

"For Osmer."

"Yes, sunny Osmer of the Singers. A twelve-day trip, if Ran is kind."

"And where then?"

"Wherever our next cargo takes us, wherever the wind suffers us to go. Wind, cargo, and the thews of men, that is all a good ship needs, if it is to make a profit in this godless world of ours."

There was a sudden painful yearning in Rol, a desire to take ship with this thing and this company whose fellowship had blossomed all around him back in the tavern. To tread the seaways of the world and leave behind the Tower of Michal Psellos, the unending training for an unknown purpose. Rowen. To be clean and free and at sea again.

"You were a sailor of sorts yourself once," Gallico ventured.

"How do you know?"

"Something in the way you look up at the stars. Most men spare them a glance and no more, but you study them as if you knew them."

"I have sailed by them, a little. Coastal sailing mostly."

"So you know the sea."

"I lived my life by it and on it once. Seems a long time ago now, but it is not so long."

"Time goes slower when one is young. I have seen out a century, and am but half-grown."

"What—forgive me—what are you?"

Gallico laughed, a great boom of good fellowship. "I am a relic, a piece of flotsam. Men call my kind halftrolls, but that is only a name. I have Old Blood in me." Gallico stopped, considered. "As have you, my young friend."

They stared at each other, Rol in dawning wonder, Gallico nodding.

"The Elder Race, of whom it is better not to speak. That ancient blood reveals itself in strange ways, odd forms. Demon or angel, it is in us all."

"You know, then, how I was able to save your wages."

"You preserved Woodrin, which means more to us. But yes, I am not so surprised. Men do not fear us for nothing."

"Your shipmates do not seem to fear you."

"That is because we are of the company, Seahawks one and all."

"Seahawks?"

"The name of our brig, though to my mind she's more of a pigeon. We are of a dozen different nations and races but our allegiance is to our ship, and each other."

Once again that odd pain in Rol, the feeling that he was

somehow missing something, lacking a quality Gallico and his shipmates possessed.

"I must go now," he said.

"Are you truly a man of this city, Rol?"

"I'm not a man of anywhere."

"Then you could do worse than seek a home on the sea. We're short several hands. The company would welcome you, I know."

Rol bowed his head, realizing how easy it would be. By this time tomorrow he would be at sea with men who seemed to esteem him. He would be *clean.*

"I cannot. I have things to do here in Ascari. Unfinished business."

Gallico's paw was surprisingly light on his shoulder. "I thought as much. But if the business becomes too bloody, make your way to Spokehaven on Osmer. Every year at the fall of the leaves, captains from all over the Wrywind put in for refitting there."

Rol looked up, his face very young in the starlight. "The Seahawks also?"

"We also. Fare well, my friend." And Gallico turned, bent, and re-entered the tavern at their backs, the door closing behind him on the lamplight, the laughter, the reek of beer and sweat of men.

Rol gathered his cloak about him, and began walking uphill, out of Eastside. Away from the sea.

Nine

THE FEAST OF HARVEST

TIME PASSED, THE SEASONS FOLLOWED ONE ANOTHER IN their particular order. Summer came and went, and the snows on the Ellidon Hills receded, and then began to creep seaward again toward the flushed fires of the turning woods. The coastal fishermen brought in their wherries and beached them beyond the reach of Ran's Rages, and in the markets of Ascari apples and hazelnuts and half a hundred other foodstuffs were mounded in colorful profusion on the stalls. Another harvest had been brought in, another season on the sea survived. Men gave thanks in drunken feasts up and down the city, where city-dwellers who barely knew what it was to plant a thing and watch it grow and harvest it sat down with fishermen and farmers and gave thanks for the largesse. It was a tradition as old as mankind itself.

Psellos hosted a grand feast in the finest suites of the Tower as he did every year, and so lavish were the preparations that it seemed he must denude the stocks of provender for miles around. Convoys of wagons brought in load after load of food and drink so that the lower levels were piled high with barrels and crates and sacks and earthen jars. Whole vintages were unearthed from the cellars, dusted, and set forth like ranks of soldiers; an entire bakery was hired to turn out pies, pastries, and cakes of every description; and as the fishing season was over, half a hundred deer were culled from the inland estates, along with pheasant, partridge, hare, and piled wicker baskets of larks and starlings.

The protracted preparations grated on Rol's nerves, as did Psellos's air of supercilious bonhomie. Rowen had taught him how to ride over the past few months, and he used every excuse he could find to saddle up the aged bay gelding that was his teaching mount, and trot up the hillside, beyond the sprawl of the city, into the green growing light of the hills and the clamor of the dying leaves. Once there, he would rein in and be able to see the whole shallow arc of Ascari bay, the headland beyond, and a world in which even Ascari's teeming streets seemed a small and untidy blot on the hugeness of the earth and the mantling sea.

The sea, the sea. He had read stories of how the Weren had become enamored of the young world they had been born into, and how some had taken to the gray stone of the mountains, others to the deep fastnesses of the woods, and some to the shifting, ever-changing oceans of the world. Many of the creatures that roamed this diminished earth owed their existence to the early works of the Elder Race. Dolphins, it was said, had their origins in a dream of Ran. Horses were the puissant valor of the earth made flesh. And peregrines had been sired by the spirit of the west wind.

Legends only, but there was a rightness about them that made Rol hope they were true.

Another rider making their way up through the woods

toward him, passing from light into shadow and back into light again, all dappled with the pattern of the sleeping trees. It was Rowen on her black mare. He mouthed the gelding backwards behind a wide gray beech and watched her as she gentled her mount up the root-strewn slope, kicking up saffron leaves as though they were flakes of autumn sparked by her horse's hooves. She thought no one watched, and her face was open and alive—she loved her horse, all horses—and Rol heard her speaking to the young mare, cajoling, soothing, praising in tones warmer than she ever used with any human being. A small, helpless sense of mourning rose in him, and unwillingly he kicked the gelding forward again, out of the shelter of the tree.

Her head snapped round in a quarter-second and a long throwing knife appeared naked in one fist. The mare half reared and laid her ears back, alarmed by the change in her rider's mood. But then Rowen saw who it was, and sheathed her knife, and clicked her mount onward.

"You are missed down in the Tower," she said coldly. "I was sent to fetch you."

"What use am I down there?"

"Perhaps they need another wine-pourer. How would I know? Come. The Master is waiting. The guests will arrive soon."

"The guests? And who are they, I wonder? The great and the good of lovely Ascari, come to enjoy the largesse of the Monster of the Tower."

Rowen looked at him. "Come, Fisheye. Time to go."

He set his hand on Fleam's hilt at the sound of the old nickname. Something white and cold and ugly seemed to rise up in his voice.

"And you, Rowen, what is your role in the festivities of the night? Will you take them two at a time in the Master's bed? Or are the flags of the kitchen good enough for you? How many will you service tonight, Rowen? Will you let them beat you, or will they be more old-fashioned than that?"

Her pale face went paper-gray.

"When you are ready, get you back down. There is a change of clothes waiting in your room. No arms to be carried tonight, not even by you and me. The guests will begin to arrive at dusk."

She turned her mare and with nudges of her heels set it trotting back down the slope to the city. Rol watched her go, black desolation burning a hole in the walls of his heart.

There was a bottle of Cavaillis, the fragrant brandy of Cavaillon, in his room. A gift from Psellos, it was older than half of Ascari. He broke off the seal of the bottle and slugged the potent liquor straight from its neck, feeling it burn a bright path down his gullet, warming the chill of his insides. He stank of horse, for he had pushed the old gelding hard at the last to get back to the Tower in time. A splash in the silver basin some maid had filled for him put paid to that, or so he hoped. He drank deeply of the brandy again, then turned his attention to the clothes lying neatly upon his bed.

A silk shirt, dark as a raven's back, woolen breeches, and a sleeveless tunic. There was embroidery about the tunic's neck, black on sable, silk thread. Two horses entangled in a repeated but variegated pattern, their necks entwining, side by side sometimes, in other places running headlong at each other. He admired it, drank from the brandy bottle, admired it some more. He must buy Arexa some frippery for this; it was exquisite.

He dressed hurriedly, set Fleam in her place by the head of his bed, and took a deep breath.

Your time approaches.

It was the sword, speaking to him.

It is right and fitting that you be here. You can follow any path in life you wish, but in the end it is inevitable that you come into your full self. You can be master in a place such as this. Only command me.

It was the brandy. He grinned at the blank walls, drank again of the Cavaillis, patted Fleam affectionately, and left the room, his shoulder striking the doorframe as he exited.

They came two by two, in coaches, in hired barouches, on horseback, with liveried servants behind them and armed retainers shadowing them up the tortuous Cartsway. The great and the good, trooping obediently to Psellos's door. They avoided his laughing eyes and were reluctant to shake his hand, but they came anyway, drawn by the glitter of their fellows, like moths to a flame irresistible. And perhaps Psellos's reputation only made the occasion more delectable. There were Feathermen lurking in every side street, producing a delicious shudder in the passing carriages. The occupants did not know that the King of Thieves had been paid to make this evening inviolate. Not so much as a beggar stirred in Ascari without his leave, and he had been bribed to ensure that there would be no hitches on the road to the Tower.

Rowen was dressed in a tight-laced bodice that emphasized her slim form and lent sex to its strength and athleticism. Her raven hair was piled up upon her head with silver clasps and her arms and shoulders were bare. The scars upon those shoulders had been powdered out of existence and the black velvet of her skirt hid all but the toes of her iron-buckled boots. She and Rol did not look at each other as they stood with Psellos in the massive atrium of the Tower and welcomed the entering guests.

Ascari, and by extension Gascar, was an oligarchy of sorts, ruled by the heads of half a dozen noble families who had been powerful in the city for time out of mind. These tolerated Psellos much as they tolerated the King of Thieves; because he was useful, in his own way, and because his eradication would take far too much blood and treasure for it to be contemplated. The Tower in which these worthies stood was older by far than the foundation of the city that men knew. Rol had learned that it was a place of the Elder Race, a hollow stronghold constructed by them in the lost millennia of the current world's shaping. Psellos had found it derelict and forgotten half a century before, and had taken it as his own—even then he had possessed the funds to make a capital city turn a blind eye. Now only graybeards remembered it as anything other than Psellos's Tower. Rol could not help but wonder whether Psellos had found more than he claimed in the rubble-choked lower levels of the place's foundations. The Tower had had a name once, he was sure of that, but no surviving record revealed it.

That was by the by. This night the ancient structure was nothing more than a grand place to hold a party, holding a frisson of half-remembered fear for the assembled guests, but not much more. Psellos had told Rol that even the most privileged of life's travelers must feel fear, or what they think is fear, every now and again. No man is content with ease and leisure and plenty, even the most indulged libertine. Especially the most indulged libertine. Which was why some of them had paid a fool's ransom to bed Rowen. Because she made them afraid.

I have come to understand many things since eating dried fish on board *Gannet,* Rol thought. But the knowledge of these things I would sooner do without.

He smiled and bobbed his head and shook hands with limp-wristed rich men, brushed his lips across the knuckles of their preening wives (many of whom eyed him with open lasciviousness) and wondered at the display of delighted interest that Psellos maintained in front of this endless stream of *cattle.*

The splendid windowed chamber Rol had only seen once before had been cleared of all its more grisly contents and now a massive U-shaped table had been assembled within, the closed end backing onto the windowed wall. It seated sixscore with ease, with room left over for extravagant table displays of flowers and silver and marching lines of silver candlesticks. Hearths were uncovered and lit along the straight wall and ornate hangings bright with gold leaf hung between them. Servants scurried hither and thither like dispatch riders on a battlefield, marshaled by the increasingly shrill cries of Quare. Dozens, scores of people milled around accepting dainties from proffered trays, savoring the most mellow of Psellos's wines, running their eyes along the riches on display with some wonder and not a little envy. Rol found himself wondering how many of those present had bought and tasted his blood, or Rowen's. Partaking of the monster. A small, bleak smile curled upon his face like a cat in a warm place. Then he caught Rowen's eye, and her utter indifference wiped his face clean again.

He left the grand chamber, bowing to those who seemed self-important enough to justify it, and made his way down the Tower stairs to the kitchens. The brandy was singing in his veins, and the wine he had drunk on top of that had not helped the bright detachment of his mind. They would not be sitting down to eat for a long while yet, and he felt the need of some ballast in his belly.

The activity in the kitchen resembled that within a command post at the height of a major battle. Gibble—this would be his last Harvest Feast—was bellowing orders, consulting lists, clipping the kitchen scullions' ears, and dipping his grubby finger into various bubbling pots, whilst all around him his subordinates were plucking, gutting, slicing, dicing, and mashing as though their lives depended upon it. There was one small island of calm, however. In the corner farthest from the fire a ragged man with a threadbare cap pushed back on his head sat eating and drinking nonchalantly at a small table. From the cap a single bedraggled feather dangled. Every so often one of the many extra serving-men and -women Psellos had hired for the night would come up to him and speak quietly in his ear. The ragged man would nod thoughtfully, as though filing away information for future use. He looked up as if he had felt the weight of Rol's appraisal and his face split in a yellow smile. He waved Rol over.

"Well, if it's not the apprentice. Sit, lad, take the weight off your boot-soles. You look as though you had seen a spirit. Have some wine—one glass will do us both, I'm sure."

Rol did as he was bidden. He needed the wine. The King of Thieves tore the flesh from a drumstick and leaned back in his chair. His eyes were black with no discernible iris and his unshaven chin was shiny with grease. He looked Rol up and down casually, but Rol had the feeling that the black eyes noted every fold and thread of his clothing.

"I am called Canker. You know me, I think."

"I know you."

"Fine work, that little job you pulled off in our guildhouse. Even had Psellos not bought your life from us, I'd have been inclined to let you live out of sheer curiosity."

"I—I never thought—" Rol stammered. "If I had known—"

"Yes, yes. That is all water down a drain now, though"—and here his avuncular manner wore thin—"it would not be wise to try such a stunt again. I have a reputation to think of, after all."

Rol nodded and drank from the grease-rimmed glass.

"But you have made a very personal reparation, so we will let bygones be bygones, eh?" He saw Rol's puzzled look, and chuckled. "Your blood, my boy. We've had quite a taste of it. It's fitting enough—life for life, you might say."

Rol's stomach turned, and the wine seemed to curdle within it.

"We miss Rowen, though—that is a thoroughbred filly if ever there was one. Psellos has done his best over the past while, of course—he has promised a dark-haired little seamstress for tonight. I dare say she's on her way to the waterfront already."

Something in Rol's eyes made the King of Thieves flinch and push back his chair. One dirt-blackened hand reached under his rags.

"Yes, Psellos is right. There's a lot to be done with you yet. Hood those eyes, my lad, or someone will have them out."

Rol rose slowly, hands clear of his sides. "Enjoy your meal," he said to Canker, and backed away, the black stare fixed on him like that of a snake. Finally he turned and left the kitchen, ignoring Gibble's wave, the maids and scullions making way for him as though his touch would burn them. In a way, he thought, it might.

Psellos had sat Rol on his left, Rowen on his right. The clothing of all three, though rich and beautifully worked, was an exercise in sable, a deliberate contrast to the plumaged finery of the guests. Before them the long arms of the U-shaped table ran out into a haze of candlelight and the gleam of silver and gold. A small army of waiters danced attendance on those present, making sure no glass was empty for long, and a succession of courses arrived with smooth efficiency. Venison, rare and red, wild boar, wildfowl of every description, and a cornucopia of fruit and root vegetables and sauceboats.

Rol's left-hand neighbor was one of the council elders, and he kept leaning across him to talk to Psellos. Finally the Master introduced them. "Councillor Pachydon, allow me to present my—ah—protégé, Rol of Dennifrey."

"So this is him! He's a trifle young, Psellos. Is he up to the job?" The councillor was a portly man with protuberant, bloodshot eyes which looked as though they were about to pop out of his head.

Psellos stared at Pachydon in icy silence. At last he said, "This is not the place to be discussing business, Councillor."

"It was a fair question."

"You will find that Rol is perfectly capable of providing complete satisfaction. Now, please, I think you will find that this next course begs your complete and undivided attention."

Rol stared whitely at the Master. He was about to get up from the table when Psellos's iron-hard grip pinched the nerve behind his knee. His lower leg went numb.

"Not now, my young friend, we have a show to put on," Psellos murmured. "Remember your manners."

"My turn to be pimped out now, is it?" Rol hissed.

"Shut your mouth, you young fool. I'll talk to you when we rise from table and not before. Until then, keep a civil tongue in your head or remain a mute."

A long night. There were speeches to sit through, praising the host and his hospitality. Some speakers were pious and invoked the gods; others were raucous and lewd with drink. Several young blades sent notes to Rowen via salver-bearing waiters. By the time the cloth had been drawn she had a little pile of them sitting beside her glass, all unread. Psellos swept them into his pocket.

At the end the Master rose himself, and proposed a toast to health, commerce, and the continuing prosperity of Ascari. His listeners applauded politely or thumped the table, but they seemed to like the sound of their own voices better than his. At last the diners rose and began to drift toward the bright firelit hearths at the back of the chamber, some more steadily than others, whilst the worst of the debris was cleared from the tables and fresh candles lit. Scores of stools were produced and on these the ladies sat fanning their painted faces, for it was close in the room and many of the gentlemen were now smoking pipes of whitherb. The servers went to and fro freshening drinks and collecting glasses. Some looked more like prizefighters than waiters, and they seemed to linger near knots of conversation, fiddling unnecessarily with the stuff on their trays. Psellos watched Rol's frown follow their movements, and smiled.

"The Feathermen are an adaptable bunch, are they not? Canker and I gather more information on this one night of the year than on the rest combined."

Of course. There must always be an angle, some advantage to be gained.

Rowen had disentangled herself from the attentions of half a dozen young noblemen and joined Rol and Psellos. The three stood apart from the chattering crowd and watched them, as a shepherd will look down on his sheep. With a kind of proprietorial detachment.

I, too, Rol thought. I do it now.

"Not even the inauguration of a new council gets a throng as well-bred as this," Psellos said with relish. "A good night, in all."

Then he turned to Rol, cold and entirely businesslike.

"Pachydon is one of the richest Mercanters of Gascar. The long and the short of it is that he wants a man killed. Tomorrow night."

Rol felt the muscles of his face tighten. "And I am to do it."

"You are to do it. Consider it a kind of final examination. Rowen's phase of your instruction is almost over. Soon you will have a new tutor."

"Who?"

"Our mutual friend, the King of Thieves. He will put the final polish upon you."

Rol glanced at Rowen. She kept his gaze for a moment, and something opened in her eyes, a kind of pity.

"Who is the man I am to murder?"

"His name is Canoval. Lord Canoval to such as you and me."

"Why?"

"Ah, Rol, that is the one question you must never ask. *How,* by all means, *when,* certainly, but *why*? No. There is no need for that one."

"Where does he live? How do I recognize him?"

"That's more like it. As to recognizing him, he is here tonight, and I will make sure you meet him. The where of it will be handled by Canker. He has been monitoring the lordship's movements for several weeks now, not that these aristocrats are anything but predictable. Canker will be your mentor in this thing, he will hold your hand, as it were. It is a test in killing, but not simply some inane slaughter. You must show us that you can practice some finesse." Psellos had not looked at Rol once as he spoke. His eyes were ranging about the chamber, alighting with interest now and again, registering faces.

"What if I refuse to do it?"

Psellos sighed. "Rol, must you be so tiresome? You should be growing out of this petulance by now. Rowen, tell him. I am off to mingle with the great and the good. Be with me at the door when it is time to see them out, both of you." And off he went, a lean, elegant figure all in black, with shining wolf-teeth.

"Well?" Rol asked Rowen.

"There are two types of men in the world," she said, "those who prize their own skins above all else, and those who . . ." She paused as though searching for words. "Those who prize the thing they love above their own lives."

"I don't understand."

"He knows you are not one of the former. So, he has said that if you do not perform this deed, I am to spend a month in the guildhouse as the plaything of the King of Thieves." She cleared her throat. "It is probable that I would not survive."

"He wouldn't do that."

"He would do anything."

"So I love you more than my own life, is that it?"

"That is what he thinks."

"And what do you think?"

"That is unimportant."

"I do love you, Rowen. You know this. You have known it a long time."

She looked him in the eye again at last. "Yes, I have."

"Then there is nothing more to be said. I must end a life to preserve yours."

"You may look upon it that way if you will."

"Damn you! Are you flesh and blood at all?"

She walked away, and he seized her arm. It came limply, as though the will had gone out of her.

"No," she said quietly. "Not here."

She allowed herself to be led out of the chamber, through the streams of servants coming and going. Finally Rol found a quiet space a few levels down. The noise of the party was faint above them. He took Rowen by the shoulders. "Listen to me. I—"

A pain in his belly. He looked down to see her pushing a blade against the silk of his shirt.

"Do not do this." Her voice broke on the last word.

He said nothing, but deliberately pulled her close, staring into her face. The pain intensified for a split second, and then was gone. There was a metallic clatter on the floor and he could feel blood running down inside his shirt.

Those gray-steel eyes staring at him, unfathomable. He wanted to make them change, to see something new come into them. He took her face in his hands and kissed them shut. And tasted salt as her face betrayed her, tears on the face of a statue. He raised her chin and kissed the lovely mouth. It came alive under his lips, a moment he would never forget. They buried their faces in each other's bodies and stood thus a long time, heedless of everything but the sudden peace each gave to the other. It seemed to Rol that he had found something of home again, a fixed point in the black whirl of the world.

* * *

He raised his head, and glared at her tear-streaked face. "No more pretense. It is you and I, Rowen—whatever it takes, it will be you and I together from now on."

She nodded, matching him glare for glare. But her warm fingers entwined with his. "So be it. I have had enough. I am tired, Fisheye; you cannot know how tired."

"I love you," he said, as though the words were some magic healing spell.

"I know. I think I have always known."

"You hid it well."

"Not well enough. Now listen to me—"

"No—you tell me, who is this Lord Canoval?"

"He has just been elected head of the council. He proposes to close down the operations of the Feathermen."

"Could that be done?"

"There is a lot of money involved. With enough money, anything is possible. Canker and Psellos have been working hand in glove for many months now, but they have become greedy."

"How much support does Canoval have in the council?"

"They are sheep, and he is their shepherd. There was a secret ballot. When they are ready they will make it public. A mercenary flotilla is rumored to be docked on Andelys already, awaiting the word to sail."

"Gods! It will be a war. And will killing Canoval stop this?"

She shrugged. "Quite probably. None of the rest of them has the sand to stand against both Psellos and the King of Thieves, and there are some among them who believe Canoval cannot either. Pachydon is one—Psellos's creature, body and soul." She looked away from him. "He is the front man, and will take the fall, if anything goes wrong. If things go well, he will be council leader."

"How was he bought?" Rol asked harshly, though he knew the answer.

"With me," she said. She tried to draw away, but he would

not let her, and he was the stronger now. She leaned her head on his chest. "This carcass of mine has been pimped out a thousand times, Rol. Are you sure you want it?"

"You called me Rol."

"Did I?" That small, rare smile which so transformed her face. "It is easier on the ear."

He kissed her again, knowing that for this woman there was nothing he would not do, no crime he would not commit.

But there was a question he had to ask. "Why entrust me to do this thing?" he asked. "I am untried, and this will be life and death for Psellos, the killing of this man. The King of Thieves must have experienced assassins aplenty who could do it. And then of course—" He stopped, and the training made its leap intuitively.

"And then there is me." She moved out of his arms, dry-eyed now. "I am the best in the city—not even the Feathermen come close."

"He wants both his own killers there."

"Yes. I, too, will be busy that night. The King of Thieves and Canoval will die together. Psellos will take over the Feathermen, and his creature, Pachydon, will lead the council. Our master will be ruler of Ascari, and hence of Gascar. He will have become one of the princes of the world."

"If we do as we are told."

"If we do as we are told."

"What hold has he over you, Rowen?"

"The hold is twofold now, and identical to that he has over you. He claims to know who my parents are—the history of whatever family spawned me. And he threatens me with the extinction of one I love."

Rol's mouth tightened even as the knowledge blossomed wide and bright in his heart. "How long—"

"A long time. I don't know how, but I think Psellos knew it would happen. He enjoyed watching it, playing us one at a time. He has always relished such diversions." She reached up with one hand and touched the embroidered collar of his tunic. "I, too, have some skill with a needle."

He pulled her close again. Something deep within him woke up and began to snarl. Whatever remnant of boyhood he still possessed withered away.

"Psellos must die. Let us kill him." His voice was thick with the desire.

She set her fingers on his lips. "Wait now, think about this. Psellos is a sorcerer, an assassin of great power. It is possible both of us together might best him, if we caught him unawares. But there may be a better way."

"I want to feel his life give out under my hands."

"You think I do not? But I want to live. I want you to live. That is more important. Trust me."

He kissed her forehead. "I will trust you. But *he* must die."

Ten

THE HEIR

CANOVAL, THE CATALYST FOR ALL THE SLAUGHTER THAT followed, was a short, dark terrier of a man with a lively smile. As the line of guests left the Tower he shook Rol's hand perfunctorily, Psellos's with rather more force than was necessary, and Rowen's he kissed with a combination of relish and reverence. An hour by the water-clock the three stood there saying fare thee well and well met to a crowd of men and women who feared and despised and desired them all in one. When at last Quare had a pair of footmen slam shut the great oaken doors of the atrium, even Psellos looked relieved. He tugged at the collar of his shirt and stretched his arms toward the ceiling. "Ye gods, but they are a tiresome crowd, these men of substance. Do they eat their gold, to become such heavy going? Rol, come up with me and have a nightcap. Rowen, you were delightful and perfect as always. I shall see you in the morning. Quare, lock up, and see that our guest workers are well looked after."

Quare and Rowen bowed. As she straightened again Rowen's fingers brushed Rol's. The warmth of that tiny gesture was still with him as he entered Psellos's private apartments near the summit of the Tower. The stair-climb and the revelations of the evening had cleared his head, and he watched the Master pour Cavaillis for them both with an even mind.

"Tiresome, these occasions, but necessary," Psellos said, handing Rol a glass and collapsing into a well-stuffed armchair. One of the housemaids had lit the fire, knowing that the Master hated a cold room, and it cast beating wings of shadow about the walls. These were lined with books, but Rol had been in here before, and he knew that the volumes on display could be bought from any good antiquarian. The real knowledge, the important texts, were housed elsewhere, in some secret chamber Rol had never seen.

"Gods, boy, you are getting tall. Take a seat. You'll crick my neck for me if I have to crane it any more."

He did as he was bidden, wondering as he sat if hatred could be smelled, if it had a particular redolence. If so, this room must stink of it.

Psellos was rolling his glass between his hands, staring into the fire. For the first time, Rol noticed that there was gray in the forelock that overhung his narrow face.

"You will meet Canker in Candlemas Street tomorrow night—no, it is tonight now, I suppose. He will take you to a back entrance of Canoval's manse. It will be unguarded. He sleeps on the second floor, in a room with a red door and his arms emblazoned upon it, the ass. His wife will be with him. She also must die."

"He was alone tonight."

"She is something of an invalid; a fall from a horse a few years ago." He smirked. "In any case, she will not be running anywhere for help."

"What about servants, bodyguards?"

"There will be a few, but no more than you can handle. Kill them or bypass them, I care not. But Canoval must die as swiftly and silently as possible. A matter of style, I'm sure you'll understand."

"It must look as though it was child's play to accomplish."

"Exactly." Psellos sipped his brandy meditatively, looking Rol over as a woman would regard herself dressed unfamiliarly in a mirror. Finally he spoke with great deliberation.

"Amerie, your mother, would be proud of you, Rol. With this final test, you will have grown up into a man."

Dumbstruck, Rol merely stared. Psellos seemed rewarded by the expression on his face.

"I have need of loyal lieutenants, and I have no sons of my own. These things are better kept in the family, I have always thought."

"Family?" Rol managed.

"Amerie was my sister. We are of one blood, you and I, not only because we share in our inheritance from the Elder Race, but because we come from the same stock."

"I don't believe you."

"Why do you think old Ardisan sent you to me with his dying words, nephew of mine? He knew it was time. He kept you hid as long as he could, but at some point you were always going to end up here. It is the only way you would ever approach your true potential."

"My father—who was he?"

Psellos frowned. "I'll be honest with you—I do not know."

"You're lying."

"No, in this I speak the truth. I have nothing more to gain by keeping these things from you now. You have apprenticed yourself here because of the promise of knowledge, and because your youth made you afraid to strike out on your own. And then there is Rowen, of course. But you are a boy no longer, and thus it is time to tell you what I know."

The fire cracked and spat brightly. Rol could not look at this man who purported to be his uncle.

"Amerie's husband in life was Bar Hethrun, one of the great men of Bionar. The Blood was in him, but so was that of the line of Bion himself. There were those who thought he would have been king, had he not fallen in love with a raven-haired sorceress out of the Goliad, the birthplace of Man. The Bionari did not like the idea of a witch's brat sitting at the foot of the throne, and there were plots to discredit Hethrun and his house, assassination attempts. He forsook his high estate and took to the seas with your mother and many others of his household, meaning to live in peace somewhere beyond the reach of whispers and pointing fingers and knives in the dark. Cambrius Orr all over again, you might say. But the little fleet he had put together was broken up by storms in the Bionese Sea, and most of the ships were scattered and wrecked, their crews drowned or cast up on beaches from Perilar to Osca. Amerie was lost in the disaster, and Hethrun spent years searching for her as a humble captain of privateers. He found her, or she found him, and she would not speak of the lost time they were apart. The pair spent what was left of their lives at sea, but the Bionari learned of their survival and sent out men-of-war to track them down, for there was a new king on the throne of Bionar, Bar Asfal, and his grip on power was not sure enough to allow a pretender to travel freely about his coasts. Their son therefore they sent away with Amerie's parents, and her brother, to be brought up somewhere in safe anonymity. Amerie and Bar Hethrun died. At the last they were hunted down and murdered by agents of the Bionese crown. Their son disappeared, and the story became a tragic ballad to be played in inns across Bionar. The King-That-Never-Was. The Lost Heir. Bar Asfal has reigned for over twenty years now, and he has struck up a treaty with the Mage-King of Kull, who even as we speak has certain suspicions about the identity of one Psellos of Gascar. His suspicions have not yet hardened into certainty, but one day they will, and there is nowhere on earth one can hide from the doppelgangers of Kull."

Rol was silent for a long time. At last he said: "You deserted them."

Psellos smiled. "Your grandparents? I had a different life in mind, that's all. But I am doing my duty by you now, Rol. The thing is"—and here he leaned forward, the firelight saffron-yellow in his eyes—"I do not believe that you are the son of Bar Hethrun, the Lost Heir of Bionar. So you can strip those bright dreams out of your head. No, you were born soon after Amerie came back to Hethrun—too soon for you to be his child." He sat back in his chair, sniffing at the fragrant brandy. "And your blood is too pure to have any of his within it. It is purer even than my own. No, you are a bastard of a different stock."

"This family of mine—of ours. Who were they? My mother's parents, and yours. Where did all this begin?"

"In the Goliad, as I said. It is a blighted wilderness now, for wars have carried back and forth across the face of it for centuries, but still a few nomadic clans with the Old Blood in them survive. Golgos itself is a ruin within which squats a Bionese garrison, a mere way station for ships coasting down to Oronthir. One would think that there was nothing left to fight over in the reed-beds and the dried river valleys of that ruined paradise, but myth is a powerful thing. It is said that out of the Goliad will come the mightiest of the kings of men, and so nations bleed to possess it, generation after generation."

"If my father was not this Bionese nobleman, then who was he?"

"I have told you—I do not know. It is a question I am itching to get to the bottom of—a conundrum. Grayven and I have knocked heads together over it with little result. Amerie was strong in the Blood, stronger perhaps than I. Even had she bedded a normal human, their progeny would have been powerful. But by the makeup of your blood your father, Rol, could only have been a Were, a full-blooded Ancient of the Elder Race." Here Psellos stared into his glass and chuckled like a man pressed to accept an absurdity. "And of course that is impossible—no such creature has walked upon the earth for millennia."

Impatiently, Rol said: "What of Rowen? How did she come to be here?"

Psellos continued to peer into the bottom of his empty glass. "Rowen is a foundling. I chanced across her begging in the street, barely strong enough to stand, and took her in, for I could see the Blood in her."

"And took her to your bed."

He sighed. "Yes. And why not? Don't tell me you would not like to sink between those white thighs, Rol."

"But you are supposed to know her parentage."

"I lied. I know only that I found her on the streets of Ascari one morning, alone in the world."

"If you cannot tell her what she wants to know, then she'll leave you."

"I don't think so."

"I will tell her the truth."

"I know you will. But from now on she will not be staying here to discover some absurd family tree—she will remain here because of you."

If he had expected to shock, he was disappointed. The triumphant smile wavered on his face as he realized events had evidently moved faster than his calculations. He blinked rapidly.

"She loves you, don't ask me why. She has loved nothing on

two legs in her entire life, I think. She is a queen amongst women—and she loves you. Think on it."

All of Rol's fine hatred had burned away to ash. He knew that Psellos was not telling all the truth, but he knew also that much of the truth was there.

"Why have you done such things to her?" he asked tiredly.

Composed again, Psellos waved a hand. "Why is a sword beaten upon the anvil? I made Rowen into a beautiful, pitiless weapon. She is my creation, and will never forget that."

"You enjoyed it."

"Yes, I did. Over my long life I have acquired many tastes, some of them beyond the ken of short-lived men. One must always seek diversion somewhere." Here Psellos rose out of his chair and stood staring into the fire, his hands on the hot mantel.

"Hate me if you will, Rol, but look beyond this night, beyond your love for Rowen and your outrage at her treatment at my hands. You, too, have a long life ahead of you, if the gods are kind—longer than mine, for your blood is purer. I have found with the passing decades that all that once seemed important—riches, women, the esteem of one's fellows—falls away. In the end, all appetites can be sated save one. We hunger after knowledge. Where did we come from, what black night are we walking toward? For half a century I have devoted myself to the pursuit of knowledge, and the fruits of that pursuit are housed here, in this ancient tower."

"For such an ascetic, you make a good fist at playing the sybarite."

Psellos laughed. "I need power, I admit. If I am to defy the Mage-King in my quest, then I cannot do so as a barefoot scholar. I need men to fight my battles for me. One day, I will rule Gascar, and even the Mage-King will hesitate before killing the ruler of one of the Seven Isles. I will have the shield I have been seeking.

"I want you to rule it with me, Rol, and after me. This thing I am asking you to do tonight is the beginning of it. Rowen is yours now, and from tomorrow onward you are my heir." He turned back from the fire and produced from his pocket a long, glinting key. "As such, you will receive this, to use as you will."

"What is it?"

"The key to my library and laboratory. The last of the secrets."

Rol's fingers had sunk into the arms of his chair. He could not move, so tangled were his thoughts.

"I don't know—"

"Kill Canoval tonight, and by morning I shall be ruler of Gascar in all but name, with you by my side, and Rowen at yours."

"As simple as that?"

"As simple as that." Abruptly Psellos returned the key to his pocket, turned away. "You had best get some sleep while you can. It's been a busy day."

Rol rose shakily to his feet. "Why should I believe you? This could all be a lie."

Now it was Psellos who sounded tired. "It could be, but it is not. You ought to be able to sense that by now. Go, Rol. Make love to Rowen—you have earned her. Tell her all this if you please, it matters not. But be ready in Candlemas Street tonight."

For some reason, he wanted to set his hand on Psellos's shoulder, so bereft did the Master seem in that moment. But in the end Rol left without another word and stumbled blindly down the endless stair of the Tower to his room.

"He knows," Rowen said. "He knows we mean to betray him."

She leaned back into Rol's arms and the sweat dripped from his face down her shoulder. He kissed salt from the nape of her neck and held her closer while about them in the half dark the steam billowed in strange shapes. It was the only place in all the myriad rooms of the Tower where they were sure of secrecy, and there was something comforting in the darkness and the wet heat.

"You think he meant it—everything else?"

"I don't know. I might, if I had been there. He is lying about my family, though—he knows something he would rather not say. As for the rest . . ."

"It is somewhat fantastic."

"With Psellos, even the truth is never very far from falsehood."

"What do you want to do?"

She turned, sliding moistly in his arms so that their faces were close enough to feel one another's breath. Those startling eyes, cold as the blade of a knife. She kissed him on the mouth and her tongue darted in over his teeth. One strong hand descended and gripped his member tightly, making the air gulp in his throat. It stiffened in her grasp, filling out with blood. He could feel a heartbeat pulsing down there against her fingers.

"I want to stop thinking and plotting for a while, just a little while." She pushed him on his back and became a mist-wreathed shadow backlit by candleflame. Her eyes glittered. In one fluid movement she straddled him and he slid up inside her. Hot warmth, a liquid ecstasy. He breathed in deeply and she leaned forward, balancing her palms flat on his chest. She began moving, minutely at first, and then with gathering momentum. Rol set his hands on her hips and closed his eyes, the sensation rocking him away into some place he had not yet seen.

Eleven

A KILLING

CANDLEMAS STREET WAS A BROAD, TREE-LINED THOROUGHFARE that lay southwest of the harbor. Here the Ellidon Hills flattened out into isolated drumlins and knolls atop which local chieftains had constructed their ring-forts in ancient days. Now it was a graciously apportioned district of gridded streets and houses reared in well-masoned stone. The light of the dying sunset honeyed their square courses and sparked out glints from diamond-leaded windows nestling half-hidden in ivy. No one lived in the Candlemas area who was not well rooted in Ascari society. Courted though Psellos was by the nobility, they would never have countenanced his existence here.

Another rain-loud night. Rol pulled the oilskin cloak tighter about his shoulders and tugged its hood lower down his face. All to the good. He was just one more shadow among many hurrying home out of the rain.

Fifty yards to his rear, the shape following him paused when he did, and melted into an ivy-hung wall.

He stopped. The Canoval manse was set in its own gardens, and these in turn were surrounded by a twelve-foot stuccoed wall, its top arrayed with iron spikes. A massive ironwork gate provided the only means of entrance or egress, and it was slightly ajar.

Rol cast aside his hood and cloak and bundled them tight, then tied the roll to his belt. He felt with one hand behind his right shoulder and met the reassuring coldness of Fleam in a back-scabbard. Then he moved up close to the gate. The soles of his boots were thin enough for him to feel every gap in the flagstones of the street and a suit of black hose clung to him head to foot like a second skin.

Just within the gate, Canker waited patiently, his cap feather drooping and soaked, his eyes bright as sea-gleams. Rol moved gently as a stalking cat, thinking his veil of shadow into place about him, but Canker merely nodded.

"You are on time. That's good. Stop prowling like a second-rate burglar and follow me. A filthy night, but then it's a filthy deed." He grinned brightly in the pouring dark.

Deflated, Rol followed the King of Thieves into Canoval's garden. Mature trees shrouded the lawn and well-graveled paths formed bright lines in the grass. The pair halted under a massive beech five fathoms from the back door.

"There you are, lad. I can't do much more if I'm not to lead you through it by the hand. I will be here when you return—if there is no alarm. Cause a scare, and I'll take off."

"I have to talk to you, Canker," Rol said, pitching his voice over the hissing rain. He wiped water out of his eyes irritably.

"Talk is cheap, time is precious. Get on with the job."

"You are to die tonight."

Canker paused. He did not seem surprised, but he seemed to grow taller, as if everything in him had tensed.

"I see. Why this night as opposed to any other?"

"You and Canoval both. He protects the Feathermen from a crackdown, and takes them over, all in one night."

"Either that, or his young protégé has reasons of his own for wasting my time."

Rol nodded over Canker's left shoulder. "Ask her."

The King of Thieves spun round in a twinkling, a blade opening in one palm, but he found one black-metaled stiletto light against his jugular and another pricking up under the edge of his tunic. This second moved slowly inward until he sucked breath sharply through his teeth and the heels of his boots left the ground. Rowen smiled, but her eyes were cold with murder.

"Drop the blade."

He did so, face calm again. "The lovely Rowen. It has been a long time. I remember those luscious lips well. Last time I saw them up close they were working hard round my prick."

Rowen smiled. "There is something different at your prick now. One move, and I'll blind that eye for you."

Canker's gaze never left her face. "I have but to raise my voice and half a dozen Feathermen will be on your backs."

"You would be dead before they got within ten feet of us, you know that, Canker," Rol said. He surveyed the dark, rain-swept garden but could see nothing.

"He's not lying," Rowen said. "I count five, and I may have missed one or two. Our friend the King of Thieves came prepared. But he is willing to talk, or we would be dead already, and his manhood would be sliding down his leg."

"I am rather attached to it," Canker admitted. "Put up your weapons, the point is made."

Rowen stepped back but kept her stilettos loose in her hands. "He's telling the truth. I was to assassinate you tonight, at the same time that Rol was to kill Canoval."

Canker bent to retrieve his dropped knife. When he had straightened his face was hard and ugly. "That is a pity. I had hoped we might work together, Psellos and I. But you two who are his foundlings, his orphans—why would you choose to tell me this?"

"We no longer choose to serve him," Rowen said evenly.

"Then who will you serve?"

"No one and nothing. We are done with Ascari."

"Ascari without the charms of the beautiful Rowen would be a duller place. If you will not serve, then you must lead, surely."

"This is not a debate. We are here in good faith as far as you are concerned. What would you have us do?"

"What is this? Are you mine to command now?"

"For tonight. We're all in the same crock of shit now."

Canker stared at Rowen for what seemed a long time, face expressionless. At last he said: "All right, then. To my mind, Canoval must die, if we are not to have a war. And so must Psellos, of course."

"That is what we thought," Rowen said. "Rol will kill Canoval tonight as planned."

"But not his wife," Rol said quickly. "I am not a murderer of crippled women."

Rowen and Canker stared at him with the same look on both their faces: a kind of puzzlement. Canker shrugged. "As you wish. And the other?"

"Psellos is a different pot of fish entirely," Rowen said. "We shall want your help with him, and it must be done swiftly, tonight. That is the price for Canoval's killing."

"You could not do it alone?"

Rowen shook her head. "He's too strong."

A flicker of something passed over Canker's black eyes, and was gone. "I shall have it put about within the hour that I am dead, assassinated. These lads with me are trustworthy, but if Psellos is confident he can lead the Feathermen after me then he must have suborned many of the others, including some of my lieutenants. If word of my death is spread it will cause an upheaval in the city, but that cannot be helped. Psellos and his traitors must be convinced. Then you must get me and these lads with me into the Tower. We'll do it together, and may the gods be behind us." He held out a hand.

Rowen shook it, holding his eyes. "So be it."

The thing began as Canker had said it would, and if Rol had not seen it for himself he would not have believed it possible. The little group of Feathermen went about their disseminating work with amazing speed, running from tavern to brothel to gambling den, down the hill toward the stews and slums near the waterfront. The news spread like wildfire. Canker was dead, and his kingship was vacant.

When a Thief-King died, all contracts were canceled. The common merchants and shopkeepers and tavern-masters were left on their own to face the leaderless predators of the slums, or else they must needs stump up huge amounts of ready coin to win over the Watch and persuade them to do their job. But the Watch were scarcely less rapacious than the gangs they were supposed to suppress—this was a chance to settle old scores, to rob and murder with impunity, and few in Ascari who could would resist that temptation. Rol thought that Canker was grimly amused by the thought of his own putative demise.

"Let them see what Ascari would come to without me," he said.

Canoval's death was as quick and quiet as Rowen's training could make it. A hand on the sleeping mouth, a blade in the heart. Rol watched the eyes spring open white and shocked above his fingers. The arms came up, but there was not the strength in them to do anything about their extinction. A life going out under his hand, lips working against his palm, trying to scream. The arms sinking again.

His wife stirred, smiled in her sleep, and laid a hand on her husband's dead shoulder. Rol withdrew the knife—always let the heart stop beating first if you want to avoid a lot of blood, Rowen had told him—and then stood silent in the ornate bedroom a moment. He could still feel Canoval's dying lips moving against the palm of his hand. Last words.

A hired bodyguard knocked on the head, Rol was back in the garden minutes later. Rowen looked at his white face, and touched his arm. "Well done."

"For killing a man in his sleep?"

"For making a neat job of it. There's not a drop of blood about you and there was not a sound to be heard either. Any fool can take a life."

"Where is Canker?"

"Gone to the Tower with the best of his men. Come, we must go too."

Rol did not move. The rain was still pouring down but the trees above sheltered them from the worst of it. They stood in a dripping shadow, the rain all about them like a curtain.

"Rowen, let us not go."

"What?"

"Let Canker and Psellos kill each other if they will. We are free. We could be on a ship tonight, and all this astern of us, the whole wide world before the bow."

Her face was white as marble with the rain shining upon it. She set a hand upon his cheek. "I cannot."

He had expected that, of course. Perhaps it was true of him also. If there were to be any symmetry about this, any sense of completion, then it would be found in the Tower.

"I know." He kissed her cold face.

They banged on the postern gate together and it was opened by Quare; a nervous, silent Quare who had smelled something in tonight's wind perhaps. He took their wet cloaks and said diffidently: "The Master awaits you both in his study."

They nodded, but as the manservant turned to go, Rol

detained him, smiling. "I almost forgot. I have something for you."

Fleam flashed out of the back-scabbard and settled at Quare's throat. His Adam's apple scraped the tip as it moved up and down convulsively.

"Master, Mistress, I do not know what—"

A slight push, and the strange-colored steel parted his skin, sliced through his esophagus, and halted, scraping in the vertebrae of his neck. He looked down in disbelief at the bar of bright metal under his chin, and then his weight grew heavier on the blade until Rol turned it to one side and he slid off, to crumple on the floor.

"No more beaten maids," Rol said with a satisfaction that was somehow hollow.

He caught Rowen's eyes and was chilled by them. Before he could say anything else she went to the postern and opened it again. A low whistle, and then she stepped back to allow Canker and six other Feathermen to enter. The King of Thieves and his followers had donned metal-studded byrnies of hardened leather. Three of them wielded small hand-crossbows, the rest swords of one kind or another and many knives in scabbards strapped all over their torsos.

"I am glad to see you well prepared," she told Canker dryly. "Follow us, but remain outside the door until I give the word." The King of Thieves nodded, his lips drawn back from his teeth in what might have been a smile.

Rol and Rowen led them up the stairs, checking their weapons as they went. There was a peculiar quiver in Fleam's hilt, like anticipation. Rol could only marvel at Rowen's composure. She was as calm and collected as if she were going to dinner.

"Do you think he knows?" Rol asked her.

"He knows this is one ending, else he would not have promised you that key. By now he will have received word of

Canoval's death, and Canker's. I hope that will persuade him we have come round to his way of thinking. It is our only edge."

"That, and seven Feathermen," Canker said behind them.

"They barely even the odds," Rowen retorted.

Canker and his followers fell back after that. Passing a maid on the stairs, Rowen knocked her senseless with the butt of a dagger and laid her down carefully. Then the little group continued, until at last the door was before them. Rowen knocked smartly upon it.

"Enter."

Rol and Rowen looked at each other, faces expressionless but for the light in their eyes. It was Rowen who opened the door, Rol who closed it behind them.

The familiar firelit room with its leaping shadows, shelves of books about the walls, wing-backed chairs and gleaming decanters. Psellos was sitting staring at the fire with an opened scroll held in his hands.

"The King is dead. Long live the King. I hear rumors the night went well."

"It is not over yet," Rowen told him.

He looked up at that, and smiled. "Join me by the fire, children. Rol, pour us some wine. We have things to discuss."

Neither moved. After a while Psellos looked up from his scroll. His smile did not waver, but something in his eyes changed.

"So, it is like that, is it? I feared as much. Ah, but it is a pity, you two. We could have had such fun together, playing games with the world." He bent to his scroll again, and Rol saw his lips move. Then he stood up, dropping it into the chair. He was unarmed, dressed in his customary black hose and velvet.

"You had best kill me and have done with it."

The oddest reluctance overcame Rol, a sense of waste. He had so many questions still to ask of this man, and if truth were told, Psellos had never done him any harm. Rowen he had debauched and debased, yes, but to Rol he had been firm and generous—even kindly. The very sword at his hip was Psellos's gift.

"Rowen—" Rol said hoarsely.

She unsheathed her stilettos. "He's spelling us." And louder: "Canker!"

She was moving even as the King of Thieves barreled through the door behind her. The white hands whirred in two blurred arcs and the stilettos hissed through the air. They buried themselves in the spines of books above the mantelpiece. Psellos had moved with blinding speed first one way, then another. The chair wherein he had sat came flying across the room. Rowen threw herself flat on the floor and it crashed into the wall above her. Wild laughter filled the place, and a wind whirled ash and smoke out of the hearth. Psellos was a black marionette of shadow moving so fast the eye could barely follow him.

The Feathermen who followed their king into the room appeared to be fighting sparks from the fire, cursing and batting them aside. One of them screamed as a darting glede smote his eye and burned the socket black. He fell clutching his face. Crossbow bolts snapped through the air like mad bats, standing quivering in the wood-paneled walls.

"Stand fast!" Canker shouted. "Don't let him out of the door!"

The laughter was all about them, as though baying out of the very walls. Rol stood with Fleam naked in his fist, turning this way and that, clinking airborne coals away from his face. Something made him peer upward, and looking down upon him was Psellos's face, grinning diabolically. He was clinging to the ceiling as lightly as a spider.

"Rowen!" Rol screamed. He threw himself backwards instinctively. Psellos's tongue shot out like a black whip and cracked the air where his head had been.

"Weren!" Canker bellowed in alarm. "Great gods above, he is Weren! Get out, lads, get out!"

"No!" Rowen shouted. Her hands moved, and a fusillade of gleaming steel stars went out of them. Psellos cried out in pain and anger, and leaped.

Clear across the room he went, turning in midair. He caught a Featherman in passing and the fellow went hurtling backwards with a slashed throat. Psellos landed on all fours by the door and sprang up again as easily as a bounced ball. He came at Rol next, and Fleam jumped into the air between them, a living thing of steel. The metal barely touched him, but blood spattered Rol's face as he bounced away again, snarling.

They backed away toward the door, swords pointed outward.

Psellos's tongue flicked out and caught a Featherman round the calf. He slid across the floor and was thrashed into a broken carcass; pieces of him flung up to fleck the walls. The Master careered about the room scattering books, his silver eyeteeth dark with blood. He capered across the ceiling on all fours, laughing again. He feinted, and a flurry of knives buried themselves in the plaster where he had been. But he came at them from the side, a boneless, spinning thing. Another Featherman fell, hamstrings slashed at the back of both knees. Canker dropped his sword, clutching at a hole in his side with a yell of shock and fury. Rowen's sable leathers were sliced in ribbons from her back. She spun and it was as though her fingers had grown blades. A scream of pain, and Psellos was clear across the room again with the gore of his wounds a dark mist in the air behind him.

Coals came hailing out of the fire in a bright barrage, striking flesh and sticking to those they smote, burning inward. Men shrieked and tried to pick them out of their own smoking bodies. A terrible stench filled the air and the smoke grew thick as fog. Psellos's insane laughter hurt their ears.

The surviving Feathermen were tumbling over one another to get out of the door. Canker had fallen to one knee and held a single long knife in one fist while the other was pressed to his punctured chest. Rowen's hair was flying about her face like a banner and her hands were full of the tiny metal stars whose fellows peppered the ceiling.

"What, leaving so soon?" Psellos's voice said. A shelf-load of books sailed through the air and pelted the fleeing Feathermen, opening up like pale-winged birds, flapping about their heads. The heavily bound volumes knocked them from their feet and fell, opening and closing feebly on the floor about them. The door slammed shut on the last of the Thieves with preternatural force and pinched off his feet at the ankles. They could hear the rest of him shrieking on the landing outside.

Psellos dropped lightly to the floor again in front of Rol.

"I'll have that sword back," he said, and his fingers fastened about Rol's arm with horrible strength. Fleam jerked back and forth between them and Psellos's tongue darted out at Rol's eyes. Rol snapped his head aside and it seared a length of skin from his temple. A light sprang up in Rol's face, a bright, furious disgust. He released the hilt of the sword, throwing Psellos off balance, and with his scarred left hand clutched the curved blade near the point. It should have sliced his hand in two but Ran's scar turned the edge. He pulled the blade to one side in one clean movement and the metal sliced clear through the Master's snaking tongue. A yard of black flesh wriggled to the floor. Psellos gave a great gargling cry, and Fleam clanged to the floor between them. A gush of blood steamed out over the Master's lips and he staggered backwards, the stump of his tongue flailing.

Rowen came to Rol's aid. Together the pair grasped Psellos's kicking body under the armpits and ran it forward as if they meant to batter a door open with his head. They thrust it into the blazing hearth and held it there, seized the Master's hose at the buttocks in tight fistfuls, and propelled him further into the fire. He leaped and bucked in their hands as they held his face down on the burning coals. Acrid, sickening smoke billowed out of the hearth. His hair took fire and his skin blackened and withered on the bones of his skull. He twitched, the long fingers snapping and curling in spasms, scrabbling at their legs. Finally they dropped to the floor. A shudder went through the Master's body and he was still.

Rol straightened, retrieved Fleam, and stabbed the bright blade double-handed between Psellos's shoulders. The blood jetted out smoking and black and Fleam trembled in his hands. A kind of charge went through the weapon, transmitting itself to Rol's loins in a momentary flash of ecstasy. He groaned, closing his eyes.

When he opened them again the fire in the hearth was obscenely bright, and what was in there seemed shapeless as a hewn log. Rowen was sprawled on the floor with her hair a matted curtain around her shoulders. Beyond the bodies that littered the room Canker sat with his back leaning against the door, his face bloodless and gleaming.

Rol straightened. His foot clicked against the spindle of the scroll Psellos had been reading. He picked it up, but the parchment was blank. Something curled itself about the toe of his boot. Psellos's tongue, still writhing feebly. Disgusted, he transfixed it with Fleam's smeared point and it joined the Master's carcass in the fire.

There was blood in Rol's mouth. His precious blood, worth so much. He spat it hissing into the fire, his head burning where Psellos's tongue had stripped the skin from his temple. Rowen raised her head, and he saw the blood pooling behind her back as she sat. But her eyes were clear. She looked up at him and smiled one bright, unclouded smile of pure joy. He wished, then and later, that he could have smiled back.

Twelve

THE KEY

THEY HAD TO HEAL THE OLD-FASHIONED WAY, WITH the help of time and the resilience of their own bodies. The Tower was emptied of its entire staff except for Gibble, who flatly refused to leave when he saw their state, and the fat little cook tended their wounds as one by one Rol, Rowen, and the King of Thieves descended into raving fevers. Some poison had entered them through their injuries and it festered and fed upon their spirits for days, whilst beyond the walls, Ascari descended into chaos.

Rol remained lucid longest, and he helped Gibble tie his companions down on their beds whilst the sweat coursed down their stark faces and their eyes glared sightlessly and they screamed gibberish at the tops of their hoarse voices. He felt the fever rise in him like the nausea of an evil memory but was able to secure the postern against the roaming gangs outside and leave

Gibble orders that the upper levels were to be left undisturbed. They had piled the bodies in Psellos's study and nailed shut the door, but not before Rol had prised a key out of the Master's black, melted flesh.

The key remained clenched in his fist for the next eleven days as Rol fought the raging fever that Psellos's venom had kindled within him. He shouted and raged and wept and was tied to the bed in his turn as all reason left him and his mind became a howling wilderness. Gibble's exhausted and frightened face was the only recurring image in the succession of nightmares that trooped through his brain.

At last, however, another face appeared in his vision, and it seemed to be not some shrieking travesty, but something reassuring and beloved. A white face framed by hair dark as a raven's wing, a cool hand on his forehead. The foul sweat was wiped from his eyes. He was thirsty and was given water to drink, and he slept a real sleep without the torment of dreams.

There was a pain in his hand. He brought it in front of his face and opened his creaking fist and a key fell out. It had carved a purple divot in his palm.

He sat up and the tall candleflames that lit the room stabbed pain into his aching head.

"Welcome back," a voice said, and he turned to see Rowen sitting wrapped in a rug near the foot of his bed. At the far wall a shape snored soundly in another, mounded in blankets.

"Canker?"

"His fever broke yesterday, mine the day before. But we are all as weak as half-drowned kittens. I sent Gibble off to get some rest. He's not had more than a few hours' sleep in the last fortnight."

"It's been that long?"

"We almost died. Psellos was pure poison, or the spell he read had made him so."

"The scroll, of course. But the thing he became—"

"That was no spell, it was the nature of the Blood in him coming out."

She stood up, naked under the rug she had pulled about herself, and joined him on the sodden bed.

"Your wounds?" Rol asked. There had been a lot of blood, and his recollection of her hurts was hazy.

"Gibble stitched them up for me. He has had much practice." She took his hand, her fingers cool and sure. The long fever had pared away every scrap of spare flesh and her face was gaunt, the tendons standing out on her neck like cords.

He kissed her chapped lips. "It's over."

"The worst is, yes. But Ascari without a Thief-King is an unpredictable place. Canker has been off the streets too long. I think he will not find it so easy to come back from the dead. Psellos's reputation is the only thing that has kept the looting mobs from the door."

"The Feathermen can't be the only glue that holds the city together."

"They were the most effective one. The Watch has disintegrated, except where some of the richer Mercanters have hired a company here and there. The militia was chased out of the lower city like pike-bearing rabbits. Another Thief-King should have been elected by now, but Psellos's bought Feathermen are unaware of his death and are holding things up. So the Feathermen are now fighting amongst themselves like all the rest of the rabble. Gibble has been out for supplies once or twice—the rumor is that Canoval's mercenary fleet is already at sea, and will be here soon to restore order, whilst inland the council sits and drafts troops from the ranks of the smallholders. Ascari may yet become a battleground."

"So it was all for nothing."

"Yes."

He had murdered a man in his bed for no good reason, left a wife lying asleep beside her husband's corpse.

"No more training, Rowen. No more knives in the dark and blades in the back. From now on when I fight a man it shall be face-to-face and fair and square."

Rowen's mouth twitched. "How very laudable of you. It's as well the world is such a simple place."

"I'm sick of murder. Great gods, the way Psellos died! Was he in any way human at all?"

"He was tainted; I never suspected how badly. Do you know what it means?"

"I knew there was something wrong there. That black tongue of his." And as he saw the puzzlement on her face he asked: "You mean you never noticed it before?"

"Never."

They looked at one another, both baffled.

"The way he appeared, at the end," Rowen went on, "means that he could only have been of the folk of Cambrius Orr; the Fallen. If his tales of your background are true, then—"

"Then it must run in the family. There is a monster inside me also. Is that what you are saying?"

"No, you fool. Think. The taint that produced the Fallen came from interbreeding with Man, but your blood is astonishingly clean. You are almost pure Were."

"So?" Rol was sullen. He wanted no more revelations.

"So your bloodline and Psellos's must be very different."

"He was my uncle, not my father."

"Uncle by blood, he said, not marriage. Somewhere along the line, Psellos has lied to you, or at least not told you the whole truth."

"You surprise me."

She leaned back with some of her old hauteur. "Now is not the time, I see. But we should use that key of yours to hunt out a few secrets."

"Very well. But after that we're taking ship. Ascari can eat itself, for all I care."

With a bath and a change of clothes, Canker was almost unrecognizable. His burly form was well muscled despite the wastage of the fever, and filled out one of the Master's tunics to bursting point. When the filth had been scrubbed from his face it was possible to see that he was not out of his fourth decade. Only the black gleam of his eyes was unchanged, as cold as those of a serpent.

"The sooner I get out and about the better for the city," he said through a mouthful of pickled fish. Reaching for the relish, he winced. Rol passed it to him wordlessly. Canker's wound had touched the lung.

Rol, Rowen, and Gibble sat with the ex–King of Thieves at the kitchen table, wolfing down the choicest cuts in the pantry and washing them down with the Master's wine. Since they had recovered their feet, the convalescents' appetites had seemed bottomless.

"It's a disaster out there, to be sure," Gibble said. "Some of the big houses on Cartsway are burning, and they're lynching nobles at the corner of Grescon Street, where they had the fish markets."

Rowen, also, had braved the streets. "The nobles have withdrawn what militia has stayed with the colors, and have barricaded themselves in the hill districts. The lower city has been left to its own devices."

"Civilization hangs by a more slender thread than we ever suspect," Canker said. He seemed almost gratified that news of his death had produced such chaos.

"They are tearing the feathers down from over all the doors," Rowen told him. "Your followers are too preoccupied with slitting one another's throats to care."

"What of those mercenaries?" Rol asked.

"A few days away. Or so they say, and they have been saying that for a week now."

"Gascar always wore its government lightly," said Canker. "Things will calm down in time."

"When the city is looted to the bone maybe," Gibble protested. "Begging your pardon, but your lordship had better do something. We may be all snug and safe in this here fortress, but the common folk is suffering something cruel. They're leaving the city in hordes by the North Road. Another few weeks of this and Ascari will be nothing more than a bunch of footpads squatting in a ruin."

"Then it will have returned to its origins," Canker said sharply, and Gibble shut his mouth.

The next morning Canker took his leave. "I go to steal back a city," he said with a grin, and he bowed to kiss Rowen's hand. "Will you really leave this tower and all in it for the scavengers?"

"We have a little scavenging of our own to do first," Rowen told him.

"Good luck, then." He hesitated a second—rare for him—and then spoke with odd formality. "Since it is just possible I owe you my hide, or some portion thereof, I promise that this tower shall remain inviolate, in case you should ever return."

"We will never return," Rol said quickly.

"*Never* is a long time, lad, even to your kind. I will give this place my protection nonetheless." And he left them without looking back.

"It is easy to give what one does not possess," Rowen said, closing the postern gate behind him. "Still, he may survive."

* * *

They packed bedrolls, tinderboxes, spare clothing, and weapons, anything light that might be of use on a journey. Braving the putrefactive charnel house of Psellos's study once more, they discovered a cache of gold ryals and silver minims, enough to allow a king to travel in style. The Tower echoed darkly about them as they labored up and down within its entrails by the flicker of torchlight. Already it seemed a forsaken place, save down in the kitchens, where at night they ate and drank by a cheering fire and savored the best vintages of the Seven Isles and beyond, Gibble producing them from the depths of a cellar with the pride of a midwife who has delivered twins.

"It is all very well to have a key," said Rol, "but what about the door it opens?"

"It must be on this level somewhere," Rowen insisted. "Either that, or there is yet another level below us."

"How many levels can a place have?"

She did not answer him, but raised the lantern and scanned the stone wall of the passageway yet again.

The stonework this far below the surface was different from that farther up. The usual conglomeration of construction styles, accumulated over the repairs and additions of centuries, had given way to stark oblong blocks set in perfect lines without mortar, not a chisel-mark to be seen upon them. The stones looked as though they had been laid down the week before, and their edges were sharp and clear as if they had been cut from clay, not hewn out of Gascarese basalt.

"These foundations are ancient," Rowen said with something like awe in her voice.

"The Weren built Psellos's Tower, or so it's said," Rol reminded her.

"Yes, but I thought that was all market gossip, old wives' tales. I thought—Wait. I have something here. Hold the lantern closer."

She drew out a poniard and scraped lightly at the join between two of the Cyclopean stones.

"There's a gap, but it's squared off. I can feel something against the tip of the blade."

There was an audible click, and the stones before them seemed to vibrate for a second. They both stepped back quickly, but nothing more happened. Rowen inserted the dagger-point again, to no avail. It was just an odd hole between two courses of stone.

"Give me the key."

It looked to be made of age-blackened white metal, weightier than silver. She slipped it into the tiny hole, and the click came again, louder now. She turned the key and there was a rapid succession of them, like a stick being dragged along palings. The huge weight of stone before them began to move, a shower of grit falling onto their heads, the floor trembling under their boots.

"A door," Rol breathed, and inexplicably he laughed.

"Weren engineering," said Rowen. "I wonder what lost artisans of the Elder Race made this, and for what purpose? All this time, Psellos has been sitting in a Weren tower, ferreting out its secrets. No wonder he was unwilling to leave." She seemed to collect herself, and touched Rol's shoulder. "Shall we?"

He nodded. The stone door had moved back ninety degrees, scraping against the dust of the floor. Rowen tried to retrieve the key, but when she took it out of the slot the stones began to close again, so she left it there. They both stared at it, thinking the same thing: if the key came out of the slot while they were inside they would be entombed.

The passageway before them was twice the height of a tall

man, and wide enough for a wagon to be drawn without bumping its axles. The stonework was of the same perfect workmanship. The whole slanted downward perhaps a foot every two fathoms.

"Another level, after all," Rowen said.

They walked steadily, all the time descending. There was not so much as a drip of water or patch of mold to break the monotony of the chiseled stone. The air was dry and wholesome.

"There must be ventilation shafts somewhere, leading to the surface," Rol said. "The air here is as fresh as in the wine cellar, and it must be eighty or a hundred feet above us."

"The Ancients needed to breathe, even as we do. I've heard they could create bubbles of air about themselves and walk along the bottom of the sea," Rowen said.

The passageway came to an abrupt end in an arch of buttressed stone. Within the arch a decrepit wooden door stood ajar. It was hinged and reinforced with bronze, but the wood itself was crumbling. Rol touched it, and the grain blurred into dust under his fingertips.

"I could poke a finger through it," he marveled.

"Try not to. This door is later than the stonework. See here? The hinges have been bored into the rock—a cruder job."

The lantern-light swung around them, a cocoon of comfort in the echoing spaces. Beyond the door the passageway opened out into a wide chamber with a high, vaulted roof. Corbels upheld rafters of solid granite. In the opposite wall another door stood closed, also of wood, but of recent construction. Rol began to step out into the looming massiveness of the chamber but Rowen set a hand on his arm.

"Look," she whispered.

She angled the face of the lantern upward, and Rol saw something perched on a corbel high above. The lantern-light cast a fearsome shadow of it upon the curved roof.

"What is it?"

At first glance, a crouching shape with the body of a man and a bat's wings folded upon its back. The head was that of a crested lizard and a long tail curled about the corbel it sat upon. But it was all carved in dead, gray stone.

"A gargoyle?"

Rowen shook her head and swept the lantern about the chamber. Another of the statues perched at the opposite end of the room.

"Haunhim," she hissed. "Watch-demons summoned and enslaved by Psellos, set to guard his sanctum. If we try to approach the far door they'll tear us in pieces."

Rol studied the grotesque shapes, fascinated. "Are they actually made of stone?"

"That is what Psellos has given them to animate. If the stone can be shattered, then they will be sent back whence they came—but one does not break stone with sword blades."

Rol began unslinging the coil of rope at his belt. "They guard the approach to the far door, you say?"

"I think so."

"You'd better be right."

He stepped into the chamber gingerly, keeping close to the wall. Hefting the coils of his rope, he tied a loop at one end. Feeding the far end of the rope into it, he created a running loop and began swinging it open around his head.

"What are you doing?"

"I made *Gannet* fast to a rock like this once, after we had lost the anchor and the tide had taken her." He tossed the spinning loop lightly into the air and it came down over the neck and wing of the haunhim. Both Rol and Rowen dropped instinctively into a crouch, but the thing remained as motionless as the statue it seemed to be.

Rol took the other end of the rope and fashioned a second noose. This time the loop landed clear round the second haunhim and he drew it tight about the thing's back legs and tail. Then he took up the slack between the pair of them and rejoined Rowen at the door.

"Punch out that rotten wood and loop it about the hinges—they seem solid enough."

They coughed and sneezed as the ancient wood splintered into a cloud of fragments under their fists. Then they wrapped the rope about the stone-bound bronze of the hinges until it was taut, and tied it off in a bulky knot. Rol drew Fleam and kissed Rowen on her tight lips. "Shall we?"

They padded across the stone of the chamber floor warily, staring upward. When they were halfway to the door they heard a grating sound, like someone moving heavy furniture across a flagged floor. In the eye sockets of the haunhim bright green lights began to burn. Despite himself, Rol halted, and Rowen tugged him on. "Too late now. Move."

They sprinted the last ten yards, and behind them they heard a rushing noise like the hiss of sliding scree, and then the beat of wings filling the tall chamber.

The door had neither keyhole nor handle, but was blank. Rol threw himself at it and felt the heavy wood move minutely. A gale of wind blew his hair about his face and the lantern cast a mad gyre of flapping shadows.

"Rol!"

He turned from the door in time to see one of the haunhim swooping down upon him, stone jaws wide. Fleam leaped up in his hand and met it point first. The metal of the blade jarred against the back of the thing's throat and the shock ran all the way up Rol's arm. He cursed as his hand went numb, and dropped the scimitar. The haunhim was beating and snapping in his face, the wings propelling great gusts of dry air up at him. His rope was tangled about its feet and whipping tail, holding it less than a yard from Rol's eyes.

The other creature was a hobbling, flapping shadow on the floor of the chamber. One of its wings had been encircled by the rope and was crushed to its side whilst the other beat madly, crashing off the floor with deep clunking booms.

"Get the door before the rope gives way," cried Rowen. She had set down the lantern, and now both of them heaved at the stubborn wood with all their strength. The door groaned open six inches, ten, a foot. It was enough.

Rowen went through first. Rol retrieved Fleam from the floor but as he was reaching for the lantern the nearest haunhim broke free of its restraining rope and crashed full tilt into the door. It was jarred open another foot and the lantern was smashed to shards of glass and metal wire and blazed up a yard into the air. The flames caught Rol's arm and set it alight. He threw himself backwards, held up Fleam, and the haunhim's snout clashed against the steel, slid down it, and ripped the flesh from his knuckles. He beat down on the thing's head but the blade clicked off it harmlessly. Then he was hauled through the doorway by the scruff of his neck.

"You're on fire," Rowen said calmly as she stepped over him and beat out at the enraged haunhim with the pommels of her stilettos. Her hands moved in a fusillade of blurs that cracked the iron bases of the knives about the snapping head of the thing in the doorway. It seemed unhurt but confused, snapping out left and right and missing her fists by inches. It slipped in the burning oil at its feet and Rowen's foot flew up and caught it on the shoulder, toppling it backwards.

She retreated quickly and in one easy move slammed the door shut. They were left in total blackness, their heads filled with the smell of Rol's burnt clothing.

Thirteen

A PARTING GIFT

ALL SOUND CUT OFF BUT FOR THEIR HARSH BREATHING. A sense of space about them, a dark echo.

"As well it closed more easily than it opened," Rol said.

"I'd guess it was made that way, so Psellos could slam it in the face of a pursuer and leave him to the haunhim."

"How in the world are we going to get back past them?"

"That's a worry for later. Where are you? Stick out your hand."

He did so, and felt her cold fingers entwine with his. "We need light," she said.

She helped Rol to his feet. His right arm stung and had begun to stiffen, but seemed serviceable.

"Rowen," he said, wondering, "I can see."

They were in a vast chamber, as large as the vaulted space within a cathedral. Buttresses of solid rock upheld the ceiling and splayed out into hundreds of tendrils of stone overhead, like the branches of trees. And that was what they had been modeled on, Rol realized. The cavern had been carved out of the solid gutrock in such a way as to mimic the floor of a forest. Every soaring pillared bole of stone had been chiseled with the distinct bark of a woodland tree, and far above, the roof was a filigree, a tracery of twigs and leaves, all hewn out of hard rock.

"Gods, it's beautiful," he said.

"I cannot see it," Rowen told him. "It's night-black in here."

"What? Surely you can. It's quite bright. I don't know where the light is coming from, but—"

Can you see in the dark? Psellos had asked him.

He stared at Rowen's face. She was turning it this way and that, like a dog hunting for a scent. He waved his free hand before her eyes and she made no sign. This gift was his alone, it seemed.

"Stay here," he said. "I'll see if I can hunt up a candle or something."

For an instant her fingers tightened on his, and then she released them. "Very well."

He kissed her. It was hard to walk away.

The floor of the cavern, or chamber, or hall was perfectly smooth in some places, rough in others. It had been worked in the same manner as the roof. There was a paved road beside a rough-cut channel that looked as though it was meant to hold flowing water. Outcrops of boulders lay tumbled about the roots of the stone pillar-trees. There was grit underfoot. When Rol bent to cup some in his hand he found it to be bone-dry dirt, soil that had not seen a drop of water in countless centuries. He wondered if things had somehow grown here once, back in the heyday of the Elder Race. No notion seemed too fanciful for a place such as this.

He came at last to the far wall of the cavern. The place was huge, perhaps three hundred yards wide on the narrow side, and lengthwise it disappeared into a darkness even his eyes could not penetrate. There were windows and doorways carved into the wall, three and four storeys high. Windowsills and doorsteps, but no doors, no glass.

He followed the tracks in the age-old dirt at his feet and entered a doorway that was reached by a series of shallow steps. A short empty hallway, and then he was in a long room with a stone gallery two-thirds of the way up the walls. The room was crowded.

Tables, chairs, bookcases, chests, jars, shelves, cupboards—an orderless jumble of furniture and artifacts. The smell of rotting cheese drew Rol to a pantry set off to one side, or at least Psellos had used it as such. Apart from some pickles and salted fish, everything was spoiling and rancid; evidently the Master had not been down here for some time prior to his death.

Books, scrolls, and unbound manuscripts heaped in careless profusion, the paper of some crumbling at a touch of Rol's fingers. Others were crafted out of more durable vellum. Writing paper, quills, ink of a dozen colors, sealing wax. Vials of what looked like blood, specimens preserved in jars, half-constructed skeletons of unknown animals. And at last, a lamp with some oil in the well. Rol lit it with a few strikes of flint and steel into his tinderbox, the fragile flame held trembling against the wick as it caught. And as the light grew and he replaced the glass cover of the lamp, his preternatural night-sight left him, and the limits of his vision were circumscribed even as Rowen's were.

"So this is the font of secrets," Rowen said. She sounded disappointed. "It's like an old man's attic."

They had lit half a dozen lamps and candles and the galleried room was bright along its length. They had shared a half decanter of decent port, taking it in turns to drink from the single crystal glass that Psellos had kept down here. As she drained the last of it Rowen smashed the glass on the floor and ground the fragments under her heel. Then she had insisted upon pouring olive oil over Rol's burnt arm and wrapping it in linen torn from her own shirt. Thus refreshed, the pair had begun rooting through the contents of the room.

"I don't even know what I'm supposed to be looking for," Rol complained. "Gods! What a pig he was when he had no maids to clean up after him."

"Old Waric," Rowen told him. "I can't read it, but I'll know it when I see it. Look for characters that resemble runes, but read north-south instead of west-east. You could mistake them for an engraving, or a geometric design."

"Psellos knew the language of the Elder Race?" Rol asked.

"Some—he said so, at any rate. He was from the Goliad, don't forget, and it is said that there are rocks in the wastes there that still bear traces of it. In here it will be on vellum, or slate. If they wrote on paper, it all perished long ago."

"Why look for inscriptions in a language we have no hope of understanding?"

"Someone somewhere will understand, and if we found even ten lines of original Waric, it would be priceless. I doubt there's enough of it left in the world to make a shopping list."

Piles of books fell over as they moved through them. A few were in Gascarese: *A Gramarye of Ancient Symbols, The Alchemy of Blood,* and even *Sailing Directions for the North Wrywind Sea.* But most were in languages Rol did not know. He wearied of the task long before Rowen and began hoking through cupboards, sniffing the contents of jars. He tapped the side of one and the sudden flicker of movement within made him cry out.

"Rowen!"

Set on a lamplit table, the liquid within was a bright carmine, like arterial blood. But it was not opaque, and something swirled within, occasionally tapping on the glass. Rowen lifted the lid gingerly, and, too quick even for her superb reflexes, the glistening thing inside leaped out and landed with a wet splat on the tabletop. Rol drew Fleam and tried to stab at it, but the bright point buried itself in wood as the creature twisted aside.

"No, let it be," Rowen said. She set a hand on Rol's sword arm.

"So you have killed me, then," the thing said, and its voice was recognizable: that of Michal Psellos.

They backed a pace, openmouthed.

"Ah, my brave assassins, my lovely pair of killers. What a picture you make."

It was a foot high at least, a bulging bag of glistening muscle and corded sinew that wheezed and twitched with life. There was a steady rhythm to its contractions, and in the echoing dark they heard the pulse of the liquid that was coursing under the flayed meat of its skin.

"Psellos?" Rol rasped.

"Part of him." The thing sprayed globules of blood from tiny gaping orifices, and with the blood the breathy, bronchitic voice issued, like that of a man with water on his lungs.

"I am his heart, the thing that beat his blood for him once upon a time, until he found a way to put me here. For safekeeping, you might say. So long as I exist, Michal Psellos survives, in some form." Quaking tendrils issued from the flesh like chopped ends of offal, and tapped the tabletop in delicate motions.

Rol fought his rising gorge, the urge to stamp this monstrosity out of existence.

"You found the key, and passed the guardians. For that I congratulate you. Perhaps you are ready for the world." A pause. "And now you stand in a veritable midden of wisdom. Are you impressed? Did you think that Psellos had untold sheaves of secrets neatly cataloged down here? You have such tidy minds."

"I think he wanted us here," Rowen said.

The thing bubbled and contracted to itself, an unnatural

horror surrounded by an accumulated chaos of junk and learning, the magpie hoarding of decades. Somehow it seemed to sense their disgust and disappointment.

"There are men in the world who would pay a king's ransom to pick over the bones of this room, and to you it is nothing, a mound of rubbish. It is to be expected—neither of you completed your training, and it is in neither of you to attempt its completion. A waste, after all. You will come to realize this yourselves, in time."

"Why would he want us here?" Rol asked.

"To hear the truth about yourselves. A parting gift. It is the least he—I—can do."

Rol knew suddenly that he did not want to hear the thing speak further. "Let me kill it, Rowen," he said.

"No, let it speak."

"Ah, Rowen, you have a fatal flaw," the thing gurgled. "Deep within you there is a great compassion, well concealed. A need to love. Whereas, in this boy there is a hardness you will never match. Ultimately, he will give nothing of himself that he cannot afford."

"You ugly little lying bastard," Rol said hotly.

"And yet you are both so similar in many ways, which is hardly unexpected. You are, after all, brother and sister."

Rol and Rowen froze as though the thing's words had turned their blood to ice. It gurgled with laughter again.

"Amerie was mother to you both. She gave Rowen to Psellos—to me—to look after, and Rol to her father, Ardisan, hoping that in separating you she was increasing your chances of survival. You must forgive me, Rowen; guardian or no, you were too beautiful to resist, even as a child. But know this also—in you the blood of Bion flows true. You are rightful heir to the throne of Bionar, daughter of Bar Hethrun himself. May you have joy of the knowledge—I know you have been seeking it a long time.

"Rol, your father was someone or something else, unknown to me. I was close to finding out, but my untimely death has put paid to that. May you live in ignorance always, you murderous little ingrate."

The thing's soft flesh crumpled slightly, as though weary. But there was a malign triumph in the awful voice. "*Now* you may kill me."

Rowen drew forth her poniard as though in a trance, but this time it was Rol who restrained her. "No. He's lying. He has been false in everything, and so in this too."

"She knows the truth when she hears it, Rol Cortishane. I do not lie, not at the door of death itself. In Waric, the word *rowren* signifies queen. She was named deliberately."

"What does his name mean?" Rowen asked, and her voice was cold and lifeless as glass.

There was a hesitation. "It means king."

Rol picked the creature up. His fingers sank into the clammy flesh and his lips stretched back from his teeth in disgust.

"Kill it," Rowen said.

"No. There is a better way."

As it realized what he intended the thing began to squirm and wail in his hand. He stuffed it back into its jar, slopping the evil-smelling liquid all over the tabletop. Then he found the lid and screwed it closed again. The thing that had called itself Psellos's heart writhed and flattened itself uselessly against the glass, the black mouths in its flesh opening and closing.

"Let him rot there for all eternity," Rol said.

They sat a long time in silence, knowing that they had fallen for the last of Psellos's many ruses. There was no longer any wish in them to go ferreting through the piles of books and manuscripts and scrolls for lost knowledge. They knew too much already. When Rol went to take Rowen's hand she moved away from him, shaking her head.

"Leave me be."

At last the candles burned low, and the last of the oil began to gutter in the lamps. Rol had the sudden fear that if the darkness returned they would sit here like this until the flesh withered on their bones, but he could not think how they were to get past the waiting haunhim. He stood up. The thing was still struggling in the jar. He set it inside a cupboard and closed the door.

"We must go now."

Rowen did not reply. Leaving her, Rol began to explore again listlessly. The heavy silence of the gutrock seemed loud as a dog's whine in his ears. But there was a different sound also.

He left Psellos's room and wandered down the cavern again, his eyes attuning to the dark as soon as the lamplight was left behind. The noise grew stronger; it was the distant churn of running water. He followed it like a hound on the scent and tracked it down to a hole in the cavern wall. Within the hole was a brightness, a skein of movement. He entered and found himself enveloped in a fine spray of moisture, impossibly refreshing after the dryness of the cavern. There was a river running through the rock, an underground stream tipped with fast-moving flashes of foam. Bobbing against the stone jetty he stood upon was a boat, a flat-bottomed punt with a wooden pole rolling in the bottom. It was made fast to a stone bollard with a length of rope. Rol laughed aloud, and the sound was ugly in his ears. Psellos always left himself another way out, it seemed.

The last of the candles had died and Rowen was sitting in darkness, turning her knife over and over in her hands. When Rol set a hand on her shoulder, she sprang up under it and the knife kissed his throat. He pushed it away gently.

"There's another way out, a river with a boat on it. I think it'll take us to the surface. At any rate, I'd rather chance it than go back out the way we came."

"You go. I'm staying here with the rest of the trophies and specimens."

"Rowen—"

"Don't touch me."

"He was lying."

"No. It fits. A thousand small things have suddenly made sense to me. He enjoyed watching us draw close, knowing he held the breaking of us in the palm of his hand."

"I love you, Rowen."

"There is not one thing I have that is not sullied and besmirched and debased. I thought he would allow me to have you, but I should have known better."

"Rowen, listen to me—"

"*Do not touch me,* or I think that I shall kill you."

They left the cavern with nothing more than they brought, save a battered lantern and the burden of their heritage. Rol untied the mooring rope and the punt was seized at once by the current and began coursing downstream. They had to crouch close to the thwarts to avoid hitting their heads on the stone overhead, and now and again their craft would crack off the rocky wall of the river-course with the crunch of wood, until Rol learned to fend off the walls with the pole. They spoke no more word to each other in all of that long, subterranean voyage, until at last they came out from under a screen of hanging willow and found themselves floating on a broad river toward the sea, with an autumn sky bright and blinding blue above them.

There was smoke rising over Ascari. They beached the punt and climbed a small hill in the yellow morning light and all about them the Ellidon Hills were loud with birdsong and the trees were flame-bright with the turning year.

Rowen peered northwest to the smoke which sullied the sky. "I hope it burns to the ground, every stick and stone of it."

Reluctant to speak, Rol said at last: "We have to go back. We need money, gear. It's all in the Tower."

"You go back. I'd rather beg by the roadside than enter that place again."

There was a rising panic in him, a sense that he had stepped over the edge of a cliff and had no way to halt his fall; he must merely await the moment of impact.

"I'll go back on my own, then, and you wait for me here."

"No. I'm done with waiting too. It's time to be gone."

"Then where shall we go?"

She looked at him, and he felt his hopes hit the ground within him.

"I go alone." This was the girl who had booted him off the steps of Psellos's Tower all those months ago, as cold and unknowable as a statue.

"Rowen, whatever that thing says we are, I do not care."

"I do, Fisheye. I care very much. I can't love you, for what we feel is as flawed and perverse as all the rest of my life has been. I've had enough of all that shit. I want to be clean. It ends here."

"You can't mean that."

She looked away from his incredulous boy's eyes. "We were brought together for his entertainment, no more. You were lucky, you had only a year of it. He took my life and shaped it like clay and set it up on a little pedestal and mocked it and charged entrance fees for others to do the same. I have had men piss on me for their entertainment. I have been passed from beast to rutting beast and had them violate me three at a time and then I have dressed like a lady and sat opposite them at dinner. There is nothing left inside me now that has not been covered in filth. Well, so be it. I shall take my chances elsewhere. Alone."

She began walking away, downhill toward the fishing villages on the coast. Rol watched her go in disbelief. He ran after her, grabbed her by the arm. She spun round instantly, her knife naked in one white fist.

They looked at one another, and he knew that she would kill him if he spoke one more word. He released her arm. The knife came up and stroked the side of his face in a caress. Then she turned and resumed her way downhill. She grew smaller in his sight, and finally disappeared into the tawny patchwork of the trees. He never saw the tears streaming down her set face, nor the bloody stripes she was cutting mechanically into her forearm with the keen edge of the knife.

After a while, an age it seemed to be, Rol forced himself to take a step, and then another, and then he stumbled into a walk, a march, and finally he was running through the woods, northwest toward the smoking horizon. Finally he was sprinting, one hand on Fleam in her bouncing scabbard, the other punching the air before him as though its momentum could increase his speed. He ran like one pursued, like a felon fleeing the scene of a crime, and he did not stop until he was hoarse and panting and had to bend over and swallow his gorge and wipe the sweat and tears from his face. Then he ran some more, until he was passing through the shapeless outskirts of Ascari, and the dirt roads turned to cobbles, and the sky above became a narrow slot between houses, and the stink of ordure and smoke was all about him.

He drew his sword, for there were gangs roaming the alleyways breaking down doors and carrying off valuables and women. He saw street urchins running wrapped in tapestries, footpads holding a man's hands in the red hiss of a brazier while he screamed and told them the shop was empty. A woman bent half-naked over a barrel by a group of slavering beggars whilst her husband was beaten to a crimson pulp beside her.

Rol shut his ears to the shrieks and laughter and picked his way through the riotous chaos of the streets, climbing always uphill toward the Tower. A pair of men made the mistake of shouting at him to stand fast and give over his purse. They were drunk, and slow, but he took fierce pleasure in lopping off their hands one after the other and leaving them to squirm and bleed behind him. He began to run again, assailed by some sense of urgency he did not understand. Here and there a knot of militia stood guard over a rich man's house, but otherwise the streets had become a murderous free-for-all.

There was a mob in front of the Tower. They had forced the postern and were already inside. On the ground in their midst lay the bodies of two Feathermen, their blood trodden into a mire. Canker had at least tried to keep his word.

Lying beside them and beaten into raw meat was the body of Gibble, a kitchen knife still clutched in one bloody fist.

The last rags of Rol's restraint blew away. He let the training take him over completely, and a white-hot sun of grief and rage within him fueled it to the brink of madness. Fleam was a thing of pure, bestial joy in his fist, and as he fell upon the rear of the mob like some berserk angel, he heard the sword singing.

Those who were intent on forcing their way within the fabled Tower saw a bright light behind them, and then a storm of steel broke upon their ranks, and it smashed bodies to right and left, cutting men in two, amputating limbs, decapitating, disemboweling, blinding. They streamed away from the Tower in panic and the thing came after them, cutting them down, making a charnel house of the street, splashing blood as high as the eaves on nearby houses. Bodies and limbs and the ropes of entrails were strewn in scarlet ruin for a hundred yards and the survivors fled down the hill in abject terror, climbing over one another to get away from the light, the singing blade, the terrible eyes.

The light faded as quickly as it had come. A boy was left leaning on a bloody scimitar in the street, his face a wilderness of pain streaked with other men's blood, his clothing soaked scarlet. He dropped the sword, fell to his knees in the puddled gore, and began to weep.

There were crowds of townsfolk on the wharves mobbing the gangplanks. Every ship's master docked in Ascari had jettisoned his cargo onto the quays and was taking on passengers instead, charging a fortune for every square foot of his hold. Enterprising longshoremen were taking others out in cutters and longboats, sculling them down the coast to quiet backwater Gascar.

Rol had entered the Tower and chased out the looters within. It had not been necessary to shed more blood; they had taken one look at his eyes and had made off, dropping their plunder. He had walked the gutted corridors, treading on priceless manuscripts and the tattered remains of ancient paintings and hangings, kicking aside empty bottles, crunching over broken glass. There was little left of the gear he and Rowen had gathered together to aid them in their proposed journey; the bag of money was long gone.

He gathered up what he could, nonetheless. An oilskin cloak, a tinderbox, a change of clothing, a loaf of bread, a wooden flask which he filled with Cavaillis and drank a swallow of in memory of Gibble. Then he went to the uppermost levels—the looters had not ascended this far—and managed to scrape together a purseful of copper minims, and a few silver, from Psellos's apartments.

He entered Rowen's room, a place whose threshold he had

never crossed before. It was bare as a hermit's cell. A narrow bed, a table, a chair, a rack for her swords. A wardrobe which he opened. Hanging within were all the fine gowns Psellos had insisted on buying her. Rol buried his face in them, smelling her, unwilling to leave off the pain, like a dog that will lick a wound into fresh rawness. His heart was a burnt-out cinder. There was no one left even to hate.

Rol secured a berth on the *Seahorse,* a leaky, overcrowded caravel that was bound for Borhol to the southwest. The only reason he was allowed aboard was because they were shorthanded, and he was able to convince the captain that he knew his way about a ship. As they cast off, a collective wail went up from the crowds on the quays. He belayed a loose point and staggered slightly as the wind took the caravel and nudged her from the dock. A southerly, it was blowing fresh and true and had been all day. Just as well, for all the harbor cutters were ferrying passengers and were too busy to tow anything beyond the mole.

"Why are they so desperate to take ship?" Rol asked the captain, a lanky, gray-haired Vryhedi named Kyle Gavriol. "They could just walk out into the countryside. The rest of Gascar is peaceable enough, isn't it?"

Gavriol spat over the ship's side. "Peaceable for some, not for all. There's an army has arrived in the west, mercenaries from Andelys hired by the council. Rumor has it they're to purge Ascari of everyone the council dislikes or is afeard of, and that's a long list of people. Running to the hills won't help—once your name is on the list they'll hunt down the whole island for you. So half the miscreants in town are running mad and the other half are trying to get to sea in anything bigger than a rowboat. It's a sorry state of affairs. Where have you been not to know this, my lad, under a stone?"

Rol turned and looked back inland, to where the hill of

Ascari loomed and Psellos's Tower stood half a league away, a monolith silhouetted against the sky. "Yes, that's just where I have been."

The *Seahorse* pulled out of Ascari harbor, past the white-washed stone of the mole, and the southerly picked up and began to make the caravel dance under their feet. By the time Rol could look up from his work on the yards again, Ascari was a white smudge overhung by a dark one, and Gascar was an island in truth, just one part of a larger horizon.

Fifteen days to Borhol, and Port Borr, for the southerly failed at last, and the winds, though strong, boxed the compass for near on a fortnight, and Gavriol's caravel was an unhandy vessel with a tendency to make as much leeway as headway. For a time they were close to being blown onto the rocks of western Dennifrey, but they clawed clear on a black, spray-flashed night and managed to beat out to sea again. In the hold the passengers spewed and wailed by the dozen and in their seasickness pleaded with the captain to let the ship sink, but Gavriol laughed, and congratulated Rol on his seamanship, and stood watch after watch at the tiller with his eyes red and smarting while the *Seahorse* did her best to send them all to the bottom.

Port Borr at last, one evening as the rags of the gale blew themselves out behind them and the western sunset burst in a calm fury of flaming cloud that filled half the sky. A small, mean place after Ascari, a fishing port loud with squalling gulls and peppered white with their guano. Stone-built quays with the fish boxes piled high and stinking all about them, and thirty or forty fishing yawls and bankers moored snug up against them while their crews haggled with inshore fish merchants and smoked whitherb in silver-lidded pipes. Gavriol was known here, and recommended Rol's abilities to the master of a small brigantine, the *Westauk,* and thus before his legs had even accustomed themselves to the unmoving nature of the land Rol was at sea again, bound for Corso with a cargo of sheepskins and several barrels of Borholian beer. From there it was a gaff ketch to Arbionn, and he was entrusted with command of a watch. And then an ancient carrack with rotten yards and a hair-raising passage to Osca across a white, furious Westerease Sea, with Rol commanding the ship after the master lost himself in the bottom of a bottle five days out and the first mate was washed overboard. In Osca, the land of the White Horses, he halted awhile and hiked inland through the grazing sheep to where the Ancients had carved vast pictures out of the turf of the hills, the white chalk underneath rendering them visible for miles. Horses indeed, but also winged lizards and sea-serpents and walrus and bears, the inhabitants of men's primitive dreams. And Rol slept without covering on the soft grass of the chalk downs, heedless of the autumn rains washing over the world. In the gray mornings he rose and walked himself dry and accepted the hospitality of shepherds' bothies, for they like all primitive men believed in showing unstinting hospitality to strangers. He would leave them some copper minims nonetheless, and part with a wordless nod.

He walked west because the brash sunsets of the fading year drew him, and so came to a region of deep, rock-strewn inlets bitten out of the raw stuff of the earth's bones. He was looking at the Bionese Sea, last of the charted seaways of the world. Beyond this horizon was the great mountainous country of Gidior, famed for its ores and its metalworkers and its deep mines, and beyond that was Tethis, the limitless ocean which girdled the world of men, unknown, uncharted, uncrossable. He sat for a long time on the shore there, while the sea crashed in white-fanged fury on the rocks about him and the gulls circled shrieking overhead. When he rubbed his hand over his face, yawning, he could feel the stubble of a beard on his chin, and scratched at it in wonder. Finally he rose in the dark of the night, set the wind at his back, and began retracing his steps to the fishing villages of the east coast, where he might work a passage back to the crowded places of the world.

PART TWO

THE SEA

Fourteen

USSA'S MANE

THE HAMMERING ON THE DOOR JOLTED HIM OUT OF sleep. Beside him his scented bed partner groaned and tried to snuggle closer, but he was already out of bed and on his feet. His scimitar was naked in his fist before he said: "It's open."

"Who were you expecting?" Prothero asked with a raised eyebrow. He stopped in the doorway and leaned against the jamb, a jaunty, dark figure with a face as triangular as that of a stoat. His eyes flicked appreciatively to the girl in the bed who was groggily coming awake.

"You never know," Rol said. He scabbarded Fleam and began to get dressed. To the girl he said, "Get out. The money's on the chest by the window."

Sitting up now, she pouted, and glared at the grinning Prothero who watched her dress with much relish. She took the minims from the chest-top and stalked past him with her head high. "You're no gentleman," she huffed at him as she left the room, and he laughed.

"You have me there, child."

Rol buckled his sword belt, yawning. "What's the time?"

"An hour to the turn of the tide, is what the time is. Riparian is tugging out his hair in wonder and dismay at the absence of his first mate."

"He worries too much. He might have known I'd be here."

"If it's Mamertos, then it must be the Flamingo House. Yes, you are a creature of certain habits. Who was she?"

"She's new, only started last month. If you like, I think you have time to—"

"Not now. I had my fill last night after we split up."

"Aha. Where'd you lay your head?" Rol was stuffing oddments into his canvas seabag and scratching his hair into a shaggy mop of gold. He leaned his face into the ewer by the bed and emerged with water dripping from his beard.

"Mother Abbe's."

"That hole? You're lucky they didn't smother you."

"There's a girl there has this trick—"

"All right, all right, tell me on the way. We'd best be off before Riparian sails without us."

Mamertos was a bustling port of some quarter-million people, the capital of lovely Auxierre. Rising in white-walled tiers from the waterside, the city resembled nothing so much as an onion sliced into rings and spread out on its side. It was stone-built, for there were rocky hills just inland, and extensive quarries had been burrowed into these for generations. Mamertine marble was sought after all over the world, and Auxierre's rulers had made free use of it in beautifying their capital. Red clay tiles covered the roofs of the houses from hovel to mansion, and gangs of city-sweepers kept the filth on the streets within acceptable levels. The city was an ordered place of tree-lined avenues and public parks. Even the waterfront was tamed, and all the brothels and inns thereon were licensed by the Crown. There were still a few independent operators, however, and both Prothero and Rol had always preferred these to the more sanitized license-holding establishments.

"Not a patch on Urbonetto," Prothero said, looking around him. They were within a stone's cast of the wharves and everywhere before them the masts of ships rose in a long forest webbed with a million lines of rigging.

"I've never made it that far," Rol admitted.

"No? Ah, that's right, you joined us just after the last of the Bionese runs. You were lucky. We used to have all the Westerease to beat across, and never a sight of land between Perigord and Bionar itself, except for Kull black as smoke on the horizon. Ever since Riparian won that Mercanter contract it's been glorified coast-following, and long may it last."

"I don't know," Rol said. "I don't think I'd mind a spell on the open ocean."

"The Armidon Banks are open enough for me," Prothero snorted. "You're young, that's all."

"You're my elder by a bare three years, you little squint. Don't try to pull the hoary old mariner act with me."

Prothero laughed. Rol's shipmate was a native of Laugro in southern Cavaillon, Cavaillon of the Vines, where the world's best brandy was made. The region of his birth was a backward, insular land so mountainous that the vineyards were planted on terraces hacked out of the sides of the hills. A place where the women were brown-skinned and black-haired and the men all bore the long knives known as *sabrons* and lived by a code of honor so arcane that feuds between neighboring families might last hundreds of years. One such feud had so disgusted the young Jaime Prothero that he had run away to sea, and had never been back since. When drunk, he would sing mournful songs of his own hills and tearfully speculate as to the fate of his brothers and sisters, his elderly mother, his stern father. And then he would spit on the floor to avert any bad luck for them. He was a small, lean man, deadly quick with the *sabron* he kept tucked in his sash, utterly fearless, and incapable of betraying a friendship. He had been Rol's shipmate for going on seven years now.

Seven years. In that time Rol had worked his way up from deckhand to first mate, and now he knew the seas from Corso to Aringia as well as any man could. He had sailed the Westerease, the Caverric, the Armidon Banks, the Inner Reach, and the Southern Wrywind, and he knew the fleshpots that lined half a hundred ports up and down their shores. The passage of time had seen his already formidable frame bulk out with muscle and reach its full height. He was a swaggering, bearded mariner now, with spiderweb wrinkles at the outside of his eyes that spoke of years peering into the wind.

Of his boyhood, he thought as little as he could, pushing down the memories, bright and dark. The pain of Rowen's rejection, once all-consuming, had become a barely registered ache. He still had a weakness for tall, dark girls with quiet smiles, but in seven years he had never spent more than one night with any of them.

"Where in the name of the gods of the Twelve Seas have you been, you cold-eyed big bastard?" Riparian was furious. He leaned over the quarterdeck rail of the *Cormorant* and shook one veined fist at Rol and Prothero.

"Saying good-bye to your mother," Rol snapped back, and stalked up the gangplank. "What's this?"

A group of sorry-looking ragged men were standing in the waist of the brig whilst the ship's company went about their tasks all around them.

Riparian shrugged. "Extra hands. We're short this trip."

"They look like convicts."

"That's because they are. Privateersmen, if you please. The gaol released them to me—given a choice, they elected to serve out some of their sentence aboard the *Cormorant* rather than rot in the quarries."

"Pirates now?" Prothero was scowling. "You trust these sons of bitches not to slit our throats in the graveyard watch and take the ship for themselves? We've run the gauntlet of bastards like these up and down the Westerease, and had we been caught they'd have tossed us overboard without a second thought. And now we give them a place before the mast and are supposed to share our grog with them?"

"Yes," Riparian said flatly.

"All right, then." Prothero grinned.

"You men," Rol said to the ragged group, "what were you? Able seamen?"

One touched his forelock. "I was a carpenter, your honor."

Riparian clapped his hands together. "Capital! I shall rate him carpenter's mate. Gastyn has been crying out for one this age."

"What about the rest of you?" Rol asked. He did not like the look of these fellows. Pirates were the curs of the earth, murderers and rapists all, and he would have as soon tossed them overboard as have them pollute the planks of his ship.

"I was a quartermaster."

"I was a topman."

"I was a master's mate."

Rol looked sharply at the one who had said this. "An officer? On what ship?"

The man hesitated. He looked to be in his forties, and his hair and beard were black, streaked badgerwise with gray. He had eyes dark as sloes and a scar broke one eyebrow in two. There were unhealed sores on his wrists and his bare feet were black with ingrained dirt.

"Come now, don't be backward. It's all in the past, we know.

You're a Cormorant now, it seems. But what was your ship before you were captured?"

"I was master's mate on the *Barracuda.*"

Prothero whistled softly. "Mathuw Creed's ship. I thought the Armidians crucified the lot of you."

"They did, mostly, but I was only fourteen at the time, so my sentence was commuted to life in the quarries of Keutta. Then the Mercanters of Auxierre took over the penal contract, and I wound up here, breaking stone for them instead of the Armidians."

"Fourteen? That's too young for a master's mate. How long have you been in the quarries?"

The man looked up at the towering masts of the *Cormorant,* and his chest inflated so that Rol thought he was about to shout. But he only said quietly, "Eleven years."

Rol and Prothero exchanged a glance. "We'll rate you able seaman for now, in the starboard watch," Rol said. "Rest for a couple of days and get those sores seen to." He looked at Riparian, and the master nodded. The penal quarries of the Mamertine League were widely regarded as a delayed sentence of death. Most men survived two or three years before succumbing to disease, starvation, or the sheer brutality of existence there.

"What's your name?" Rol asked the man.

"Elias Creed."

"Mathuw's brother?"

"His son."

"I'm surprised you weren't crucified, youth or no."

"They never suspected who I was. The survivors told our captors I was a cabin boy."

Rol studied the man. There was a calm purpose to him he liked, but his late unlamented father had been the bloodiest pirate-captain for half a century, plunderer of at least sixty ships before the Armidians dispatched a flotilla to hunt him down. If there was anything of the father in the son, he would bear watching.

They cast off from the wharves and were towed out of the harbor of Mamertos by a pair of twelve-scull cutters. As soon as the wind began to creak the yards Riparian had them let fall the topsails. These were sheeted home and braced round with the smooth efficiency of a veteran crew. The cutters were cast off and waved away with the traditional catcalls deep-ocean sailors reserved for inshoremen. The *Cormorant* took the wind like a greyhound on a scent and her stem began to throw back packets of spindrift along the fo'c'sle as her pitch increased and the tall swells of the Armidon Banks began to roll under her hull.

The sea. *Ussa's Mane,* some called it, and half a thousand other names besides. It seemed to Rol in this moment that a life spent entirely on land was a life only half lived. There was an eternity in the sea, something about the endlessness of the movement in that vastness that both set the soul at rest and kindled within it the desire to emulate, to rove the changing face of the waters, to travel for the sheer novelty of new horizons.

Riparian packed on sail steadily, the brig staggering as each new stretch of canvas was unfurled and her speed increased. He looked up at the mizzen above him. They had a northeaster, a following wind, and the mizzensail had been brailed up to let the air at the main and forecourses. The master met Rol's eye and they grinned at each other. Three days in the taverns and brothels of Mamertos had been enough. This was where real life began.

The *Cormorant* was a sleek packet-brig, a low-decked, sharp-nosed vessel built like her namesake. Her cargo was compact: the return correspondence of a thousand prosperous letter-writers from Osmer clear through the Mamertine. Land deeds, bills of credit and of sale, the reports of spies and merchants and soldiers, the haggling of diplomats; they were all packed in waterproof bags in a sealed cell below the waterline, bound for greedy readers in Oronthir. The *Cormorant* flew the pennant of the Mercanters, that worldwide network of secretive, sophisticated businessmen who, it was said, could buy and sell whole kingdoms if they chose. They had commissioned Riparian to carry their correspondence in safety and with dispatch and in return he collected a fat fee, plus better than usual cooperation from harbormasters up and down the Mamertine, who liked to keep on the right side of those with money and influence. Hence the swift compliance of the local authorities when Riparian had told them he was short of his complement. Rol was willing to bet that the local gaolers had looked down their muster-rolls for those with maritime experience and had not concerned themselves too much about how that experience had been gained.

As soon as the *Cormorant* was out on the open ocean, naval routine took over almost every aspect of the lives of the ship's company. Riparian had once been a quartermaster in the Armidian navy, and he liked to try to run things naval fashion—the crew divided into two watches instead of three so that each man worked four hours on and then had four hours off, round the clock. The brass of the little four-pounder swivel-guns was to be kept gleaming, as was that of the ship's bell, and officers of the watch handed over to their relief with a formal statement of the ship's course, her speed, and the behavior of the wind. It was all very man-of-war, though the *Cormorant* carried no heavier metal than the swivels, and Prothero for one thought it all an absurd eccentricity of the master's. Rol liked it, however; the men were easier to manage than on some ships he had served upon, and obeyed all orders without question. He and Prothero had been with the *Cormorant* for almost two years now, having sailed in a variety of vessels and under some truly execrable masters. For all his foibles, Riparian was a fine seaman, and he valued his first mate and master's mate enough to indulge their occasional late return from shore leave.

At two hundred tons, the *Cormorant* was on the large side for a brig—a two-masted, square-rigged vessel. As a rule Mercanter ship's companies averaged one man per ten tons of ship. Riparian had thirty men under him, including the convicts. The heavier crew meant, however, that sail-plans could be altered with greater speed, and the efficiency of the ship was increased. At times speed was everything in this game, as there were sometimes large bonuses for making the run in a certain number of days. But by and large there was time on most runs for a couple of days onshore—if all the company made it back to the brig in time to catch their tide.

West-southwest was their course, along the green coast of Auxierre. They gave themselves a clear ten leagues of sea room so that all they could see of the land was the blue haze of the Mamertine Hills running northeast to southwest, the spine of the kingdom. It was the spring of the year, and the herrin yawls were out in large numbers, towing their glass-buoyed nets behind them and accompanied by clouds of screaming gulls. The *Cormorant* sailed past them like a racehorse gliding by a flock of sheep, and Riparian altered course to due west so they had the breeze on the starboard quarter and could unfurl the mizzen-course. The land bulged north here in a slow, curved sweep of wooded lowlands, and there were reefs to port, calling for a hand at the bow and another in the foretop, both scanning the undulating surface of the sea for the telltale flash of foam or a darkness near the surface which would rip the keel out from under them. Riparian took the helm himself at times like these, and when the lookouts yelled aloud their sightings he would swing the ship's wheel one way or another, eyes half closed, feeling the movement of his vessel under his hands, gauging the answer of the rudder.

By late evening of their first day out of Mamertos they had the reefs and rocks behind them and were in green water. They had covered thirty-five leagues, so brisk had been the northeaster and so attentively had Riparian pushed his ship. Now they were clear of the Auxierre coast and were in the Armidon Banks proper, running southwest with the wind aft again, the stem pointed toward the Caverric Straits which separated the northernmost tip of Cavaillon from the southern extremity of Armidon. The Straits had been the site of naval battles for centuries as the sea-canny Armidians sought to invade Cavaillon. Sometimes they had succeeded, sometimes they had failed, but their attempts at annexation and colonization had never taken. Perhaps it was because of the character of the Cavaillans—men like Prothero who would never forgive a slight or forget an injury.

Beyond the Straits was the Inner Reach, one of the Great Seas of the world, and a haven for pirates since time immemorial. Depending on the winds, Riparian would either follow the coast of Cavaillon around its periphery or cut straight across the open sea to Ordos in Oronthir, their destination. The former was more usual, for it meant less outlay on provisions and a chance of fresh food and water from the fishing villages along the coast to the Gut. Either way, the *Cormorant* had a good four weeks of sailing ahead of her, if the winds were kind.

The ship's officers had dinner together that night in the master's cabin, with the brig's wake phosphorescent as moonlight in the stern windows at their backs. Riparian was no gourmet, but he liked to keep a few chickens and goats on board for eggs and milk, and they were rarely so far from land that they must subsist on the salt horse and hardtack that were the staples of the foremast hands. He was not a wine drinker, though, and the glasses were filled with Kassic rum, well watered and flavored with lemon.

They pushed the plates back whilst Riparian lit his pipe and then they indulged in the small talk of a ship at sea, discussing the crew, the provisions, the weather. It was virtually a tradition, and Rol listened much more than he talked. But as well as the concerns of the *Cormorant,* Prothero and Riparian also liked to debate the matters of the world, as though they had some say in them.

"It's a world of men," Riparian said. "I don't think much of these myths we hear of the Elders and such—where the hell are they now, is what I want to know? All bedtime tales for children. Rol—have some more rum."

Rol and Prothero smiled at each other. Riparian was a blunt, straight man with nothing in his life except his ship and the cargoes she carried and the men who made that possible. In this he was almost admirable. Sometimes Rol envied him his certainties.

"The world is what men have made of it, that's plain," Prothero said. "But who knows what was here in times before men walked the earth? The history of Umer is longer than we give it credit for."

"What are you now, a seer?" Riparian asked with a contemptuous snort.

"Would you call Kull a figment of the imagination?" Prothero countered.

"The Mage-King is a fact of the waking world, there's no denying that. But who's to say what he is? Who has ever seen him and lived to tell of it? He may just be some reclusive madman with a madman's following. There are many examples in history of half-baked ne'er-do-wells hoodwinking the gullible and declaring themselves king of this and heir to that. Look at Bionar now. I had word off Gilcom of Omer before we sailed that it's at war again."

"Bionar at war," Prothero said. "That's about as remarkable as sunlight in summer."

"Ah, but this is different—Bionar's not invaded Oronthir again, or such as that. This is a civil war, Bionari killing each other by the thousand, and armies marching across the Myconian Mountains, and Urbonetto has closed her landward gates."

"What's the occasion of all this?" Prothero asked, interested despite himself.

"Some girl has been going about the kingdom saying she's the rightful heir to the throne, and Bar Asfal naught but a usurper, a killer of his own kin."

Rol looked up from his glass. His face seemed to have grown suddenly cold.

"A beauty, she's supposed to be, but a killer also. She leads her followers from the front rank, and slays Bionar's doughtiest champions like sheep. It's been brewing for years, apparently—she's seduced half a dozen of the mountain cities to her cause and they're where Bionar gets its iron, where the royal manufactories lie. So she's outfitted her forces in the best gear the kingdom can produce, and I hear she's even brought a few pieces of artillery down out of the mountains with her to batter the walls of Myconn with."

"There are madmen for all seasons, I suppose," Prothero said, draining his glass. "If she stops the Bionari from marching over half of Umer, I for one will be well pleased, so good luck to her. And now, gentlemen, I believe it is my watch on deck."

"Don't trip over your own feet," Riparian warned, for Prothero was swaying where he stood.

"My feet can mind themselves, old man."

The Caverric Sea went by in a succession of fresh sunrises. Rol liked taking the morning watch, from the fourth hour to the eighth, and watching the sun begin as a gray hint in the dark, and rise red through the cloud until it was broad yellow day and his body seemed to cast off the weariness of the dark hours as though the sunrise itself were some form of roborant.

His mind had been busy all through the dark hours, gnawing on memory, savoring past pain. Rowen was trying to make herself ruler of the most powerful kingdom in the world—for it was Rowen Riparian had been speaking of, he had not the smallest doubt. The Lost Heir of Bionar—it was like something out of an old story. As he often had over the course of the last seven years, Rol wondered how it was for her, if she had any peace at night, or any kind thought in her mind for him. The memory of her scalded his very spirit—her face, her taut body straining against him. Her smile, the rarest gift in the world.

And as always, when he could bear it no more he finally halted the arid conjecture and wondering in their tracks by staring out at the early morning on the surface of the waters, and finding there some form of quietude.

Elias Creed was supposed to be holystoning the quarterdeck but he got up off his knees and bent a crick out of his back with a faint groan. A year or two older than Rol, give or take, he had the face of a worn middle-aged man. His body, though lean, was a framework of pure muscle, the result of years spent breaking stones in the quarries of Keutta. The convicts had been issued sailcloth and had made their own clothing with the aid of a few of the other crew members who were handy with a needle. They had shaped up well, despite regaling the fo'c'sle with gory tales of past misdeeds. The men they were boasting to had heard it all before, however, and were not so easily impressed. Creed in particular was turning into a valuable hand, uncomplaining and swift to anticipate the orders of the ship's officers. Now he looked out at the birthing morning much as Rol did.

"I never knew the Caverric so well," he said. "For us it was the Inner Reach, the Westerease. We never went beyond the

Gut either. The seas of my youth. I will see them again soon." He looked at Rol inquiringly.

"Within a few days, if we make it through the Straits without mishap, and Ran is kind." He paused. "What happens to you once we reach Ordos—are you to stay with the ship?"

Creed shook his head, smiling. "They have quarries in Oronthir also, the Mercanters. Your captain will register my comrades and me with the harbormaster in Ordos and we'll be in shackles again, breaking stone. Still, it's been something, to have had a deck under my feet again, no matter for how short a time."

Rol turned away, frowning.

"You think I am a murderer and a thief, do you not, sir?"

"You were a privateer. That's what they do, I hear tell."

"Yes. Yes, they do. But they are not all monsters. They are merely men, most of them left without a choice in the manner they live their lives."

"How so?"

"I know that on the *Barracuda* the main part of the crew, my father's veterans, were refugees from the Oronthian borders, some from the Goliad. They did not choose the sea; they had all other choices taken away from them. Bionese armies had sacked their towns and carried off their wives and daughters and starved out their fathers. Perhaps our ship was a little different, but we only ever preyed on Bionar and her allies. We killed and raped in our turn, but only the Bionari and their fellow-travelers."

"Very discerning of you," Rol said dryly. He turned and regarded Elias Creed closely for the first time. The man had the same sense of calm confidence about him that Rol had remarked at their first meeting. He had possessed it then even though he had been standing in shackles. He had trimmed his hair and beard since and was dressed in sailors' canvas and his sores were on the way to healing. But the eyes had not changed. Somehow Creed had not lost faith in the goodwill of strangers, even after eleven years in Keutta.

"If you were not returned to the quarries, what would you do?"

Creed did not hesitate. "I would take to the sea."

"As a pirate?"

Here, Creed looked away. He turned to the ship's rail and leaned thereon, the muscles bunching around his shoulder blades.

"I don't know." And then: "Have you ever heard tell of Ganesh?"

Rol searched his brain. "It's an old name, is it not? For the southeast coast of Bionar."

"Yes. The Myconians come down to the sea there in steep woods and high crags of granite. There are a thousand coves and bays in that part of the world, and though the Bionari have claimed it, they have never truly set a footprint on the place." He turned back to face Rol. "That is where I would go, where no marching army could ever reach me. There is a city in Ganesh, it's said, a secret city to which no road leads. Ganesh Ka."

"I've heard of it. It's a legend among mariners."

"Yes." Here Creed drew closer, as if he were imparting a secret. He lowered his voice so the quartermaster at the wheel might not hear him.

"My father told me he had been to Ganesh Ka in his youth. He said it was a real place. A pirate city where free men lived who could not stomach the hegemony of Bionar. They had a fleet of warships, and they ruled their own affairs and welcomed all the lost and fleeing peoples who came to them in desperation or despair and gave them succor, and a new homeland."

"You believed him?"

Creed's nostrils flared. "He was my father. He went to the scaffold having never told a lie in his life."

More gently, Rol said, "You believe it still exists? The Bionari have tramped their bloody bootprints over most of the continent at one time or another, and this place cannot be more than a hundred and fifty leagues from Myconn itself."

"The Myconian Mountains have shielded it, and the impenetrable forests on their slopes. Ganesh is no place for armies. It is there, believe me."

Rol nodded. It was not his place to convince Creed of the absurdity of his beliefs. The convict had the face of a man who has not yet lost hope, despite having nothing to hope for.

Fifteen

THE PASSAGE OF THE NARROWS

"WHAT'S TO HAPPEN TO THE CONVICTS ONCE WE PUT into Ordos?" Rol asked Riparian in the middle watch that night. The two stood by the taffrail watching the stars wheel round overhead and listening to the night-time creaks and plashes and murmurs of the living ship beneath their feet.

The master yawned and scrubbed at his beard with one hand. "I turn them over to old Haremn at the docks. He'll put them to shifting cargoes or something until the Mercanters decide."

"They'll go back to breaking rocks?"

"Most probably. Piracy is not something the Mercanters look kindly upon. It's a pity; there's one or two of them have shaped up well, biddable as goddamned lambs."

"Rip, they're our shipmates now. Is there no other way?"

The master looked sharply at his first mate. "Don't

start getting ideas on me now. I admit it's a damned shame such men are to rot their lives out in the mines and quarries of the penal towns, but they made their own bed when they began slitting throats and burning ships up and down the Twelve Seas. There's naught to be done about it, not by such as us."

Rol nodded, and stared up at the uncaring brilliance of the stars, every one a red and blue flicker in the clear sea-night.

"That's what I thought."

They were two and a half weeks at sea, a slower passage than usual, and were coming up to the approaches of the Caverric Straits when Ran turned his face from them and began to build up black cloud in the skies over southern Armidon.

Rol, Riparian, and Prothero stood on the quarterdeck and silently watched the weather close in. The rest of the ship's company were going about their business as usual, but a few of the old salts had also paused to eye the growing threat of the sky. Elias Creed was studying the northeastern horizon with them, and then shifted his gaze to the trio on the quarterdeck. He could smell what was in the wind.

"How long, you think?" Prothero asked the master.

"A few hours, not more. We'd best get ourselves battened down, lads; we're in for a blow or I'm a farmer."

All hands were called up on deck, the drowsy, cursing larboard watch roused out of their hammocks below and set to storm stations. The two small cutters on the booms were frapped with extra layers of cordage, the swivels secured, and hawse-bags laid over the cable-ports. Every scuttle and hatch on board was sealed and overlaid with a canvas covering, and to everyone's obvious reluctance, they were ordered to shorten sail. Soon the *Cormorant* was flying along with a jib and the mainstaysail, no more. The wind veered round to east-nor'east, striking the brig on the starboard quarter near the stern. She began to dig deeper into the gray swells.

The Narrows of the Caverric Straits were less than five leagues ahead, and were a hard passage at the best of times, for there the waters of the Caverric Sea came funneling in with a crash to meet head-on the currents of the Inner Reach. On a quiet day there was white water for ten square miles about the Narrows. Today the wind was whipping up that confused mass of ocean into a fury, and the *Cormorant* began to pitch and roll as the first white-tipped breakers broke under her keel and lifted her high into the air.

The wind picked up further, a shriller note in the rigging. They rigged extra preventer-stays to the masts and deadman's lines to the ship's wheel. Already there were four men at its spokes, straining against the roll and push of the seas under the rudder to keep the brig on course.

"Ran is restless today," Riparian said with a grin.

Cavaillon to port, Armidon to starboard, two dark, rocky masses with the sea wolf-gray and white between them. The clouds had gathered and thickened overhead with a speed that Rol would once not have thought possible, but he had seen storms come fastening upon ships quicker than this, black squalls that could pass over a vessel with the speed of a galloping horse to lay her on her beam ends, and then rush on. Ran in one of his rages, in a hurry to smash down on some distant coast, tossing ships aside in his wake like toys.

There was a branched flare of lightning, as many-limbed as the roots of a tree. The thunder rolled after it seconds later. Over the Straits the knuckled mass of the storm stopped and hovered, thrashing up the Narrows into an intense fury of white water. There was no rain as yet; it was still boiling in the slate monsters ahead. The lightning flashed out in forked glee, beating what sunlight there had been from the sky. Rol saw the men at work about the decks of the ship in staggered instants of white light, roaring darkness between. He felt a backstay; the cable was rigid as wood. They would have to run before the wind and hope for the best—there was no beating back in the teeth of a blow like this. Thank the gods it was east-nor'east. There was a chance it would pop them through the Straits like a cork from the neck of a bottle.

"Lifelines fore and aft!" Riparian bellowed over the shriek of the wind. The ship leaped up in the air under him, and he bent his knees with the unthinking reflexes of a man inured to the sea. Two of the convicts were not so quick, and left the deck bodily. One went rolling into the scuppers like a ball, and the other was flung over the ship's rail, too astonished to even cry out.

"Man overboard!" Rol yelled for form's sake. There was no way to heave-to for him, not in this.

"It's times like these," Prothero shouted in Rol's ear, "that I wish we had a nice high sterncastle to cover our arse."

Rol looked astern. The waves following up behind them had metamorphosed into vast, murderous mountains, gray and solid-looking as stone with foam flying off their tips in smoking fringes. If the *Cormorant* could not keep her head to the wind, they would swallow her in a heartbeat and turn her end over end in their depths. A two-hundred-ton ship was a scrap of matchwood set against the brute majesty of those waves.

"What do you reckon she's making?" Rol asked Prothero. They had given up on the log-line some time ago.

"If it's less than fourteen knots then I'm a Kassic bumboy."

"We're setting a record, then."

"Yes. I'm so pleased. When we've sunk to the bottom I'll write my mother a letter." Prothero roared with laughter, and Rol smiled back. There was something splendid in it, after all, the valiant battle of their stout-hearted ship, the pitting of their frail bodies against the might of the gods, the rage of the waters. Had men never felt this, they would never have gone to sea. Looking down into the waist where the crew were rigging lifelines, Rol saw Elias Creed look up at him with that ruined, bone-lean face, and saw the same gladness within it.

"Steady," Riparian roared to the quartermasters at the wheel. The ship had slewed round, staggering under the onslaught of a crosscurrent from the Straits. This was the most perilous part. The wind might be going one way, but the sea beneath it was hacked and churned with several different currents here as the swells of two seas met and vied with each other.

The *Cormorant* groaned like a sentient thing as the water hammered her hull timbers, corkscrewing round. The wheel spun wildly, sending the helmsmen flying, breaking ribs and snapping the deadman's rig.

"Rol, Prothero!" Riparian screamed, and the three threw themselves upon the spinning wheel. Prothero cried out as one of the spokes clapped his wrist and snapped the bone in two. Rol and the master strove together to bring the head of the brig round. Through the tiller ropes it was possible to feel the titanic forces working on the rudder; a judder of movement—the ropes were sliding on the drum beneath their feet.

They hauled the wheel round and brought the brig before the wind again, Prothero helping them with his good arm. Elias Creed ran up the companionway and threw his weight into the struggle; he was immensely strong, and with his help they were able to ship fresh cables to the spokes. A roaring crash of spray came over the brig's stern in a pummeling torrent that washed them off their feet and sent them sliding against the quarterdeck rail. Rol regained his feet first and grabbed Prothero before the master's mate disappeared into the foaming chaos of the sea.

"I'd get writing that letter if I were you."

Prothero's mad humor seemed undimmed, though his hand hung useless as a rag from his wrist. "I think I'll have to dictate it."

The *Cormorant* was under the looming sea cliffs of the Narrows now. Two hundred fathoms they soared up, and seabirds fought to keep aloft near their summits, white against the dark sky. At their foot the seas hammered and smashed in furious abandon, breakers splintering half a cable up the rock, so white in the gloom that they seemed to have a light of their own.

The master wiped water out of his eyes and shouted at the quartermasters to get back to the wheel. Creed helped them, for two of their number had broken bones and bloody faces. The *Cormorant* swept on with a speed Rol had not seen or experienced before at sea, and in pursuit the following waves of the Caverric came thundering onward, lightning striking their crests. Five-fathom swells towering in line after line like attacking battalions, and as the Straits came together in the white-choked teeth of the Narrows so their assault became a frenzied battleground of broken water, waterspouts, whirlpools, and crosscurrents.

Looking upon that field of devastated ocean even Prothero's wit failed him. The ship's company had tied themselves to the butts of the masts, lines of sodden cordage wrapped round their chests. Some sat head down and silent, others had their eyes open and were peering into the lightning-fractured sky. Beneath them the brave *Cormorant* powered on, her tortured hull groaning and creaking, the strain on the yards rising to a shriek.

There was a rending crack, clear even over the tumult of the storm, and then a mass of timber and cordage came crashing down on deck. Three of the starboard watch died under that avalanche, and whips of severed rigging flew viciously in the wind. The maintopmast had gone by the board, and the mainstaysail with it. It was blown from its bolt-holes and disappeared ahead. The brig shuddered and yawed, and every man on the quarterdeck heaved on the wheel to keep her on course. Half a mile to the Narrows. A thousand batteries of artillery could not have produced a more fearsome barrage of explosive force than that which lay ahead.

Rol tied Prothero to the quarterdeck rail. The master's mate was white-faced with pain. A fall had brought the bone out through the bruised skin of his wrist and it was jetting blood. When Rol tried to tie some whipcord about the wound he was shoved away roughly. "Don't mind me—see to the blasted ship, will you, you great oaf!"

The stern of the brig was catapulted into the air a hundred feet as the huge mass of water she rode upon was hurled at the rock of the Narrows. The *Cormorant* twisted in midair and for a few seconds was actually falling free of the water. Rol's feet left the deck but he managed to seize a backstay and swing there. A sickening impact and the tearing shriek of rent timbers. The foremast came down across the bows, slewed round, and laid waste to the fo'c'sle. The brig hit the water again and was buried in water. It foamed up round the waist and up the quarterdeck ladders. She wallowed there as all about her the white water turned and spun in a weltering mass. Still spinning, the sea spat her out again, on her beam-ends this time. The brig's starboard side was underwater and the stumps of her masts were at ninety degrees. Men slid free of their lifelines and disappeared into the foam.

Slowly, slowly, she began to right herself. Had she been a man-of-war her gun-ports would have been stove in and she would be on her way to the bottom by now. But she was a light ship with no heavy cargo to move around, her ballast not the usual mass of rock and gravel, but pig-iron bars bolted to her bottom ribs to make her stiffer under sail. So she began to right herself where any other vessel would have continued the roll and capsized.

All that remained in the way of yards was the bottom part of the mainmast and a ten-foot stump of the foremast; everything else had gone by the board. There was not a scrap of sail on the brig now and so she was flung forward through that awesome sea like a twig lost in a millrace, still turning widdershins as the water below her keel whirled in confused fury. Rol looked along what remained of her decks. Prothero was unconscious, still tied to the rail. Creed and two others were tangled in the cordage that secured the ship's wheel, and there were a dozen more in the waist, but many of the crew had been washed overboard.

"Riparian!" he yelled out. "Captain!" But there was no answer under all that lightning-cut sky. The master was gone.

Rain came at last, a vicious hissing downpour that leaped up from the beaten deck. The *Cormorant*'s crazed motion began to ease as it beat down on the white water, flattening the worst excesses of the broken waves. Rol raised his head, not quite believing that they were still afloat, and saw that the Narrows were astern; they were through. The sea began to assume some rationality again, and the wind veered round to east-southeast; it was now striking his left ear instead of his right. The waves were still huge, however, and if they were not going to be pooped he would have to get some sail on her, get her to run before the wind. The gods only knew how much water was in the hold. The *Cormorant*'s side was only a few feet from the surface of the sea—she must have taken on untold tons.

"Creed, Arkin, untie yourselves. We have to get a jury-rig up or she'll founder."

Arkin was a quartermaster, a mariner these twenty years, but he simply turned his face away and did not move. He had given up. Creed alone staggered to Rol's side. "The stump of the foremast?"

"Yes. If we splice it to the main it'll press down her stern, which is the last thing we want. We'll have to—" He stopped and looked out along the length of the ship. Masses of broken timber and mounds of cordage littered the decks, but out on the bow the bowsprit was in one piece. Someone would have to crawl out on that slender yard as it dipped into the waves, and make fast one end of the jury-rig.

"I'll go out on the sprit. You make fast the other end to what's left of the foremast."

"No, let me—"

"That's an order, Elias. Now come on."

They prevailed upon another stunned member of the crew to go below and rouse out a staysail from the sail locker whilst Rol clambered out on the bowsprit. Every so often he would have to grit his teeth and bow his head as the tremendous rush of water went past him and over him and strove to tear him from the yard. Then he would emerge gasping again, the line still tied about his wrist. It was slow work, but in the end he had a two-inch cable made fast two-thirds of the way out along the bowsprit. When he had finally returned to the fo'c'sle he felt more exhausted than he had ever been in his life before and the seawater was streaming out of his ears. He bent and threw up a pint of the stuff on deck.

They got up the scrap of staysail, and it was enough to bring the brig's head round and put her before the wind. Her mad roll began to ease and her pitch became more pronounced. The *Cormorant* was moving like a ship again, not like some toy set adrift in a rapid.

"It's getting light," Creed said, and looking up Rol found that it was true. Heartbreaking to look up and see nothing there above his head, no complex beautiful weaving of masts and yards and rigging. The *Cormorant* was a poor crippled thing now. More than that, she was dying under their feet. But at least the storm-dark was receding along with the lightning. It was day again. Only the wind was unchanged, still malign and shrill in their ears, whipping them forward relentlessly. And the rain—

Rol opened his mouth and it filled up in seconds, washing away the salt. Huge drops that stung the skin like hail.

He collected himself. A knot of sailors had gathered about him now that the odds seemed better.

"Man the pumps," he said. "We're not going to let her die on us."

The wind slackened, but it did not back or veer a single point for five days. During that period no member of the *Cormorant*'s remaining crew slept for more than a few minutes at a time. West-nor'west was their course, the only one they could manage to keep with the wind behind them. They got a yard up on the mainmast but any sail hoisted upon it pressed the stern of the ship lower in the water until the waves began to break over the taffrail. So they manned the pumps night and day, trying to lighten the *Cormorant*'s load. Men fell asleep with the rain hissing on their steaming backs and had to be roused with kicks and blows and set to work again.

Prothero's hand turned black and dead on the end of his arm, so Rol lopped it off with Fleam's hungry edge and sealed the stump with boiling pitch. That was the only time they could spare the effort to get a fire going in the galley, for the place was knee-deep. The men drank brackish rainwater from barrels lashed on the quarterdeck and chewed gristly salt pork raw. All the provisions had been drowned by seven feet of water in the hold.

Slowly, agonizingly, they began to win the battle with the pumps and the jets of water spurting out to larboard and starboard grew thinner and choppier. On the fifth evening, when first one and then the other of the pumps began to suck, Rol called all hands—there were barely a score of them left alive—and served out an issue of the master's rum. Then he sent them all below to their soaking hammocks while he and Prothero and

Creed manned the helm. Prothero's dark face had become a white-sculpted exercise in ivory, but his stump was clean, and under the pitch Creed had sewn flaps of flesh about the bone. His eyes were clear as he stood by the binnacle and peered forward.

"Dead reckoning?" he asked.

"What do you think?" Rol retorted.

"Eight knots."

"As much as that?"

"For the first two days, I'd agree," Creed said. "But lately it's been slackening a little. I'd say six now."

"Very well," Rol mused. "Eight knots is sixty-four leagues a day for two days, then six knots is forty-eight leagues a day for three days. That's—"

"Two hundred and seventy-two leagues," Creed told him.

"And from the Narrows to the coast of Bionar on this course is two hundred and seventy-five. Gentlemen, we've crossed the Inner Reach. I believe we are about to hit land."

"Or it's about to hit us," Prothero retorted. "If the cloud lifted we could see it by now. In any case, we'll make landfall in a couple of hours, blind as bats on an unknown coast. We must heave-to and send a cutter ashore, find an anchorage. If we don't we'll have a wreck on our hands."

"Agreed," Rol said. He wiped his scarred palm across his face. "Though heaving-to when we've naught but a scrap of staysail on her may not be the easiest task in the world."

"Drop anchor, then," Creed suggested. "Even if it's too deep, it'll slow us down, and when we hit the shallows there's a good chance it'll catch and halt us."

Rol looked at Prothero. The dark man shrugged. "You're senior now. Final say is yours."

"Splendid." Rol smiled sourly. "Very well, lads, we'll drop anchor, and pray to that bastard Ran we find good ground for it."

* * *

They dropped anchors from both bow and stern and then the entire ship's company remained motionless on deck, watching to see if their pace slowed. At last Rol nodded.

"It's taken a good three knots off us. Prothero, get a leadsman in the chains and let us see what's below our keel. The rest of you, get to work on the ship's boat."

While the crew were patching up the only cutter that had survived, Rol went below to the master's cabin to try to make some sense of their position. Riparian's cross-staff, along with most of his charts, had been broken or washed away during the storm. There was nothing left detailed enough for inshore work, just one large-scale chart of the Inner Reach and its surrounding coasts. Rol took the dividers and plotted their course as best he could on the crinkled paper, and what he found made his lips purse in a silent whistle. The unseen coast off their bow was none other than that of the Goliad.

He sat back in the master's favorite chair, wishing old Riparian were here to shoulder the problems, to give orders. The Goliad was a desert, so men said, an amphitheater for the staging of the endless battles between Bionar and Oronthir and their allies, a cockpit of Umer's many wars. But it was less than three hundred miles up the coast from Ordos, their destination. Somehow on the barren coast of the Goliad they must find the wherewithal to refit the ship.

Rol studied the odd scar on his palm. The Mark of Ran, Riparian had called it, and considered it lucky, a talisman against drowning. Rol thought of it as a curse. The storm-god liked to play with those he marked, and this was one of his games.

A hammering on the cabin door and Creed stepped inside without invitation, eyes alight. "Land ho." And then he added: "Captain."

"Where away?"

"Fine on the port bow, a league maybe."

Rol ran up on deck. The clouds had lifted and a hot, dry sun had come out from behind them. It was as welcome as a blessing to Rol's saturated clothing and wet skin. Looking forward he saw a sere mustard-pale coastline ahead, devoid of any hint of life.

"What's the lead say?" he called forward.

The leadsman in the forechains was coiling up his rope. "Four fathoms, sir, and shallowing. Sand and gravel."

The wind dropped, and Rol, looking to larboard, saw a long promontory there extending miles out to sea in a hooked curve. They were in its lee now, becalmed. Prothero nodded at it. "Ussa smiled on us today. Half a league to the sou'west and we'd be broken wood on the tip of yonder headland."

The ship came to a halt, making them all stagger slightly. The anchors had finally bitten in the seabed and were holding fore and aft. The *Cormorant* was still a mile offshore.

"Three fathoms!" the leadsman shouted. Eighteen feet of depth. Looking over the ship's rail, Rol could see clear to the bottom in the pellucid water, the shadow of the brig's hull dark in the blue-green of the shallows. Tiny fish winked silver in swarming schools and as he watched a turtle flapped its slow course through them.

Sixteen

THE SHORE PARTY

"THERE'S A WICKED REEF ABOUT TWO CABLES OFFSHORE all the way round the bay," Creed said. "High surf all about it; we barely pulled clear. There is a gap, though, to the northeast."

"Did you get through it?" Rol demanded.

"Yes. The beach is new-moon-shaped, five leagues long or so, but at the back of it there's high cliffs, thirty fathoms high at the least. Only on the southern edge do they crumble somewhat. Men could make a passage there; everywhere else it's not even a place for mountain goats."

"And sculling out again?"

"Nip and tuck. The cutter's a handy craft, but even so, we scored the bottom off her. Laden, it would be a whole different pot of fish."

There was a silence in the cabin until Rol said, "Well done, Elias. Have some rum."

The convict smiled. "An able seaman drinking in the master's cabin?"

"Consider yourself a master's mate like Prothero here, and drink something, for the love of God."

"Me, I think I'll crawl into the neck of the bottle and stay there awhile," Prothero said, cradling his stump. "We're in a cleft stick."

"Wind still picking up?" Rol asked him.

"Were it not for the headland she'd be back-broken on those reefs of Elias's as we speak. It's picking up into a gale again beyond the bay. What is it they say? *An onshore wind is the wrecker's friend.*"

"Ran is not done with us yet, it seems," Rol said. He looked sightlessly at the chart that their glasses held uncurled upon the table. They had been at anchor in the bay for three days now, hard at work twenty hours of every day. But the weather was changing again, and not for the better.

"We've jury masts now with a yard apiece, the mainmast lateen-rigged, which is good. But there's no way we could beat out of this bay in the teeth of that onshore gale. We wait it out. Provisions are not a problem—a soaking makes little difference to salt horse. It's water I'm worried about. It's so damn dry here, and there's sand in the air too. We have to land a watering party whatever the risks."

"With a fair wind we could cruise down the coast to Ordos in four, five days," Prothero protested.

"With a fair wind. Given our luck on this trip so far, I'm not going to hold my breath waiting for one. No. Since the casks were bilged in the storm we've water for another two days, that's all. I can cut the ration, but I'd rather try to find a spring inland."

"For such a big, bloody-minded bastard, you are the very soul of caution," Prothero said irritably. "If it were me—"

"Sail ho!" came the cry from on deck.

The three were on their feet in a second and piled out of the door to the waist. Rol was first up the quarterdeck ladder. "Where away?"

"Large on the port bow, sir," Mihal, a young topman, said. "Just coming round the headland—and don't they wish they may make it."

The entire crew was on deck staring intently southward to the tip of the promontory that sheltered their bay. Half a league away perhaps, a lateen-rigged two-master was trying to beat clear of the rocky shore in the teeth of the wind. The men on deck held their breaths, feeling for the crew of the strange ship, willing it onward.

"Come on, *come on,*" someone whispered.

She struck amidships, and the waves at once broke over her starboard side. They watched as first one mast toppled, then the other. The hull was lifted by the savage surf and dumped full onto the rocks. The vessel's back broke. For perhaps half a minute she was a black, turning shape in the white surf, then she was gone.

"Blood of God," Prothero said through clenched teeth. "That bastard wind-mongering whoreson. Curse you, Ran, you—" Creed laid a hand on Prothero's good arm and he caught himself, nodded.

"There may be survivors," Rol said, eyes hot and glaring. No man bred to the sea could watch the death of a ship with equanimity. "We'll start inland at once. Prothero, you stay here with a harbor watch. Elias and I will take half a dozen of the fittest men up that headland and look for her crew. We'll hunt out water while we're at it."

"It's late in the day," Creed ventured.

"All the more reason for haste. Get that fucking cutter fixed, and let's be on our way."

* * *

It was dusk by the time that Rol, Creed, and six of the fitter, steadier survivors among the crew were rowing away from the side of the *Cormorant.* They all carried cutlasses, Rol his scimitar, and a long-barreled wheel-lock pistol he had found in the master's cabin. He had enough dry match and powder for only a few shots, but thought he might try potting a bird with it. Salt pork was beginning to stick in everyone's throat.

Elias sat at the tiller and steered them through the gap in the reef he had navigated earlier in the day. The former pirate had become a quietly effective leader of men and Rol had made a vow to himself that Creed would never be breaking rocks in a quarry again. He belonged at sea.

The bottom of the cutter kissed the sand, and Rol felt a wall of heat hit his face: the close, baking dryness of the land. After being at sea, the deadness of the air seemed bizarre, enervating. They ran the cutter up the beach and stood on the sand in the empurpling light like men confused. Under their feet nothing moved, and each step jarred as though they were missing a stair. It did not seem right that the earth should be so solid.

"Matiu and Haim, stay here with the boat," Rol said. "You might want to get the casks out of her and up the beach a way. We'll make for the headland to see if any survived the wreck, and then we'll come back down if we find water."

The soft sand was hard work and they trudged up the curving strand in silence as the night quickened about them. Looking out to sea they could see the deck-lanterns glowing on board the *Cormorant* but no other sign of human activity in all that wide sweep of sand and sea and stars.

The tall cliffs reared up to one side like the walls of a fortress, and there were masses of broken rock and gravel at their feet where high tides had battered. Elias led the party without hesitation to a place where a landslide had created a precarious way up to their summits.

They began climbing on all fours, eyes straining in the

starlight, stones crumbling and ticking under their feet. Once Rol's foothold gave and he slid five yards down the steep slope, but was brought up short again by a solid outcrop of rock. Breathing heavily, he started up again.

It took them over an hour, by Rol's guess, to make their way to the head of the cliffs. They stood wiping the sweat from their faces and rubbing the raw places, and looked out at the star-shimmered sea and the *Cormorant*, a twinkling toy, a jewel set upon it. They could feel the wind here, and it quickly cooled their hot backs and made them shiver. A good reefed-topsail blow hammering in from the open ocean. Farther out in the bay they could see surf glimmering white as fangs on the reef. Had it not been for the sheltering promontory, that wind would have broken *Cormorant*'s back as it had the other vessel's. As Prothero had said, it was sheer luck they had made landfall in the lee of the headland and not on the windward side.

Almost, Rol thought he saw something else out at the uttermost reach of his sight. Lights out at sea, a line of them. The wind made his eyes water, and when he rubbed them clear he could see nothing. A couple of low stars perhaps, making their way up the sky from the sea's brim.

They turned their eyes inland and saw a wide, pale plateau carved with night-blue gullies and pocked with scattered knuckles of weathered stone. It rose steadily, until they could make out the shapes of mountains dark against the stars to the northwest. The Goliad was a vast bowl of desert upland hemmed in by the Goloron and Myconian Mountains on all sides. Beyond those mountains lay Bionar, mightiest and most hated of the realms of men.

"We've our work cut out for us, finding water here," Jude Mochran, one of the sailors, said gruffly. "It's dry as a corpse's cough."

They paralleled the beach. The others tripped over rocks and uttered muffled curses, but Rol could see as easily as if he were abroad in daylight. In the years since leaving Psellos's Tower he had neglected his exercises and his training had become little more than a memory, but he still had the sight of a cat at night. Unlike the others, he was able to see that many of the jumbled stones that dogged their shins had once been reared up in walls. They were walking through the ruin of some ancient settlement, so old that not two stones of it now stood one atop the other, and the very stones themselves had been rounded by centuries of desert wind, losing their sharply masoned edges.

The wind was stronger out on the headland, which jutted perhaps half a league into the Reach and was no more than four cables wide. There were writhen trees growing here and there in more sheltered places, their branches tilted away from the sea as though in revulsion. Their bark was gray and scaled and the leaves upon them were narrow as the tines of a fork.

Another half hour brought them to the tip of the headland. Below them the boom of the surf was loud as the massed guns of a fleet action, and they could see white flashes of foam in a line to the southwest where a second reef ran alongside the shore. The wrecked ship had been trying to beat along this, fighting for leeway, but the wind had been too determined.

"Rope," Rol said mechanically. "Who's brought rope?"

One of the shore party began unwrapping a coil of one-inch cable from around his shoulder. "You're not going down there?" Creed said.

"I am. Lower me down and I'll have a look about."

"Nothing could survive on those rocks."

"If it were my ship wrecked, my crew cast into the sea, I would hope that fellow mariners would do more than wring their hands over me from a safe distance."

With the rope tight under his armpits the men lowered Rol down the cliff-face. It was not sheer, and in many places he was able to take his own weight. The thunder of the breakers grew ever louder as he descended. When he had come down some ten fathoms the rope gave out. He untied it and coiled the end about a large boulder, then began scrambling the last few yards with the spray of the waves cool on his face. Elias had been right—there was nothing here, not even a shard of wreckage. The murderous waves had swept the rocks clear of any remnant of a wreck. He had wasted his time.

But now something was moving feebly in the white of the breakers, something huge and glistening. Were it not for his night-sight, Rol would never have seen it. It was not a man. Some great beached fish perhaps. Rol edged closer, until the waves were soaking him and the spray was exploding all about his knees.

Two green lights winked on, watching him. He thought he heard a voice in the tumult of the sea. Startled, he clambered and slithered over the black rocks and wiped seawater out of his eyes. Not a man, but manlike, huger than any man had a right to be.

The thing raised an arm and a white whirling mass of foam broke around it, tearing it from the rock. Rol saw the green lights shut off as it slid into the breakers. He clattered forward, and a club of water smote him about the head and shoulders, flattening him on the stones. He clung there as the wave receded, tasting blood, and when he was able to look up, the thing had hauled itself out of the water again. It was a fathom away, no more, and in its face—it had a face, after all—two great tusks glimmered and the emerald light of the eyes winked on and off as it blinked.

"Give me a goddamned hand, will you?" Its voice was hoarse and cracked, but deep as a well.

Rol reached out an arm and it was at once enveloped by the thing's huge paw. Then the two of them lowered their heads as another wave broke about them. When it had passed the thing leaped up the rock convulsively, and Rol braced his boots on the stone, pulling with all his might. Its legs pumped and he could hear its talons ticking and scraping on the slick stone. When Rol thought his arm was about to leave its socket, one foot found purchase and the awful grip slackened. The creature boosted itself upward and slapped full length on the slimed stone. They lay side by side and watched a huge breaker come running at them in a slathering fury of white surf. As one, they turned and scrabbled up the rocks to the foot of the cliff. The wave sucked impotently at their feet and withdrew with a rattle of gravel and stone.

The thing Rol had rescued sat panting heavily. There were scraped and broken places all over its huge carcass where the blood shone black in the starlight.

"Thank you," it said. "I'd held on there long enough."

"You're from the ship?"

"Where else?" It shut its perilous eyes and a dry black tongue licked about its tusks.

Light dawned on Rol at last. A night in Ascari, an episode from another life. "I know you. You're a halftroll. Your name is Gallico."

The thing's head snapped round and the light in the eyes intensified. "What in the world—How could you know that?"

"We met once, a long time ago. I had saved your purser from footpads in Ascari. I forget his name."

"Woodrin. By God, it's the terrible youth, the one with the Blood in him. You have grown up, my lad—the name, now, the name would be Rol, I think."

"It would."

Gallico laughed, a barrel-deep, roaring laugh that rose even above the thunder of the breakers. "Here we are years later, met by chance upon the most desolate coast in the charted waters of the world. If there's not some kind of fate involved in this, I'll leave off beer for life. Boy, you are well met and very welcome."

"Was there anyone else?"

Gallico's good humor faded. "There were, but they could not hold on. The sea took them. Woodrin was one. He never did learn to swim."

"I'm sorry."

"That's for later. For now we must get up onto drier land. I feel as though I've swallowed half the goddamned Inner Reach. I'm salt-blooded with the stuff. How did you get down?"

"My crew are on the headland with a rope. They'll haul us up."

It was approaching the middle of the night by the time they all stood on the clifftop, and when the shore party finally caught sight of the thing they had been sweating and groaning to haul up out of the breakers they stood shocked, like men who go fishing for trout and land a whale. They gave Gallico some of their precious water and Creed, who seemed less daunted by the halftroll than the others, helped bind up the creature's wounds. Gallico had been scraped raw by barnacles, bloodied by the battering of the rocks, and generally smashed about for several hours as he fought the waves, but he was alert and upright. As soon as he was able, he limped to the brink of the cliff and peered out to sea.

"That's your ship, down there in the bay?"

"Yes," Rol told him. "The storm dismasted her, but we've a jury-rig up. As soon as this onshore blow dies down a little, we're going to put to sea. But we need water."

Gallico nodded grimly. He was still peering out at the horizon. "You'd best be careful. There are two Bionese men-of-war out there sniffing for blood. They chased us down the wind, and by the time they had drawn off it was too late for us to claw clear of the rocks."

"We've a Mercanter commission. I doubt they'd trouble us,"

Rol said, remembering now the half-fancied line of lights he had seen out to sea. He wondered why Gallico's vessel had been fleeing the Bionese but was not sure how to ask. The halftroll looked down on him kindly.

"Our ship, the *Adder,* was a privateer, Rol Cortishane. You had best know that right off."

"You're a pirate?"

Gallico grinned horribly. "For my sins."

"Were you a pirate in Ascari?"

"Not strictly speaking, but times change. Now, would you rather I wandered off into the Goliad, or will you tolerate my kind in your company? You owe me nothing, whereas I owe you a life. I'll take myself off if you do not want to befriend my sort, and think none the worse of you for it."

Rol looked at Creed, but the ex-privateer's face was closed.

"Stay with us. If it comes to it, we'll find a space for you to hide belowdecks. I would not turn someone adrift in a desolation such as this."

Gallico set a paw on Rol's shoulder. "Then you have my thanks again. I will not forget it. I am your man now to the death."

Despite his injuries, Gallico could keep pace with them with ease. They made their way back down to the base of the headland and moved inland. The night sky was entirely clear, awash with constellations. There was no moon, but the starlight was powerful enough to cast faint shadows. The shore party tramped steadily inland, their ears cocked for the telltale trickle of water. They were parched, and had only a cupful left in their skins. The heat of the day had evaporated and it was bitterly cold on the plateau. Their breath steamed out before them in gray clouds.

"A cold desert," Rol said. "I did not think there were such things."

"Only at night," Gallico told him. "The heat is lost to the sky, sucked up by the stars to keep them bright."

"Have you been to the Goliad before?"

"Not to speak of. But I have walked in Tukelar and Padrass, and I would surmise most deserts are alike."

"Why did you turn pirate?"

Gallico paused a long time before answering, and watched his huge splayed feet as they stirred up the dust.

"The Mercanters are becoming too greedy for their own good. They want a complete monopoly for their ships on some of the major trade routes of the world. You know the Free Cities?"

"Some."

"They are independent, hence the name; city-states existing only for the purpose of commerce, and hence ideal bases for the Mercanters. But I have learned that the Mercanters actually control the Free Cities. Osmer, Spokehaven, Perigord, Graillor, even great Urbonetto of the Wharves. In any case, Urbonetto and Spokehaven have barred ships from taking on cargo at their docks who do not have a Mercanter commission, and it is rumored the others will soon follow suit."

"They'll bankrupt themselves."

"You underestimate the volume of Mercanter-commissioned trade, my friend. No, what is happening is that up and down the Twelve Seas, captains are scrambling for that red pennant, and paying tidy sums for the privilege of flying it. After that, they sail where they are told to sail, take on what cargoes are set out for them. There is no freedom, even for a shipowner, anymore. He is merely an employee of the Mercanters—and who are they anyway, to be set on taking over all the free trade of the world? Does anyone know?"

"I have met their agents, ordinary men for the most part."

"Yes, but who are their leaders? No one can name them, and so long as everyone is growing rich, no one has thought to ask—

it is not as though they have standing armies, or defended borders. They do not need them—other states will do the fighting for them, if that is called for. The Bionari love nothing more than to come crashing down on some small country with the complaints of the Mercanters to redress."

"You still have not told me why you turned pirate."

Gallico nodded, and the bone ridge of his brows came down almost to meet his jutting cheekbones so that his eyes glared green out of a crevice.

"We traded illegally in Spokehaven, and our ship was forfeit. They took it on the very docks, and half the crew. Woodrin, a few others, and myself took off inland, and walked all the way to the southern tip of Osmer. There we worked as fishermen for a few months, until one day a gull-winged xebec put in for water flying the Black Flag. The fisherfolk fled, but we remained. It was the *Adder,* and her captain, Harun Secharis, agreed to take us on. Initially, all we wanted was passage off Osmer, but the privateers told us that we were blacklisted up and down the Westerease Sea. No captain would employ us—and it must be said that for me at least it is not simply a question of changing my name." Here Gallico chuckled bitterly. "I have a tendency to stand out from the crowd. The others took their chances elsewhere, but Woodrin stayed with me, and I stayed with the *Adder* for want of a better alternative. That is how I became a pirate."

"And have you raped and pillaged and murdered, as sea lore has it?" Rol asked.

Gallico looked at him. "Yes. Yes, I have murdered and pillaged. The *Adder* took fourteen ships before they ran us to earth here on the rocks of the Goliad, and every one of them was a Mercanter. We killed only those who resisted us, set the crews adrift in ship's boats, took the cargoes, and burned the ships. That is how privateers do business."

"Where did you get rid of the cargoes?"

Gallico paused, looked away. "Anywhere we could. The

Mercanters may be controlling trade, but there will always be goods of dubious ownership to be bought and sold. Some cities have black markets for the Black Ships."

They walked on in silence after that. Rol's shipmates kept their distance from the halftroll—especially now they knew he was a privateer. Only Creed seemed unfazed, as might be expected. Rol caught Elias staring at him as if wanting to say something, but whatever it was, the ex-convict thought better of it. They trudged along without further talk, their tongues sticking to the roofs of their mouths, and the air burning cold on their sunburnt faces.

Gallico stopped and they straggled to a halt around him. They had been walking for well over two hours and were perhaps two leagues inland. The Goliad was a barren, sandblasted plain strewn with formations of brindled rock, the only vegetation low-growing plants with leaves like knives. Here and there odd piles of rubble were heaped in lines, and gullies spoke of a time when there had been heavy rains to carve the parched dirt of the land.

"Water," Gallico said, tongue rasping over his lips.

"Where?"

"Nearby." His nostrils flared, snorted. "I smell it."

He traced the elusive scent to the side of one of those gullies, a deeper blade of shadow under the stars. While the others stood about sceptically, Gallico went to his knees and, with his huge talon-tipped paws, began to dig.

Rol and Creed climbed up to the lip of the draw and looked north, to where the mountains rose dark against the sky. The Myconians, greatest heights of the northern world. Some great convulsion of the earth's heart had punched them up in sliding shelves of tilted stone, fifteen thousand feet from foundation to peak. They were sheer as a wall here, though Rol knew that they grew less fearsome as one went farther north and west. Myconn, the Imperial City, stood in a highland vale in their heart, reachable only by a few passes, considered so impregnable that for centuries she had never built walls to protect herself. And Rowen was out there in those heights—for a moment he thought he could almost touch her sleeping mind. Rowen, fighting to become one of the powers of the world—and she would succeed, or die trying. The demons that gnawed at her heart would never let her do otherwise.

There was a quiver at Rol's hip, and he set his hand upon his sword-pommel. Fleam slept uneasily. Perhaps she sensed more violence to come.

There was a life in the sword; Rol knew that now. It was avid, savage, and it had a voice that he half understood. What sorcery had created the blade he could not guess, but it had long passed from this world of men.

"They say the Goliad was once paradise on earth," Creed said quietly, staring up at the mountains but seeing different things. "A garden of the ancient world shaped by the hands of the Creator Himself. And in it He set the fathers of the first men, while the angels watched over them in their sleep." Creed's eyes snapped darkly to Rol's face. "They say some with the blood of angels still walk the earth."

"I was not sure if you'd noticed."

"It's in the eyes. They are not truly human."

"Gallico and I, we are the same, under the skin. Does that bother you?"

Creed shrugged, smiling. "We all have our burdens to bear. Myself, I think I shall feel the shackles on my wrists for the rest of my life—and the lash of the overseer's whip."

A cry, a tattered chorus of laughter from below. Rol and Creed ran and jumped down the side of the gully to find their shipmates gathered close about the kneeling Gallico. The halftroll was still shoveling earth out of a fair-sized hole, but his hands were glistening black now with mud and there was a tiny bell of sound at his knees, a trickle.

"Water, by all the gods," Elias breathed. "Gallico, I salute your nose."

"The hell with my nose. Get down here and help me dig."

Another quarter of an hour and they had a pool of water shining in the gully bottom and were taking turns to cup it in their hands and gulp it greedily down their dry throats. It was muddy and full of grit, but tasted sweet and cold. They filled their flaccid waterskins and drank pint after pint. One or two of the men threw it up directly, and then went back to drinking again. It sat like liquid ice in their stomachs but was welcome for all that. Finally Rol called a halt.

"Back to the beach. We have to fill the water casks. The rest of the crew are as thirsty as we, and it'll be dawn soon."

The way back seemed shorter with the good water seeping through their parched bodies. Gallico raised his head and sniffed the air again.

"The onshore breeze has dropped. It's backing round now, northeast or nor'-nor'east."

"A fair wind for Ordos," Mihal, one of the younger sailors, said.

They were still a mile from the coast when they caught sight of a strange glow on the horizon, a saffron glare like that of a tiny setting sun. They studied it in puzzlement as they walked.

"Perhaps the men at the boat lit a fire to keep themselves warm," Elias said.

"What are they burning, sand?" Gallico retorted. His face had clenched shut again.

It was Mihal who said it.

"It's the ship. The *Cormorant* is burning."

Such a stupid thing to say. Ships sailed, they went aground, they capsized, they sank. Ships did not burn. Men burned ships.

Rol began to run.

"Do not do it!" Gallico shouted, loud as a trumpet blast in the night.

Rol ran. The land dipped under his feet and he sped through a hollow filled with black stunted trees. Their sharp leaves furrowed his brow for him but he did not slacken his pace. He ran as fast as the burgeoning fury in him could catch light. He found the cliff path and scrambled and half fell down it, a cloud of stones and gravel tumbling with him, racing past his feet. His boots hit soft sand and he ran on. He ran past the bodies of the men he had left on the beach, the stove-in timbers of the ship's boat. He hit water with a white flare of spray, and began swimming as though water were a necessary irritation, another medium of transport. He swam as he had run, without thinking, his mind one big white space.

Prothero.

The *Cormorant* was ablaze from truck to waterline, and crucified to her sides were Prothero and the shipmates Rol had left behind to look after her. A dozen men twitching in the flames as their muscles and sinews contracted into cinders, their skin already blackened, hair alight. The pitch on the end of Prothero's stump blazed like a torch, so that it seemed he was bleeding fire. His eyes were already withered and the heat had shrunk his face to the size of a child's.

Rol swam to the ship's side and trod water, staring up at the conflagration. The *Cormorant* groaned and creaked in her final agony and flaming pieces came tumbling off her jury-rigged yards like little comets, hissing into the sea all about him. There was a sharp bang on board, and the brig shuddered, timbers fountaining up into the air like fireworks as one of the small powder-charges for the swivels caught light. The ship began to list and the fire hissed venomously at the waterline, fighting the cool dark of the sea.

Rol dragged his gaze away from Prothero's shriveled face and swam around the *Cormorant*'s stern. The glass in the stern windows was exploding with high-pitched cracks and the flames rushed out hungrily to lick round the taffrail. His fury cooled, sank cold into ash. He peered out at the horizon where the lightening sky spoke of morning, but could see nothing. He was too low in the water, weighed down by his sword and the master's wheel-lock at his waist.

He floated there by the dying ship that had been his home, ignoring the pleas and cries of the shore party as they found their own way down onto the beach. Finally, as the sunrise paled the roaring flames, he turned in the water and began swimming for the shore again, tired to the depths of his bones.

Seventeen

THE BIRTHPLACE OF MAN

"WE SAW THEM. FROM THE SEA CLIFFS THEY WERE HULL-down on the horizon," Elias Creed said, his face pale beneath the red peel of his sunburn. "Two Bionese cruisers, sailing sou'-sou'west. They must have sent boats in through the reef during the night."

"We were a Mercanter ship," young Mihal protested. "What were they thinking?"

"No pennant—it went in the storm," Rol told him in an even voice. "They mistook us for the privateer's consort, and sent in the marines without asking too many questions. They crucify pirates, and pirates is what they thought we were." He looked at Creed and Gallico as he spoke, and then looked away again, ashamed of the meanness of his thinking.

"I do not blame you if you are bitter," Gallico said. "The *Adder* brought this upon you, and for that I am heartily sorry."

"Sorry!" Jude Mochran said, red-eyed. "My brother was on that ship. He made it through the storm when many another didn't—and then they killed him like a common murderer!" Mochran was a small man, but he bunched his fists as though he meant to take on Gallico there and then.

"Enough," Rol said sharply. "We've two shipmates to bury, and we must salvage what we can from the cutter."

"We're on the shore of a desert hundreds of miles away from anywhere," Bartolomew Geygan, a young sailor from Corso, said, quiet but cold. "What in the world is the use?"

"You can sit here and cry into the Reach if you want," Rol snapped, "but I intend to live through this. Now get on your feet, all of you."

"You can't command us," Mochran said, "your commission went down with the ship. You're nothing to us now."

"Then go your own way, Jude," Rol said calmly. "I won't stop you." He knelt in the sand and began to dig with his hands. At once, Gallico and Elias joined him, and after a few moments the other four Cormorants did so also. The tears ran down Mochran's face as he hurled the sand aside, but he said no more.

Two years, Rol had been with the *Cormorant,* and many of those who had gone down nailed to her burning hull had been shipmates all that time. Prothero he had sailed with for three times as long. For some reason, as he knelt in the hot sand with the rising sun beating fierce and unpitying upon his back, he felt that his past had somehow caught up with him again. There was something to his life that would not let go of him, as unyielding and ineradicable as the mark on the palm of his hand. It had slept, these seven years, but now was waking again. So he dug deep in the sand, making a grave for things other than the two corpses. There were tasks to fulfill now, and the white fury of his rage would help him accomplish them.

The cutter had had planks chopped out of her hull and her

thwarts were smashed into splinters. Even if they had possessed a full complement of carpenter's tools, it was unlikely they could ever have got her to float again. Most of the casks had been stove in also, but one was whole, and this Gallico roped to his back, straightening under it as lightly as if it were a rolled blanket. They also salvaged a few sheaves of dried fish which all the boat lockers of the *Cormorant* held against emergencies. Thinking of the *Gannet,* Rol smiled grimly, and made a pack for them out of a swatch of canvas, slinging them across his shoulder. The sailors had their knives and cutlasses, Rol the master's pistol as well as Fleam, and there were two full waterskins and some tinderboxes in the party, but aside from that they possessed only the rags they stood up in. When they had mounded up the sand over their murdered comrades they stood about the graves like men amazed, and then their heads came up and all but Gallico stared at Rol for inspiration.

"We make for Ordos, I suppose," he said. "It's three hundred miles as the crow flies." But it did not feel right as he said it. Going to Ordos would not bring him quicker to any revenge.

"There may be somewhere closer," Gallico rumbled. "Northward up the coast from here there is a place where I know we will be welcome. But once we go there, there can be no going back. You should all know that."

"What is this place?" Creed asked, eyes bright.

"Men call it Ganesh Ka, the Pirate City. I have been there in the past. It's a hard road, by land, but shorter than the way to Ordos."

"Pirate City! It's a tale told to children, and drunken landsmen in seafront taverns," Mochran said.

"No. It exists, believe me. But when a man enters the city, he cannot go back—from that moment on he must become a privateer or perish, for no one is allowed to leave unless they take to one of the Black Ships."

"So we must all turn pirate?" Sayed Rusaf said. The oldest of the remaining Cormorants, he was an experienced topman, and might find employment anywhere on the Twelve Seas with ease.

"It is the law of that place," Gallico said. He was watching Rol closely.

"I'll go," Mihal said. He was young enough to perhaps find the idea exciting.

"And I," Mochran agreed. "For my brother's death."

"I will not," Rusaf cried. "The Bionari made a mistake, it's true, and our shipmates paid for it, but we are still alive—no need to throw our lives away as well."

The last of the four original Cormorants was Bartolomew, the hot-tempered youngster from Corso. "How do we know this thing is telling us the truth?" he asked, eyes flashing under a ragged mop of black hair. "It could be he's leading us into some kind of ambush where a few of his mates are laid in wait somewhere."

For the first time Gallico's temper rose. "You stupid little fool—what in the world do you have that is worth stealing? I am offering you a way to find a new life. Trek across the mountains to Ordos alone if you will—the eagles will be feasting on your eyes ere a week is out."

"What does the skipper say?" Rusaf asked. "Rol, what of you?"

Rol looked over them all, his eyes lingering a moment on Creed's transfigured face.

"I believe Gallico. Unlike all of you, I have met him before. If there is a hidden city, he will lead us to it. There is nothing for me now in Ordos or anywhere else; the *Cormorant* was the only home I knew, and now it is gone. I want revenge. I will throw in my lot with the Black Ships."

"We have no choice, then," Bartolomew said bitterly. "We must all turn pirate or else die here out in the waste."

"It is more of a choice than our shipmates had," Rol told him. He looked sidelong at Gallico. "Perhaps something can be worked out when we get to Ganesh Ka, some deal struck. Do not give up hope—we are alive, after all, when so many are not."

They gave in after that, and grudgingly agreed to follow Gallico's lead. There had been no need to ask Elias his opinion; it had been clear to see in his eyes. The little group labored back off the beach and up the cliff to the plateau above once more. They were tired now, having walked through the night, but Gallico insisted they make some distance between themselves and the charred, sunken hulk of the *Cormorant*. "We'll rest at noon," he said, "in the hottest part of the day, and then continue after dark. First we must go back to the spring I dug up, and fill this cask. One cannot dig out water every time one needs it."

So they trudged inland. Rol and Gallico took the lead, then Creed, and behind him Mihal and Mochran. Bringing up the rear were Rusaf and Bartolomew. They retraced their steps under the burning heat of the morning sun, their eyes screwed up against the glare of the light on the pale, naked earth. Rusaf, who had been born in Tukelar, plucked a dry leaf from a tree and held it between his teeth to prevent his lower lip from blistering. The others peeled off their ragged shirts and draped them over heads and shoulders against the blast of the sunlight.

The spring had turned to cracked mud, but Gallico dug it out once more and held the bunghole of the cask under the bubbling water. It was awkward going until they hit upon the solution of emptying their waterskins into the cask and refilling them. By the time the cask was full and their skins also, and they had all drunk as much as they could hold in their swollen bellies, the sun was halfway up the sky. Gallico shaded his eyes and peered north along the coast. The great plateau jutted out into the sea there for ten or fifteen leagues and then broke off suddenly in sheer sea cliffs. On the other side, clear to see even through the gathering shimmer of the heat haze, the Inner Reach bit into the land again in a wide blue firth.

"We are north of Golgos, which is good, because there is a Bionese garrison there," Gallico said. "I'd wager those two cruisers are going to put in there also to refit; our stern chasers mauled them somewhat before they ran us on the rocks. This plain ahead is named the Gorthor Flats; fourteen leagues across, and there will be no water there, but it must be faced. Beyond it is the Firth of Ringill. We must follow its shores northwest, toward the mountains. Across the firth is Ganesh, the ancient land which legend holds was once a fief of the Goliad, but which is now a wilderness. We have a journey of some two weeks before us at least, for Ganesh Ka is much farther to the north."

Rol looked at the desolation of the blasted land about them, a shimmering ochre waste where the only movement was that of wind-reared dust-clouds. "How in the world do armies fight in a place like this?"

"By losing as many men to the heat as to the enemy," Gallico said. "The Goliad is the only real place to land an armament between Ordos and Urbonetto; everywhere else is too mountainous for a baggage or siege train. Plus, if one heads inland there are passes through the Myconians that lead to Myconn itself. Battles have been fought for possession of those passes for time out of mind, with armies of Oronthir and Cavaillon and Armidon and the Mamertine League all seeking to come at Bionar through its underbelly. All have failed. Even a century ago, the Goliad was not the place you see now; it was a rolling savannah, with herds of deer and bison and wild asses. But the grazing of countless army horses and the feet of passing soldiers have stripped the grass from the earth and the wind does the rest. In this part of the world rain comes fast and hard in the autumn of the year, and the rest of the seasons are dry. With no vegetation to protect it, the rain washed the good soil away, and now the wet season brings no life to the place because the life is not there to germinate."

Rol eyed his companion with some wonder. "You seem tolerably well-informed for a pirate."

Gallico grinned. "I like to read."

They walked on in silence after that, their pace steady but slow. Gallico told them to breathe with their mouths closed to keep their tongues from drying out and when they drank he made sure it was a few gulps at a time, no more.

The land fell and then rose again, a long, hard slog in the rippling heat. At the height of the slope Rol looked down on the blinding glare of the Gorthor Flats and thought he saw black figures moving in the heat-shimmer. He pointed them out to Gallico, who nodded.

"Ur-men. They prowl the Flats in packs."

The name brought forth a prickle of memory in Rol's mind and no more. "What are they?"

"Creatures of the wastes, manlike in some respects, but not remotely human. Experiments gone awry, some contend. They are dangerous to one alone, or a small party unarmed, but so long as we keep a good watch out we should hold them at bay."

The Flats began like a white sea lapping round the shores of the rockier hills. They glittered with salt in wide pans, and reflected the heat and light of the sun with pitiless ferocity.

"Rub the hollows of your eyes with dirt. It'll help with the light," Gallico told them, and they used some of their precious water to create a muddy paste which all save the halftroll smeared over their faces.

"There are ruins a few leagues out on the Flats," he went on. "We will march to them and then lie up until dark. Only the Ur-men walk far upon the Flats in daylight; any man who tries will go blind in a few days."

"Is there no way to go round them?" Creed asked.

"We could, but it would take us up into the foothills, fifty or sixty leagues out of our way. I'm hoping we can reach the firth in two marches. The land is kinder after that; we'll have left the

Goliad behind us, and there are woods and rivers; we may even be able to take down some game."

The heat slammed into them like a wave as they ventured down onto the Flats. They screwed up their eyes against the harsh light and the mud in their faces cracked and flaked despite the sweat that was soaking into it. When Rol's palm brushed against the lock of his pistol it burned like the handle of a skillet left over the flame.

The earth was fractured in a million angular cracks, as if the Flats were a shattered, burnt-out mirror the ages had covered in dust. "This was a lake, once," Rol said, "or a lake-bed rather."

"If it was, it was in a time before men were here to see it," Gallico said. He was moving somewhat stiffly, and Rol could see the shine of new blood oozing out of his dressings. He wondered at the endurance of the halftroll.

"Are there many like you walking about in the world?" he asked.

"Not many. Small communities here and there who share similar deformities. I am not part of a different species—I am a man, but one whose frame has been skewed by the potency of the Blood. My parents were not like me, though they would not have been considered human either." He glanced at Rol and seeing his eyes said: "I come from a village in the Myconians, on the Perilar side."

"Hence your knowledge of the Goliad's history."

"It is said that one day the Goliad will be a garden again, and when that happens the Creator will come back to the forsaken earth and give every man a life beyond death. A pretty story, but stories are cheap. I like to find out the truth of things. I have spent days in the Turmian Library in Myconn itself, back in the days when my kind was welcome there. But they say that all the learning in the world is as nothing compared to the archives of Kull, the isle of the Mage-King."

"Who is the Mage-King?"

"You might as well ask the Name of God, or how He made the world. For myself, I think he is a Were, the last of the Ancients. The last angel on earth, you might say."

"Is he evil?"

"I don't know, Rol—no one knows what it is he wants from the world. His agents come and go unseen amongst us. He has no armies, he fights no wars, and yet nations tremble at the mention of his name. I have heard an old man in the Myconians insist that he is merely waiting for some change to come upon the world, after which he will leave his island and walk amongst men again, but the old man was half crazed and half drunk. As I said, stories are cheap."

"Why did you leave your village in the Myconians?"

"The Bionari burned it in one of their habitual forays into Perilar, slew everyone in it. They paid a dear price for their temerity, though; we Folk of the Blood know how to go down fighting, if nothing else. I think the Perilari were glad to see the back of us. As our numbers grow fewer, so men grow more afraid of us." Gallico paused and looked over his shoulder at the remainder of the party. The low hum of aimless talk had ceased, and the Cormorants were eavesdropping without shame.

"The Bionari take a lot upon themselves," Rol said darkly, oblivious.

"They have always been a quarrelsome lot, it's true. But they're in a fix of their own making now."

"How so?"

"This civil war they've started. Arbion and Phidon have declared for the rebel queen, and huge battles are being waged across the Vale of Myconn itself. Last I heard, Bar Asfal had fled the capital to raise more troops in the north."

Rol walked along mutely, his mind jarred into startled silence.

"She has a chamberlain who is also one of her generals, and he speaks Bionese with the accent of Gascar. He calls himself

Canker, and they say he is an assassin. At any rate, several of Bar Asfal's most talented commanders have been killed in odd circumstances."

"What do you know of this rebel queen?"

"Rowen Bar Hethrun she is called, a great beauty, but cold as frost, and a wicked hand with a blade. She's won over many of the nobles through a combination of fear and lust—rumor has it half of Bionar's aristocracy has sampled her charms at one time or another in the past five years. It's how she built up her support to begin with: in the bedchamber. But the strangest thing is that she has the Blood in her, or so it is rumored. Imagine—Bionar ruled by a monarch with Weren blood. God knows, it might be an improvement."

"It might. It might not." Rol felt sick at heart.

"There's something ahead," Creed said, the dust clicking in his throat. "Something out on the Flats."

Gallico shaded his eyes and nodded. "The ruins, and not before time."

Rearing up out of the haze were the crumbling remains of a large building. As they drew closer they could see that it had once been a high tower of some sort. Closer still, and Rol realized with a shock that it was familiar—the shape, or what remained of it, was a direct duplicate of Psellos's Tower in Ascari. Here it had been built upon a plain, not set into the flank of a hill, and he could see the huge unmortared joints of the perfectly sculpted stone at its base. They seemed inviolate, unworn, but as the eye traveled upward their massive courses were disrupted and broken so that the tower looked as if it had been broken off halfway up by the hand of a giant, and all about it the tumbled blocks lay scattered and piled in mounds half buried in blowing dust and sand.

"This was a Weren place," he said.

"Yes," Gallico agreed. "*Turrin Ra,* I have heard it named, which is merely an old way of saying the High Tower."

They drew closer step by weary step, the men eyeing the ruins with a mixture of curiosity and distrust. The sweat had dried into white salted rings upon their clothing, and the light boots and shoes they wore were already flapping upon their feet; they had been made for the timber of a ship's deck, not the raw grind of a trek across a desert.

As they entered the naked gateway of the tower the sun was cut off and they sighed with relief at the blessed shade. The stone of the ruin was cool to the touch despite the heat of the day, and they laid their hands upon it, forgetting their qualms. Gallico led them up a surviving stairway and they found that half of one upper floor had survived more or less intact. Here he bade them stretch out and rest. The company collapsed like a puppet show whose strings have been cut, too tired even to bicker amongst themselves. There were five or six hours until dark, and they fell asleep almost at once, sprawled on the stone, but Rol sat looking out of the perfect archway of one huge empty window, his gaze traveling across the sunblasted Flats to the blue heights of the mountains beyond, pale against an empty sky. Gallico sat with him, blotting the fresh blood from his wounds and studying his face.

"You should sleep. We'll walk all night."

"I'm all right."

They shared a few swallows of tepid water from one of the skins and Rol helped the halftroll bind up his dressings again. The scraped skin was already closing beneath them, and the deep gashes made by the coastal rocks had closed like brown-lipped mouths.

"You heal quickly."

"You and I both, and all who partake of the Blood."

Irritated without knowing why, Rol slumped back down again. "*The Blood.* I wish I had never heard of it. I was a fisherman once, living a small life on a small island."

"Dennifrey. I hear a touch of it in your voice. But you were never going to be a fisherman, Rol; I sense that in you at least. You are here for a reason. It is why I suggested Ganesh Ka. Do you think I would lead these others to it, were it not for you?"

"It's such a special place, then?"

"It is a haven, one of the last for folk such as you and I. My village was another such place, and they burned it. They will not be happy until we are consigned to legend, and the Lesser Men have the world to themselves. Man has always feared what he cannot understand. You can try to bury yourself among them, but you will never succeed."

"I succeeded well enough, these last seven years."

"Is it so long since we drank beer together in Ascari?"

Firelit good fellowship in a smoke-filled tavern. The laughter of men. "Yes. It seems like a whole lifetime."

"You have seen something of the world since then."

"I am—I was—a mariner, nothing more. That is all I wanted out of life."

"But no longer? Well, who knows—you may find something else to occupy you in Ganesh Ka. It, too, is old, and there are folk there who know much of the world past and present."

"A city of pirates and scholars, no less."

"If you like. Now I'm for sleep if you are not. Wake me if you begin to nod—someone must stay alert." And with that Gallico's massive head sank forward on his breast. Within moments he was snoring gently.

The sound of the sleepers' breathing was the only thing Rol could hear. The Flats were concave, though over miles it was hard to realize. The wind might be blowing somewhere up in the washed-out sky but here it was dead and still as the air in a cellar.

Rol wiped sweat from his face, fought the urge to drink more water, and cursed himself for not letting Gallico take the watch. He was exhausted—more than that, he was *worn,* so that the very workings of his mind seemed dulled and leaden. He occupied himself with cleaning the grit and dust out of Riparian's pistol. Retrieving a coil of match from his pocket, he found that it was almost dry despite its submersion that morning. He loaded the weapon—he had but four lead rounds to his name—and, finding his tinder wet, spread the filaments of wool and bark out on the stone to dry. Then he drew Fleam and checked the lustrous blade. It was, had he known it, the exact same storm-shade as his eyes, and there was no speck of rust upon it. He ran his finger down the hollow of the blood channel with something like affection, and then leaned forward slightly and kissed the metal. It was refreshingly cold, and he felt that shiver in his loins as it met his lips, the sort a boy might feel upon glimpsing the nakedness of a beautiful woman for the first time.

"What are you?" he murmured, but the sword was silent, cold. He slid her back in her sheath and felt the hungry disappointment through the hilt.

Something in his brain left off working, however, and when he opened his eyes again it was fully dark. The air was chill and blue about him but the stone of the tower had retained the warmth it had absorbed during the day and was pleasant to the touch. Everyone else was still asleep. But something else was moving, somewhere.

Again—a tiny scrape on the stairs, like someone's foot shifting. Rol rose to his feet with all the stealth he could muster from the rags of Psellos's training, and padded noiselessly to the top of the stairway. It was pitch-black now, though if he looked out of the tall surviving window of the place he could see the paleness of the earth below and, raising his eyes, the hard glitter of the stars. A lighter patch on the world's rim spoke of the rise of the moon to come; it would be a mere sliver, a new moon. There was no breath of air to stir the dust in his throat and when he swallowed it felt as though he had sand coating his tongue.

He looked down the stairway, his night vision soaking up the blackness and making sense of it. There was someone standing at the foot of the stairs. Even his preternatural sight could make out only that it was a man or manlike, short in the legs and long in the arms, the limbs very fine. A shapeless lump of a torso, and a head oddly sunk into the shoulders, almost domelike. No neck to speak of, or any feature where the face should be. But he knew it was watching him. He was not afraid; in fact, he felt the strangest sense of pity.

"Who are you?" he asked.

The thing disappeared so quickly he almost lost track of it. He drew Fleam, the moment of calm broken, and pelted down the stairs. Out of the ruined gateway he ran until the vast bright arch of the night sky was all above him, the welkin ablaze with more light than he had thought stars could make, mare's tails and filigrees of diamond in the black. The Gorthor Flats ran out all around him in a featureless blank, and closer to, the broken fragments of the tower lay in skewed lines and mounds. There was no sign of the visitor and the night air was icy and still.

Gallico appeared at his shoulder, fast and quiet despite his size. "What was it?"

"I don't know. An Ur-man perhaps. I've never seen anything like it."

The halftroll sniffed the air and it came out of his gaping nostrils again in two gray spumes. "Yes, they have been here. Time to go. They may be a while gathering yet."

"Gallico, it was not threatening. And it ran from me."

"To fetch its pack-brothers, you may be sure. They never hunt alone. Come—let's get the others on their feet. The tower is no longer safe."

The party set off across the Flats, cursing the brevity of their interrupted rest and shivering in the cold of the desert night. All but Rol and Gallico found themselves tripping and stubbing toes on the deep cracks of the Flats as they set a fearsome pace northward. It was bitterly cold, and hunger had begun to bite into their strength despite a hurried meal of dried fish, wolfed down on the move. They had a mouthful each of water, gulped down as they half jogged in Gallico's wake.

"What's the rush?" Bartolomew complained. "Is this some kind of race?"

"Yes," Gallico said shortly. "Keep your wits awake and your weapons to hand."

"Who's to attack us out here?" Rusaf complained. "Lizards? Beetles?"

"There," Rol said, pointing. Gallico followed his arm. The flicker of movement was so brief as to be dismissed as a trick of the eye, but he nodded.

"They're coming up to larboard."

"I'd rather stand and await them than have a running fight," Rol said.

"That's what they want, with a small group such as this. Stop for only a few minutes, and they'll use that time to gather in their hundreds. No, they are like wolves. A stalled prey only emboldens them."

"What in the world are you two talking about?" Rusaf hissed.

"The locals," Rol told him with a thin smile. "They're about to pay us a visit."

Ten yards in front of them the cracked planes of dirt reared up like trapdoors in the ground, and out of them swarmed a mass of shadows, noiseless, swift as snakes. Rol had a split moment to take in their features before he had drawn Fleam and she was leaping forward in his grasp with the distinctive whistle that sounded like the laugh of a woman.

They had heads like moles, eyeless, with delicate snouts and snuffling nostrils set at the very tip. Below the heads were wet holes that might have been mouths. Aside from that they were featureless. Their thin arms ended in four digits, all tipped with long claws. Their bodies were gray, lighter on the belly and darker on the back. The backs and shoulders were covered with fine fur, like the stubble of an unshaven man's chin.

They came in from all sides, thirty or forty strong. The Cormorants drew their cutlasses, faces white as bone in the darkness.

"Stand fast," Gallico said. "Make a ring, and do not let them inside it."

The Ur-men circled, uttering a high-pitched ululating warble that hurt the ears. More of their fellows were running and lurching and limping across the Flats now, dozens and scores.

"Should have stayed in the tower," Gallico spat. "This is new to me, these numbers. I have never seen—"

The black ring closed in on them.

The party fought silently, murderously, beating away questing talons, stabbing out with the bright points of their blades. A nick here, a shallow stab there, the sharp, horrified intake of breath as Rusaf saw his forearm laid open from wrist to elbow. Rol edged his way left to close the circle. It was like fighting a gale-flapped thornbush. The Ur-men would move in, dart back, bob and duck and leap up and chance a swing with their claws, then scurry out of the ring to let another in. Rol stabbed out in growing desperation, to meet nothing but empty air. Out of the corner of his eye he saw Gallico's towering frame, fists barreling through the air. The water cask was sliced from his back and fell to the ground behind him. He turned for one moment and the creatures leaped on his back, howling. Others scampered through his legs and pummeled the cask itself, breaking in the timbers with a splash and a splinter. Creed impaled one on the ground, his cutlass bending in the thing's spine.

Fleam sliced off one questing, clawed hand that had come seeking Rol's face, and its owner shrieked, high and awful. It lifted its snout and spat out a gob of liquid, which spattered against Rol's shoulder. He beheaded the creature with one long sweep of Fleam's curved edge, fluid gouting up in two steaming jets from the thing's severed shoulders. The acrid smell of burning made him pause. There was smoke writhing from the shoulder of his tunic. Even as he stared at it, astonished, the pain hit him as the ichor burned through his clothes and seared his skin. He cried out loud. It was as though a hot coal had been dropped inside his shirt.

The creatures were thick as a hedge all about them now, and the party was fighting desperately back to back, cutlasses flickering. Gallico was outside the ring with one of them still clinging to his back, stabbing its claws into his corded muscles again and again so that his blood ran down, and then putting its wet mouth to the wounds and sucking ecstatically. The halftroll twisted, agonized, smashing Ur-men to mangled wreckage right and left. Up and down his huge chest little crackling streams of smoke were writhing and he was bellowing with pain and rage as he fought.

Rol ducked below the swipe of another Ur-man's claws and stabbed Fleam upward through the delicate snout. The steel emerged glistening from the thing's head and he let it slide off the scimitar, booting it aside. The agony in his shoulder was overmastering him; it felt as though his flesh were being burned deeper and deeper, some fire there seeking his heart. He reversed Fleam in desperation and grasped the blade in his scarred hand, then dug the point into his own body, digging deep, seeking the hot mote that was tunneling there. Then he flicked the blade outward, tearing free a gobbet of smoking flesh. The pain was bearable again, that of a normal wound.

He lunged forward out of the ring of mariners, and flailed into the crowded enemy about Gallico. The scimitar sang joyously in his hand and seemed lighter than ever before. He hacked and sliced and slashed with his own blood soaking him from shoulder to thigh, and cried out as he saw Gallico fall to his knees, the halftroll tearing at his own flesh in his agony, ripping away ragged collops of burning meat from his body.

The ring of men fell apart. Rol saw Mihal yanked from his feet to disappear into a scrum of the enemy, legs kicking uselessly. Creed and Mochran were fighting grimly in a little war of their own, and Bartolomew was standing over Rusaf's body with a bloody cutlass in each hand. Gallico was buried under a squirming mass of Ur-men, the ground puddled with his blood.

A light began to shine in the depths of Fleam's blade and in Rol's eyes. They flared white and seemed to smoke without heat. The black desert night was transformed into a capering chiaroscuro of leaping shadows as the radiance grew. Rol cried out, but the sound was strange, too deep for a human chest to hold. His eyes were two holes through which the sun of another world speared its unbearable brightness. The Ur-men hesitated, backed away. Rol's cry grew until there was no vestige of humanity left within it. There was a terrible stink of burnt flesh. Fleam was a spike of pulsing argent that stood vertical one moment, flickering so that it no longer seemed bladelike at all but had the silhouette of something else that shrieked with the fevered laugh of a woman. It came down again in Rol's fist and began to scythe through the Ur-men as though harvesting corn.

To Elias Creed and the others watching, cutlasses momentarily forgotten in their limp hands, it seemed as though Rol grew in stature and his very face changed. In his grip the scimitar steadied and coalesced again until it was a molten bar five feet long which he wielded two-handed, and he towered above them as it snicked and clicked through bone and meat and sinew, scattering body parts and black gore far and wide, dispersing his attackers. They saw a terrible, mirthless rictus on Rol's face, and the light spilled out of his body until it seemed they were watching some towering creature with luminous wings that arced and beat with thunderous concussions high in the air above their heads. All but Creed cowered on the ground, hiding their eyes. The Ur-men gave a collective shriek, and those who could began running as fast as their wiry legs would take them, but the winged furious light followed them and slaughtered them left and right, hovering above the ground and hunting them down by the light of its terrible eyes.

Eighteen

THE GORTHOR FLATS

CREED FOUND HIM HALF A MILE FROM THE FIGHT, having followed the trail of gore and body parts, a dark road of slaughter. It was coming on to dawn and there was a light behind the horizon in the east. Soon the sun would spring up to begin its daily battery of the parched earth.

Rol lay on his face with his sword beneath him. When Creed turned him over he could see the burnt hole in the shoulder of his tunic, but there was no other mark on him. He pulled the charred material to one side, to find nothing greater than a small rose-pink scar on Rol's flesh. He was soaked with black blood that was crackling and dry now, but not another mark was on him. He seemed to be asleep.

Creed rubbed his filthy hands over his face, and then trickled a few drops of water from the skin he carried onto Rol's eyes. They opened, blinking at once, and

Fleam came up defensively, halting a handspan from the convict's nose. "Welcome back to the world," he said quietly.

Rol sat up and seized the waterskin, squeezed a stream out of its nozzle into his mouth. He shut his eyes again and said, "Tell me what happened."

"Mihal is gone—dead, I suppose. Rusaf is hurt, but will live if his wound does not go bad. Gallico . . ." He hesitated. "I do not think he will make it through the day."

The eyes opened again. As they did, the first dawn light sprang swift as an arrow's flight above the flat pan of the horizon, and kindled in them a luminosity, a brightness that had nothing human about it at all. Then the swift-rising sun rode up farther, and they were Rol Cortishane's eyes again, striking, but those of a weary man, no more. Creed took back the skin, corked it, straightened with his own small hurts shouting for attention all about his arms and shoulders.

"We cut the spittle that burned out of Gallico, and bound up what we could, but they have carved his back to bloody rags. He lost more blood than I ever saw any creature lose and live, and they sucked it out of him too."

"Take me to him," Rol said, and he stood up, sheathing the marvelous scimitar. He set a hand on Creed's shoulder and Elias had to make an effort not to cringe from that touch.

"You remember what you did last night?"

"Partly. It happened once before, or something like it." Then he grinned weakly at the expression on Creed's face. "I am not a ghost, Elias, nor a demon either. You need not fear me."

"Well, you saved our lives, at any rate. They'd have slaughtered us all if you—if that hadn't happened."

They walked back to the dark knot of men huddled on the white blazing blankness of the Flats.

"Bartolomew and Rusaf want to turn back for the coast and make for Ordos. They say this place is cursed."

"They are right," Rol said mildly. "But no one will turn back."

Creed studied him as discreetly as he could. It was the same Cortishane he had come to know and esteem in the past few weeks, but there was something different, all the same. Something in the *Cormorant*'s first mate had hardened. Whatever had occurred in the night could happen again—would happen again. Would the white winged light always know friend from foe when it came burning out of this man's eyes?

They murmured and backed away from him as he approached, Rusaf, Bartolomew, even Jude Mochran. Gallico lay at their feet, a felled giant. He turned his head and his eyes blinked on and off.

"We owe you our lives, I think."

Rol knelt beside him, ignoring the others. "Can you walk?"

"I think so. How far is another matter."

"We'll help you."

"Leave him here—there's no way we can support the weight of a thing like that," Bartolomew said hotly. "We must go south—this place is a cursed wilderness. He brought us here on purpose."

"No," Rol said quietly, not lifting his head.

Rusaf, Bartolomew, and Mochran backed away from Rol one step, two. In all their eyes the fear shone stark. Spittle had gathered white at the corners of their cracked mouths. They looked like horses about to bolt.

"You stay with him if you like—you're both monsters together." That was dark-faced Rusaf, voice shaking. "We want no more to do with any of you, or your goddamned pirate city. We're men—decent men, not pirates, or... or... We'll split the water. Fair's fair." He wiped a raw knuckle across his lower lip.

Rol stood up. He was very calm. "You are all going to do as I say. We will continue north, and Gallico is coming with us. We are going to Ganesh Ka."

"Who or what in hell are you to command us?" Bartolomew

exploded. "You're not even the captain—a first mate is all you were. We're not your chattels to be told where to go and when."

Rol strode forward with a blurred swiftness that startled them all. He took Bartolomew by the collar. The youth's eyes flashed white, like those of a calf caught by the slaughterman.

"That may be so, Geygan, but I promise you this: if you do not obey me in this thing I will kill you. Do you understand? I will kill you." This last was said with such quiet intensity that even Creed backed away, hand on the hilt of his cutlass. "Now help Gallico to his feet. The night is gone, so we must march in the day. Elias, you lead. Our course is due north. Bartolomew and Mochran, you will help Gallico. Rusaf, you next. Carry the waterskins. I will be at the rear."

Not another word was said. Gallico heaved himself up, leaving the ground dark where he had lain. Jude Mochran and Bartolomew Geygan supported him one to either side, and the party set off once more. Already the carcasses of the Ur-men were beginning to stink, and glass-blue flies the size of a man's thumbnail were settling on them in clouds.

They stumbled through a baking purgatory of heat. It poured down relentlessly from a shadowless sky and beat up again in reflected waves from the ground. All about them the horizon became a ripple of swimming mirages. Creed fell back down the little column.

"Look," he said, pointing.

Black beetlelike figures moving across the Flats. Impossible to tell how far away, with the torrid atmosphere rippling in between.

"They'll leave us alone for a while, I think," Rol said. He seemed dizzy, and swayed slightly as he walked. Creed's own tongue felt too large for his mouth. He passed it over the cracked skin of his lips.

"We have two half-full skins of water."

"Fourteen leagues, Gallico said the Flats were across. We must do it in two more marches at most."

Creed looked at the trio of Mochran, Bartolomew, and Gallico. The halftroll was taking most of his own weight but his helpers were wearing down fast. "We'll be lucky," he said.

They halted to rest every hour, and Rol supervised the periodic rationing out of the water—a mouthful per man, and twice that for Gallico, no more. Then he and Creed took over from Mochran and Bartolomew, and they continued on their way.

It seemed impossible that the halftroll should still be alive. From the waist up, every inch of his torso seemed ripped and torn in some way, and though these wounds were drying in the sun, the deepest still oozed clear liquid. He spoke little, and his face was a granite clench of agonized determination. Occasionally he stumbled, and his weight bore down on Rol and Creed like that of a sinking hill.

The sun coursed across the sky, and finally approached the featureless horizon in the west. As it did so, it lit in stark silhouette the sharp-peaked ranges of the Myconians, bringing them to life out of dust and haze as though they had sprung fully formed over the brim of the world just that moment, and then it dipped behind them in a matter of minutes, leaving a roseate residue in the west, and the first glitter of the stars.

The cold deepened quickly, at first refreshing, and then debilitating. They kept walking. Rol and Creed had been counting paces for the first half of the day but had lost count in the afternoon as they labored under Gallico's immense arms. Creed thought they might have made some five leagues, but it was wishful guesswork, no more.

Rol allowed the party to sleep for a couple of hours and they lay huddled together on the barren plain, shivering with closed eyes. Creed woke up toward the end of that time to find Rol standing with drawn sword looking south across the Flats. He hauled himself to his feet.

"What do you see?" He had realized by now that Cortishane could see in the dark, and Gallico too.

"They're on the move, but keeping their distance. Small bands of not more than half a dozen apiece. They're afraid of us now."

"Just as well," Creed muttered. He yawned. He thought perhaps the lack of water bothered him less than the others—in the Keutta quarries there had never been a lot to go round. "Shall we wake them?" The others looked corpselike in their exhausted sleep, save that every now and again a flicker of emerald light would peep from under Gallico's eyelids and the pupils within could be seen moving under the skin.

"Give them a minute yet."

"Would you have killed him?"

"Who? Bartolomew?" Rol smiled unpleasantly. "I hadn't thought of it. It was something to say."

Creed studied his face. It was still that of the young, bearded first mate of the *Cormorant,* but something in the eyes had become indefinably colder. He looked away. "They will desert you at the first opportunity. Perhaps not Jude Mochran, but the other two, certainly."

"And you, Elias Creed, convict, pirate, what about you?"

"I will follow you. You are going to the place I want to see above all others. And I have nothing but life to lose." He met the cold eyes squarely. Rol nodded.

"You're like me, then. All right, let's get them up. We need a lot of miles under our belt ere the dawn."

The men ate some fish and drank their meager water ration without speaking, though they all watched Cortishane as though he were some breed of dangerous animal that was padding about in their midst. Gallico seemed in much better condition. He refused their support with one of his old grins, and limped along under his own power. They made much better time as a result. Creed watched the sky and found Gabriel's Fist, then tracked half left until he found the Compass-Star. They followed it north like pilgrims set upon some crack-brained quest. No one spoke, and Cortishane walked at their rear as silently as a ghost, his strange eyes gleaming as they caught the light of the rising moon.

"Have you ever traversed these Flats before?" Creed asked the halftroll.

"Not all the way. I have never been to their heart—I doubt few men have. But I have been some distance in from both north and south."

"Why—why would anyone want to come here? It makes the Keutta quarries look like a garden."

"The Bionari have chased me in here from time to time, or rather I led them. It is a good place to lose people, if you can make good speed and are well provided with water. Not everyone has a mariner's knack for sniffing out the compass points, or for following the stars."

The party walked all night. By the end of that time Gallico was flagging and they had to take turns supporting him again. Rol called a halt just before dawn and they collapsed to the ground as if their legs had been cut from under them.

"I need to sleep," he said quietly to Creed. "Take a watch, will you?"

But Creed was exhausted also. He nodded in and out of sleep like a fever victim, finally succumbing a little before daylight. He was woken some time later when the sun leaped up above the flat eastern horizon and smote his forehead, levering open his crusted eyes and dazzling his fuddled mind. He cursed himself, lurched upright like a stiff-limbed marionette.

"Rol, Gallico," he croaked.

They came awake slowly, fighting their way out of sleep.

"They've gone. They took the water."

The waterskins had been tied to Cortishane's wrist. The lashings had been cut free in the dark. The hard earth held no sign except a few scuffed bootmarks.

"Mochran too?" Rol asked, blinking stupidly.

"All of them. They took the water."

The trio stood up and scanned every direction under the white glare of the morning, squinting. There was no sign of their erstwhile comrades.

"They'll have taken off for the south," Rol said wearily.

"Then they're fools—we're over halfway now. How do they think they'll get past the Ur-men?"

"Perhaps they think them cowed. Perhaps they fear me more. I am sorry about Jude Mochran. He was a good man. Gods of heaven, I slept like the dead. I felt nothing."

"No use crying over it," Gallico said. "They have taken their chance, now so must we. We'll not last another two days without water. We must get off the Flats by nightfall."

They stood, momentarily paralyzed. It would be very easy to lie back down on the ground and bury their heads in the dark of their arms. "Come on, then," Rol said at last.

Creed had marked out their course by the stars the night before with an arrow of flaked earth. They set off now three abreast. In the scant minutes before the heat haze leaped up to dance on the lip of the sky, he thought he saw the blue shade of high land to their front. Then it was just the tantalizing mirage of nonexistent water-shimmer again, the silence of the blasted waste about them. Not a breeze stirred; the very air seemed cowed by the glare of the sun.

They plodded on doggedly all that day, their throats parched into uselessness. Creed staggered like a drunk man, walking at length with his eyes screwed shut against the awful glare, one hand on Gallico's forearm. They did not halt or rest and seemed to have agreed by some form of osmosis that they would walk till they dropped.

And Creed did drop. It felt like flying, like being whirled around in the heat of an oven. He dimly felt his face hit the earth and knew there was grit in his teeth, but was completely detached from the beginnings of his own death. When he opened his eyes he could see nothing but whiteness. A voice said *Drink,* and he felt himself raised up. His lips touched hot flesh, but it was wet and dripping also and he sucked on it without conscious volition. The liquid he ingested was not water, but it allowed his tongue to move against his teeth again. There was something else in that coppery fluid. It seeped into him like a draft of good brandy, but was cool as a fountain on a summer afternoon. The white blindness receded and the stabbing pains in his head faded away. He saw Cortishane leaning over him. He was being cradled like a baby. Cortishane's forearm was dripping blood, and Creed knew now what the taste was. His gorge rose feebly but he had not even the strength to retch.

"What in God's name—"

"Don't speak. Gallico will carry you for a while. It's not long now, Elias."

He was lifted up onto the halftroll's lacerated shoulder and had not the will to protest. It was like perching upon a moving tower. He could see more clearly than before—he felt as though Cortishane's blood had chilled the bubbling heat of his arteries and veins, allowing his mind to cool, to work again.

Their shadows, attenuated and fantastic-looking, streamed out to their right as the sun began descending toward the mountains. The capering haze before them thinned out with the wearing on of the day, and Creed, nodding stupidly, saw something that had not been there before. A different color inserted between the broiling white of the Flats and the deepening sky above them. He stared at it for long minutes while bobbing up and down on the halftroll's shoulder.

"Land ho," he rasped at last, pointing with one corded arm. "Two leagues maybe. Dear God, I see—I see trees."

"I wish you joy of the sight, my friend," Gallico rumbled with something approaching humor. "Where there are trees there is water. We will make it yet."

They stumbled off the Gorthor Flats as it came on to dusk. The white dry-packed earth ended in frozen breakers of stone and piled dirt, and the land rose beyond it with a browner hue, green in places. There were patches of sharp-toothed grass, stunted acacia and live oak, juniper bushes. They staggered uphill like creatures unable to halt in their tracks, this new country dipping and rising under their feet. Stone began to thrust up through the scanty earth, crumbling in avenues and tumbled hillocks. They found flowering things at the base of the rocks, and then heard the liquid rill of running water, sweeter than any music. A bright ribbon of water gliding and flashing between banks of gray stone. They fell to their knees before it, and drank on all fours like beasts.

Nineteen

THE HIDDEN CITY

THE HIGHLANDS OF GANESH WERE GOOD TO THEM. UNtouched, unpopulated, they fairly teemed with game, animals so unafraid it seemed almost a shame to kill them. With the master's unwieldy pistol Rol wounded two plump young bucks badly enough for Gallico to be able to run them down and break their necks. These were gralloched and skinned, and their livers eaten warm and raw by the famished castaways as the halftroll jointed the remainder. Then the trio lay and slept the night through with their feet turned to the warmth of a high bonfire, too exhausted to care who might mark the man-made blaze in the darkness of that vast wilderness. The nights were not so cold here as on the Flats, but still chilly enough to warrant the gathering of grass and heather for bedding and the sheer luxury of a good wood fire to keep the frost from their bodies. They were high up, and when dawn came they could look out on a great panoramic view of the Inner Reach, as grand as kings.

"I see ships," Creed said, looking into the bright fire of the eastern dawn.

"Where away?" Rol asked.

"East-southeast. Three—no, four, ship-rigged and in convoy."

"Men-of-war," Gallico said somberly. "Probably part of the flotilla that pursued the *Adder.* The Bionari are taking an almighty interest in this coast all of a sudden. I wonder if it's anything to do with their civil war."

"This city of yours had best be well hid," Rol told him.

They walked northward along the coast for thirteen days and in all that time they saw no further sign of man or his works. On their right the Inner Reach swept white-tipped to the horizon and on their left the hills rolled in rumpled, rocky succession to the heights of the Myconians, draped with dark forests of pine and poplar, fragrant with wild thyme. Rol buried the master's pistol, having run out of bullets for it, and Gallico fashioned a sling out of deerhide that knocked down rabbits and birds for their nightly meals. They raided birds' nests, nibbled wild sorrel and bracken shoots, and drank from every stream they came across, finally satiating their inordinate thirst. Their wounds healed and the constant walking and short commons pared down the flesh of their bodies until they became tireless creatures of muscle-wrapped bone, at home in the high woods and mist-shrouded crags of this quiet world.

They came upon Ganesh Ka at evening, rounding the bluff of one outflung arm of the mountains that towered above the spear-straight poplars at its foot. There was a gap in this tall buttress of granite, as square and sheer as though cut with a knife, and once through it the land descended steeply to the sea over a mile below. The last sunlight was disappearing behind the Myconians, and below them, purple and blue with evening shadow, was the perfect circle of a deep bay surrounded on all sides by honey-pale cliffs about which thousands of seabirds circled and wailed. Its only outlet to the open sea was a narrow gap in the circle to the east, scarcely half a cable wide.

But on the landward side the cliffs were less steep, and seemed to have been broken off short. They had been hewn back and shaped in a way that made it hard to guess whether their fashioning was the work of man or a freak of nature. Tunnels or caves riddled them at sea level, but there were no signs of life in those black-shadowed holes.

Slender blade-shaped towers of darker rock were perched on the crest of the cliffs like stone-sculpted poplars, at once part of and distinct from the landscape about them. The tallest of these reared up twenty or thirty fathoms from base to sharp tip and they were built in orderless clusters that had nonetheless a pleasing kind of half-glimpsed symmetry about them. Looking closer, Rol saw that about the base of these towers was a talus of deeper shadow, coigns of light and dark—streets and roadways. If they had an overall pattern, then the knots and copses of trees that grew amongst them obscured it. Overall the place had an eerie, forbidding quality, like a monument erected to forgotten gods. Though there were no lights in the towers, no movement in the tree-clogged streets, Rol could smell woodsmoke, carried past them by the onshore breeze.

"Ganesh Ka," Gallico said with satisfaction and a weary kind of relief.

"It looks deserted." Rol frowned. If truth be told, it did not look like a city at all, more a geological formation, an immense abstraction thrown up on a whim by the Creator.

"Come full dark, you would see it come to life with lights, but only on the landward side. The cliffs are tunneled deep, and could house many thousands with ease. Most choose to live in the towers."

"How many live here?" Creed asked. As he spoke, he saw the flicker of lamps being lit far up in the spines of the towers, tiny yellow gleams dwarfed by the massiveness of the stone. It was an unsettling sight, like seeing movement in the skin of a megalith. The windows must be so deep-set as to be almost invisible.

"Some thousands," Gallico said. "It varies, depending on how many ships are at sea. The tunnels at the base of the cliffs lead to a vaulted underground harbor with wharves of solid stone. Fifty men-of-war could tie up there with ease. The whole city is built inside the circuit of a half-drowned crater, formed in some past catastrophe of the ancient world."

The moon was rising, well on the way to becoming full. Out at sea a band of translucent pink cloud was smeared across the eastern skyline and the light was climbing red up the pinnacles of Ganesh Ka's towers whilst below the sea grew dark with the onset of night. More lights were kindled in those tall spires of rock, and as the day dwindled the lights stood out alone in the gathering dark, a spangled tracery soaring up out of the sea.

"It's beautiful," Creed breathed. He looked like an exile within sight of home, his face transfigured. "I have dreamed of this day." His voice choked and he bent his head. Gallico laid one great paw lightly upon his shoulder.

"The work of the Ancients, yet again," Rol said, oblivious. "I am to wander from one Weren relic to another, it seems." He turned to his companions, cold eyes unreachable. "Well, let us go down."

There had been a wall once, more a demarcation than a defense, but this had crumbled and was now little more than a rockery for dense thickets of lavender and juniper and a few stunted olive trees. They clambered over it without difficulty and found themselves in the skeleton of a town. Roofless walls delineated narrow guttered streets. Doorways opening into nothingness, windows of blackness. Rol was at once reminded of the cavern below the foundations of Psellos's Tower where his former life had come to ruin. The same perfect masonry, utterly devoid of any life or sign of use.

A dog barked somewhere and shattered the silence of the shadowed streets. Rol could smell rotting food, ordure, burning wood with the tang of resin in it. The trio tramped down the street like ghosts surrounded by a world they could not see, only hear and smell.

And halted as a band of shadows became solid before their eyes, materializing out of the side streets with no sound to mark their appearance except the click of metal and scuff of leather on stone.

"Who goes?"

Gallico grinned, his green eyes gleaming. "Who in merry hell do you think, Miriam?"

"A face like that could only have been made the once; God does not repeat His mistakes." The speaker stepped forward. She was a tall, lean woman with a long face above which sprouted an untidy thatch of bright-colored hair. She smiled, revealing a wide gap between her front teeth. It gave her speech a lisping quality, though her voice was melodic as a harper's. In her hands she held a long-barreled musket, a weapon Rol had seen only once or twice before in his voyaging. Her clothes were of worn buckskin, as were those of her companions. They all edged forward now behind her, and there was the gleam of more musket-barrels.

"Hold hard there a second," Miriam said, raising one white bony hand. "You we know, Gallico, but who are these followers of yours? Been collecting vagabonds on your travels? What about old Woodrin, and the rest of the Adders?"

Gallico's face closed. "All dead. These two are my friends. I will vouch for them with my life. One is Mathuw Creed's son, the other a mariner from Dennifrey. They saved me when the

Adder was wrecked, but the Bionari torched their ship, and we walked across the Gorthor Flats to get here."

A murmur of talk behind Miriam. Her eyes widened. "So? The Bionari are a busy crowd of late. Gallico's word is enough for me. Come, and be welcome to Ganesh Ka."

Miriam left the rest of her band at the wall and led them downhill into the ruined city proper. All about him now, Rol could hear the voices of a multitude, but apart from Miriam and her fellows he could see no sign of the inhabitants. Looking up, he saw that the towers above were riddled with lights, but only on the landward side. To the east they presented a face of blank stone. The streets themselves were an empty maze; the more so since the buildings that enclosed them were open to the sky. This was later construction, not the consummate masonry of the towers, and was choked with tumbled stone and broken blocks.

He caught the woman Miriam staring at him as he lowered his eyes from the towers. She held his gaze coolly for a second, then looked away.

"We'll go to the square. There's a good gathering there tonight, because Artimion's *Prosper* has just come in, looking as if Ran has been using her for a toothpick, I might add. You are not the only ones to have had a run-in with the Imperials lately. We've the *Albatross* and the *Swallow* on the wharves, too, come a-running with their sheets flying, tails between their legs and twelve-pound cannonballs rolling in their scuppers. They won't be fit for sea again this side of midsummer."

"This coast must be getting crowded," Gallico said.

"Aye. We'll have the faint-hearts and grandmothers up on their hind legs tonight, you mark my words. Something is up in the palaces of the world, and they'd like to take it out on us for want of an easier enemy."

"How long have you been in this place?" Rol asked Miriam.

"Since my master's ship was taken by Artimion and the

Seasnake. Ten years ago if it's a day. God bless that old brig, she's on the bottom now."

"I mean everyone—how long has Ganesh Ka been a haven for pirates?"

Miriam stopped in her tracks and looked Rol up and down. "This cold-eyed friend of yourn is free with his insults, Gallico." The musket-barrel came up. Her own eyes were hazel, hot and bright.

"He's still learning, Miriam," the halftroll said, pushing down the weapon's muzzle gently. To Rol he said: "We do not like the term *pirates* here in the Ka. We're privateers, if you must call us anything."

"My mistake." He held Miriam's gaze and some momentary tussle of wills was set aside. She smiled.

"Whatever you think of us, friend, you are one of us now, like it or not."

They resumed their way downhill. "Twenty-five years or so," Miriam said, "that's how long we *pirates* have rattled around in this old mausoleum. The irony is, I've heard tell it was a Bionari, an Imperial, who set it up, come here fleeing his betters."

A tunnel-mouth opened in the ground before them, stone steps leading down and firelight somewhere at the bottom of the darkness. Miriam extended a hand and leaned on her musket. "Do come in."

Rol counted sixty steps. At their foot the tunnel-mouth opened out into a wide cavern or carved vault at least fifty fathoms wide and thirty feet from roof to ceiling. Fires burned on raised hearths in the middle of the space within, and all about them hundreds of people came and went. The air was thick and warm, stinking of close-packed humanity and woodsmoke and roasting meat. Rol's eyes smarted and the fug seemed almost unbreathable after the cold, clear air of the Ganesh highlands.

"The square," Miriam announced grandly. "Or so we call it.

The gods know what the Ancients used it for; they seemed to like rock over their heads, at any rate. Eat and drink as you please—the *Prosper* took a Mercanter wine barque before she was mauled by the Imperials and there's fifty tuns of the stuff floating around—the best Auxierran you could wish for. I'll tell Artimion you're here."

She stalked off, a willowy, russet-haired shape with the swagger of a longshoreman about her.

"A city?" Rol said. "It's a squatters' camp. Who's in charge?"

"The ship captains," Gallico told him without meeting his eyes. "Without them we'd be down to flint axes and bows. Do not judge us too harshly, Rol—these are humble folk for the most part, many of them freed slaves or convicts like Elias here. We're not setting ourselves up as one of the powers of the world." His eyes gleamed dangerously.

Rol set a hand on Gallico's massively thewed forearm. "I know. I am sorry." Perhaps more of Psellos's training remained in him than he had thought. Or perhaps he had expected something different. This was no legendary city—it was a bolt-hole of refugees.

They joined the crowd about one of the fires and were given venison and roast hare to eat and a plump skin of wine. Gallico was slapped and hailed and hooted at and the numbers around the three castaways grew as news of their presence spread. Soon there were three- or fourscore packed tight around them, squatting on their haunches and gnawing meat from greasy bones, tossing back beakers of dark wine and laughing and talking all at once. Gallico made no mention of their ordeals yet somehow managed to make a tale of his adventures since last leaving the city—a tapestry, a bright story without shadows. It was a romance of half-truths and imagination, but it was what these people needed, Rol realized. Their lives were cut too near the bone to allow otherwise. Watching them, he was reminded of nothing so much as the kitchens of Psellos's Tower, and the scrum of kitchen scullions competing for scraps after one of the Master's grand dinners. These people were of all ages except for the very old and the very young. They were dressed in cobbled-together rags and half-cured animal skins for the most part, though some sported incongruously fine attire edged with lace, or stitched with pearls, no doubt part of some ship's stolen cargo.

A girl wormed her way through the malodorous press and sat herself by Rol's elbow. No more than ten or eleven, she had disturbingly mature eyes. He levered her hand gently out of his crotch and looked appealingly at Gallico.

"Now, Jenra, none of that. Give him a kiss and have done."

She tugged down Rol's face and planted a kiss on his lips, then smiled a beautiful vacant smile and curled up beside him, asleep in minutes.

Gallico's bestial face was ill suited for compassion, but his eyes burned. He patted the sleeping girl's golden head as though it were that of a dog. "Jenra spent some time as a plaything of Bionese infantry. She was sold onto a Mercanter slaver, and liberated by Artimion. He crucified the captain of the ship that carried her, and fed the crew to the sharks. I think he was merciful."

The girl whimpered in her sleep and an older woman with a ravaged face lifted her and took her away, crooning softly.

"All of these folk have tales like it to tell," the halftroll went on relentlessly. "This is the continent of Bion we are on now, not the Seven Isles, or the Mamertines. Man took his first steps here, on Bion, and it's said by some he will limp his last here also."

"In the wide world, when one thinks of Bion, it conjures up a picture of the old empire, of fabled armies and glorious battles," Rol said. "I had no idea the Bionari were still like this."

"When they find the time," Gallico grunted. He nudged

Creed. "Hi, master convict, don't be too free with the wine just yet. The night is young."

Creed wiped his lips. He had not uttered a word since entering the city. "Elias," Rol said. "You're all right?"

Creed nodded, but his eyes were suspiciously bright. "I've not drunk Auxierran in over eleven years. I have found my way to the only place in the world where I am free of looking over my shoulder for the overseer's whip. This night I will drink whatever I can hold." But he did not sound like a man intent on celebrating; more like one trying to forget.

Miriam came elbowing through the throng with her musket held over her head. Beside her was a black barrel-shaped man in salt-stained leather with the rolling walk of one lately come off the sea. The crowd made way for the pair, calling out ribald greetings. They halted in front of Rol.

Miriam's companion stared at him frankly. He had a face dark as wet rawhide, a wide nose and full, folded lips, but his eyes were an icy blue that seemed to take light from the fire and hold it writhing in the pupils. With a start, Rol realized that this man had the Blood in him. His eyes reminded him of Rowen's—there was a cold implacability about them.

"I am Artimion. Gallico, let us go elsewhere," the man said, his gaze not unlocking Rol's for a second. "There are things to say that cannot be said here." One hand rested on a curved short-sword at his belt, the fingers thick as sausage.

"Bring your friends."

Artimion had a room farther down inside the hollowed-out cliffs that butted onto the bay. It had a wide window, glassless, but otherwise perfect in the sculpted stonework of its construction. It might have been set in place just that morning. A fire burned in an equally wide hearth, logs hewn out of Ganesh's illimitable forests. For furniture there was a table upon which olive oil lamps burned, and a series of three-legged stools. A sea-cloak unfurled upon a pile of heather and brush served as a bed and a cross-staff was propped up in one corner. The moon was high and white and cast a silver-speckled track across the bay beyond the window. Rol stared at it, at the almost unbroken barrier of the sea cliffs in their caldera. He could smell sea salt in the wind. It seemed like a breath from another world. Here, at least, he could feel the sea air on his face.

"A fine view, fit for a prince," he said.

Artimion did not reply. He had set a series of clay mugs on the table and was pouring wine into them. Alongside stood a fine goblet of beautifully chased silver. This he gave to Gallico, though the thing looked far too fragile to be gripped in the halftroll's vast taloned fist. Gallico lowered himself cross-legged on the floor but did not touch his wine. Creed sat staring owlishly into the fire and Miriam remained standing by the door, leaning on the muzzle of her musket. Rol moved away from the window. For some reason he felt as though there was danger in the room, and his hand dropped automatically to Fleam's cold hilt.

"Drink with me," Artimion said, and held out two clay mugs brimming dark.

They drank together, their eyes never leaving one another's face. Rol knew that this man was the ruler of Ganesh Ka, as surely as Canker had ruled Ascari.

"I knew Mathuw Creed," Artimion said casually, not looking at Elias. "He was a wastrel, a whoremonger, and a liar. He cheated at dice, and stole other men's women. He reveled in cheap finery and could not hold his drink." As Elias raised his head, blood filling his face, Artimion smiled at him. "He was my friend. As his son, you are most welcome here. I drink to his memory." And he did so. After a confused moment, Elias did likewise. The wine trickled incontinently over the black and gray of his brindled beard.

"And now you," Artimion said, his eyes sharpening their cold light. He smiled again, this time with no trace of humor. "You with the Blood staring out of your eyes. What in the world am I to make of you?"

"Artimion—" Gallico began.

"Hush, Gallico. I must make up my own mind here. I have no doubt this man is your friend, that he has behaved admirably, that he is a true companion. But he is here in our home with some cloud hanging over his head. I know it as sure as I stand here. Of the five of us in this room, three have the Blood in them, but in this fellow it runs perilously close to true. I can smell it."

Miriam blew casually over the muzzle of her musket, a hoarse mote of sound. Rol relaxed, hands hanging wide of his sides. He began to breathe deeply, listening to Fleam's hungry voice. Automatically, his mind mapped out the position of everything in the room. There was almost a joy in it.

"You have been trained," Artimion said. "By whom, I wonder?"

"I am a mariner," Rol told him. "Like you." Why this feeling of danger, the creeping closeness of the walls closing in on him—too many people around, the fire too bright? He began to sweat.

Artimion nodded. He set down his wine. "Everyone who comes to Ganesh Ka has left something behind or is fleeing something—it is hard to tell one from the other at times. There is no shame in it. But you, Rol Cortishane, have brought with you that which you are trying to leave behind."

"And what might it be?"

"The blood in your veins, for one. You are not to be blamed for that—many with the Old World in their flesh wish to ignore it, or even cut it out in some kind of exorcism or other. But the thing is, I have been talking to a man, a man with a feather in his hat, and he has offered me a huge amount of money—a ransom in ryals—if I will but bring him news of a young man named Rol with the Blood bright and strong in him, trailing a past as dark as his shadow. This man was named Canker, and he is the right hand of she who would set herself up as queen of all Bionar. I see that name is known to you and that you are the Rol he named."

Fleam slid out of her scabbard with the scrape of ice on wood. There was a light in her that gleamed pale and yet illuminated nothing. The blade hissed like a cat.

The lock on Miriam's musket snicked back with a well-oiled click in reply. The long barrel pointed now directly at Rol's heart.

Gallico stood up, the silver goblet clinking to one side. "What in the hell is this?" Creed sprang to his feet beside the halftroll and drew his cutlass, swaying. Artimion ignored them both.

"How do you know Canker?" Rol asked, to gain time and because he was genuinely curious.

"We were in the Guild of Thieves together at one time, upon Corso. Yes, I was a Featherman in my youth, before I found the sea."

"In our youth we all do things we regret later."

Artimion laughed, an odd, snapping sound. "By God's breath, you are right there. And I am no longer a youth." Now he deliberately took up his cup and drank deeply from it. "I am not a betrayer either. Put up your sword, Rol Cortishane. Drink with me again and fear nothing. You are safe here—from us at least." He jerked his head. "Miriam, put down that damned contraption before somebody gets hurt."

Rol stood irresolute for a second—Fleam quivering and eager in his fist—and then he looked at Gallico and Creed, and sheathed the hungry edge of the sword. "I still do not understand," he said, not touching the wine.

"*Mine enemy's enemy is my friend,* it is said. I have been making contacts with the rebels on this last trip, and Ran knows I was startled enough to find that my old cellmate Canker is now chamberlain to the woman who may well win Bionar for herself. I have made an alliance with them—why should I not? But the king's forces have got wind of it, and now there are warships gathering on the shores of Ganesh." Artimion's face grew sober. "I have backed the winning side, I am sure of that, but the winning side are up in the mountains and midlands of Bionar. The losers are out there in the Reach in their floating argosies, and are hungry for blood."

Despite his claims, Rol knew that Artimion was not done choosing sides yet. The black man's face was smiling, but something about it spoke of hidden decisions. Deliberately, he sipped at the wine in his cup. Miriam had set down her musket but had her long fingers about the hilt of a throwing knife at her waist. Rol smiled. If there was one thing he knew well, it was the way of a throwing knife.

And if Canker wanted news of him, then it was because Rowen had bade him seek it.

"Fair enough. But what, then, is my place in the game?" Rol asked equably. "If you will not give me up for this king's ransom, then you must have something else in mind for me."

Artimion looked at him quizzically. "I suppose I do. I am offering you the chance to stay here and be a captain. You will help these people around you—you will safeguard Ganesh Ka as I have done these twenty years. Cortishane, you are welcome here." He smiled again, with no whit of warmth in the gesture. "Is that so hard to understand?"

Of course it was. Who gave away anything without asking something in return—especially someone in power? But Rol nodded nonetheless.

"Excellent. I accept."

Twenty

THE *REVENANT*

I AM LIVING IN A TOWER ONCE MORE, ROL THOUGHT. IT must be my fate.

There was room and to spare in the city for all, and Rol had chosen his living quarters quite deliberately. They were close to the harbor tunnel but high enough up one of Ganesh Ka's strange towers to ensure that few would ever feel the need to walk past his door.

Not that he had a door. Grand though the apartments might be in a skeletal, resonating way, they were wholly bare. A flap of deerhide closed his rooms off from the dark passage beyond, whilst a bolster stuffed with heather was his bed. On the mantel of the vast hearth a clay lamp burned smokily, flapping shadows about the naked stone of the walls. There were no other furnishings as yet. Creed had a room one level down but Gallico lived somewhere close to the wharves of the underground waterfront.

"There's a communal firewood pile near the foot of the next tower," Creed said, entering with an armload of faggots. "But we can only light fires at night lest the smoke be seen by the Bionese cruisers. It's coming on to summer anyway." He dumped his load by the cavernous fireplace and looked about him. "I still think somewhere lower down by Gallico's rooms would have been better. This place echoes like some lofty tomb."

"It's too busy down there, like struggling through a goddamned bazaar," Rol said irritably, hauling off his boots one by one.

"Anyone would think you were avoiding the common herd, Cortishane," Creed said, eyes dancing.

"I do my best, but they follow me with piles of firewood."

"Ah, but we all help out one another here, don't you know? Some are hunters, others are choppers of wood and haulers of water, whilst at the top of the tree are the mariners, who bring in the little luxuries that make life worth living."

"Is it what you thought it would be, Elias?"

Creed picked at the bark on a beech log. "I suppose not. But it's better than Keutta."

"It seems to me that our friend Artimion's word is the law about here, and what's more, he begins to fancy himself a power in the world. He's mistaken there."

"How do you know?"

"If I know anything, then—then this rebel queen is only using him as a means to distract her enemies. And how big a distraction can it be? A few lightly gunned privateers who cannot even hope to take on men-of-war in their own backyard. No, Artimion is setting these people up for a fall, Elias."

Creed stared at him, frowning. "Perhaps he thinks to bargain."

"I believe he does."

"With what?"

Rol smiled dourly. "My precious hide. The rebels want it, Artimion has it."

"You think he would do that?"

"Never trust anyone who has responsibilities beyond his own skin. Anything can be rationalized when it is for the general weal."

"He said he'd find you a ship."

"My grandfather once promised me a pony. I believed him, but I was a child then."

Creed threw his hands up. "So what do we do?"

"*We?* Elias, we have come to your journey's end. I don't claim any loyalty from you or anyone else."

"You have it nonetheless."

"And if I don't want it?"

Creed's reply was cut short by a clatter in the passageway, and then ducking in through the doorway and throwing aside the flap came Gallico.

"By God, you hide yourself well, Cortishane. Are you allergic to company?" The halftroll had a large seabag of weathered canvas in his arms. He dumped it on the floor and flexed his scarred arms.

"What's this?"

"Shipmates must stick together. I'm moving house, taking the rooms opposite Elias."

Rol stood up. "What is this, a conspiracy? Damn it all, Gallico, if I wanted neighbors I'd have taken a cubbyhole alongside that carnival downstairs. And since when have we been shipmates?"

"I speak metaphorically. I, like you, am without a ship for the moment, and I pick my captains carefully." He lowered his voice. "Artimion is a good man, but he has many concerns above the heads of the likes of us. I would feel better if Elias and I messed below—that way anyone coming to see you must first get past us."

Rol held the halftroll's gaze steadily. "Very well, then. It seems I am to be burdened with the pair of you. We'll get settled in later." He bent and began pulling on his boots once more. "Gallico, take us to this much-lauded harbor of yours. I want to see what floats there."

"Precious little at the moment."

"Nonetheless. Somehow or other, I intend to find us a ship."

The stone of the sea cliffs had been hollowed out into nothing less than a warren, though one constructed on a vast scale. A series of ramps led down a gentle incline into the gutrock, the roadway as smooth as a dinner table. They passed a stream of people coming and going, some pushing handcarts laden with timber, others rolling empty casks downhill with a rattling thunder that jabbed at the temples. Rol saw a gang of sweating, cursing men easing a light culverin on its carriage down the slope, and Gallico stepped in to give them a hand as it threatened to slip free of its tackle.

The tunnels opened out into an incredible space, a cavern so large it had its own air currents. Light came in from a series of sea gates, enormous arches cut out of the stone on the far side, each tall enough to admit a fully rigged ship. Long moles of stone extended out into the waters within the place, and tied up at these were half a dozen vessels of various rigs. These moles and the wharves they ran out from were piled high with all manner of cargoes, and crammed with men and women loading and off-loading, provisioning, hauling on dockside cranes, heaving sacks and barrels and generally creating a picture of chaotic industry.

Behind the wharves there were dry docks with spring-loaded doors of stone that seemingly still worked. Around these were clustered scores of shantylike huts of wood and hide warmed by a series of high bonfires. There was a heavy smell of smoke, and Rol saw women manhandling long poles upon which fillets of ablaroni hung brown and brittle. Others were stretching deerskins on wooden frames and scraping them clean and yet more were sewing nets and gutting fish. A layer of rubbish covered the perfect stonework of the place. Fish bones, scraps of rope and wood, discarded lengths of rawhide. The whole place was nothing less than a manufactory for the convenience of ships.

"What's moored at the moment, Gallico?" Rol asked. "With your head up there you can see better than I."

"A few fishing smacks, off-loading. Artimion's *Prosper,* a brigantine, and then the *Albatross* and the *Swallow,* two big schooner-rigged pinnaces."

"Are there many more at sea?"

"I know that Jan Timian's *Osprey* is still out, and Marveyus Gan's *Skua.* A few more I can't recall."

"You burn the ships you capture, do you not?"

"Mostly, though if they're handy craft we'll board a prize crew and bring them in. The average merchantman is too slow for our liking, and draws too great a draft to make it up to the wharves. We never moor vessels outside the ship-cavern; it's too risky."

"So much for the chances of a ship going begging. Let's walk about, now we're here. I've never seen so many so busy at one time."

They made slow progress through the crowds, for everyone knew Gallico and made it their business to wish him good day. The halftroll showed Rol and Creed the magazine, where the store of powder and shot was kept. Rol studied with interest a set of a dozen twelve-pounder sakers beautifully forged in long-barreled bronze, taken from the hold of a Bionese munitions ship. The magazine was guarded by a pair of Miriam's musket-armed compatriots, the closest Ganesh Ka came to regular soldiers. They greeted Gallico brightly but reserved cold stares for Rol and Creed.

"Unfriendly fellows," Rol said as they left.

"Miriam likes to pick the sober ones for her militia, and there's a waiting list to get in."

"Where did the muskets come from?"

"Same place as the sakers. Bionar has armed us nicely these last few years, though the city is low on good powder. We tried making our own, but it was poor-grained, unstable stuff. There are ancient lead mines in the hills, though, so we smelt our own shot."

They wandered their obstructed way toward the rear of the cavern and the dry docks. In one of these a mastless hulk floated in scum-thick water and rats skipped about her decks. Intrigued, Rol boarded her over a narrow gangplank for a closer look.

"What is this?"

"An old Bionese dispatch-ship. She was badly mauled in the taking, some five years ago now—though not so badly as she mauled three of our vessels—and she's rotted here ever since. We cannibalize her for the wood; she's built of Kassic teak, black timber that's hard as iron and as difficult to work; but it lasts forever."

Rol ran his hands up and down the hulk's side, feeling the heavy grain under his palms. The scar on his hand tingled oddly, and he felt a momentary thrill, but his face did not change. "What do you think she would gauge?"

"She's bigger than most privateer craft. Three hundred tons, I'd say."

"Let's look below."

"Rol, she's been gutted time and time again. What's left is probably rotten and worm-bored."

"Indulge me, Gallico."

The companion ladders were long gone so they dropped through the gaping main-hatch and made their way aft, Creed groping in the darkness behind them and cursing under his breath. "We're not all cat-sighted wonders."

"There's light ahead," Rol told him. "They made a clean sweep of the orlop anyway; that's the stern windows."

They came up against the stern locker and looked over the heavy mantels of the windows. Turning back, Rol saw the noble sweep of the ship's shape loom out before him in the dark. All the interior compartments had long been stripped away and he could clearly see the graceful lines of her construction, and the massiveness of her ribs.

"How was she rigged?"

"Eh? Oh, ship-rigged, I think. A lateen on the mizzen. Blast you, rat." The halftroll kicked out at an overfriendly rodent.

Rol nodded, eyes shining. "Gentlemen, we have found our ship."

"You're jesting," Gallico said in disbelief.

"Have you seen her scantlings, or looked at her knees? You couldn't push a knife blade into them, they're so solid. She's been stripped, yes, but what remains is sound—I'd bet a king's ransom on it. Let's check out the hold."

They trooped to the orlop hatch and peered into the blackness below. There was water there, rats swimming through it.

"See? She's got a fathom in her if it's an inch," Gallico said.

"We'll rig pumps and get it out." Rol stamped his boot on the deck timbers. "I'll bet you anything you like it's nothing more than her normal workings—there's no real leak in her, or her decks would have been awash long ago. A dispatch-runner, you say? But she's built like a man-of-war."

"She's old, sixty or seventy years at least. They built heavier vessels in those days, and the Kassic teak forests are long gone."

"Those sakers in the magazine—anyone have a claim on them?"

"They're too heavy for any vessel of the Ka. Artimion was thinking of rigging them up on the clifftop as a shore battery, but it would be a hell of a job getting them up there."

"This ship could bear them," Rol said, smiling. "Damn it, Gallico, this is the one."

The halftroll rubbed his chin. "The work involved would be fantastic."

"Have you more pressing employment?"

"What about a crew?" Creed asked. "A vessel like this, with twelve of those guns, would need... say sevenscore men, if she's to be run man-of-war fashion."

"Less than that," Rol said. "We'd only man one broadside at a time. No, I'd undertake to sail her with a company of a hundred, if they were the right seamen."

"A hundred men," Gallico said thoughtfully. "Well, there are mariners aplenty here in the Ka, but you will need gunners, carpenters, blacksmiths—a shipwright if there are any major defects in her hull."

"Then we'll find them. Today. Gallico, you know every ragamuffin about this place. You are going to be our recruiting sergeant. I want artisans first, carpenters as you say, but plenty of willing backs for the donkey work too. Anyone who works on her will be eligible to be picked as crew."

"You're liable to annoy the other captains, if you go poaching experienced men off the wharves."

"Too bad."

They came at first out of curiosity, and because it was Gallico. Many of the more experienced sailors took one look at the hulk and turned away again, shaking their heads and laughing, but enough were unemployed and bored and sufficiently intrigued to remain, and form work parties under Rol's direction. He poached supplies and equipment from the wharves—few men would argue with Gallico when he breezed in with a dozen others at his back and demanded pitch, oakum, leather-hosed pumps, coils of cable, sailcloth, adzes and saws and hammers and ten-inch spikes. A cornucopia of naval stores built up on the dock about the hulk and within three days there were thirty people working on her—but they were common sailors and curious landsmen, no more. Many were handy with a saw or a handspike, but Rol needed specialists, and a forge.

They drained the dry dock first, so it lived up to its name, and had an unpleasant time propping up the hulk's sides so she would not tip over in the evil-smelling ooze the departing water revealed. Her rudder was gone, and she settled on her keel with a rending groan that had Rol's heart in his mouth as he waited for her to hog, or, worse, break her back entirely. But the Kassic teak held firm and a series of custom-hewn baulks wedged her tightly in the dock on all sides so that she stood upright as a model ship yet to be inserted in its bottle.

It took them eleven hours, watch on watch, to pump out the hold, and in the bilge they found the skeleton of a tall man with his armor rusting about his bones. This rattled many of the more superstitious of the workers, until Rol had the thing set up on a stake at the dockside, the empty sockets of its skull staring at them as they worked around the hull. The skeleton became a mascot of sorts, and created a sort of grim camaraderie among those who labored there.

The hull timbers were remarkably sound. Whatever was in the water of the docks, it discouraged *teredo,* the wood-boring worm that was the death of ships. Creed raided the wood stores of the city for deck planking and fittings and at the same time had experienced men out in the hills looking for the largest and straightest tree trunks they could find, for no mast in the stores was big enough to fit the butts of the hulk.

Miriam visited the dockside on the fourth day with two of

her militiamen beside her. She looked over the swarm of men and women working on the hulk with a raised eyebrow, and asked where she might find Cortishane.

Rol was belowdecks aft, drawing rusted spikes from the transom timbers whilst about him Creed and several others were levering the salt-rotted rudder gudgeons loose. The hulk was iron-sick, for not enough copper had been used in her construction and parts of her hung together more through luck and stubbornness than anything else. He edged out of the tight space about the transom, wiping his rust-orange hands and frowning, to find Miriam squatting on her heels behind him, her musket slung shining on her back.

"Artimion wants a word."

"I'm busy."

She blinked. "You've been appropriating a lot of things that are not yours, Cortishane. The least you might do is answer to the man for your actions."

"I thought we held everything in common in this place," Rol told her with a feral grin. She backed a foot, then steadied. "You have a monster's eyes."

"Yes. It broke my mother's heart. Where is he?"

"On the dock." And as Creed rose to join Rol she said: "Cortishane alone."

"It's all right, Elias," Rol said, and he followed Miriam up on deck, straightening with a groan and knuckling the base of his spine.

Artimion nodded curtly in welcome. "You have found a project, it seems."

"It's coming along. I'm still short of a few things, though. People mostly."

"What exactly are you hoping to achieve, Cortishane?"

"I'm bringing a ship back to life. A good ship, better than any you have tied up at the wharves."

Artimion's eyes flashed coldly. "You take a lot upon yourself. Less than a week in the city and you are setting yourself up as some kind of captain."

"I thought that was the general idea."

"How long have you had at sea?"

"Long enough." Rol met Artimion glare for glare.

"And you have commanded a man-of-war, have you?"

"I've smelt powder, if that's what you mean. And I've fired great guns before."

"That's hardly the same."

"It'll have to do."

Artimion looked about at the gaggle of workers on the dockside who were listening, some covertly, some openly. "Walk with me," he said.

They ambled away from the dockside toward the busy wharves beyond and the blinding white arches of the sea gates. Men nodded at Artimion as he passed, without speaking. Rol saw respect in their eyes but not a great deal of affection; a far cry from their reception of Gallico, who was universally loved.

Artimion seemed to have read his mind. "Without the support of Gallico you would not have had a single pair of hands at work on that hulk."

"I know. I've always been lucky in my friends."

"I do not wish to be your enemy."

"There's no reason why you should be."

Artimion smiled. "You put two dogs in the same kennel and one is always going to try to piss higher than the other. You are strutting about Ganesh Ka like some form of royalty, and it sways the weaker minds among us. Were you delicately brought up?"

Rol laughed heartily. "I have been educated in the finer things in life, it's true."

"Do not try to jump too high too fast, Cortishane."

"All I'm trying to do," Rol said quietly, "is rebuild a good ship."

"And that you cannot do without my goodwill."

Rol stopped, and they stared at each other. Again, that momentary contest of wills in the contact of their eyes. Again it was put off, postponed. But it would not be so forever.

"All right, so I've been like a bull at a gate about it," Rol conceded. "But if I know anything, it's that your little fiefdom here has rough weather ahead of it. The Bionari are sniffing up and down the coast, and have been for months from what I hear. They will find this place eventually."

"They've been looking for it for nigh on a quarter of a century to no avail. Why should they chance across it now?"

"Because you've thrown in your lot along with the rebels. You are part of their politics now, and they cannot ignore that."

"We have always been part of their politics. It was Bar Hethrun himself founded this place, before leaving for his death at the hands of betrayers. And now the woman who purports to be his daughter wants you delivered to her—so you are not above politics either, it seems."

Rol stared in surprise at Artimion, and finally managed a strangled laugh. "By Ran's beard, you have no idea."

"What brought you to the coast of Ganesh?"

"The wind, what else?"

Artimion stared at Rol thoughtfully. "There is a shadow hanging over you, Cortishane. I have heard it said that when one with the Mark of Ran upon him comes to Ganesh Ka it shall be the harbinger of doom for our city. An old sailor's tale, no more, but even old tales may have the lick of truth about them. I think it best you do not stay here."

"Are you going to throw me out?"

"I owe you for saving Gallico's life, if nothing else. No, I will let you stay until you have your hulk made seaworthy in some fashion or other, and then I would have you leave us. You are bad luck."

"Maybe I am," Rol said soberly. "But you'll help me get this ship to sea?"

"I will. You may have the labor of any carpenter or blacksmith you desire, and the run of the storehouses—so long as it does not interfere with the provisioning of our regular vessels."

"I suppose you cannot say fairer than that." Rol held out a hand and Artimion shook it, unsmiling.

He was as good as his word. Two good ship's carpenters, Jon Lorriby and Kier Eiserne, were released to work on Rol's hulk, and with the news that Artimion himself had blessed its rebuilding, more veteran mariners came trickling to the dry dock to offer their services, for Ganesh Ka had experienced sailors by the hundred, and not enough ships to employ them all. Rol set Gallico and Creed to weeding out the chaff from the real professionals and within a fortnight he had sixty good, thorough-paced seamen on his muster-list and a portable forge had been set up on the dockside to turn out ringbolts, chain, and new rudder-pintles and gudgeons. The carpenters built oak carriages for the sakers, and these were trundled up to the magazine, and the guns bolted upon them. Then the whole contraption was trundled back down again, the wooden wheels squealing with the protest of new wood. But the most delicate business was the getting in of the lower masts. These were massive pylons of heavy timber, the best the Ganesh highlands could provide, the mainmast almost a yard across at its base. Sheerlegs were set up on the dockside and it took eighty men all told to haul on the tackles that lifted these massive yards into place. One false move and the masts would have dropped through the hulk's bottom like spears, and it took a sweating, cursing, shouting three days to get them in. Once they and the bowsprit were in place, however, she began to look like a ship again. Another two days saw the shrouds, forestays, and backstays in place, and the sluice gates of the dry dock were opened. The ship's company (for such they had become) stood in a crowd and cheered as the hulk's keel lifted from the stone and the baulks that supported her hull were knocked away one by one by Gallico, half drowned in foam and rushing water. She was afloat; she was alive again. A ship of black wood, long and graceful as a thoroughbred, and larger than any other in Ganesh Ka. A Man of War.

"Have you thought what you might call her?" Elias asked Rol as they stood in the midst of that cheering throng and watched Gallico haul himself up the ship's side, his grotesque face all agrin.

"I have." Rol looked back at the skeletal warrior in his stained armor who had watched over their labors. "We brought her back from the dead with the dead's blessing, so it's only fitting that she should be named the *Revenant.*"

Seven weeks after Rol had first clapped eyes on her, the *Revenant* was near ready for sea. Her topmasts were in, a new ship's wheel had been rigged up to her rudder, and two small cutters were made fast to the booms across her waist. They warped her out of the flooded dry dock to the wharves of the ship-cavern, and over a thousand people gathered there to see her topgallantmasts hauled up and lowered into place with tackles to the crosstrees. She had glass in her stern windows, a good bower and two kedge anchors, and a full load of ballast: piles of rock from some of the more ruinous galleries in the tunnels of Ganesh Ka. Rol, Gallico, and Creed had begged, borrowed, and in not a few cases stolen whatever they needed to fit her out, but they were still critically short on essentials. Sailcloth for one; they had enough for a full sail-plan, but not much in the way of reserves, and what stuff had been bent to the yards was a trifle worn for Rol's liking. Cordage, also, was in short supply, and there was a lot of twice-laid stuff in the rigging which a full-hearted gale would play havoc with. But the worst deficiency was in gunpowder. Here Artimion's indulgence had failed. They were allotted six small barrels, no more; enough for one moderate engagement.

"We need a shakedown cruise," Gallico said, "a week or two at sea, preferably with a bit of a blow to see how the men shape up. And gunnery practice. They've all fired ship-guns before, but the gun-teams are new to one another and to the ship—and those sakers are nine feet long and weigh a ton and a half apiece, heavier metal than most will be used to, unless they've had a spell on a man-of-war."

"We're still thirty men short of complement," Rol told him. "We could barely man a broadside and sail the ship at the same time."

"Who said anything about broadsides? Ran's teeth, Rol, we're not looking for a fight—we just prowl up the coast a way and take her due east into the Reach, deepwater sailing. We've enough food and water on board for a fortnight at least."

"If we run into a blow, it'll go hard with us; the running rigging is a hand-me-down cat's cradle, and I could piss through some of the topgallantsails."

The halftroll grinned. "Creed is right—you are an old woman."

They were seated in the captain's cabin, a beautiful space of white-painted, curving wood with the noise of the wharves rattling in the open stern windows. Several of these had cracked glass, which had been sized to the frames with a liberal amount of putty. One good following sea would burst them through and have the stern cabin flooded. They would have to ship deadlights in anything but the mildest wind.

A cot and a lantern, both hanging by ropes from the deckhead, swayed minutely with the restless movement of the water beneath the keel, for the tide in the bay beyond the cavern was on the ebb, flowing back out to sea. Rol and Gallico felt that small motion through their feet and smiled at each other. There was living water under them again.

"It's been a long time since I had a deck move below me," Gallico said.

Rol was about to agree when Creed swung open the cabin door. "Something's going on along the wharves. Looks like Artimion's making some kind of speech, and the ships' companies have all been mustered."

They went on deck, where their own crew were gathered in a body forward. Rol hailed his carpenter. "Kier, what's afoot?"

"Bad news, skipper. The Bionari are here."

Twenty-one

MEN OF WAR

THEY WERE STILL GATHERING BY THE HUNDRED ON THE wharves. Artimion had piled up a couple of crates and was standing atop them. About his feet stood Miriam and a few of her musketeers. All work had ceased, and the yards of the ships in dock were black with sailors, listening.

"They're troopships, no more, and their escort is only a pair of brigs," Artimion was saying, his baritone echoing in the eerie silence of the ship-cavern. "But if they manage to land Bionese regulars onshore, then we are lost. We must meet and destroy them at sea."

"Two Bionese men-of-war? *Swallow* and *Albatross* and *Prosper* cannot take them alone," someone shouted, and there was a general murmur.

"You damned fool, how do you think we had word of them? Timian and Gan are out there in their own ships, shadowing this flotilla. The *Osprey* and the *Skua* carry nine-pounders. With their help we'll take the brigs and sink the transports."

"How many soldiers in these transports?"

"There are eight troopships in the convoy, so bank on a full regiment, sixteen hundred men." Another murmur, disquieted and more widespread. Some women began sobbing. Artimion held up his hands.

"They're still thirty miles out at sea, so if we're quick we can meet them a good distance from the Ka. There is no reason to believe they know where we are, not yet."

"Then why embark a marine regiment?" a burly mariner called out. "They're not on board those troopships for their health."

Artimion's face grew grim and closed. "We must sink them all; drown every one of the bastards in the Reach. Not one must get back to Bionar, not one. We do that, and Ganesh Ka's secret is safe."

A general growl of approval met this.

"But we must plan for the worst also. We're clearing the decks and holds of every fishing boat and launch in the Ka, and I want all those not in a ship's company to prepare to leave the city."

A roar went up; fear and anger in the wordless chorus of a thousand voices. Once again Artimion raised his hands amid the upcry, and the levelheaded about him began shouting for silence and cursing their more histrionic neighbors.

"Those who cannot or will not find a berth in the boats must take what they can inland, into the hills. When this fleet has been destroyed we will make contact with you as soon as we can. You shall return to your homes, I swear it. I will sink these enemies of ours in the Reach, down to the last man, or I will die in the attempt."

A stillness fell over all that serried host of men and women. Some were nodding determinedly, others seemed sunk in resignation. A child cried out and was silenced by its mother.

"That is all. We are getting under way now, the men of the ships. May Ran be kind to us, and may Ussa of the Swells watch over us."

Artimion jumped down from his box and the crowds began to part reluctantly. There was no panic, only a purposeful current of movement. The mariners began filing to their ships, and the decks of the *Prosper,* the *Swallow,* and the *Albatross* were at once crowded with busy men. Rol, Gallico, and Creed looked at one another, and then as one they left the *Revenant* and began forging through the milling throng to Artimion's brigantine. They caught up with Ganesh Ka's de facto ruler just before he boarded the gangplank.

"Where do you want us?" Rol asked.

Artimion turned round, eyes bright in his black face. "You are free to leave the Ka without obligation, as we agreed. I do not hold you to its defense."

"The hell you don't, Artimion," Gallico began.

"Ask your captain, Gallico. You are his man now, not mine."

"We'll take our place in the line of battle with the rest of you," Elias said hotly.

"No. I do not want you in it."

"Why not?" Rol asked. "Surely this is no time to allow personal animosity to sway judgment."

"My judgment is sound," Artimion flashed. "Your ship has not even undergone sea trials. You are short in your complement, and your men have not yet worked together under your command—you would be more of a liability than an asset. This is not your fight, Cortishane. Stay out of it."

"Is that your last word?"

"If you wish to be of use, take on as many of the common folk as you can and get them out of here until the thing is done. Otherwise, you're just wasting my time. Go waste your own elsewhere."

He turned and walked over the gangplank, closely followed

by Miriam and half a dozen of her musketeers. Rol watched him go white-faced, but he put an arm out to stop Gallico following. "It's no use."

"I never thought Artimion small-minded until today."

"He may be right. We're not ready to take on Bionese men-of-war in open battle. Not yet."

"We have a ship and a crew to sail her."

"Oh, we'll sail her, all right. Never fear."

The little flotilla of vessels left the Ka towed by lighters from the wharves and cheered from the dockside by almost the entire population. Rol's crew stood watching from the decks of the *Revenant,* sullen and low-spirited. Gallico was clenching and unclenching his mighty fists as though eager to wrap them round a throat. Elias came running along the packed dockside and pelted up the gangplank as though pursued.

"Well?" Rol asked, still watching the yards of the departing ships, stark silhouettes against the bright sunshine beyond the sea gates.

"I spoke to one of Artimion's master's mates. The enemy are sou'-sou'east of here, nine leagues. The wind's from the west-nor'west, a fresh breeze. They're beating up into it, tack on tack."

"So that's why he's so confident," Gallico said. "He has the weather-gage. He'll swoop down on them at the time and place of his choosing."

Rol stood considering. "We're putting to sea, all the same. We'll make some offing from the coast and take a wide course down their starboard flank, make sure everything is going to plan."

"And maybe get in a few licks of our own?" Gallico asked, eyes dancing.

"If we can. We'll play it by ear. Elias, go you to the far docks and hunt us up another lighter—we'll need a tow to get out of the bay same as Artimion. But we'll leave it until he's made it beyond the cliffs. No sense in antagonizing him. He has enough on his mind."

Ganesh Ka was not yet in a panic, but it was a close-run thing. Its population had divided into those who sought safety on the boats now being cleared at the wharves, and those who were fleeing pell-mell for the hills. Experienced mariners were numbering folk off to each and every fishing smack, cutter, launch, lighter, and hoy that stood at the docks. It was an ordered process, but in the queuing lines there was the growing stink of desperation. Rol did not doubt that it would turn ugly before long.

A gaggle of men and women turned up on the dock alongside the *Revenant* and hailed the ship in shrill voices. The gangplank had been taken up preparatory to casting off but now these unfortunates were wailing in a body at the busy ship's company.

"Take us aboard of you, sirs!"

"I worked three weeks on this here ship!"

"For pity's sake, you have room enough in the hold; let us aboard."

"Lower the gangplank," Rol said to Creed, his hand on his sword hilt. "Gallico, how many could we get below the waterline?"

"We pack 'em in tight among the cable-tiers and the water casks, I'd say fifty maybe."

"Count the first fifty on board and then raise the plank."

Those on the docks cried out their thanks and came aboard in single file, their arms full of their meager possessions. Men, women, and bewildered children, some sobbing bitterly as they boarded. Creed led them below bearing a ship's lantern and stowed them in the depths of the hold, where they lay weeping and gabbling in the near-darkness. When the gangplank was raised on the last of the fifty the remainder of the crowd stood staring hopelessly at the ship for a while, and then shouldered their burdens and left quietly. Rol felt a kind of shame as he watched them go.

"No lights to be allowed below," he snapped as Creed came back on deck bearing his lantern. "We may have loose powder coming and going later on. Gallico, how long can we fight?"

The halftroll scratched his chin. "We've enough for eighteen or twenty full broadsides, fighting only one side of the ship. Both broadsides are loaded, though, and we've plenty of match, no fear about that."

"If we haven't won with twenty broadsides we're beat anyway," Rol said. "Sidearms?"

"A brace of pistols in your cabin, courtesy of the magazine. For everyone else it's cutlasses, pikes, and axes, and don't they hope we won't need 'em."

The lighter was alongside, its twelve-man crew resting on their oars. They had their seabags piled about the thwarts; clearly, once they had towed the *Revenant* out of the bay they meant to keep going.

"Cast off fore and aft!" Rol shouted. His heart was thumping madly. "Bear a hand with the towline forward. Helmsman, stand by at the wheel."

His orders were well-nigh superfluous, for every one of the crew was an experienced seaman, and they had anticipated him. Beneath their feet, the ship began to move. Achingly slow at first, she built up a momentum through the water as the lighter crew strained at their oars. They edged away from the docks, toward the blazing brightness of the sea gates and the wide blue disc of the bay beyond.

The sunlight made them all blink like owls as they passed out of the shelter of the stone. Rol had almost forgotten that it was early summer, and the day was not yet old. He let fall topsails as a shimmer of a breeze passed over the enclosed bay, wrinkling the water, and the lightermen made better speed with the help of the sails. They steered directly for the gap in the encircling cliffs.

"We're on the tail of the ebb," Creed said, shading his eyes with his hand. "Lucky for us. Another hour and they'd have been hauling against the tide."

The *Revenant* passed through the gap, the shadow of the cliffs cutting out the brilliant sunshine for a few minutes. But then she was through, and at once her motion changed, grew livelier. There was a stiff west-nor'west breeze blowing from the land and she had it on the port beam. The topsails bellied out taut and the creak of the rigging picked up a note.

The lighter crew cast off the towrope and stroke oar rose in his seat and waved his cap at them as they pulled away from the smaller craft. He shouted something but it was lost on the wind. Rol breathed deep. He could see Artimion's ships fine on the starboard bow, some three or four leagues away already. He would keep his distance.

"Jib and courses—but reef the mizzen, lads," he called out to his crew, and the men started up the shrouds, their sullenness evaporated. They were grinning and laughing as they climbed out on the yards, and the huge creamy masses of canvas fell like clouds, to be braced round and sheeted home with a minimum of fuss. Rol met Gallico's eye, and nodded.

"Well, they're seamen, all right." He turned to the quartermaster at the wheel. "East-southeast."

"Aye aye, sir. East-southeast it is." The quartermaster was smiling like a man whose wife has given birth.

"Now let's see what she can do," Rol said to Gallico. "Get a log-line to the forechains."

The *Revenant* was chopping through the swells, rolling and pitching as the offshore breeze met the eastward-rolling waves of the Inner Reach. She rose nobly, her heavy construction a bonus. Rol stood on her quarterdeck and grasped a backstay as was his wont, feeling the living movement of her beneath his feet, gauging the pressures working on her hull and masts. The spray raised by her bows came as far aft as the waist and in the white wake of her passage a miniature rainbow bloomed. Out here in the sunshine her hull timbers seemed even darker than in the gloom of the ship-cavern, such was the contrast with the blue sea, the unclouded sky. She was truly a black ship. His ship, the first he had ever truly taken to heart, having sweated and agonized over her resurrection like a midwife at a breech birth.

Rol closed his eyes, and felt her move under him. Felt the long creak and groan and fall and rise of her. It was like taking a strange woman into one's bed, a new body to explore.

"By God, she has a heart," Gallico said.

He opened his eyes at once. "Yes, she's remarkably stiff. They knew what they were doing, those shipwrights who cursed over the teak in her ribs. Log-line there, what's she making?"

The beardless youth who was being soaked in the forechains held on to the knotted log-line and shouted back aft. "Seven knots and one fathom!"

Gallico thumped the quarterdeck rail in sheer satisfaction.

"We'd best take in sail," Rol said with studied casualness, "or we may well overtake master Artimion." And then they both laughed like simpletons.

Rol sent lookouts to the mastheads; on a day like this they could survey a twenty-mile horizon. He looked back over the starboard quarter at Ganesh Ka, and saw a strange formation of mighty stone, the towers mere geological curiosities, the gap in the cliffs almost invisible. He realized in that moment that Ganesh Ka had always been a place of refuge, even back in the far distant days of its building. The Ancients had windows and fireplaces, they needed stairs and roadways, but their motives and concerns were utterly lost, completely alien. How old was

Ganesh Ka? Ten thousand years? Twenty? No one knew. There was something maddening in that, not because of the Ancient blood that ran in his own veins, but simply because the loss of this knowledge, which he felt to be important, seemed almost criminal. What a world, he thought, what an awesomely crass world that can have such monuments erected in it, and not wonder about the minds that made them.

He faced forward again, the ship rising and falling under his feet. There was something in the sea, some ageless rhythm, which all men hearkened to even if none understood. He did not know if Ran's Mark had put the sea yearning in his heart or if it had always been there, but he knew that here, now, at this moment, he was as happy as he had ever been in his life.

He looked skyward, and in his mind the bright ocean became a flat gaming board upon which pieces moved in obedience to the vagaries of the wind. There was the ragged Ganesh coast; deep-bitten and rock-strewn, death for vessels that did not know it well. There was Artimion and his ships, swooping down upon ten other vessels, the Bionese regiment and its protectors. Rol breathed in slow, remembering what Psellos had told him.

Most men think in one straight line. They see their own actions as a single thread unraveling, and the impingement of others upon their life as nothing more than stray knots in the thread. They look at things through one set of eyes: their own. It is a gift you must learn, to look at your own situation from the viewpoint of another. It is not hard, nor is it complicated. But it is necessary, if you are to survive.

For a moment Rol thought of Rowen, now a rebel queen vying for the possession of a kingdom. His sister. Why would she want him brought to her, now, seven years after she had walked away? He did not believe it was for love. Whatever she was now, it was not the woman she might have been had they remained together. He knew somehow that she was an enemy. That knowledge broke the boy Rol's heart, but the man Psellos had trained nodded thoughtfully and filed it away for future use.

Then the training went to work on the task in hand. Assemble the information, and ask yourself how it all got there. Why is this happening? Crude questions, and pyramids of factors in the answers.

The Bionari are beating up the coast, into the wind, which means they have come from the south. What is in the south? They have a garrison in Golgos, and—and that's it.

Rol opened his eyes.

The embarked regiment is the Golgos garrison, and it has taken ship because it has received intelligence about the region in which this elusive pirate city can be found. From where would it receive such intelligence?

And he knew. The knowledge leaped up in his brain even as his heart sank under the weight of it.

His erstwhile shipmates must have been picked up by the Imperials. For the first time, the Bionari knew in which region the Hidden City lay. And now they were sailing up the coast looking for it.

Artimion was right, he thought. I am bad luck. I have brought this on their heads. And his joy in the bright blue day and the ship leaping under his feet was diminished.

"Sail ho!" the lookout on the foremast cried.

His mind emptied. He was instantly alert. "Where?"

"Broad on the larboard beam, skipper. Topsails up. I believe she might be ship-rigged."

Rol was running aft in a moment. He clambered up the weather shrouds of the mainmast, heaved himself into the maintop, and then started up the topgallantmast. He got close to the truck, hooked an arm in the hounds, and peered east.

Yes, she was three-masted, though not ship-rigged. A barque, square-rigged on fore and main, fore-and-aft sails on the mizzen. More than that he could not make out.

He roared down at the quarterdeck. "Helmsman there! Bring her three points to larboard. Course due east!"

The *Revenant* turned smoothly under him, his lofty perch leaning and then straightening, dipping and rising. The strange ship could be a Mercanter, minding her own business, but somehow he did not think so. And in any case, she had the weather-gage of Artimion's little fleet. Rol would have to intercept her if she was not to come upon the other ships of the Ka from the rear.

Ran, let her not be a man-of-war, he prayed silently. Not now.

It was a glorious day about him, a fine day to be at sea. After the confines of Ganesh Ka's somber stone, the outside world seemed vast beyond measure.

This turning earth, as limitless as a madman's imagination.

He could see five leagues in every direction, and if he looked east, this entire world was naught but a bubble of blue space. Turquoise sea, the breeze caressing it into a wrinkled swell that caught the sunlight in a vast shimmer. And a sky so dark above his head it might almost be purple, shading down to the far horizon and meeting the ocean, merging with it at the edge of sight. A blue world, empty of everything but air and water. And that nick on the edge of the horizon, the strange ship that might be harmless, or might spell his doom.

Heart rushing in his throat, he looked down. Far below him there pitched a tiny, crowded wooden world. The deck was covered with men, cordage, and the crouching shapes of cannon tied up close to the bulwark, like bronze beasts kept prudently in check. The men below paused, and he could see scores of faces tilted upward at him, and then out at the horizon.

He could not take the risk. Rol closed his eyes for a second, and bellowed, "Beat to quarters!"

A moment of stillness, and then the dry rattling of a drum started up, and the crowd of men on deck exploded into a circus of activity. The ship's wake began to curve in a graceful arc behind her as she answered her rudder, and changed course to converge with the approaching vessel. Her bow dipped and plunged with a hissing roar and scattered packets of spindrift along the fo'c'sle. Below him, the rigging creaked and groaned, the timbers stretching and straining as though his ship were stirring into wrathful life, a woken titan.

The *Revenant* was running now with the wind on her larboard quarter, with her mizzen brailed up, the topsails full and drawing tight. His crew were hauling in the mainsail and fore-course—when there was action ahead, it was best not to have canvas billowing too near the muzzles of the guns.

Rol grasped a backstay and slid back down on deck, Ran's Mark keeping his palm from burning. At once the close-packed activity surrounded him, and his world grew small and busy.

"Don't run them out, lads," he shouted at the gun-crews. He wanted the port-lids to remain closed until the last moment, when the *Revenant* would bare her teeth at her enemy by running out the six twelve-pound sakers of her larboard broadside. Below his feet the ship answered the urgent impetus of the wind with a will.

There—the chase's topsails had come farther over the curve of the horizon and were visible on deck now. A pennant flying from the mainmast like a spit of far-off saffron, edged round with black. The fighting flag of Bionar.

"Ran's beard," Gallico said softly. "She's a warship."

"We'll need your twenty broadsides after all," Rol told him, smiling. He sniffed the air. The wind was still nor-nor'west, and the *Revenant* was making a good seven knots before it, whilst the barque was close-hauled, running into it at an angle, the yards braced round until they were almost fore-and-aft like a schooner's. Rol studied her progress.

"A slow way to sail, it must be said. I doubt she's making three knots."

Gallico nodded. There was a tight grin on his face that held no humor in it at all.

"Deck there!" a lookout bellowed. "She's altered course a point—seems she means to close with us."

"Stand by to run out the larboard broadside. Elias, run up our colors. Gallico, go you to the fo'c'sle and see about assembling some boarders."

"Aye, sir," Gallico snapped, winking, and lumbered off with a swiftness startling in one so huge.

The *Revenant*'s pennant was run up the mainmast halliards, and the breeze snapped it out like a frenzied snake. It was a ragged length of sable linen without device. The Black Flag. If she struck after this, there would be no quarter asked or given.

"Larboard crews, run out your guns!"

The port-lids that lined one side of the ship were raised up, and sweating teams of men, six to a gun, hauled their massive, brutal charges outboard with a groaning of rope and thunderous rumbling of wood and iron. A ton and a half apiece, the twelve-pounders' collective weight canted the ship to one side as they shifted. Sand had been scattered across the deck so that the barefoot sailors might not slip in their own blood (if blood was shed), tubs of water had been set out round the butts of the masts, and the coils of slow-match that would touch off the cannon were already smoldering away in iron buckets beside every gun-team. The acrid, pulse-quickening smell eddied about the waist of the ship. Rol breathed it in as though it were perfume and took up his battle station at the break of the quarterdeck, close to the ship's wheel. His four quartermasters stood grasping it, keeping the ship on her course. At the quarterdeck rail two more men stood manning the wicked little two-pound swivel-guns.

"You might want these," Creed said, proffering a pair of flintlock pistols with a wry smile. "They're loaded and primed; I did it myself."

Rol nodded, and tucked them into the sash at his waist.

Everyone else had a cutlass at his hip, but Rol had Fleam. As the two ships drew closer together, he fiddled unconsciously with the leather-bound flints of his firearms, blessing the breadth of Psellos's education.

"Steady." This to the helmsmen. They were doing well, but then most of them were born to the sea. Many had seen action before. He looked up and down the decks, and saw his men standing ready and poised. There was no talk. Gallico had picked them well.

"Elias, the people in the hold—"

"They've been warned to stay below. They're quiet as mice. They've taken the children into the bilge—not too pleasant, but safer."

The oncoming barque was less than three cables away now. At the last moment he would put the *Revenant* about and present his gleaming broadside. She would have to heave-to then, for fear of being raked. Once they had pounded the tar out of her, Gallico would grapple her forestays to the bow and board her—and every man-jack of the crew would be—

"Skipper—she's not heaving-to," one of the helmsmen warned.

"Mind your course."

The barque's crew were crowding forward onto her fo'c'sle. Rol saw the gleam of metal on blades there; and then all along her hull the port-lids opened and the sinister shapes of heavy guns were run out. She was going to plow straight on and meet them yardarm to yardarm.

"Hard a starboard!" he yelled, hoping he had not left it too late.

The helmsmen spun the ship's wheel frantically and the *Revenant* turned, growling and smashing waves aside. But the run-out guns on her port side slowed the turn. The deck canted and they groaned against the tackles that held them in place. A water bucket slithered into the scuppers and overturned, and one unhandy lubber lost his footing on the sand-strewn deck and followed it.

Too slow.

"She won't make it. Gun-crews there—lie down on deck! After her first broadside, fire as they bear!"

"Ran be merciful," one of the helmsmen muttered. He and his fellows had to remain standing to keep the ship on course.

The barque put about her helm a scant half cable from the bow of the *Revenant,* and then her entire side vanished in a huge fuming storm of yellow smoke. Half a heartbeat later came the tremendous roar of her full broadside, and then the air was screaming and alive with iron and wood and sundered flesh. The cannonballs struck the *Revenant* fine on the port bow and traveled almost the full length of the ship, slicing rigging, smashing the boats on the booms to fragments, rending her hull, and blasting men to bloody pieces. One shot, which shrieked along the quarterdeck, cut two of the helmsmen in half and burst the ship's wheel into jagged shards of wood. The two surviving quartermasters fought to regain control of the shattered wheel whilst Rol picked himself off the deck and, panting, yanked a wicked sliver of oak out of his thigh.

"Fire!" he shouted, maddened with pain and fury.

The ship was still answering her rudder, and completed her turn to starboard with barely a check. With blood streaming from her scuppers like that of some wounded giant, her own guns thundered out in savage sequence. A bank of smoke as tall as the mainyard rose up in a billowing cloud, shot through with flame. In the waist the heavy sakers jumped back one by one as their crews jammed smoking match into the touch-holes.

"Pour it into them, boys!" Rol yelled. And to the surviving helmsmen: "How does she steer?"

"She's all right, skipper."

"Then make three points to port. Take us right up the bastard's throat."

Chaos all the length of his ship. A gun overturned there in the middle of the waist with the corpses of its crew a mangled pulp about it. Men throwing water over a burning heap of cordage, others tossing bodies overboard. The mizzen half shot through, and up on the fo'c'sle a bewildering maze of broken timber and rope with Gallico and his men trying to hack it free of the bow-chasers. Rol looked up. The foretopgallantmast had gone by the board. Sailors were up in the shrouds with axes already, trying to cut away the wreckage that was strangling the *Revenant.*

God damn them. His beautiful ship.

"Skipper, we've half a dozen holes just on the waterline. I need more men for the pumps." This was Eiserne, the carpenter.

"You shall have them, Kier. Take half a dozen from the larboard gun-crews—no more, mind. Can you plug the holes?"

"Aye, no fear of that. But she's a fearful mess down below. Some of the passengers have copped it."

"As long as she floats. Go to it now." Rol clapped the man on his shoulder, and the carpenter scurried off down the companionway.

Another broadside from the barque. This one was less devastating, as the two ships were side by side now, slugging it out on even terms. Another saker dismounted, and three gunports beaten into one jagged hole on the larboard side, murderous splinters of wood spraying across the deck and knocking men down like skittles. The enemy was firing low, into the hull. When going after a prize it was usual to aim high, at the rigging, and so avoid the risk of sinking a valuable vessel. These men were not out to capture, but to kill.

Rol saw a cannonball rolling along the deck—an eighteen-pounder by the looks of it. This was heavier metal than he had ever thought to encounter—he was outgunned.

But the men who served the *Revenant*'s guns were not novices, and their blood was up. Broadside after broadside continued to roar out, and they heaved at their sakers with sweat streaming down their naked torsos, faces black with powder, blood trickling from minor wounds.

The broadsides were ragged now, though. Only four guns still firing on the larboard side, and those thinly manned. Damage-control parties were working steadily; putting out fires, plugging shot-holes, splicing rigging, and heaving bodies or parts of bodies over the taffrail. This could not go on. The heavier metal of the barque would prevail, in the end.

The two ships were still cruising side by side a cable's length apart, the air between them a fuming cataclysm of smoke and hurtling iron. The *Revenant* had the wind on the starboard beam and thus possessed the weather-gage: in theory she should be able to close with her enemy anytime she chose.

Rol turned to the two surviving helmsmen, who were still holding steady the splintered wreck of the ship's wheel.

"Hard a port!" he shouted.

The *Revenant* obediently turned to his left, and with the wind now on her starboard quarter she picked up speed, closing the two hundred yards that separated her from the barque with breath-catching rapidity.

"Brace yourselves!" Rol bellowed, the second before the two ships collided.

The *Revenant*'s bowsprit smashed through the barque's bulwark just aft of her fo'c'sle and exploded into a splintered nightmare of wood and rope. The *Revenant* kept going, and the hulls of the two vessels came together with a concussion that knocked every man aboard them off his feet. Rol found himself flung over the quarterdeck rail like a discarded child's toy, and landed in a pile of canvas and bodies. There was a searing crack, and the *Revenant*'s entire foretopmast came crashing down over the waist of the barque, entangling the two ships hopelessly and forming a bridge that Gallico and his boarders now clambered shrieking across.

The cannon-fire had stopped for the moment as the two ship's companies picked themselves up and collected their wits. Rol wiped blood out of his eyes and drew Fleam. The scimitar was trembling in his hand. "Come on, Revenants—get the guns going. Don't go to sleep on me now!"

The dazed crews stumbled back to their sakers and mechanically began reloading. On the barque, a confused scrum of men were fighting viciously to repel Gallico's boarders. A surf of shouting and screaming rose up out of her hull. Rol picked his way through the wreckage of the waist and climbed up onto the fo'c'sle. It was like navigating through a storm-felled forest. Behind him, the *Revenant*'s guns started up again. A damage-control party was hacking at the tumbled topmast with axes. Creed was in their midst, shouting orders and looking half-demented.

"Forget about that now, Elias. Follow me. Gallico needs a hand."

He gathered a motley crowd of perhaps twenty men and led them across the topmast that joined the two ships together. One man lost his footing and fell into the dark, choppy sea between the vessels' hulls. The rest did not pause, but followed Rol onto the barque, brandishing axes, cutlasses, and boarding-pikes and yelling like maniacs.

Gallico was there, towering over everyone else in the melee, his face transformed into a demonic mask of battle-rage. He was laying about him with a massive baulk of broken timber, cutting men down as though they were corn, sending bodies flying to left and right. He was the apex of a solid wedge of Revenants who were struggling to advance down the waist of the barque. Resisting them was a mass of the enemy crew, some in the loose garb of sailors, others in the breastplates and helmets of soldiers. In places, men of both sides were so tightly packed together that they could not even raise their arms to strike one another. An enemy officer stood at the barque's quarterdeck rail urging on his men. He wore black-trimmed scarlet hose and his breastplate shone like a mirror. His handsome, bearded face was framed by a cascade of raven ringlets and there was lace on his cuffs.

Rol drew forth one of the pistols at his waist, cocked it, and shot the man in the throat. He tumbled head-first into the affray below.

A cry went up, and the barque's crew seemed to flinch. Instantly, Gallico waded forward, and the men facing him retreated hurriedly. Some moral advantage seemed to have passed to the Revenants. The fight opened out. Rol led his men into the gap, shot a raging soldier with his second pistol, skewered another through his open mouth, and kicked a third aside whilst ripping his sword free. He found himself at Gallico's side. The massive halftroll grinned horribly, his eyes two green windows into hell.

"Well met, Rol. A hot day's work."

"Too damned hot by half." Rol slashed out at an enemy sailor, opening up his bowels. The man shrieked despairingly as they poured steaming down his thighs. Gallico crushed his skull with one blow from a gnarled fist.

A wicked, vicious melee in which men hacked and clubbed one another to death and the deck of the barque ran slick and scarlet with their blood. Rol, Gallico, and Creed were in the forefront of the Revenants, battling their way aft to the barque's quarterdeck. The enemy sailors streamed away but the armored soldiers in their midst gave a good account of themselves; they were Bionese marines, some of the finest professionals in the world. They asked no quarter and did not retreat, but gathered in knots and fought stubbornly, and Rol's unprotected mariners were no match for them. The fighting swayed backwards again, and the Revenants began to waver. Though Rol, Gallico, and Creed fought on in one tight, unyielding triangle, the rest of the crew were retreating back to the fo'c'sle.

The enemy marines gave a shout and pressed home their advantage, slipping on the bloody deck, tripping over bodies in their haste to hack at the unprotected backs of the Revenants. Rol turned his head to shout, to rally his men, and the flat of a sword blade struck him just above his left eye. He fell to one knee, and the jubilant marine would have had his head off in the next second had not Gallico's fist smashed the man backwards. Rol staggered, vision blurred, head ringing, and as he collected himself, he could *feel* something stirring inside him.

It was terrifying and exhilarating at the same time. He laughed out loud as raw bull-like strength flooded his limbs and a white rage began to rise behind his eyes. In his fist the new-moon length of Fleam began to shake and shine, bloody over the hilt. *"On me!"* he shrieked in a voice that did not sound like his own, and rising to his feet he powered forward alone.

One sweep of the scimitar's wicked edge cut through the breastplate and ribs of an enemy marine and laid his heart bare. Rol reached in and plucked the beating muscle from the man's chest, ripped it free and threw it at his comrades. The awful laughter continued to cackle out of his throat, and from his eyes now the smoking whiteness spilled out and Fleam began to glow white and the blood boiled off her hot steel. To those about him it seemed their captain grew in size, and looming white wings of flame rose from his shoulders. His sword arced back and forth in a brightness painful to look at, and the Bionese marines about him were cut to steaming pieces by the snick of the terrible blade.

The marines broke and began climbing over one another to get away from the terrifying light. Even the Revenants turned tail on their captain and began clambering back over the tangled wreckage to their own ship. Only Gallico and Creed remained at Rol's shoulders. He pursued the fleeing enemy back to the quarterdeck rail, to the ship's wheel, and finally to the very taffrail itself, where they crowded like sheep yammering before a wolf. They threw away their weapons and jumped over the barque's stern, or stood slack-jawed with terror and were cut to shreds. Fleam came down on the back of the last as he was trying to clamber over the stern and sliced clear through him, burying herself in the wood of the taffrail. The marine toppled overboard in two pieces.

For a moment it seemed that the white, winged light would rise up over the ship's stern and fly away. The wing-shapes, almost too bright to look at, seemed to curl and smoke in silver tendrils, feathered blades sharp as frost. Then they began to shrink again.

The light went out. Rol Cortishane stood breathing hard, staring at his scimitar buried to the hilt in hard oak. He tried to wrench her free, failed, finally succeeded on the third attempt. The radiance in his eyes dwindled. He tottered, would have fallen had not Gallico's great paw steadied him.

"It's done, skipper," Elias said quietly, and set a hand on his arm. The Revenants were clustered about the fo'c'sle of the barque, their faces gray with fear and shock. Rol seemed to come back to himself with a physical effort. He blinked, glared disbelievingly at the carnage about his feet. The cracking boom as one of the *Revenant*'s sakers fired again, sending splinters flying from the barque's hull at the waterline.

"Revenants, 'vast firing there!" Gallico shouted out across the bulwark to the gun-crews of their own ship.

The cannons went silent. Suddenly there was no noise but for the bubbling groans of a few wounded, and the creak of the two grappled vessels, the slap of the sea at their wounded hulls. Rol's ears hissed and rang with the after-echoes of gunfire. In his eyes colored after-images swam as if he had been staring clear into the heart of the sun. Gallico stared into his face, searching there for the man he knew.

"Rol. Rol, come back."

Cortishane blinked stupidly. Fleam slipped from his grasp to the deck. His eyes rolled back in his head.

"Gallico, we must be quick. This ship is sinking under us," Elias Creed said, and the halftroll scooped Rol's body up into his blood-smeared arms.

Twenty-two

THE BITERS BIT

A PATCHWORK OF IMAGES, BARELY FIT TO BE CALLED memory. At some point he knew he was being carried, and he heard the urgent chorus of many axes working frantically on timber. Men and women were screaming in pain but they were at one remove. He knew that he was being stared at, and whispered about, and he heard Gallico's voice raised in anger.

He was in his cot, and it was swaying with the pitch of his ship. Beside him Elias Creed sat methodically reloading his pistols. The *Revenant* was moving through the water about them with the graceless lunge of a crippled bird.

Rol drifted away again, and this time the *Revenant* was left far behind. There was a woman with him; they existed together in some indefinable space. She was beautiful and dark and rounded and her white flesh melted against his. She had eyes the color of Fleam's gray-green steel, and her eyeteeth were long fangs of gleaming silver. She moved against him with a delicious building friction, her skin satin-soft. He wanted her more than anything else in the world, and set his mouth against hers, crushed her dark lips against the white fangs. When he drew breath their mouths peeled apart as if glued, and he saw that there was blood all over her lips and teeth and he could taste it in his own mouth.

"It's all right, Orr-Diseyn," she said. "Prince of Orr, Lord of Demons. You come into your own, day by day, and I will be here always to watch over you."

"Rowen?" Rol asked softly.

The woman's face changed; it grew hard, and he could see the bones beneath her flesh, the skull within its beautiful shell of meat. For a second she was no longer what she seemed, and Rol had a glimpse of some shambling angular beast. Then she was gone completely.

He stood on a high mountain; he could feel the rareness of the air as it sidled unwillingly in and out of his lungs. But it was hot and bright all the same, and he looked down onto a green country below, a riotous forest of trees and plants he did not know. Beneath their canopy there was a hidden world.

The violent jade-green of the forest was bisected by the wandering course of a mighty river, brown and slow. His eyes followed the meander of its sinuous turns and twists, and far out on the edge of the world he thought he saw a glimmer of what might have been the sea, great Tethis. This, he knew, was the land of Orr.

A thing stood beside him. It was manlike in many respects, but not a man in the remotest sense of the word. It stood shrouded in a dark cloak with a tall helm of iron on its head, and within the helm two green lights blinked.

"You have been sailing in ancient waters," it said. "The first men launched their canoes upon the waves of the Inner Reach, and it was by sea that they spread to the far corners of the world, not over the mountains. For what remains of the One

God is in the sea, and thus men listen to Tethis and are moved and know not why. The sea was here at the Beginning and shall be here at the End, when all things shall return to it."

The iron helm turned and the lights within it burned brighter. "Now, feast your eyes on the jungle-brightness of Orr. One day you will find sanctuary here. You are the son of my blood, but not the child of my heart. For her it is too late, but for you there may yet be a chance."

Rol shrank from the chill of his companion's regard. It was like staring into an abyss without end.

"There is no need to be afraid of me. Be more afraid of what is festering in your own marrow. Orr-Diseyn, do you not feel it working within you?" The thing gestured at the wide jungle-hid land below. "Do you not know what you will find here?

"No. Of course you do not. You are yet young, a stripling. Ten thousand leagues of the sea have yet to go beneath your keel." He paused. "Your vessel was well named. She will carry you far, your *Revenant.*"

"Sail ho!" a voice shouted.

Rol opened his eyes, sucking in air with a hoarse gasp.

"Welcome back," Creed said, smiling. "I don't know where you went, but you were gone deep."

Memory flooding back, no longer a tattered patchwork thing, but a full-blooded torrent. "The ship, Elias—"

"She floats. It would seem—"

Rol leaped out of the hanging cot and ran along the companionway. He came out onto the sunlit quarterdeck, and found himself looking forward at a strange, disjointed mess of a vessel: scarred decks, broken wood, and a makeshift series of sails sheeted from the foremast to an ugly lumpen stump of bowsprit. All about the ship's guns a great crowd of people gathered, cowering at his approach.

This ship. My ship. This, here, is my world. I want no other.

"Gallico!"

I want nothing more.

"Here, skipper." The halftroll raised a hand.

Rol stood swaying, empty-eyed. It seemed to him that the world was not what it had been. As though some other place floated serenely behind the sun and he was now aware of it.

He knuckled his eyes. "What sail? Where away?"

"On the port beam, a small boat and some kind of jury-rig." In a lower voice Gallico said, "Are you well?"

"Quite well," Rol snapped, suddenly aware of the entire crew staring at him, their work forgotten. There were filthy-faced children on deck chewing ship's biscuit, and a throng of the passengers who had importuned him for a passage back in Ganesh Ka.

"Gallico," Rol said again, fainter this time. He mustered his feet under him and made it to the lee scuppers before throwing up. His vomit was blood-red. He leaned on the ship's rail.

"Tell me, Gallico." And in a stronger voice: "Damage report."

"We've fished the mizzen and jury-rigged the foremast. There's what's left of the foretopmast serving as a sprit, though it's too damn heavy and is pressing down the bow. We lost twenty-three men killed or wounded. The barque sank half a watch after we got ourselves cut free of her. We have no powder left, and we're making water fast, but the pumps are keeping pace with it. The orlop is ankle-deep, so I brought the passengers up on deck. I set course back for Ganesh Ka, west-nor'west, the wind on the starboard bow." He stopped, and seemed to grope for words. "Rol, we just sank a Bionese man-of-war."

"So I understand."

"You don't understand. No single privateer has ever bested a man-of-war in even fight—never. And with a new ship and untried crew."

Rol managed a smile. "You look like a bloodied cat who's kept hold of the cream."

"They mauled us, yes, but by God—" He thumped the quarterdeck rail in a gesture that Rol was coming to see as a habit. "Wait until Artimion hears about this. It was like something out of a goddamned song."

"Deck there!" a lookout cried. "There's people on the launch to larboard, waving and such. I believe they're friendly."

"Heave-to," Rol said. He straightened and wiped his mouth. Many of the crew were still staring at him, but what he had first mistaken for fear now looked more like awe. He shook his buzzing head. "Heave-to, I say, and set down a cutter."

"They're all in splinters," Gallico told him.

Rol sighed. "Gallico, close with the bloody boat and get them on board, will you?"

The halftroll grinned. "Aye aye, sir."

It was Miriam in the launch, along with a dozen others who were slack-jawed with exhaustion, having pulled into the wind for some twenty-five miles. Artimion lay in the boat, his bloody head resting in her lap.

"The fleet is gone," she said, having gulped cloudy water out of a scuttle-butt. There was a black bar of gunpowder darkening her face from the corner of her mouth down her chin. Her eyes were red-rimmed as cherries.

"Jan Timian ran for it, but the others piled in yardarm to yardarm. The brigs were sunk, and the transports scattered. I think a couple went aground in the surf. But they beat us up something terrible. *Albatross* and *Swallow* were dismasted and had to put about before the wind. They're running south, trying to get new masts up or something. *Prosper* sank under us. We got the launch over the side and Artimion into it. I do not know if he will live. Where *Skua* is I do not know. There was too much smoke, too much confusion. But we beat them. The Ka is safe."

In the hesitant outbreak of cheering that followed she

seemed to look about herself for the first time. "Are you listening to me?" And then: "What happened to you?" Her voice was near breaking.

"We also had some trouble, Miriam," Gallico said gently, and bending he lifted Artimion's body from the deck and into his massive arms.

"Does he live yet?" Miriam asked. A harshness throbbed behind her words. She looked close to breaking down.

Gallico closed his huge paw about Artimion's throat. "There is life beating here. We must get him below."

He and Miriam disappeared down the companionway. The rest of Miriam's companions were sitting all about the waist, heads bowed. The Revenants had fallen silent. Even the passengers did not speak.

"It's a lot to take in, I suppose," Creed said.

"Get them back to work, Elias," Rol said sharply. "The ship will not fix herself." He looked up and down the crowded decks, and his heart lurched at the devastation there. His beautiful ship. Well, she would be rebuilt. But first he must get her back to Ganesh Ka.

She will carry you far, your Revenant.

Gallico and Miriam were bending over Artimion's body in the light of the stern-cabin windows. They had laid him in Rol's cot and were peeling off layer upon layer of filthy bandages.

"How is he?" Rol asked.

"Shot through the lung," Miriam snapped. "Plus a splinter scalped the side of his head."

Artimion's dark face had taken on a livid hue, and white bone gleamed at his temple. Rol touched his own head, remembering the blow there, but his flesh was unmarked. The wound in his thigh had disappeared also.

"Gallico?"

"I've stopped up the hole—there was air coming out of it—and I'll sew his scalp back down. The rest is up to him."

"The Blood is in him," Miriam said. "He'll not go easy."

Artimion opened his eyes, and Miriam stifled a cry. The black man stared at them one by one, his gaze resting last on Rol's face.

"I thought so. Miriam, are we—"

"The day is won." She took his hand and clenched her white fingers about it. "The Bionari are sunk or scattered."

The eyes closed again. The tense, glistening face relaxed somewhat, though it tightened again in pain as the breath left his wounded lung. "Oh, thank the gods." Then Artimion smiled. He met Gallico's bright eyes once more. "I thought you would get into the middle of things somehow."

"Of course."

Artimion stared at the deck-head. He looked puzzled. "This is not the *Prosper.* What ship is this?"

"The *Revenant,*" Rol said quietly. "My ship."

"Cortishane. So you took her out after all."

"I took her out. She came in useful, as it happens."

"She sank a man-of-war," Gallico said quietly. But Artimion's eyes had already closed.

The three of them left him sleeping and came on deck again, glad of the clean air and spray after the powder-reek, the charnel-house atmosphere below.

"He will live," Miriam said fervently. "He must. Without him, Ganesh Ka is finished."

"The Bionari will not stop looking," Rol said quietly. "They have an idea now of where we are."

Miriam regarded him coldly. *"We?"*

Gallico was running a paw up and down the quarterdeck rail. "We've put our blood into this ship. She's truly ours now."

"That's one way to look at it," Rol said. He was very tired.

"The refitting will take three or four weeks at least."

"So I figure."

"We are the only ship the Ka can count on now, Rol. All the rest are sunk or fled."

"We're not so far from sunk ourselves, brother," But Rol's attempt at jocularity fell flat.

Gallico looked square at him. "We must go home now. We must gather up our people."

Rol did not look at the halftroll, but surveyed the multitude that populated the ruined deck of his ship. Men, women, children, squatting amid the gore and the wreckage. Miriam, glaring at him with a fine-boned face full of mistrust and doubt. Elias Creed, the sun catching the white in his beard. So many faces, and all of them looking his way.

"I suppose we must," he said.